THE DEVIL'S HAND

THE DEVIL'S HAND

N.D. Andrews

PLANCHETTE PRESS

Published by Planchette Press

Cover illustrations from original artwork by N.D. Andrews

For permission requests, contact the author: ndandrewsauthor@outlook.com
Twitter: @ND_Andrews Instagram: _ndandrews

Planchette Press is an imprint owned by N.D. Andrews

First Printing, 2020

ISBN 978-1-9163892-0-5

10 9 8 7 6 5 4 3 2 1

To Joany. I'll carry a piece of you with me forever. You'll forever be a part of me, and then, you'll never really be gone. Because if you're never forgotten, how can you have ever really left?

To Peter. The most wonderful human.

The Girl in the Black Lace Dress

'There are moments that change your life forever, for better or worse. Usually, it's the ones that aren't seen coming — the unexpected — that make the biggest impact. The death of a loved one, the meeting of a soulmate or life-changing injury; these moments live on forever in the minds of those who experience them. No-one knows how they'll react until it happens. But a time, a place — even if no longer in existence — can be revisited, in just the blink of an eye, or snap of a finger.'

☙✤❧

<u>Wednesday 10th September 1997, 23:15pm, ASHFIELD, LONDON.</u>

North London, 1997. Cloud hung thickly in the night sky, but the half-moon was still clearly visible. Its aura strong, it cast brilliant beams of silvery light down on the damp streets below as Detective Inspector Michelle Davey tensely trekked through the unseasonable cold, heading home.

Still, the bracing walk was more appealing than the offered lift from Kevin Gunn – her partnered colleague. Only that lunchtime Michelle had called him a *'male chauvinist pig,'* under her breath. He'd asked that she repeat herself, but chickened out to say, *'stale seeded bread.'* Regrettably, Michelle's own car was out for repair at the garage, in the capable hands of Thierry, though she'd been disappointed it was not his brother, Nikos, who was to service this time. Over the years and the high number of times Michelle had visited the garage, she had grown rather fond of Nikos – his face, his capable hands and arms. That's where her mind now stalled. She mentally undressed him for thirty seconds or so before returning her thoughts to work.

Aged forty-two, it had felt as if her career had plateaued, until recently. It was no secret that Detective Chief Inspector Malcolm Goodfellow was soon to take early retirement, but with many potentials clambering to take up the position – herself and Kevin included – Michelle feared the odds were against her. Everyone was out to impress, and everyone was out for themselves. Hopefully, the extra hours Michelle was putting in would aid her.

Michelle turned left between two houses and quickened her pace along the alleyway nestled there. She took note of the time – seventeen minutes past eleven – as her stomach rumbled. She thought of home and the microwave curry that patiently awaited her return.

The alleyway opened out into a street flanked by terraced red-bricked houses. As always, Dragnell Lane was crammed with cars, which only emphasised its narrowness and the fact that this Victorian street had not been designed to accommodate them. Only a yellow builder's skip – piled to the brim – broke the neat assembly.

Michelle crossed the road, and, jumping the gutter's puddles, clipped her toe. She didn't think to inspect the damage – any scuffs could be disguised with the aid of a black marker. Michelle didn't own any polish; although, with the opportunity for promotion, perhaps she should invest.

Under the glow of a lamppost, a gust of wind hit Michelle's face, causing loose strands of brown hair to brush coolly against her cheeks. She paused and pulled the collar of her trench coat up higher. This was far from the Indian summer that had been promised.

Something then caught Michelle's eye: a disc of white flesh, as bright as the moon. A woman's face – or rather that of a teenage girl – bore out of the shadows from behind the windscreen of a parked car. A dark-coloured hatchback, it was a Renault of some kind. Michelle laughed off her initial fright and flashed the girl a wide smile, slackening her posture, as she resumed her approach.

Clad in a black lace dress, the girl had long and curly auburn hair. She showed no acknowledgement of Michelle's presence and simply continued to stare blankly into the night, through sunken eyes. A ghostly sight; the girl's skin appeared unblemished, almost paper-like, as if it could easily be torn. Michelle's smile faltered.

Looking away, Michelle reclaimed her thoughts, allowing Nikos and her microwave curry to swim lazily back. The two, interchanging, ultimately combined. Maybe one day she would share a curry with Nikos? Perhaps on a date—

Michelle tripped.

She immediately steadied herself. But now beside the Renault, Michelle felt suddenly overcome by a mesmerising curiosity that she could neither fight nor explain. She lowered herself to its passenger window.

As she drew close, only the girl's head pivoted ninety degrees. Her body had remained still. With no interlinking action, the movement had been instantaneous. Like a television, she had flickered, becoming scratched and yellowed – translucent – like an old photographic negative.

Shocked, Michelle fell back against the low brick wall behind, dropping her handbag to the pavement. She gulped, as the girl's body then jumped to catch up with its head. Michelle gripped the wall tighter; a pang of emptiness creeping through her before crashing. All she wanted was to run away as fast as she could, but she didn't … she couldn't.

The girl jumped again and from nowhere a bottle appeared in her hand.

Michelle slumped to the pavement beside her bag, breath rasping between her lips as the girl brought the juddering glass up to meet her own. Michelle squinted at its label. Fingers covered its name, but the picture was visible. A hand? Yes, it was a clawed-hand. As for the liquid's true colour, Michelle couldn't be sure, for it and the girl continued to flicker.

The girl jumped once more, and the bottle disappeared completely into the ether. As she began hammering upon the window, she looked fraught, yet made no sound. Determination – sheer self-preservation – silently screamed out from her contorted face.

Michelle choked on tears as drain water gushed upwards from the gutter and over the curb. It sloshed around her bare ankles before rising further to reach her backside, bringing years' worth of sludge and half-decayed leaves bubbling along with it. Raindrops too began to fall. Sporadically at first, then much heavier, as the heavens quickly opened into a downpour.

Her hair plastered to her scalp and cheeks, Michelle looked on as flames suddenly leapt up around the girl. Her apparent disconnect from the natural world was now instinctively irrelevant. Michelle had to help.

Pulling herself up, Michelle slid and staggered the few feet over to the car. She attempted to open the passenger door, but to no avail – it was locked. The fire was bright but gave off no heat and nor did it crackle. Still, the girl begged to be freed and so Michelle frantically ran her fingers over the car's surface, feeling for any gap, weakness or opening. Again, this was useless; the windows were closed, and the car was solid. Michelle ran around the car's perimeter three times, kicking up dirty water as she went.

Impossible as it was within the time that had passed, the entire road had become flooded. A flash flood, it was of proportions Michelle had never witnessed – or indeed ever heard of – in North London.

There was nothing for it: Michelle would have to break the car's window. With gritted teeth, she slammed clenched fists to the glass as rain pounded her face – ruining make-up and streaking mascara.

Thump.

Thump.

As if she was punching brick, it was futile. The only damage Michelle inflicted was to her own knuckles. Desperation rising with the road's water, she looked this way and that. Time for this girl was surely running out, if she didn't act fast.

Michelle spied the builder's skip a few doors down and she waded over to it. At knee height, water rushed through front gates and floated garden gnomes. Atop the skip – which now resembled an over-flowing bathtub – was a lump of masonry, formed by a trio of house bricks. Michelle lifted it with both hands and, with muscles spasming, returned to the car.

The entrapped girl remained in peril. Facing away, she seemed unaware of the detective inspector's efforts to free her. It was now or never. Michelle hoisted the masonry over her right shoulder and flung it with all her might at the driver's side window. Eyes closed, she prepared herself for impact.

Splash.

Michelle's eyes sprung open to a tsunami of odorous water. With grubby hands, she blinkingly wiped her face clean, but the car was nowhere to be seen and neither was the girl in the black lace dress. The masonry simply lay in an empty space between two other cars, with water softly trickling over it. No longer flooded, the road looked just as it had before.

Michelle Davey, the supposed very ordinary detective inspector, stood confused and shaken, herself hunched and dripping. She collapsed into a heap on the camber, quite literally head in hands and with her skirt riding unceremoniously high. The contents of her discarded handbag scattered out around her, the usually plucky and courageous officer had been forever changed within that moment; reduced to a mere shadow of her former self.

Within that moment, it was as if curtains had been parted. Michelle's view of the world had been remastered in high definition. The aspect ratio had altered, as the past could be seen in the present.

*

The mysterious girl's unexplainable disappearance left but one other ghostly face in Dragnell Lane, and that wasn't Michelle's. A middle-aged woman, thin from months of worry – yet most certainly corporeal – stood motionless inside the front bedroom of number 23. Looking down upon the detective inspector's crouched figure, she slowly and precisely rearranged the nets from behind which she had just viewed, what she'd believed to have been, a grown woman suffering some sort of mental breakdown.

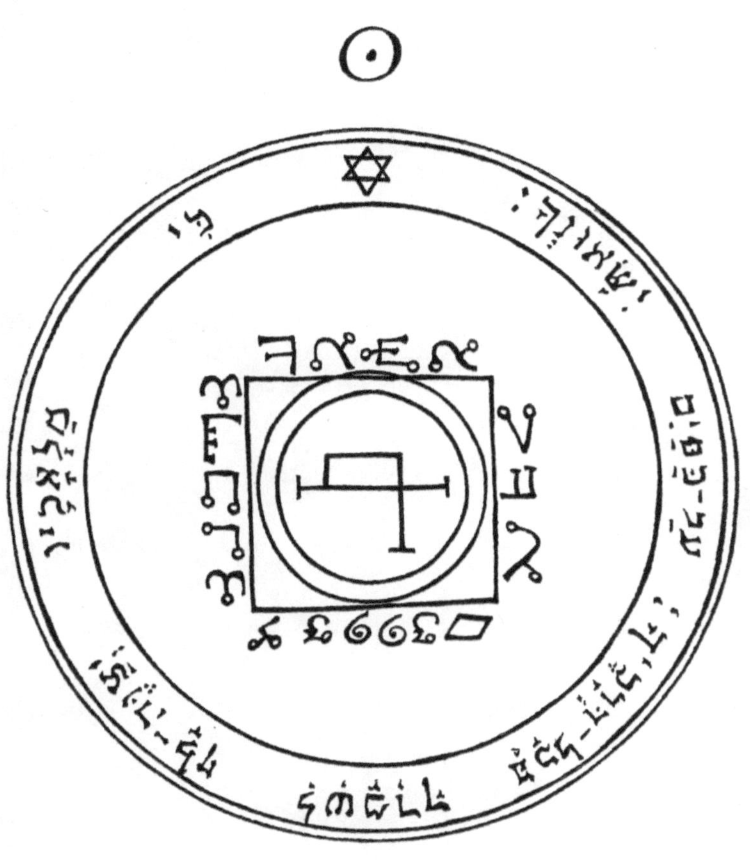

ACT I

CHAPTER I

Rye Turpin

Eight days earlier …

<u>Tuesday 2nd September 1997, 19:43pm, SULLEN WOODS, ASH-FIELD, LONDON.</u>

Cassette tape spinning in her Walkman, Savage Garden's 'I Want You,' flooded fifteen-year-old Rye Turpin's ears through headphones. A person who'd often take long walks in nature alone, she was the type to envisage life's montage to musical accompaniment. And it was one of these walks that had led her down to the lakeside in Sullen Woods, where she sat mermaid-like in the shade of an old oak.

The stone Rye threw hit the water, sending out ripples of concentric circles. Blonde hair tousled by the light breeze, she watched as the projectile sank to murky depths. Head tilted and pondering, her hand hovered over the bank's wide selection of pebbles before selecting her next target; a flat, black and circular one. She immediately set about dislodging it from the earth's firm grasp by scraping away at the dirt with her fingernails.

Rye loaded the stone into a grubby palm – it fit perfectly. Hopeful, she drew back her arm and fired, slinging the stone across the lake's surface. A couple of dozen feet and this, just like the others, refused to skim and plopped. Rye released her bated breath with a sigh. And it was then that the sun caressed the treetops – her cue to leave. With evening's onset, Rye's sister, Pris, would soon start to worry. Not just a school night, tomorrow was September the third and the start of a new school year.

Standing, Rye brushed herself down and inspected a fresh rip in her jeans above the left knee. It wouldn't need mending, but Pris would insist that it did. She'd be pissed for sure, or as Rye dubbed it, 'Pris-*ed*.'

Pris was elder by five years, not that – in the mind of a younger sibling – that should dictate any superiority. But for as long as Rye could remember, her sister had acted as such.

This was because Pris was not just Rye's sibling, but her guardian also. Their parents had died when they'd been aged seven and two, respectively, and, even at such a tender age, Pris had always striven to protect.

Ever since they'd both been taken in by their father's cousin, Veronica Tremaine, and her husband, Harry, Pris had truly been the one to step up, and she continued to do so. Thirteen years later and, with herself verging on adulthood, Rye had come to misconstrue Pris's overprotectiveness as meddlesome nosiness.

Music still playing, Rye tamed her hair into a ponytail by use of her emergency scrunchie and commenced the walk home. Weaving in amongst the trees, the trail she followed was overgrown, and much narrower than the track she'd taken down to the lake.

Her thoughts meandered with her path, inevitably settling upon school once more. To say that Rye was dreading its start would be overly dramatic but like most teenagers, she was hardly thrilled. A distinctly average pupil, teachers would rather describe her as a tryer than an achiever, which was quite incorrect. Rye didn't achieve – this was true – but nor did she try. If she did, then perhaps she would.

Several golden leaves fluttered down before her and Rye readily snatched out to catch them. Alas, this proved yet another unsuccessful attempt to bend nature to her will. Another fell and Rye chased it to the woodland's edge. From here she could see the church and tower blocks in the distance. At the summit of the adjacent field's hillside, this cluster marked the north-most periphery of Ashfield.

Rye's fingertips had just caressed the leaf when her cassette cut out. With music stopped, so did she, as the power dropped from her heart. She opened the player's battery compartment and gave them a twist—

Crack.

The undisputable snap of a twig echoed throughout the tranquillity. As Rye jolted then froze, the batteries fell out to the ground. Though initially shocked, she wasn't greatly perturbed, attributing the sound's origin to a heavier woodland creature than the squirrel that had bolted up the nearest tree. A rabbit, or muntjac deer, perhaps?

Cra-ck.

Drawn-out, this sound was much closer and softer. Rye looked back over her shoulder, sliding her headphones down to around her neck. Scanning the trees and undergrowth, it was impossible to discern any separate entities from the growing tangle of shadows that were slowly creeping with the setting sun.

'Hello?!' Rye called out, bravely.

A bird abruptly took flight from a treetop and she flinched. Disgusted at her own cowardice, she tentatively took a few steps towards the area where the latest noise had emanated. She homed in on a holly bush and took another step, her eyes ever focusing. A further step and the bush began to rustle. Slow at first, the rustling then grew in intensity and volume until the bush was practically a hum of vibration that sent dying leaves flying in all directions.

Frantically retreating, Rye tumbled onto her backside and the cassette player that was clipped there. Dumbfounded, and with her sense of fear rising, she lay sprawled, gaze transfixed, as the vibrations began a process of transference from bush to bush. Rye tracked its path, shuffling around upon the ground. The source of the disturbance somehow remained concealed as it encircled her by near one hundred and eighty degrees. Whatever it was now posed an obstacle to her escape through the open field. All movement then ceased and all of nature held its breath.

Seconds passed, preceding a violent shudder that shook loose another deluge of leaves. This was followed by a high-pitched and gleeful laugh that broke Rye out in cold sweats; forehead, neck and pits. She stood, quivering from head to toe. Her fear was apparently being enjoyed – lapped up, even. The laugh didn't sound human. Its tone was playful, yet far from innocent.

Then it spoke.

'Must look. *Look* for what we're told.'

Little more than a whisper and almost auto-tuned, Rye could not distinguish gender. Blood drained from her face.

'Listen to the pretty girl,' it sang louder, and Rye's heart quickened. '*Listen* to what she knows.'

The sun, ever sinking, stretched out the gloom.

'Not kill her!' exclaimed the voice louder still, followed by a pause and the quietest of whispers, as if to remind itself. '*Kill* for what we're told.'

At this, Rye took flight. Forcing her legs into cooperation, she ran around the bush from where the voice had just spoken. She dared not look back.

Faster, faster, Rye increased her speed up the field's hill past the bandstand, her cassette player bouncing. The sound of hooves – heavy and strong – pounded the grass mere feet behind. Her vision shaken and unfocused, Rye's eyes were quick to become watery and blinkered, as her own breathing and heart reverberated to intersperse the rhythm of the chase. With the church and tower blocks looming, she raced for them. Rye had never been good at sports – a natural runner, she was not.

Forty feet.

Thirty.

Twenty.

Ten.

Now on the pavement, in a dozen or so streets, Rye would be home. But her feet left the curb before she'd seen the car hurtling along the lane. Swerving to avoid her – tyres screeching and horn slammed – its dark-colour blurred past. Lit up like a Christmas tree, the car disappeared around the corner as a beer can was thrown to the gutter.

Rye regained pace, spurred on by her near-brush with death. But her aching legs only allowed her to run the length of the next road before grinding to a halt. In the midst of stereotypical suburbia, all the houses here had well-maintained gardens and neatly painted front doors. Hands-on knees and wheezing, Rye turned around and around on the spot in search of her pursuer. There was no-one, however – no sound of hooves – and she couldn't be sure when they'd relented. The freakish voice repeated itself over and over in her head as resonance. It had to have been some sort of trick – a prank, she thought.

The wind, stronger and cold, whistled between the houses to ruffle hedgerows. Rye shivered and with her legs protesting, launched into a fast walk, intending to not stop again until she was home.

A little over five minutes later and Rye was passing through Ashfield's town centre. Still, she continued to check back over her shoulder. She crossed the busy high street, this time ensuring to look both ways.

Like moths to a flame, groups of unruly teens clogged the pavements, clustered around brightly lit fast-food outlets, smoking, drinking and clutching bags of fried chicken. Amongst the tracksuits, white trainers and oversized jewellery, Rye stood out like a sore thumb in a grass-stained T-shirt and torn jeans.

Tensed, she kept her head low and shoulders high. Rye's headphones quiet, they were nonetheless replaced atop her head.

And sure enough, her tried and tested method of flying under the radar worked a charm, until—

'Oh, Rye,' a voice close by cooed.

Thoughts of Sullen Woods fresh in her mind, Rye spun, headphones slipping, fists raised and ponytail flicking.

'Oooh, why so scared?' Trinity spoke again, sickly sweet.

Simultaneously the most popular and unpopular girl at school, Trinity Fry headed up a trio that smirked, bullied and backstabbed their way through life. What they lacked in personality, they more than made up for in make-up. Luckily for Rye, the other two appeared absent.

Trinity leant against the side of a telephone box. Like a cat, she skulked in the shadows but in four-inch heels and a sequined boob tube. Chestnut hair curled and crimped to precision, it cascaded down past hooped earrings. She was wearing a skirt, but Rye had to double-take to be sure. Trinity clocked her staring.

'You a lesbian?'

'What? No. Why?' Rye replied, unoffended but reactionary.

Strutting out into the centre of the pavement, Trinity kissed her teeth. The movement was intentional intimidation. If Trinity was a cat, then Rye was her prey.

'You oughta get your legs out,' she mused. 'Or, perhaps not, if what I've seen in the changing room is anything to go by.'

Trinity's comments bounced clean off Rye. She had no qualms about her developing assets; she just chose not to show them off.

'I'm going home,' Rye said, simply.

And with that, she walked away.

'I'm waiting for my boyfriend, anyway!' Trinity called after her, indignant. 'Guess you wouldn't know about … that's right! Walk away, orphan!'

<u>Tuesday 2nd September 1997, 20:27pm, TURPIN RESIDENCE, 32 KYNASTON GARDENS, ASHFIELD, LONDON.</u>

Another fifteen minutes and Rye reached home, at the end of a short cul-de-sac. Semi-detached, these houses were built in the thirties and large enough to boast both front and back gardens. Suffering months of neglect, their own was jungle-like and so Rye ducked an overhang and leapt some creepers as she traversed the path to the door. She retrieved the spare key out from under a cracked plant pot, whilst desperately hoping that Pris wasn't home.

Midway through re-taking her A levels at a local community college, Pris also worked shifts at a bar. Although Rye tried, she could never quite remember her sister's ever-changing rota, but she suspected today was her day off.

Rye quietly closed the door behind her and headed straight for the stairs. The hallway, like the rest of the interior, was smartly decorated, albeit dated and twee. Predominately pink, it was ridden with crocheted doilies.

Rye was less than halfway up the stairs when Pris emerged from the sitting room, her face like thunder. A blonde also, though through repeated use of cheap peroxide, the look did nothing to soften her prominent features, particularly whilst riled.

'And where have you been?' she demanded.

'I've been at Zach's,' Rye replied, thinking on her feet. 'I'm sorry, I should have called.'

Rye hated to lie but her sister was always so frantic.

'No, you haven't,' Pris dismissed, producing the cordless phone from behind her back. 'He just called to ask if you wanted a curry.'

Rye sighed, her chest and heart sinking. She didn't have the energy. Slouching against the bannisters, she prepared herself for a lecture.

'Oi – Rye – look at me when I'm talking to you.'

Seeing she was being ignored, Pris rolled her eyes, tutted and continued.

'Just let me know where you are – that's all! It's that simple. A note – a phone call—'

'If I had a pager, I could have paged you,' Rye sniped. 'Everyone else has one. You have one.'

'If you want a pager, you can get a job and then maybe you'll be given one. And don't change the subject. Six months, Rye. Six months, Veronica and Harry have been gone. What if something had happened to you?'

Pris had begun dramatically speaking with her hands – a habit she possessed, and one which Rye despised. Rye also despised that on this occasion Pris was right – something had happened to her.

'You're overreacting a little, don't you think? It's only eight-thirty.'

'It's dark. You know the rules.'

Each sister – equally as stubborn – held a glare.

'Is there anything else?' Rye asked, business-like.

'Do you want dinner?'

'I'm not hungry.'

Without another word, Rye turned and resumed her climb.

'Well, best be sure you're awake and on time for school tomorrow,' warned Pris, voice raised. 'I'm out early for beer delivery, so don't rely on me to get you up. We don't want to draw attention to our situation and have Social Services sniffing around!'

Rye would face round two with Pris tomorrow, no doubt when the rip in her jeans was discovered, but for the time being her concerns were elsewhere. She could think of nothing but the haunting voice from Sullen Woods.

The doorknob to Rye's bedroom squeaked as she turned it and the door creaked open. A large room, at the back of the house, she'd only occupied it since spring. Before then, it had been Harry's study.

Six months. It had been six months since Veronica and the ladies of her book club's syndicate had won on the National Lottery, and Rye remembered the night of the Saturday draw clearly. By ball four, Veronica had slammed shut her works of Daniel Defoe. Final ball and the book was airborne, as she screamed, '*Fuck you, Friday, and screw you, Crusoe! I'm goin' cruisin'!*'

And so, she had. It had come as no surprise when neither Rye nor Pris had been invited along for their travels, but it had when they realised they'd been left without a single penny. Weeks passed, bills piled up, and with no hint of Veronica and Harry's return, Rye had taken it upon herself to upgrade from sharing the box room, as Pris took it upon herself to obtain employment. It was only with encouragement that Pris had also upgraded herself, to the master bedroom.

Striding into the room, Rye made a beeline for the windows. She peered out with caution before closing them. All appeared as it should. Her eyes' focus shifted onto her own reflection and Rye exhaled. She felt silly and berated herself for it. Drawing the curtains, she forced her fears aside with them and without bothering to change, withdrew to bed.

Having to yet dismantle and move the frame from out of the box room, Rye's bed was a single mattress on the floor's centre. Essentially, she camped there, surrounded by just a few cherished belongings. After over a decade of living in the house and Rye was still without a wardrobe. She lived out of tattered cardboard boxes. Just as this house had never truly been her home, no room would ever truly be hers either. There was nothing typical of a teenager within; no posters adorned the walls, no knick-knacks or books of her own.

Rye groped at her bed's covers, patting and parting them until she found what she'd been searching for – her diary. An old Maths exercise book, its blue cover was a mass of doodles, stars, spirals and song lyrics. As Rye flipped through its pages, a photograph slid out, as it did every time, of herself as a baby, a young Pris and their parents. The only photograph still in existence of their original family unit, Rye kept it here as to ensure it wouldn't fade – a location and logic that Pris was kind to allow. It was striking how Rye had grown to resemble her mother. Both naturally blonde and slender with slight features and a thin mouth, the only difference was that Rye was yet to need glasses.

Though it had been made well-known to the sisters how very hard Cousin Veronica had fought to spare them from a life of foster care, it was also no secret that she'd always yearned for children of her own – a fact frequently referenced by both sides during arguments. Whatever Veronica's initial motive had been with taking them in, it became obvious over the years that it was regretted. Realised through neglect. Harry, on the other hand, had despised them both for as long as either sister could remember.

Heart aching, Rye slipped the photograph back inside her diary and turned to a blank page. After hastily scrawling the date, she held her pen poised – unsure – as her mind swam backwards. Seconds passed – a whole minute, in fact – before Rye finally committed pen to paper. Tongue held between her teeth; she furiously transcribed the evening's peculiarities in detail.

Initially a tangled scrawl, Rye was left to edit her lengthy account so as to ensure its legibility. By the end of her third read through, her eyelids had grown heavy. The sound of a train rushing by in the distance and the faint hubbub of the main road acted as an urban lullaby. Rye was unaware of her head having even touched the pillow, but before long she had plummeted into a deep sleep.

Hours later, the door to Rye's bedroom creaked open once more – slowly this time. Moving quietly, a solitary figure entered, to stand over and study her.

'Rye?' spoke Pris, softly. 'I've got you something to eat.'

Except for the few strands of rogue hair that twitched with every exhaling breath, Rye remained still. The corners of Pris's mouth pulled into a tired smile. Carefully, she placed a packet of cheese and onion crisps on the floor beside her sleeping sister, then folded over the patchwork quilt.

'Goodnight,' whispered Pris, as she leant in to kiss Rye on the forehead.

Inadvertently flopping a delicate hand over her diary, Rye conveniently concealed her latest entry from wandering eyes and so Pris left the room, leaving the door ajar. Whilst unconscious, the subject of Rye's writing preyed upon her dreams before they were ultimately hijacked.

- CHAPTER II -

September the Third

<u>Wednesday 3rd September 1997, 07:09am, HEATHROW AIR-PORT, LONDON.</u>

Alexis 'Ally' Monaghan walked briskly through the airport terminal. Her white blouse bore streaks of neon green and its pits were stained with yellow sweat. Her dark hair was sticky. Despite this, she remained effortlessly pretty, if somewhat fatigued. A short skirt and knee-high boots – both black – completed the look.

Appearing older than her years, Ally had only recently turned seventeen – not that she knew it. Her fraudulent passport stated she'd been eighteen since the twenty-second of March, and that was the date she had come to adopt and honour. But she would not adopt its name. There was something about 'Patricia Valery' that made her hungry.

Knuckles white, Ally held onto a black leather briefcase in her left hand. It did not belong to her, it belonged to Mick – the same man who'd provided her with the passport – but she had stolen it and the money within, and fled Barcelona, leaving him for dead. Certainly, Ally feared Mick – everyone did – but by leaving, she'd proven herself stronger.

Ally turned off right of the corridor for the toilets. Therein, everything gleamed. Everything, except for Ally. She paused by her reflection. Having been pummelled black and blue, Ally had tried her best to conceal all visible damage with make-up. Many of her bruises were unseen, however, hidden beneath her clothes and in places she'd rather not dwell. For a minute, she stared off against herself.

Placing the briefcase in a sink and both hands on either side, Ally leant ever closer to the mirror. Lips aquiver, she willed them to form words of self-motivation.

'Fucking pull yourself together, Ally,' she hissed, in a Scottish lilt. 'You don't know where you're going, but that's OK – you never have. You look like shit,' she observed, prising apart her eyelids. 'But that's OK, too. You've got the money and you've got your freedom – *almost.*'

Ally slid a cheek across the glass, eyes closing, as she crumpled. Oh, how she wished she could sleep. She hadn't managed to on the plane.

'Mummy, is the lady crazy?'

Ally jumped back away from the mirror and, turning, was faced with a mother and child. The mother, standing legs apart, clasped her son close.

Anxious, Ally snatched up her briefcase. In an act of composure, she wiped her palm down from her forehead to her neck, but in doing so, unknowingly smudged concealer to reveal a purple blotch above her collarbone.

'Are you—' began the mother.

'Beautiful morning,' Ally breezed. 'Perfect conditions for landing. Everyone clapped.'

Eyes wide, Ally then swept past the pair, feeling the woman's gaze linger upon her as she exited the lavatories. Only after she'd re-joined the bustling throng did Ally realise that she hadn't peed. *Beautiful morning,* Ally thought. Never had she said such a thing.

Several more twists and turns, and the disembarked passengers filtered into lines for European and Non-EU Internationals. Ally's heart thumped against her ribcage. A mix of emotion, her anticipation at the prospect of a new life began to build. She moved forward a step and the corners of her mouth twitched. Another step and Ally brushed her hair behind her ears. Two more steps and she straightened her blouse. Finally, giving in to temptation, Ally beamed. Next in line; she could practically taste freedom.

The black woman in the booth at passport control waved Ally forwards and she obliged, passport extended. One-on-one, a prolonged silence ensued.

'Enjoy your holiday?' the woman finally spoke, matter-of-factly and in a strong Jamaican accent. Her tag revealed her name as Helen.

'No, not really,' Ally replied with a stretched smile, her own accent strengthening, as she scraped away at her cuticles. 'I'm just glad to be home.'

'Did y'go far?'

'No. Why?'

Teeth gritted, Ally's smile was frozen.

'I was jus' wondering how far you got on dis t'ing?' Helen replied, dryly.

Head still, Helen's eyes swivelled between Ally and the passport. After repeating the action several times, she beckoned to a man in uniform.

Ally's eyes remained fixed and staring. Gut clenched; her smile had completely faded. As sweat reformed on her brow, it felt as if a rug had been pulled out from under her. Ally did not hear any of what was said between Helen and the uniformed officer. All she heard was the deathly silence that had infected the crowd, and it was consuming her. The officer then addressed Ally directly and his one sentence was enough to bring both her eyes, and thoughts, back into focus.

'You'll have to come with me, miss.'

Escorted by the arm, her briefcase confiscated, Ally was led back through the airport and away from passport control. Whispers followed the pair as bystanders pointed and craned their necks for a better view. Ally stole a look over her shoulder – a glance – at her fading route to freedom.

'I'm sure there's no problem,' said the officer, but Ally knew this to just be spiel. 'This is only procedure—'

It was in a moment of desperation that Ally elbowed her captor in the stomach. But the thought of being sent back to Barcelona – back to the consequence of her actions – awoke an animal instinct for survival within her.

Amid gasps and screams, the winded officer's grasp slackened and was easily shaken off. Ally extracted her briefcase from his hand and thwacked a corner – hard – into his crotch for good measure. She then ran, her sights set, back towards passport control.

One man, a would-be hero in his twenties, ducked out from the queue and adopted a stance for a rugby tackle. But he lacked the strength and build, and with momentum on her side, Ally bowled through him as if he were a pin.

Quickly gaining ground, Ally could see Helen once more. Having climbed down from off her high perch, she appeared in a battle against her booth's door. A further obstacle to Ally's escape, a group of three – two women and a young girl – to whom Helen had just been attending, stood dumbstruck in the pass.

The recovering officer audibly in pursuit, Ally increased her speed. She locked eyes with Helen, and woman's fumbling grew incensed. If looks could kill… Undecided which way, the two other women pulled the young girl by the wrist and in opposite directions, as the teddy held by her limply swung.

The race came to a head in the final split-second. With one of the women winning the tug-of-war, the trio ultimately parted. Dropping to the floor, only the girl's teddy was left behind, which Ally jumped over. Helen burst through her cubicle's door just as the pursuing officer misplaced a step and skidded on the stuffed bear, to take out her legs. Both cursing, they were left in a painful, tangled heap, as Ally hopped the railing of the staircase.

One floor below, Ally blindly ran. Yells rippled out as she pushed and shoved her way. She had no plan. Tripping over an elderly man's foot, Ally stumbled and fell into the back of an Asian gentleman dressed in a sharp suit. The blonde in five-inch heels who accompanied him shouted abusively at her in a foreign language and Ally darted between them.

Through a mass of orange baseball caps, Ally could spy baggage reclaim and it was then she was hit by an idea. All that stood between her and its execution was this group of teenagers in their matching coloured T-shirts. Accidentally kicking a younger and much shorter girl in her struggle, Ally persevered.

Reaching the nearest luggage belt, Ally dived headlong onto its moving conveyor to ungracefully land with a somewhat comical thud. Bruises forming atop bruises; the action hurt even more than she'd anticipated. She crawled against the motion, scrambling through vertical strips of hanging plastic.

Awkwardly, Ally hoisted her skirt higher, itself threatening to split, as she was forced to kneel, flop and roll – anything necessary to manoeuvre past the endless stream of travelling baggage. All the while she held onto her own briefcase.

Ally roamed for what felt like an eternity. Like a child lost within a maze, she repeatedly chose the left tunnel whenever the conveyor split, until she feared ending up where she started, and so turned right.

Like trying to move through custard, it was as if time itself had slowed, as it always felt when someone was in a hurry to be somewhere other than where they were. This, and the fact that the conveyor was moving in the opposite direction to herself, although it too had seemed to slow.

Eventually, Ally quite literally saw the light at the end of the tunnel and so made her final scramble. She hurled a large holdall over her shoulder as she then plopped down onto tarmac.

On all fours and blinking, Ally took in her new sur-roundings. Beside a forklift and piles of luggage, she'd emerged at the edge of the airstrip. Eyes coming to rest on a pair of thin legs clad in scruffy trousers, she followed them upwards past an equally scruffy shirt to meet the pockmarked face of a young man staring back at her. Statue-like, he stood mid-action, ready to chuck another case. Ally gave her blouse a sharp tug, allowing its top two buttons to pop open.

'What the – are you alright?' the young man asked, finding his words and Ally's face.

'Wouldn't mind a hand,' she replied, holding out her right.

Reciprocating with his own, the man helped Ally to her feet. She straightened up and rearranged her skirt by way of slinking it down her thighs with an emphasised shimmy.

'How did you—'

'Would you believe it? I just *fell in* and the conveyor – it wouldn't stop moving. Quite hazardous really – I could sue!'

Thoroughly gormless, the young man nodded his concern. Ally was surprised to see that, despite the mechanics involved, he had apparently bought her explanation.

'Try the next one!'

Ally's eyes widened and she gulped. The shouting had come from close by.

'You should really see a medic,' the young man continued. 'Have yourself checked for—'

'That won't be necessary,' Ally assured him. 'I'm perfectly fine.'

She flashed him a seductive wink and gave his bottom a firm squeeze. He gasped but smiled at her touch. Breaking into a run, Ally then dashed under the aeroplane's wing, leaving her aide doe-eyed and dizzy.

A quick look to her right and Ally could see a gaggle of airport security. Gaining on her fast, she was alarmed to spot that they carried pistols. Immediately, Ally turned left. Proceeding to sprint the runway, her boots pounded the tarmac.

The morning sun beat down upon her. And the horizon bounced a sea of grey and green, as an aeroplane came in to land. Ally veered diagonally left again. Whipped up by the wind, hair stuck to her face as sweat trickled and dripped from her cheeks. Reverse thrusters roaring from the descending aircraft, the sound ripped through the words shouted after her.

'… LAST …'

'…WARNING …'

'… MUST …'

'… NOW …'

'… STOP …'

Still, Ally ran. Her legs wanted to buckle and fold right there and then, but still, she ran. Fast approaching the edge of the airfield, Ally could make out the airport's entrance. As she made it her target, it dawned upon her; she had not thought this through. There was no way in which Ally could enter the building in order to escape.

Tearing up the grass, a bullet collided with the earth a foot behind her left boot, splattering its leather with dirt. Multiple shots; Ally heard the bullets' whistling. Sharply, she turned the corner of the airport's main building, only to come face-to-face with a thirty-foot-high chain-link fence.

Fear and panic took hold as Ally began to run her hands all over it. Up high and down low, she moved her palms across it in search of a miracle. Surely, this was the world's worst hangover, she thought.

❧🖑❧

<u>Wednesday 3rd September 1997, 07:30am, BATEMAN RESIDENCE, 52 BELLAMY AVENUE, ASHFIELD, LONDON.</u>

The sound of the alarm rang loudly through Fred's dreams, ending them suddenly and waking him. Rolling over, he wrapped his pillow around his head. The ringing persisted, of course, and so he begrudgingly set out across the room to where his clock was purposely placed. Tiptoeing, Fred navigated every book, dirty mug and loose cassette tape, his stance emulating that of a zombie.

Fred's hand was a hare's whisker from the top of the clock when a flash of dark-brown streaked across the back of his desk. A misplaced step and he quickly lost balance. Fred fell to the floor with a heavy thud. Spread-eagled and now fully awake, he tilted his head sideways. Looking down at him from atop a stack of open books was his sister's pet gerbil. It snuffled its tiny nose and Fred narrowed his eyes.

Standing, Fred slapped the clock, then proceeded to scoop the rodent up, simultaneously ripping the topmost page free. Head throbbing, and holding them at arm's-length, he descended the stairs and padded through the hallway into the kitchen. His younger sister, Mollie, was sat at the breakfast table. Their father sat opposite. Unconcerned by the appearance of his son, Stan Bateman's fat and bald head remained buried in the newspaper.

'Molls, your rat shat in my textbook,' Fred declared.

He thrust the tiny mammal towards her with one hand whilst dropping the parcelled excrement into the bin with his other.

Mollie clambered down from her chair, dropping her feet to the floor. While she was – as Fred always teased – small for her age, he by comparison, was amongst the tallest in his class. Though alike in looks – both had hazel hair and eyes to match – this was where any similarity ended. Mollie was only six, but that was no excuse for forgetting to lock her pet's cage door, thought Fred.

'You should keep a better eye on it,' he criticised, depositing the gerbil into her cupped palms. 'Mum nearly vac-uumed 'im up last week.'

Far from scaring sense into his little sister, Mollie's miniature face instead became a picture of fury, her cute cheeks ablaze with colour.

'Say *her* full name!' she demanded, her mouth full of cereal.

Hardly a third of Fred's height, Mollie stood a pint-sized version of their mother.

Having rid himself of Fudge Cindy Coco Pops *(Mrs)*, Fred decided to skip breakfast. A likely consequence of his friend Zach's choice of takeaway the night before, his stomach felt a little worse for wear.

Withdrawing to the sitting room, he curled up on the comfy sofa. As the first day of a new school year, Ashfield Community did not open until the second period. Ipso facto, Fred deemed an hour's channel surfing justified.

'Can we watch the music channel?'

Her voice eager, Mollie skipped into the room, to sit cross-legged on the floor directly in Fred's line of vision. Physically constrained within the lap of her white fluffy dressing gown, the gerbil fought valiantly.

'Let's watch the music channel.'

'Not now,' replied Fred, flatly. 'Meerkats.'

He gestured at the television.

Mollie went to snatch the remote from Fred's hands, but he was too fast for her. He held it aloft his head, far out of her reach. In retaliation, Mollie leapt onto the sofa and onto Fred himself. The pair's fingers wrestled over the buttons and the television obediently switched between stations:

'After suffering an accident at work, Suzanne — the Starling population has dropped — reports of a security breach at Heathrow Airport — Garibaldi, Dorothy? — down eight, from number eleven, it's Meredith Brooks with, Bitch.'

Pre-empting Mollie using her teeth, Fred suddenly let go of the remote in surrender. He left the room silently fuming, and leaving his little sister bouncing and twirling to the chorus of a track that his mother would no doubt deem inappropriate. Fred, however, found its title aptly fitting. Fudge zoomed about the room in every direction, as Mollie waved her arms around in time to the beat.

Returning to the kitchen, Fred sat down beside his father. 'Where's Mum?' he asked.

'She's having a lie-in,' came the muffled reply, from behind the business pull-out.

Fred translated this to mean that she had tried, and failed, at keeping pace with Sarah's cocktail intake the previous night. Sarah was Zach's mother. *'I was just being polite,'* was sure to be her excuse later, but Fred begged to differ. The only time he'd ever witnessed his own mother drunk, both she and Sarah had whipped their skirts off to a karaoke rendition of Bucks Fizz. Fred's mother was uptight, but if anyone was able to encourage her, it was Sarah – like mother, like son.

Fred picked up the main paper – the *Daily Mail* – but threw it down after reading the headline: 'Diana Seven Face Death Trial'. There was no more he wished to read about the horrid incident.

He stared dismally at the date upon the newspaper's cover. Zach would come calling in a couple of hours, most likely without Rye. She'd probably be late, as was tradition. The same dull and dreary school year was then almost certainly destined to repeat itself, yet again, as nothing interesting ever happened to them.

*

Ally's eyes fixed on the bottom right-hand corner of the fence. There was a three-feet-high vertical slit where the links had been uncoupled from the frame. She could have sworn it hadn't been that way a second ago.

Back on all fours, Ally's head was jerked backwards as her hair became entangled in the wire. She swore loudly between sharp breaths, her fingers shaking, as she ripped strands free. A few ever more violent movements and she was detached, only to have her briefcase that she dragged pull her back again. Ally twisted it upright and it slid neatly through.

Ally half-slid, half-ran down the steep gradient that followed. The stony clay crumbling beneath her feet, gorse bushes and barbed wire threatened to tear and trip her. She dared not slow, just ensured precision. Barely able to maintain balance, she skidded onto the path below. With five lanes on either side, the adjacent road was large and awash with traffic of all sorts. Hotels and car parks lined its opposite side, and a bus station. Ally headed for the latter, knowing that her body could not go on much longer.

With a leap of faith, Ally rushed across the road to its median. Cars screeched and honked, for not only was her green-cross code way below par, but her blouse remained unbuttoned past her cleavage. She traversed the final lanes with more caution.

As Ally climbed aboard the nearest bus, she tried her best to look casual. It was a futile attempt in and of itself, without her slipping the driver a twenty under the grille.

'Keep the change,' she uttered, breathlessly.

The driver didn't disappoint and greedily stuffed the note into his trousers' pocket before ushering the next passenger to come forward.

Between commuters, Ally squeezed a path towards the back of the bus. Busy typing away on laptops or chatting into their phones, no-one took any notice of her. Cleanliness aside, Ally's attire did well to camouflage her within the young affluent professionals.

'Move,' she prayed. 'Just, *move.*'

From out of the corner of her vision, Ally became increasingly aware that she was attracting the unwanted attention of one somewhat smarmy individual. The owner of a similar briefcase to her own, it was rested in the aisle beside his seat. Complete with slicked-back hair and a hands-free headset, the man looked Ally up and down. Smiling, he raised his eyebrows closer to his receding hairline. She responded by quickly buttoning up her blouse and looking away.

'Course you're flash,' Ally whispered to herself. 'That's why you're taking the *bus* to work.'

With a whoosh and a snap, the doors closed, and they were off. Ally allowed herself to slump against a nearby pole, wishing that there was space for her to lie down. Every time the bus came to a halt, Ally extended her neck to assess the reason for the delay. Intermittently, she'd check her watch, forgetting it was broken. A recent gift from Mick; it was expensive, and certainly worth keeping, if only for resale value.

'I know that feeling,' said a voice next to her – it was the man with the slicked hair. 'Some days I just can't wait to get into the office.'

'Oh, yeah?' replied Ally, uncaring. She turned away and the man's smile faded.

It was then the bus turned a sharp right and all its standing passengers – Ally included – were caught off balance. The bus turned a second corner and Ally was flung into the lap of another commuter. Pushing herself off, she stooped low to the floor, and with her left arm outstretched, attempted to crawl back to her initial position, and briefcase. *Success*. Ally clung to the base of the pole, exhausted, but relieved.

The bus journey seemed to last a lifetime, although in truth was only half an hour. Disembarking at a random stop – someplace near Tottenham Court Road Station – Ally was a stranger in a busy street of an unfamiliar capital. After a couple of suited workers expressed exasperation, she swiftly repositioned herself at the edge of the pavement. Her full bladder a priority, she clocked a coffee shop a little further down the street.

Upon entering, Ally was quick to locate the toilet. She took one last look through the gap before shutting and bolting its door. Painted an earthy red, the window-less interior was dimly lit, which did nothing but add weight to her eyelids.

Not wishing to look at herself in the mirror this time, Ally pulled down her skirt and knickers to take a throne. Exhaling heavily, relief washed over her. Another deep breath and she lifted her briefcase up from beside the bowl. She placed its leather atop her naked thighs.

As she unsnapped the clasps with one hand, Ally ran her fingers through her hair. It was tangled and knotted – hardly surprising. Her knuckles were bleeding and raw – that was hardly surprising either. At least she was free, and she had her money. She opened the briefcase and its hinges squeaked.

Ally gasped. The money – it was gone. In its place was a stack of printed spreadsheets. Aghast, she lifted the pile out, allowing its paper to haphazardly flutter. A Polaroid depicting a woman dressed in suspenders, and laying across a desk, slipped out from between the pages. There was no uncertainty as to what had happened. It appeared that her preconceived views of the smarmy man on the bus were, in fact, correct. Sure, Ally had gained her freedom, but it had cost her. She was now penniless.

Vacating the toilet, Ally strode back through the coffee shop. Casually, she collected a half-full takeaway cup from an abandoned table on her way. A cockroach when it came to survival, Ally had more than a few tricks up her sleeve and within seconds had selected her unwitting victim. Sat outside under the awning, he was alone and had removed his blazer – as was essential, it hung off the back of his chair. As Ally walked right up to him, she loosened the coffee cup's lid.

'Excuse me?' she asked with a smile.

The man looked up from his newspaper and smiled also. This only made Ally feel worse for what she was about to do.

'Could I please borrow your phone?' she continued, in a faux English accent. 'I have a very important call to make, and mine's chosen now – of all times – to give up the ghost. You'd really be helping me out.'

'No trouble at all,' the man replied, politely, and gladly passed over his brick-like mobile from the table. 'Happy to help.'

The next stage was even easier than usual. Exaggerating a minor brush with a passing commuter, Ally fell forward – spilling, then dropping, her coffee down her already stained blouse and skirt. She yelped, faking its temperature, as the stone-cold liquid trickled over her knees.

Living up to expectation, Ally's target acted the gentleman. In a flash, he had leapt up from his seat and rushed inside, in search of a napkin. That was all the time Ally needed to slide her hand inside the stranger's blazer pocket to extract a wallet. She held it behind her back, out of sight.

Upon returning with a clump of paper towel, the man hesitated. After concluding it inappropriate for him to dry Ally's legs himself, he instead thrust them across.

'Here – take this.'

Indeed thankful, Ally began patting herself dry with her free hand.

'I'm Matthew, by the way,' the man declared, proudly.

'Patricia,' Ally lied, depositing the saturated towels upon the table in a pulped lump. 'And, thank you.'

'Do you come here often?'

'Most mornings,' Ally lied again. 'My brain usually needs the caffeinated kick-start. Not every day, mind – some days I just *can't wait* to get into the office.'

Ally really hoped this exchange wouldn't last long. She wouldn't know what to do if Matthew offered to buy her a replacement coffee.

'I'm surprised I haven't noticed you here before,' Matthew mused. 'What with you being so … beautiful.'

He flashed a perfect smile yet laughed awkwardly.

'Well, now you know to look out for me. Maybe I'll see you tomorrow?' Ally asked, feigning hope.

'Yes – yes. Definitely!'

With that, Ally turned on her heels, picking up her briefcase, whilst simultaneously moving the wallet to her front. It took Matthew longer than it should have to realise that 'Patricia' hadn't used his phone, let alone returned it.

❧❦❧

<u>Wednesday 3rd September 1997, 10:09am, LIVERPOOL ST-REET STATION, LONDON.</u>

The wallet Ally had procured contained three twenty-pound notes. Not a bad haul and more than enough for the sandwich she was gorging. Physically defeated, she lay on a secluded bench towards one end of Liverpool Street station, with only her useless briefcase for company.

As Ally ate, she rummaged through Matthew's cards, revealing his full name as, *'Matthew Daniel Withers.'* His date of birth was the twenty-seventh of May 1975. His work identification displayed his profession as, *'Software Developer,'* for a company called, *'E.Y.E.'*

'Technical bollocks,' Ally murmured, unceremoniously disposing of the lot – minus the cash – in a neighbouring bin.

With no idea of where to go from here, her gaze shifted to the departures board. She read down the list of destinations, longing to call any one of them home; Chelmsford, Tottenham Hale, King's Lynn, Clacton-on-Sea or Ashfield Town. Any would do.

Starting on the second half of her sandwich, and Ally choked. Coughing, she spat a mouthful out onto the floor. An orange and green card, slightly chewed, protruded out from between what remained of the two slices. Ally removed it, curiously turning it over in her hand. It was a train ticket.

'Ashfield Stations,' she read aloud.

A one-way ticket; it was only valid for that day.

Fear of Mick's gang spreading like a fever, Ally violently jumped up from the bench. Sinister and strange; this had to be their work, surely? They must have known where she was, but how? And if not them, who was playing with her?

Briefcase in tow, Ally ran back to the shop from where she'd made her purchase and pushed to the front of the queue.

'What's this?!' she demanded of the server, feeling frightened.

'That's your train ticket, miss,' the man replied.

Sceptical, Ally stared him down.

'Listen, I don't know what you're playing at, but—'

'Excuse me!' a voice from behind interrupted. 'There is a queue, you know?'

Defensive, Ally spun around to see a stout balding man gesture aggressively to those people between them.

'Would you hurry up, at least?' the impatient man continued. 'I want to buy my sandwich!'

Eyes bulging, he held a packet patronisingly aloft, as to emphasise his grievance. Indifferent to his tone or words, Ally was far more interested in the man's sandwich. As hers had been, it was sealed in plastic. The sandwich – *her* sandwich – no-one could have known which she'd select. Coronation chicken, yes, but the specific packet? Indeed, this was sinister and strange – unexplainable – but perhaps Mick's gang was not responsible for her ticket to Ashfield after all.

- CHAPTER III -

Integration & Dissection

<u>Thursday 11th September 1997, 09:40am, ASHFIELD, LONDON.</u>

With six days of school under her belt, Rye had taken it upon herself to strike each from off of the kitchen calendar, already with a mental countdown until half-term. Nine evenings had passed since she'd heard the voice in Sullen Woods, equating to nine diary entries that had kept her scrawling late into the night. Her sleep restless, Rye's dreams, however, were forgotten the moment she'd wake up in a sweat. For fear of sounding foolish, she had yet to share any of this with anyone.

Today, Rye awoke to her sister physically wrenching her out of bed, as was the norm when Pris wasn't working. *'Pris, don't prise,'* Rye would bemoan, all to the soundtrack of the local radio station – upon this occasion, Kylie Minogue's, 'The Loco-Motion'. It was with her teeth unbrushed, breakfast uneaten and uniform unironed, that Rye was hastened out of the door. As was the norm, she was late again.

Raindrops bounced inches off the pavement as the sky rumbled. The commencement of a new school year had seemingly brought an end to the good weather.

'Hmm, hmhm, hm, hm, hmhm-hmmm,' Rye hummed as she power-walked, her navy blazer held aloft her head as a feeble canopy.

The song's artist, name and lyrics escaping her, it's tune nonetheless had been firmly lodged in her brain for days. An eighties pop track, that was not Kylie Minogue, was all Rye could be sure of. She'd been meaning to ask Zach, and would do so later, if she remembered.

Suddenly, Rye's left ankle plunged deep into an unseen puddle and she gasped. Begrudgingly, she accepted that her shoe and sock were now saturated with ice-cold water. If only Pris could drive, she thought, then she wouldn't have to get drenched on days like these. It was a truth unacknowledged, that should Rye have been on time for school that day, she would've remained dry.

ஜ✋ஜ

<u>Thursday 11th September 1997, 09:40am, MR BULLEN'S OFF-ICE, FIRST-FLOOR, ASHFIELD COMMUNITY SCHOOL, ASHFIELD, LONDON.</u>

'What are your, erm, p-p-particular favourite s-subjects?' asked Mr Bullen.

A lifetime of self-doubt had manifested the headmaster's stutter – a trait impersonated by many of his students, it was an affliction that Mr Bullen contended with daily. Initially implemented as headmaster on a temporary basis, three years later, he remained. It would seem no other staff member wished to contend with the failing inspections, persistent drugs problem and increased rate of teenage pregnancies. True to say, Mr Bullen was a decent headmaster, although flawed. Rarely ill-tempered, he strove to find the good in everyone, albeit naively. This was clear to Alexis Monaghan, who looked upon him with a mixture of sympathy and curiosity before opening her mouth to embellishment and lies.

'Well, I've always loved History, and I've been told I have a natural flair for Spanish. I used to take part in lots of extra-curriculars at my old school too – drama, dance…trampolining.'

As far as Ally could remember, she had never attended a school before. Most of what she knew had been self-taught, such as, using one's surroundings to one's advantage. For example, hung on the wall behind the headmaster were his qualifications. Before being awarded his teaching certificate in 1966, Andrew Bullen had studied History at Durham University, graduating with honours. Out in the corridor, next to where Ally had waited, was a cabinet. It housed only a sparse collection of club trophies.

'Ah, well, y-yes – yes, erm, that's s-smashing,' Mr Bullen beamed from across his desk. It was littered with old lottery tickets. 'I think you'll be the p-p-perfect fit for Ashfield Community.'

Mr Bullen then directed his attention to Ally's 'mother'. The only other person in the room, Kathy had until then remained silent – mentally absent. As the woman was handed several forms, Ally just prayed she was sober enough to remember the briefing. The pair had only met a mere twenty minutes prior to the interview, with Ally having found her slumped in a pub's porch and swigging from a bottle. For a tenner, Kathy was as willing an accomplice as they came.

'I 'ave a letter,' Kathy reciprocated, exchanging papers.

'A letter of recommendation,' Ally interjected.

'Oh, righ', yeah,' Kathy continued through a yawn. 'My Alice is a righ' li'l' star.'

Pushing his glasses further up his nose, Mr Bullen eagerly read the fabricated letter, eyes darting from one side to the other.

Ally's previous – fictitious – school was St Christopher's, and it was simply unfortunate that its remote location in the Scottish Highlands left it cut off from all telephone and email communications. Ally had mocked up the letter at an internet café a few days earlier, and it was from there that she'd also made initial contact with Ashfield Community.

'Oh, y-yes – yes,' Mr Bullen enthused, lips aquiver. 'Great stuff. S-smashing.'

Ally sharply elbowed Kathy in the ribs, as the woman's eyes began to close.

'Money!' she began, with a start, remembering her lines. 'Uniform ain't 'alf expensive.'

Mr Bullen's face dissolved with sympathy. Ardently nodding, his combover slid.

'Say no more, s-say no more! We'll s-sort you out.'

❧

<u>Thursday 11th September 1997, 09:57am, GIRLS' TOILETS, GROUND FLOOR, ASHFIELD COMMUNITY SCHOOL, ASHFIELD, LONDON.</u>

With its paint peeling and windows grimy, the school's toilets were indeed a vile place. Rye could only assume the cleaners had given up long ago, and who could blame them? There wasn't enough bleach in the world to save them now. Rye squeezed her hair into the sink as the bell sounded to signal the second period.

Removing her knee-high socks, Rye proceeded to dry her feet with the inside of her blazer, as her eyes met those of her reflection. A sorry sight; Rye's blonde locks lay plastered to her scalp and appeared brown. Sodden; the white stripes of her tie were rendered near indistinguishable from the dark blue. All over, Rye was dripping. She cupped her hands to her mouth and exhaled warm air from deep within her lungs. Exhale then turned into a hum.

'Hmm … hmhm, hm, hm … hmhm-hmmm …'

Rye held her own stare; an endless and aching chasm of blue. Her reflection fragmented, was split right down the middle by a crack which she followed from top to bottom. Zeroing in on the misalign, seconds passed; all sense of urgency dissipating.

She thought of her long-dead parents, Pris, Cousin Veronica and Harry. Unconventional upbringing aside, Rye was a conventional teenager. She was awkward; not sure of who she wanted to be, but sure of what she did not. She deemed herself as astute as one could be at her age but could rarely translate that to true empathy. She was reflective.

Rye shivered as she shrugged off the sensation that had taken her. She slipped her bare feet back into damp shoes, and turning on the spot, binned her socks. Only marginally drier than before, she hurried her way to Biology.

❧✋❧

<u>Thursday 11th September 1997, 10:04am, SCIENCE ROOM 6, SCIENCE BLOCK, FIRST-FLOOR, ASHFIELD COMMUN-ITY SCHOOL, ASHFIELD, LONDON.</u>

'What?' yelped Fred, startled.

Having lost his friend to a daydream soon after entering the lab, Zach had resorted to kicking the leg of Fred's stool.

'New girl,' Zach whispered, more discreetly. 'What do you make of her? She's taking notes. I think she might actually be listening to this drivel.'

'I thought it was funny seeing Trinity's reaction to her uniform, and the briefcase,' Fred replied, resting his head on a hand. 'I mean, like, I know it's a bit dated, and using a briefcase as a school bag is way beyond weird, but Trinity was just staring at it, unblinking.'

'Yeah,' Zach agreed, excitedly. 'Like – like this.'

Giving Fred an unappreciated prod, Zach then offered his best attempt at a Trinity impression. Head forward, his jaw dropped in an expression of bewilderment. Outside, thunder clashed just in time to conceal their sniggers, and the pair coughed away their laughter.

From the row in front, Melissa turned to thrust a drawing atop Zach's book. She'd passed the paper back as instructed, not caring to look at the doodle herself. Zach, however, struggled to hold back a hearty laugh the second he'd caught a glimpse of it.

A crude artwork, it depicted their teacher, Mr Vincent, in an explicit scenario involving the young and vivacious science technician, Miss Fisher. Everything from genitalia, to Mr Vincent's large belly, circular glasses and paediatric shoes, were all accounted for. The artist, Tony, flashed Zach a double thumbs-up from the front row, coupled with a cheeky grin.

'Genius,' Zach chuckled.

Far from his choice of seat, Tony's place had been assigned within minutes of their first lesson last week. The new addition to their class, Alexis Monaghan, sat a few places to his right. No-one sat to Ally's immediate left or right. As the new girl, the entire class had retracted from her, not that she seemed to care. With the first page of her exercise book already filled, she sat enthralled.

The classroom door swung open and a rather bedraggled-looking Rye entered. A lone raindrop slid from the bridge of her nose to the tip and she blew it off.

'Sorry I'm late, sir,' she said, avoiding eye contact.

'I wouldn't have expected anything less, Turpin,' Mr Vincent barked in reply. 'It's bad enough you're ruining your own education, but now you're disturbing that of your peers.'

In direct response to their teacher's clichéd rhetoric, the class began hammering upon their desks, in a deliberate attempt to disprove and annoy.

As Mr Vincent struggled to restore order, Rye took to her seat without another word. Taking a mental snapshot of one boy as she passed by him, she absorbed more detail in that half-second than anyone could possibly have guessed. Hair, posture, even pencil case; bed-head, slumped, and clear with red trim. His name was Louie Morgan, and it was an active decision of Rye's, whilst embarrassed by her appearance, to ignore him.

'Late again, Turpin, tut-tut.' Zach smiled, pulling out a stool.

'Yeah, Turpin,' joked Fred. 'You're such a bad influence on us all!'

He emphasised his sarcasm by rapping his own fist firmly on the desk.

'In all fairness, you ain't missed much, except for the entirety of first period,' continued Zach. 'But that was a poke-your-finger-in-your-eye, I'm-so-bored-I-could-die, type of lesson. *Trigonometry* – yeesh.'

'Zach, I have a question for you,' Rye hastened. 'You know a lot of music, right?'

'Well, I guess so,' he pondered.

'See, I've had this song stuck in my head for days, and I can't—'

'*Days?* That's some torture. Wait, this isn't one of your pop-princess ditties, is it? Because if it is, then I probably—'

'No, no, it's not,' Rye whispered. 'Well, it might be. I think it's some eighties track.'

Zach opened his mouth to respond.

'And Alanis Morissette is hardly a pop-princess, Zach,' Rye clarified. 'At least, not anymore.'

'Then, this could go either way,' Zach mused, stroking his chin. 'Hit me.'

Rye lowered her head and quietly began to hum, floating her hand in time to the elusive tune.

'Hmm, hmhm, hm, hm, hmhm-hmmm … Anything?'

''Fraid not,' Zach replied, shaking his head. 'Kylie?'

'It's definitely not Kylie,' Rye groaned.

'You could always search the net?' suggested Fred.

'This ain't the twenty-first century, mate,' Zach rebuked, jovially. 'You can't just hum a tune to the internet.'

'Alright – alright!' Mr Vincent roared, as the class disturbance subsided. 'You've got two minutes to pair up for practical!'

He took secret pleasure in the chaos that ensued, as the students ran, panicked. His pet budgerigar, Mr Tumnus, did not, however. Fretfully tweeting from the storeroom adjacent to the lab, as far as the bird was concerned, this was the end of days.

'What's the practical?' asked Rye, quickly.

Cautious, she remembered the previous year's eyeball dissection.

'Lamb's heart,' replied Fred, meekly.

'Come on, Fred!' Zach encouraged. 'All those valves and tubes, not to mention that sweet, *sweet* smell of stale blood. What's not to love?'

Fred began to turn white.

'Thirty seconds!' Mr Vincent boomed, and the volume of negotiations intensified.

'How're we splitting?' Rye pressed. 'Three people ain't a pair.'

She looked to Zach, who in turn looked to Fred, who shook his head in objection. Time was of the essence – many students had already relocated.

'Me and Fred, you and …' Zach trailed off.

'Ten seconds!' warned Mr Vincent, as he began to distribute scalpels.

'What?!' Rye demanded.

'You *were* late,' Fred offered, weakly.

'Time's up! If you're not in a pair, I'll put you in one of my own choosing,' announced Mr Vincent, steepling his fingers. 'Let's see, we'll have … Fred and Ros. Trinity, go with Zach—'

'But, sir—' Zach and Trinity protested in unison.

Mr Vincent raised a hand to silence them.

'And Rye, let's have you with the new girl, Alexis.'

Dissent among the ranks, Mr Vincent smiled, satisfied.

Though nearly experiencing similar, Rye found it funny how Trinity's underlings had mutinied against her. Rather than face the prospect of being side-lined, Moya and Lyssa had instead formed their own alliance. This had left Trinity only momentarily speechless.

Reluctantly, Rye and Zach gathered up their books, their stools scraping painfully back as they stood. Ros, by comparison, bounded over to Fred.

Rosalind 'Ros' Pretty was also blonde. She very much lived up to her surname but her reputation as a nerd was all her peers ever saw. Having only joined Ashfield Community at the start of last year's summer term, she herself had been the 'new girl' up until this very lesson. Sidling up to Fred, Ros immediately began rearranging their entire desk.

Rye approached the front of the lab with apprehension. En route, she stole another glance at Louie, as Tony stole one down Miss Fisher's blouse. Tottering between the aisles, the science technician slopped hearts out into plastic trays. Not sure of what to say, Rye was thankful when Ally made introductions first.

'Hi, I'm Ally,' she smiled. 'Well, my name's actually Alexis, but everyone calls me Ally.'

Reciprocating with her own name, Rye took a seat beside her. As both girls titled a fresh page within their respective books, they low-key absorbed each other's presence.

Rye found Ally's aesthetic somewhat unusual. Her blouse was buttoned right up to the neck. Her tie was neatly knotted and longer than the socially accepted norm, as was her skirt. Peculiarly, the look was completed by knee-high, black leather boots. Ally's dark hair was thrown loosely over one shoulder.

Both girls then launched into a conversation at once.

'You first,' Ally insisted.

'Last time our class was allowed a Biology practical, Tony and Jake dropped the goat's eyeballs in Miss Buchanan's coffee.' Rye nodded in Mr Vincent's direction. 'I'm not sure he knows what he's in for.'

The practical commenced, and the students – many in vain – attempted to navigate themselves through the complicated instructions. Occasionally, the odd squeal would prevail above the racket, accompanied by a dramatic recoil and waving of the hands.

'Go on, Norman, have a go!' Zach persisted, as he prodded at the heart with his scalpel.

'How about, no, dickweed?' replied Trinity, through grossly audible mastication of her gum. 'What's your damage? Who's Norman?'

'You tell me,' Zach goaded. 'You're the one hitting that minty highway.'

Zach's reference to the Wrigley's television advert for chewing gum, itself a kitsch parody of David Lynch's *Wild at Heart*, was completely lost on Trinity. Up until now, she'd tried her best to ignore him, but this had only encouraged his torment. Zach prodded the heart again, and Trinity looked at him as if he were something nasty that she'd stepped in.

In truth, Zach was a very handsome boy, with his black hair and blue eyes, and although Trinity and her entourage all thought so, they would never admit it. Much like Ros, it was Zach's social standing that worked against him.

'Look what happens when you only squeeze one side,' he spoke, excitedly.

A fountain of blood spurted forth from one of the valves and Trinity let out a high-pitched shriek. She jumped back, sending her stool crashing to the floor. Plucked eyebrows raised in a mixture of disgust and loathing, she slinked off to re-join Moya and Lyssa.

Oblivious to Trinity's reappearance, her friends had been arguing for the past ten minutes over which way up the heart should go. Clearly losing her temper, Moya's gestures with her scalpel were becoming increasingly wild.

'And now to make a twenty-millimetre incision into the left atrium.' Ros narrated as if providing a voiceover to a documentary. 'Why aren't you taking notes, Frederick?' she then asked. 'If you're not going to participate in the dissection, you should at least be paying attention. You haven't even copied out the diagram — you don't even have a page thirteen in your book! Did you … rip it out?'

About to gag, Fred raised his hand.

'I think — I need some air,' he spluttered.

Not waiting to be formally excused, he rushed for the door.

'You're going to miss the heartstrings!' Ros called after him.

Thirty minutes in, the rain continued to pour. It slid from off the windows in sheets, enabled by the wind that shuddered them. Dark and overcast; little natural light entered the lab.

At the front of the class, Rye and Ally had almost completed their dissection and were about sketch their results. Sipping from mugs of steaming coffee, Mr Vincent and Miss Fisher stood a little way off. He was boring her with a story about carp, whilst she hopelessly tried to appear interested.

'So, erm, where did you go to school before?' Rye asked, desperate to drown out the dull monologue. 'Anywhere 'round here?"

'Scotland,' Ally replied.

Rye paused, awaiting further detail. None was given and so she enquired further.

'So, *not* local then. Whereabouts in Scotland?'

'It was only a tiny School — outside Kilmartin.' Ally looked up and smiled. 'You've probably never heard of it.'

'In Argyll and Bute, right?' Rye precisely expounded. 'My parents had a dig up there once. They're archaeologists — *were* archaeologists. They died when I was two — trench collapse.'

Her voice was tinged with sadness.

Ally nodded but said nothing else. For her, too, the subject of a family always came with a great feeling of emptiness.

To the girls' left, unbeknownst to them, Tony and his partner had instigated a Mexican wave that was growing in popularity. Another pupil constructed a tower out of stools. Trinity, sensing an imminent uprising, removed her gum and stuck it to the radiator. As students spontaneously returned to banging their desks, the unruly behaviour could go unnoticed no longer.

Mr Vincent began crowd-controlling procedures as Miss Fisher stood firm behind.

The room was suddenly plunged into darkness, followed by only flashes of light that bounced around the lab. Someone — most likely Tony — had begun playing with the light switches, whilst another fiddled with the blinds.

The banging quickened in pace and grew in volume, which when combined with the rain and chirping from next door, created a rhythmic tempo that fast approached crescendo. The various jars of suspended animals and plants, along with the taxidermy, cast fluid shadows. Angry, they leapt. Heavy, they fell. Faces intermittently illuminated in war cry, it was like the class were fanning the flames of a crackling fire.

Rye noticed Ally jolt upright. She turned to face her new classmate, but Ally's body remained rigid. Her eyes, wide with shock, were fixed upon their dissected lamb's heart, itself reflected. Cut open and spread, the previously inanimate organ appeared to pulsate in the half-light. If Rye was not mistaken, she could have sworn it was beating. All background noise faded, and it too became all she could see and hear. A hollow, steady thump, it reverberated in their ears, slow and deep.

- CHAPTER IV -

Alea Iacta Est

<u>Thursday 11th September 1997, 10:39am, ASHFIELD POLICE STATION, ASHFIELD, LONDON.</u>

Her legs unsteady as she made her way across the car park, Michelle Davey experienced flashbacks to the night before in Dragnell Lane. Rain. The car. The girl in the black lace dress, the bottle and the fire. The disappearance of the collective.

Michelle hadn't slept. She hadn't washed. Yesterday's blouse and skirt hung creased on her. In a trance-like state, today's rain, though evocating, did not faze her. It was her battered brolly that took the brunt.

Code entered at the station's side entrance, Michelle opened the door and was immediately subjected to the usual hustle and bustle. People shouted good mornings from behind stacks of paper and coffee cups, as others darted past, chatting furiously into walkie-talkies. The bright lights cut deep, outstripping the grey skies outside.

'Alright, Michelle?' Gary waved cheerfully at her, from his desk. 'Public transport today, was it? Hope you weren't walking.'

In the twilight years of his policing career, Gary was older than Michelle. Broad and pot-bellied, he always wore a smile. His address, necessitating response, forced Michelle to focus, whilst squashing any hope she had of lying on her timesheet. Gary noticed her pause.

'Knock back a couple last night?' he teased.

It was no secret that Michelle had backed her car into a pole on Tuesday morning. As it happened in the station's car park, many of her colleagues had heard of her regret first-hand. Michelle's reputation at the work parties was also well-known, though she wished it wasn't. It was hardly an accurate representation of her usual drinking habits.

'Car still with the mechanic, is it?'

Frustrated that Gary insisted on conversation, Michelle tapped her umbrella on the carpet, allowing droplets to slide off. It was with a sigh that she turned back to face him.

'Still with the mechanic, Gary.'

'Nikos, the mechanic? I've heard you talking to Shaz about *him*,' Gary winked.

'His brother, actually.'

'I see, I see,' said Gary, reaching for his coffee.

Before Gary could look up again, Michelle had scurried off. Taking her departure on the chin, he resumed busying himself with his morning's paperwork.

Free from the constraints of small-talk, Michelle made haste to her office, ensuring to keep a low profile. She was already behind schedule, having made a detour to the pharmacy for painkillers, and, with a plan of action, she wanted no further delay.

Shutting the door to her office, Michelle crossed the room to close the blinds. A small space, yet somehow two desks had been successfully crammed inside – Michelle shared the office with her partner, Kevin. She counted her blessings that he was presently elsewhere. It meant she could conduct her research in private.

As she sat down, Michelle pulled a notepad from her bag and started up her computer. Her bag's depths unyielding of a pen, she took to ransacking her desk, rifling through folders and loose paper. Two binders were carelessly dropped to the floor. Kevin was always stealing her pens, but instead of checking his desk, Michelle persisted. Still disturbed from the night before, she was not thinking entirely clearly.

Michelle found a biro – half-chewed – under her keyboard. With a slowed action, she clicked it, inspecting her knuckles as she did so. Grazed, they still bore the self-inflicted damage from when she'd thumped the car's window. It took constant reassurance to remind herself that she'd not imagined it all. Was this proof that she wasn't crazy?

Michelle held the biro between her teeth as she scrambled to enter her computer's login. Thoughts flooding, as if released from behind a mental dam, she then tore through her notebook. A dozen pages had already been filled since her ghostly encounter, many with imperfect sketches of the short and stout bottle, with a rectangular base, from which the girl had drunk. The clawed-hand on its label was surely unique, but Michelle had not knowingly seen it before. She was frustrated that its name had been concealed.

A quick internet search of the bottle's description proved futile. Gin, rum, whiskey or vodka? Her line of inquiry drew a blank. But Michelle was sure it must have contained a spirit.

Next, she would try her luck with the car. In a whirlwind, Michelle flipped forward several more pages in her notebook to a line and stick drawing of the girl seated on its passenger-side. All aspects of her diagram were labelled via arrows, from *'Dragnell Lane,'* *'Dark-coloured Renault, hatchback,'* *'Black lace dress; thin girl, long and curly auburn hair,'* and *'Clawed-hand bottle,'* to *'Fire,'* and *'Lots and lots of water.'* A triple question mark was in the place of the vehicle's number plate.

Michelle opened the MID database and punched in the car's manufacturer and style. Hoping for a miracle, she ticked every colour except for silver, white and yellow, then hit enter.

'Your search has returned 384 results within your criteria.'

She refined the criteria to Ashfield specifically, but returned zero results. She opened the search up by a ten-mile radius, to include parts of Essex and Hertfordshire, whilst also ticking the box labelled, *'arson'*, but once again, her attempt generated zero results. Growing exasperated, Michelle unticked *'arson'*.

'Your search has returned 29 results within your criteria.'

Another's cough; Michelle was ripped back to reality. Closing the database in a flash, her demeanour was not dissimilar to a scared teenager about to be caught by a parent.

'Meeting in fifteen, Michelle.'

DCI Malcolm Goodfellow was stood in the doorway, and Michelle's heart dropped. A tall man, with a slim frame and thick moustache, her superior cut the classic silhouette of a British officer, as if directly lifted from a souvenir tea towel. She'd been so engrossed, Michelle hadn't even heard the door open.

ॐ

Thursday 11th September 1997, 10:45am, SCIENCE BLOCK, FIRST-FLOOR, ASHFIELD COMMUNITY SCHOOL, ASH-FIELD, LONDON.

The lab's door slammed straight into Fred's backside as Rye made her hasty exit. Recovering from the dissection, he had been stood, bent-double, hands-on knees and breathing deeply. Rye's action caused Fred to retch, as he was booted into the opposite wall. Slowly, he slid himself down to sit cross-legged on the floor.

Zach was next out, followed by Ally, in amongst a tide of other students. Ally was reluctant to join the trio but had yet to gain confirmation from Rye as to what they'd both just witnessed. She didn't feel well. The feeling was familiar — she'd felt that way for weeks — but this was a distinct wave of nausea.

'The heart — it moved!' Rye blurted, distressed.

The look was intensified by her damp and crumpled uniform. Her hair had dried in thick, knotted strands.

Zach laughed, mistaking her fear for paranoia.

'What do you mean, "it moved"?' he asked, disbelieving.

Interrupting them, the lab door swung open again. This time, it was Tony. Detention slip in hand, he playfully slapped Zach on the back. And as the boys said their goodbyes, it was left to Fred to fill the conversational void.

'What?' he asked Rye, simply, from beneath them all.

'The heart – it was beating!' Rye spluttered, eyes bulbous. 'Like what a heart should do – but it shouldn't, should it? Because—'

'No, it didn't,' Fred dismissed.

With Tony gone, Zach piped up again.

'Mass female hysteria?' he joked. 'I thought it took months for women's periods to—'

'Do *not* finish that sentence,' Rye warned, folding her arms.

'I'd love to have seen your reaction to it,' Ally stung.

Silence encapsulated the group as the final surge of students exited the lab. Ros – the last to leave – proceeded to crouch down to Fred's level. Pointedly, she tapped him on the shoulder.

'I'll write up the notes, Frederick,' she happily sang, undeterred by – or, unaware of – Fred's blatant lack in interest. 'Many thanks for being my lab partner. I'll look forward to our next practical together.'

She flicked her pink feathery biro in his face before taking off down the corridor. Staggering, she was barely able to carry her hefty rhinestone-covered rucksack. Ros's words would have been patronising if they weren't so innocent. Still, Fred would've argued them, if only he hadn't felt so horrid.

'You can come across a right dick sometimes, you know that?' Rye directed at Zach, her voice cracking.

'Girls, chill out, please,' he implored.

'Like that,' Rye fired.

'Zach didn't mean it,' Fred attempted to diffuse. 'He's just being funny.'

'I don't find him very funny,' replied Ally, bluntly.

'It was probably just gas escaping,' Zach suggested, sourly, shrugging his shoulders. 'You'd been cutting it apart for the best part of thirty minutes. You probably just poked at it in a weird way and dislodged some gas. It happens all the time with corpses.'

Rye looked sceptical, whilst Ally looked down at the floor. Zach went to comfortingly squeeze Rye's shoulder.

'Get off, Zach! I didn't like it, OK? And I don't believe it. If you'd heard it speak, then—'

'"Speak"?' the other three questioned.

'*Beat*,' Rye corrected herself. 'If you'd heard it beat, you'd think differently.'

❧ ✋ ☙

<u>Thursday 11th September 1997, 11:00am, MEETING ROOM 2, ASHFIELD POLICE STATION, ASHFIELD, LONDON.</u>
Michelle quietly took her place around the large rectangular arrangement of tables. Placing her notepad and case file in front of her, she sat back in her chair, feeling tense. Headache persistent; she massaged her temples.

'Morning, Michelle,' Kevin greeted in his usual vulgar tone, as he came bouncing over to sit beside her.

The faint odour of brandy laced his speech. The hip flask in his desk drawer being no secret to Michelle, she screwed up her nose. Her only acknowledgement of him; she would waste no niceties on him today. Kevin was oblivious to her dislike, as always.

The other officers took their seats, and the weekly Thursday meeting kicked off in the usual fashion. DCI Goodfellow gave an update on crime statistics and how targeted improvements were faring – not very well, as it turned out. This slowly fed into the open cases, that all respective detective inspectors were expected to speak on.

As others spoke, Michelle skim-read her own notes, as well as the file she shared with Kevin. An irritant; he held the file's papers aloft in order to read the pages beneath those she was reading. Ultimately surrendering the file to her partner, Michelle instead concentrated upon her own notepad. Mind-wandering, however, she couldn't help but flip back to her drawings of the night before. Minutes passed.

'Thank you, DI Ismay. That was very illuminating,' DCI Goodfellow praised. 'Now, DI Davey, DI Gunn, over to you.'

The room silent, all turned their attention to the pair. Sitting back in his chair, Kevin closed the case file, then slid it across to Michelle with elongated fingers. He'd deny any malice later, saying it was because he knew she liked to lead, but that wasn't true. He'd done so because Michelle was distracted.

Caught off guard, Michelle appeared uncharacteristically unprofessional. She let out a short burst of nervous laughter. Her notepad fell from her lap to the floor, but she was too embarrassed to pick it back up.

'DI Davey, what can you tell us?' DCI Goodfellow pressed, his full moustache twitching.

Willing her brain to connect with her mouth, Michelle remained speechless. Her thoughts elsewhere, she was unable to focus. She laid a hand upon the case file, in the vain hope the information would somehow transfer itself via some osmosis-like process. The words were on the tip of her tongue.

'The Richard of York case – would you care to elaborate?' DCI Goodfellow expanded, growing impatient.

'The – erm – the em-em-embezzling,' Michelle began.

'Richard Simkins has been charged and bailed,' Kevin swooped in. 'He denied all wrongdoing, but that'll sure change. He's a tough son of a bitch, but his lawyer will no doubt advise he pleads guilty – the evidence is damning. I've had dealings with Defence Lawyer Bowen before; she's weak and incompetent at best, but even she knows his only option will be early admittance, to lessen the sentence. The prosecution will otherwise surely go in for maximum – fifty grand is a *lot* of money. He should be praying for a shitting miracle.'

'The Prosecution Service will have all the evidence, probably by next week,' Michelle chimed in. 'A December trial date for sentencing is the earliest we could expect. Should all be very cut and dry.'

'There's still a lot to collate before CPS.' Kevin side-eyed Michelle, his voice oozing arrogance.

'I'll think you'll find everything's organised,' said Michelle, through gritted teeth.

'It's getting there,' Kevin spoke directly to DCI Goodfellow. 'I just need to ensure it's watertight.'

'You just said it was damning,' Michelle fumed, trying her best to maintain an air of professionalism, now that she had found it. Her smile stretched tight.

'Yes, I said damning, not organised.'

'I'm sure I can walk you through it all again before submission.'

Patting the case file, Michelle slid it back across the desk to Kevin. Though he might not have known it, she knew his game. Kevin was good at his job, Michelle would grant him that much, but his approach was insincere. His deliverance and turn of phrase were belittling, intentional and wholly unsuited to his rank.

The rest of the meeting continued just as Michelle would have predicted, with Kevin prattling on for at least another ten minutes. DCI Goodfellow commended him highly before then dropping another hint at his own impending retirement. Anyone who thought the 'Boys' Club' mentality had ended in the eighties would be sorely mistaken. Bored of it all, Michelle took to covertly sketching in her notepad.

It was only towards the end of the meeting that her ears pricked again. Detective Inspectors Goddard and Doherty were investigating the origin of numerous cut-and-shut cars and had sought the advice of Vehicle's Specialist, Danny Malloy. As part of the National Criminal Intelligence Service, if ever there was an expert that could navigate the database and help Michelle identify the car seen in Dragnell Lane, it was him.

*

The school bell rang; the morning break had ended. The group's final minutes of freedom had comprised a heated exchange between Ally and Zach.

'Oi!'

All four turned, as Liam Pritchard came sauntering down the corridor with the swagger of a Bloodhound Gang member with dysentery. Regarded by most as a tosser, Liam was Trinity's current boyfriend. He was also Fred's worst enemy.

Fred non-too subtly looked his nemesis up and down, taking in Liam's new-found summer build. His untucked shirt outgrown, he'd evidently been hitting the gym. His trousers – beltless – were still too large, however, and had slid down to reveal a good few inches of underwear. His hair buzzed to the scalp; both that and his smirk were greasy. Fred shakily took to his feet, dragging his back up the wall for support. He glared at Liam with unique disgust.

'You look distressed, Turpin,' Liam spoke, roughly, and nodded in Rye's direction. 'Freddums – *mate* – hope you had a good summer. You know I've missed you.'

To Fred's detest, Liam leant in to give him a firm hug. Upon withdrawal, he forcibly ruffled the boy's hair with his knuckles.

'What do you want?' Rye seethed. 'If you're looking for Trin, she's long gone.'

Judging by Liam's downcast expression, Rye had assumed correctly, although he did not move along as hoped. A parody of himself, he stood, scratching his crotch.

'You might wanna crack a smile sometime, Turpin,' Liam sneered. 'You had a face like a slapped arse last week 'n' all.'

'When did you see me last week?' Rye shot back. 'Didn't you get excluded on the first day? I ain't even seen you.'

His lower jaw protruding, Liam moved the gum he chewed around to the other side of his mouth. He kissed his teeth before continuing.

'Running across the road like a proper 'tard, you was. My brother nearly hit yer.'

'Oh,' Rye responded, thoughts flashing. '*Then.*'

Despite his proximity at the time, Rye doubted Liam had been the perpetrator of the voice she'd heard in Sullen Woods. She imagined his smoker's rasp prevented him from reaching such a high-pitch.

'"Running"?' Zach repeated, questioningly, having never known Rye to run anywhere, for anything, not even a bus.

'Home. I was running home.' Rye shrugged, avoiding all eye contact. 'I was gonna be late back.'

'Well, you oughta look both ways next time, pretty girl,' leered Liam. 'I'd hate to see you splattered.'

'Is that a threat?' Zach stepped up.

'No threats,' replied Liam, his hands held up in surrender. 'Just don't wanna have to *scrape* together the shrapnel for a carwash.'

He then winked, and without a goodbye, slouched off.

'Is he always such a tumour of a human being?' asked Ally.

'Yes,' Fred droned.

He himself then departed the group, with the intention of finding a secluded place to vomit. Walking in the opposite direction to Liam, he aggressively pushed open the double doors at the corridor's end and disappeared onto the bridge that connected the science block to the rest of the school.

<u>Friday 12th September 1997, 15:29, ST BOTOLPH'S CHURCH-YARD, ASHFIELD, LONDON.</u>

Years before its own took over, Ashfield Community had been built in the shadow of St Botolph's. The school had been founded by the clergy and up until as recently as the nineteen sixties, had shared its name. With its many nooks, the churchyard was popular with the students who snuck out for a cigarette, or something harder, during break times. Overgrown, it was easy to hide within.

This afternoon, under the thick cloud, one could easily have mistaken the darkness for an evening. For the time being, at least, the rain had ceased, and the droplets left behind upon the trees' branches twinkled like fairy lights.

Over twenty-four hours since the ominous Biology practical, Rye walked home alone. She had hoped to meet Fred and Zach after the sixth period, but by a series of well-orchestrated hand gestures, it had been communicated to her that their class had earned detention.

Rye's route through the churchyard was her quickest, though she regretted her choice, and indeed not waiting for her friends. All things considered, she was still on edge – the feeling only exacerbated by her current location. Usually, it didn't bother her, but today Rye's mind conjured forms and faces from between the graves. She read the inscriptions adorning the nearest headstones as she strode by them. After four years, Rye knew them and their order well.

'William Pratt. 31st January 1866 – 5th April 1898.'

That's what the fourth headstone used to read. What once served as a monument to an upstanding Victorian gent had since become a pile of rubble. Assuming it had been unashamedly kicked to the ground by her peers, Rye sighed. *No matter who we are, we all become but a name on a stone, wherever that stone may be,* she thought.

At first, the sounds of the footsteps following Rye were indistinguishable from that of her own, as they were muffled by the leaves that had turned to mush upon the flagstones. It was only when they began to quicken, that she realised someone was running up behind her.

Ashfield easily duped the inexperienced as an innocuous, historical town, but the locals knew the truth. This suburb had fallen foul to the effects of the capital and the increased crime rate that came with urban sprawl. Let whoever it was there pass, Rye thought. Avoid eye contact and hope for the best.

'Rye!' a voice suddenly called out, and the secondary footsteps ceased.

Rye jolted and froze.

'I wanted to ask, what are you doing tomorrow?'

The soft Scottish voice that had spoken sounded skittish. Rye knew it had to be Ally, even before turning. Faceless in the growing mist, the odd schoolgirl stood a few dozen feet away.

'Jesus Christ, you scared me,' Rye breathed, clutching her chest.

'What're you doing tomorrow?' Ally repeated.

'Nothing!' called Rye, relieved.

'Shopping? Do you wanna go shopping?' Ally asked, breath clouding, as she walked closer. 'Girls go shopping, don't they?'

'Yeah, they do. I mean, alright,' Rye replied, unsure.

Making new friends did not come naturally to Rye. It had only been her, Fred and Zach for years. But the prospect of getting to know a girl was appealing, particularly one that was distinctly un-Trinity-esque. Ally had barely acknowledged her presence since yesterday, however. Was it possible she was just as socially inept as herself?

'Are you walking my way?' Rye asked.

'Yes – well, no – actually, I'm not sure. No,' Ally stuttered. 'I'll see you tomorrow, yeah? Around eleven? We can meet … somewhere around here.'

Ally was already beginning to back away.

'Can I get your number?' Rye hastened.

All too aware of her time-keeping, she thought it only polite to notify Ally, should their plan change. She also wanted the option to cancel.

'I'll take yours,' said Ally.

Moving closer again, she produced Matthew's Nokia 9000 from out of her blazer's inside pocket. It had mostly been switched off since acquirement and was due a test-run. But without a charger, it was inevitably useless, albeit not worthless.

Rye gawked, open-mouthed.

'Woahh! Oh, my – is that? I'm so jealous!'

'What?' asked Ally. 'Jealous of what?'

Without hesitation or invite, Rye plucked the mobile from Ally's hand and turned it over in her own.

'I've only ever seen these advertised on the telly, but never in the flesh. It's practically a pocket computer,' Rye enthused.

'Oh, it's just my mum's old one. She's the business type,' Ally lied. 'Feel free to add yourself as a contact.'

In awe, Rye turned the device on its side before flipping it open, as one would a glasses case. Ally smiled, looking smug.

'I'm your first contact?'

'You are?' Ally asked, façade faltering as her pride faded. 'I mean, you *are*. I've only had it a few days – a gift, for starting a new school.'

Completely believing and with no reason to suspect otherwise, Rye pressed in her home number, flipped the phone closed, and handed it back.

'Awesome,' Ally beamed, and slapped Rye on the back – much like Zach would do. 'See you tomorrow.'

Already wishing she hadn't committed – for what she saw as early on a Saturday morning – Rye watched curiously as Ally's silhouette disappeared; boots, briefcase, et al.

- CHAPTER V -

Beryl's Bargains

<u>Saturday 13th September 1997, 10:37am, LAWRENCE'S DEP-ARTMENT STORE, FIRST-FLOOR, ASHFIELD, LONDON.</u>
Ally wandered the aisles of racked clothing, ogling the stunning garments. Far out of her price range, all beckoned to be felt and worn. The shimmering satin and sequined tops, the dolly and denim dresses, and lacy lingerie. Defiantly, she passed them by, resisting the urge to try them on. In her old life, Ally wouldn't have thought twice about pilfering them. This was a fresh start, however, as she had to keep reminding herself, and she longed for the life of an average teenager.

Ally had arrived in town earlier than planned but had decided to use this to her advantage, by utilising the time to showcase her feminine side, and have some fun.

Entering the make-up department, Ally caught a glimpse of her face in a rounded mirror. Recoiling, she then backed up a few steps, to get a better look. Her face verged on gaunt and there were dark circles under her eyes. All things considered; this was worse than she'd feared.

From the sample pots dotted amongst the sealed products, Ally began applying foundation without embarrassment. She may no longer have been a thief but when opportunity knocked, Ally would surely answer. Moving onto the eye shadow, she set about selecting a colour as if they were all her own. Then onto the mascara, followed by eyeliner. Just as Ally was tousling her hair in front of another, larger mirror, a sales assistant emerged from behind the lipstick stand.

'Are you alright there?' the woman in her mid-forties droned, in a not-so-obvious tone of sarcasm.

Ally continued to examine herself, completely and utterly unfazed.

'Couldn't … be … happier,' she replied, between hair flicks and blew her reflection a kiss.

'I gather you're buying them.'

Even behind her own, sophisticated, make-up, the sales assistant could not mask the unnecessary stresses her job placed upon her, nor bewilderment.

'They're testers,' Ally replied, simply, through rouged and puckered lips. 'I'm *testing* them. Besides, what sort of person would *buy* testers.'

The sales assistant gritted her teeth.

'And what are the results of your tests?' she hissed, acerbically.

'Not bad, not bad …' Ally considered. Pausing, she finally turned to face her. 'Do you have this in a shade darker?' she enquired, holding up a lipstick. 'You know, more Shirley Manson, less Playboy bunny?'

The sales assistant rolled her eyes and unattractively fluttered her lashes.

'We do for sixteen ninety-five.'

Ally pulled a face.

'That's pricey.'

By now, the older woman had clearly had enough of Ally's smart-aleck comments and comebacks. She considered herself a respectable and dignified lady, but one simply did not have enough patience, only cynicism for the girl.

'If you don't stop taking the mick, I'm going to have to call Security.'

Eurgh, '*Taking the Mick.*' Ally replayed the phrase, all of a sudden remembering her ex-boyfriend.

'No, thanks,' she declined, disgusted, as if she'd been asked a question, rather than issued a warning.

Departing the woman's company, Ally did not meet her eyes again. She didn't judge her – not in the slightest – for she knew she had taken advantage. However, Ally also did not care.

Approaching the escalator, Ally lifted a bottle of shoe polish from off of a nearby stand. Checking over her shoulder, she proceeded to spurt the black liquid and at an unnecessary height. As intended, the rippling jets landed – mostly – upon the leather of her boots. With a joyous yelp, Ally merrily hopped upon the escalator, allowing the brushes that flanked each side to shine and buff as she descended.

ஒ❦ஒ

<u>Saturday 13th September 1997, 10:55am, ST BOTOLPH'S CHURCHYARD, ASHFIELD, LONDON.</u>

Rye tapped her heels together in beat to the unidentified tune that continued to plague her mind. Her frustration surrounding it was so great, that she'd even hummed it to Pris the evening before, during a muted song on *Top of the Pops*. As suspected, her sister was incredibly unhelpful, for Pris's musical knowledge was almost solely limited to Ace of Base.

Rye yawned. After a string of near-sleepless nights, last night she had endured yet another. At least on this occasion, she had risen early as result, and was in fact early for her meeting with Ally. Rye's punctuality unnerved her, but nowhere near as much as the eerie voice, or pulsating heart, that tugged at her consciousness whenever it was unoccupied.

The wind whistled around the corner of the church's nave, whipping up several empty crisp packets and wrappers. Rye's gaze followed their rise and fall – as if juggled by invisible hands – as they were carried up, and over the roof of her school.

'Penny for your thoughts?' a voice spoke.

All too glad to be relieved from the pit-falls of her overactive imagination, Rye happily stood up from the bench. She was unable to hide her initial shock at Ally's face, however. Beaming from ear-to-ear, Rye's classmate resembled a child who'd been left unsupervised with their mother's make-up. It was such a contrast to the previous day's aesthetic, that she almost didn't recognise her.

'Hi,' Rye mustered, stiffly, slowly adjusting to her peer's transformation. 'Any . . . anywhere in particular you wanted to go?' she asked, tentatively. 'Wait – are you wearing your school skirt?'

Awkwardly, Ally delved her hands into the pockets of her newly acquired – *stolen* – leather jacket, that hid her school blouse, and raised her shoulders a fraction of an inch.

'You know the area better than I do,' she raced, brushing past Rye's question. 'Anywhere that's cheap – not that I want to look cheap.'

'Ah, I see. Shopping on a shoestring,' Rye empathised. 'Trust me, I get it. I know just the place. Why are you wearing your school skirt on a Saturday?'

'Rye, plaid is like, still, *so totally* in.'

Giving her best attempt at an Alicia Silverstone à-la Cher Horowitz impression, Ally rolled her eyes.

Accepting the explanation, Rye giggled and probed the subject no further. As the pair set off in the direction of the high street, she still had many other questions for her new acquaintance, although most of these were quickly rebuffed. Usually the master of ad-libbing and an expert inventor of fantasy backstories, Ally simply could not keep pace with Rye's inquisitiveness. This left Rye high and dry for conversation starters, until—

'*Charity* shops?' Ally blurted, upon arrival at their destination.

Beryl's Bargains. The sign's red plastic letters were dirtied and discoloured. The letter Y was askew, with a bird's nest precariously constructed atop it.

'It's not a charity shop, it's thrift. It's vintage – *retro,*' Rye offered. 'That's still in, right?'

'What are we waiting for then?' Ally grinned.

Grabbing hold of Rye's hand, she pulled her across the threshold. Tumbling through, both girls giggled. A raucous mass of arms and legs, they bounced off the door's frame, as the bell above them rang out.

With generations of dust and life, Beryl's Bargains smelt musty, almost damp. All but empty, there were only two others within – the sweet old dear in glasses behind the counter, and a scruffy man, who left a horrid odour in his wake as he browsed.

'Good afternoon, my loves,' the elderly lady greeted them, despite it being late morning. 'Beautiful day, wouldn't you say?'

The weather was far from sublime.

Rye nodded a hearty hello in response. She knew the lady to be Beryl, and Ally assumed as much.

Stacks and racks of clothing dominated the elongated shop, which tapered into an acute angle towards the rear. Narrow pathways had been tunnelled out between the towering wares, and the girls commenced their quest by diverting down the nearest one.

Rye and Ally sifted through the tatty, over-sized and out-dated selection. Digging up to their armpits, deep into wire baskets, both contributed to an ever-growing reject pile. Girls on a mission; garments flew.

Appearing comatose, Beryl remained behind the counter the entire time. The man, moving towards the back of the shop, had taken to handling each individual woman's shoe and noisily sniffing them.

'Bloody hell,' Ally exclaimed, holding a neon-yellow dress out at arm's length.

'I think, it's meant to look better in the dark?' replied Rye, unconvinced, diving her own arm back into a basket.

'*All* the boys would notice me,' Ally joked, as she consigned the garish garment to the reject pile.

'Would be hard not to,' Rye agreed, her voice muffled as she bent-double, ponytail bobbing. 'How about this?' she suggested, almost inaudibly, before emerging. 'Looks like it might be your size.'

Panting, Rye tugged at something lodged at the bottom of the basket. As the material finally unknotted itself from the entanglement, she wiped her brow. Rye passed Ally a midnight-blue minidress, her face begging approval.

'Now that *is* retro,' Ally retorted.

Uninterested, she dropped the dress and immediately resumed her own search.

'Your enthusiasm is contagious,' said Rye, dryly.

*

As the girls continued their conversation, the rack behind them softly creaked, as a pair of scab-ridden talons slowly parted the jackets for a better view. The movement went completely unnoticed.

*

Rye retrieved the minidress.

'Why don't you try it on, at least?' she pressured, excitedly, practically hopping.

*

The jackets behind them shifted again, closing the gap to conceal heavy, rasping breath. From its position, the creature — hidden — heard Ally succumbing to Rye's persuasion, and subsequently witnessed their relocation to the back of the shop.

*

'That's not a changing room,' Ally scoffed, taken aback by the flimsy curtain.

Half of the hooks connecting the curtain to the pole were broken and the stripy material sported some questionable stains. With their backs turned, neither Ally nor Rye saw the creature stalk over to them. Each jacket, each rack, swayed in turn.

'It's a good thing you've got me then, isn't it?' Rye urged, as she held the curtain aside. 'I'll keep look-out.'

Taking the minidress from her classmate, Ally reluctantly entered the cubicle. Rye drew the curtain behind and assumed her position as a guard. The odorous man sauntered past, and so she gripped the fabric more firmly, as per camaraderie.

The man wiped his nose as he made to leave the shop. Shakily, he retrieved a black woollen hat from his pocket and pulled it on over his head. Rye suspected him to be homeless and felt a pang of guilt over her previous ill-thoughts of him.

'You done yet?' she called, her voice nasal from her crinkled nose.

The sound of a zipper could be heard, and Rye whisked around to presumptively pull back the curtain. Once again taken aback by the sight before her, she could not help but ask another question.

'Is that a tattoo?'

Clad in the figure-hugging minidress, Ally's arms were left exposed. Three stars of green, red and blue, formed a diagonal line across her right wrist, above her watch. An impetuous decision that she had later come to regret, the cheap ink had already faded. It remained a permanent reminder of a drunken night out in Barcelona.

'Did it hurt? Pris would kill me if I ever got one.'

'I think, it should have,' Ally reminisced, tenderly stroking her wrist. 'Bled tonnes.'

Rye was visibly put off. She did not consider herself a prude, but tattoos made her stomach churn.

Ally smoothed the material out against her hips. Although short, the dress covered her cleavage and fit perfectly. Without a mirror for reference, she looked to Rye for judgement.

The creature crouched lower, as it attempted to avoid Ally's eyeline. As before, its movement was subtle and easily overlooked. Rye opened her mouth to wax lyrical her praises but was beaten to the punch.

'You do look a picture!' complimented Beryl, suddenly appearing behind Rye, and bursting into life. 'Never hurt me to show a bit of leg!'

At this, the ageing pensioner flashed a portion of bare thigh – a portion bordering on what was considered socially un-acceptable – much to the girls' horror.

'Cheers, Beryl,' Ally replied, fighting back a smile.

The shop bell resounded once more, and all turned.

'Good afternoon—' began Beryl, but she stopped herself mid-sentence.

As the door slammed shut, it became apparent that no-one had entered, nor indeed left the shop. If Beryl had not suffered from cataracts, or if the windows hadn't been so filthy, she might just have noticed – what Rye and Ally believed to be – a large stray dog, streak past.

❧

Saturday 13th September 1997, 13:06pm, ST BOTOLPH'S CHURCHYARD, ASHFIELD, LONDON.

'Go on, tell me. What happened between you and Liam yesterday?' Zach asked Fred, for what felt like the hundredth time. 'You both disappeared.'

Fred scowled, anger bubbling up inside him.

'It doesn't matter, Zach. He's just a prick.'

Zach lay, casually stretched out along the very same bench where Rye had met Ally earlier. Black Converse trainers rested upon Fred's lap, Zach's demeanour was in stark contrast to his friend's, who sat forward and hunched.

'I think your nose might have more to say—'

'I know, Zach!'

Purple and shiny, Fred's nasal bridge was enlarged from injury. It certainly looked painful.

'What did you tell your mum?'

'I told her what I told you,' Fred sighed. 'And I told you, I walked into a door.'

Fred shivered as he tried to ignore the throbbing pain that coursed through his face. He was cold but would not admit it. He was inherently self-conscious. In just a flannel shirt and jeans, he felt a coat might detract from his carefully selected ensemble. Zach, by comparison, wore a duffle.

'Where's Rye and the new girl anyway? They're late,' Fred scorned.

Deliberately changing the conversation, he directed his most secret thoughts inward, in deep self-reflection.

All of a sudden, Zach sat upright and swung his lower body out from the bench, releasing Fred's lap in the process.

'They're here,' he confirmed, eagerly. 'And the new girl does have a name, Fred,' he rebuked, whilst unapologetically tracing Ally's approaching figure with his eyes.

- CHAPTER VI -

A Cosy Conversation

<u>Wednesday 17th September 1997, 11:54am, HOMEFIELD PAD-DOCK, HATFIELD, HERTFORDSHIRE.</u>
Removing the last cigarette from her pack of twenty, Michelle mentally berated herself for finishing them off so quickly. She had kicked the habit aged thirty-three. Nine years later, however, and she had taken it up once more.

Lighting up in the driver's seat of her beige Mini, Michelle took a long inhale, her eyes closing. Slowly, she let gravity drag her forehead down as to impact upon the wheel. She rapped herself against it several times and in quickening succession, groaning.

As she pressed her mobile's cold plastic to her ear, Michelle remained in position. Navigating the audio menu, she successfully selected the order of numbered options before the automated voice could even finish speaking. Michelle had listened to the message already but wanted to again, one final time, before acting on it.

'First message, received on, Tuesday, 16, September, at, six, twenty-seven pm.,' intoned the distinctly British, female recording.

'Hi Michelle, it's Danny. I'm just calling to say that I've re-queried the records as per your criteria and can confirm that all Renaults — of any colour — can be accounted for, except three. All others have either been located, did not display fire damage, or were just noted for parking tickets. The fates of three Renaults are unknown. One disappeared about three months ago — Mrs Nicholls', dark-blue — from Hatfield, Hertfordshire. The other two were reported stolen over two years ago, and on the other side of London. So, to

confirm, I would say Mrs Emily Nicholls' Renault 5 hatchback — second generation, 1984 — would be the most likely to have — possibly — suffered arson within the vicinity of Ashfield. I've called in requests for surveillance footage from the surrounding area, and ANPR, but had no luck so far. You still haven't explained why I'm—'

Michelle hung up on the voicemail. Needless-to-say, she had not returned the call, and did not intend to. Having gleaned all there was from him, Michelle no longer deemed Danny Malloy useful.

Savouring her final inhale, Michelle then flicked her cigarette butt out of the window and onto the path with a limp wrist. Far from precise policing, her off-the-record investigation did not sit well with her. It didn't help that Michelle wasn't even sure what she was investigating. Theft? Arson? Murder? Of course, there'd been no trace of Dragnell Lane — nor of the girl's description — on any of the other available databases. That would have been too easy.

Collecting her handbag from the passenger seat, Michelle exited her car, locked it, then traversed the road to the bungalow opposite. She strode up the driveway — car-less — and at the door, composed herself, rethinking her introduction. Mrs Nicholls had no forewarning of her visit, and so it was with hesitancy that Michelle tried the doorbell. Not a second after her finger had released and the musical notes of the hymn 'Jerusalem' could be heard chiming from within the hallway.

'Oh, for the love of—' Michelle complained, screwing up her face.

Patiently, she awaited the instrumental's halt, which happened after the second verse. Michelle pressed her face up against the roundel of stained-glass. Through filters of red and green, it was evident Mrs Nicholls was a fan of chintz wallpaper. There was still no sign of the lady herself, and Michelle pondered if her one and only lead might be out for lunch, until—

'And did those feet, in anc-ient time, Walk upon England's moun-tains green?'

The sweet and tuneful, albeit slightly croaky, sounds of someone singing travelled on the air from around the side of the property.

'And was the ho-ly lamb of God, On Eng-land's pleasant past-ures seen?'

The words sang weren't of great volume but there was no mistaking them. Brazen, Michelle opened the side gate and followed the path to the back garden, where she lingered at its edge. Lush shrubberies and perennials were stuffed between and cascaded over the flagstones. Thriving, and with sunlight limited, Michelle supposed them to survive solely on prayer alone.

Snug between the low flora, an elderly woman with a sharp perm and with her back turned, knelt upon a gardening mat. Secateurs clipping ten to the dozen, she continued to sing.

'And was Jeru-salem build-ed here, Among these dark sa-tanic—'

Michelle coughed, as a way of announcement, prior to speaking.

'Excuse me? My name's—'

'—mills?!'

'I'm sorry to disturb you,' Michelle spoke, louder.

Unaware of the presence behind her, Mrs Nicholls tilted her head heavenward. Enthusiastically, she hacked away at a particular protrusion, changed key, and reached for an unobtainable crescendo.

'Bring me my bow of burn-ing gold! Bring me my arrows of de-sire!'

'Mrs Nicholls!' Michelle hollered, encircling her mouth with her hands.

Singing having ceased, Mrs Nicholls still did not turn. She remained, staring at the clouds. Michelle wondered whether the lady thought that God itself had indeed spoken to her.

'Hello, Mrs Nicholls?' Michelle spoke again, trying her best to remain patient. 'My name's Michelle Davey. I'm a detective inspector with the Metropolitan Police.'

Finally, Mrs Nicholls shuffled around upon her mat to face her. She took a while to process the introduction.

'Oh, I am sincerely sorry, my darling girl. I didn't see you there.'

Her voice was confident, but her heavy green eyes were clearly wary.

'I tried the bell,' explained Michelle, reaching inside her trench coat's pocket for her badge. 'But I suppose—'

'I didn't hear it,' replied Mrs Nicholls, briskly.

'No?'

'No.'

Mrs Nicholls rose to her feet, brushed down her knee-length pleated skirt, and walked over. Her frailty misleading, she displayed much ease with regards to her mobility. Holding out a wrinkled and bony hand, she looked up at Michelle, expectantly.

'Just underneath my photo,' began Michelle, as she handed over her badge. 'There's my name, rank and—'

'Oh, yes – I can read. I've got my glasses on.'

Michelle raised an eyebrow, as Mrs Nicholls squinted through her lens'.

'How can I help you?' she then asked, curtly.

Satisfied with the means of identification, the badge was handed back.

'I'm here concerning your stolen car.'

'Oh, well, you'd better come in then,' Mrs Nicholls declared, turning on the spot and making a beeline for the back door.

She wiped her Birkenstocks on the mat with gusto, making a point of the action, as if it was an instruction for Michelle to do the same, before disappearing inside. Michelle did as was encouraged, quickly following after her.

'Have you found it then – my car?' Mrs Nicholls asked, as she moved a kettle across to a hotplate of her Range cooker. 'Do you take sugar with your tea?'

'Erm, no. Unfortunately, we haven't managed to locate your car,' Michelle admitted. 'And I take coffee with my tea – I mean, I'd prefer a coffee – if you have any?'

'Oh, that's a shame,' Mrs Nicholls sighed. 'Mind you, I do quite have my mind set on a shiny, brand new one.'

Proceeding to remove a cup, saucer and mug from the draining board, Mrs Nicholls then paused to look up at Michelle with perplexment once more. She was much shorter than the detective inspector, by so much in fact that it caused Michelle to ponder – just for a moment – what age it was a person stopped growing and started to shrink.

'If this conversation isn't going to be as straightforward as, "We've found your car", then you'd better go on through and make yourself comfortable. We can address specifics over cake.'

'Oh, of course – certainly,' Michelle agreed.

Backing out into the chintz-ridden hallway, Michelle felt a rush – a craving for nicotine. Oh, how she'd suffered whilst quitting the first time around. And being inside Mrs Nicholls' home did little to soothe her impending headache either. There was such a strong scent of frankincense, that she suspected the lady had her very own thurible.

Michelle made her way through to the sitting room and took a seat upon one end of the green velvet sofa. She was unsure whether Mrs Nicholls would deem it more suitable that they sit at the table. No doubt, she'd make it known if she did.

The kettle could soon be heard whistling. Michelle fished

a blister pack of paracetamol out from her handbag and swallowed two of the tablets, dry. No sooner had she dropped the pack back within her bag, when Mrs Nicholls emerged, preceded by a tea trolley, laden with sliced Victoria Sponge and Battenberg, teapot, sugar bowl, milk jug, teacup and saucer, and one steaming mug of coffee.

'This one's yours, my darling girl,' Mrs Nicholls confirmed, sliding the mug across the trolley and over to Michelle. 'You didn't say about sugar, so you can help yourself to some cubes. There's milk – just there. Help yourself to cake.'

Mrs Nicholls fixed her tea – three cubes and only a dash of milk – before settling into the comfortable, high-backed armchair opposite the detective inspector.

'Oh, bother,' she spoke, almost immediately. 'I forgot the side plates.'

'Oh, no – no need,' Michelle hastened, as Mrs Nicholls went to stand. 'I'll make do.'

Her host looked sceptical.

'Well, best be careful. I can't be having crumbs,' she warned.

Michelle eyed the baked treats. Seemingly homemade, they indeed looked delicious. Weighing up the risk, however, she fought temptation.

'So?' Mrs Nicholls asked, removing a teaspoon from her pinafore's pocket to stir her tea. 'How can I help in your line of inquiry?'

'Well, I know you've already covered the specifics of your car's theft with my colleagues. I'm just here to go back over your statement – check base, if you will. Unfortunately, as your car still hasn't been found, the case is still open.'

This was not an outright lie. The case, though not technically closed, was no longer officially being investigated.

'Tell that to the insurance company,' Mrs Nicholls scoffed.

'I'm sorry—'

'My actions constitute negligence, apparently. I can't claim.'

'Oh, I see,' Michelle replied, sympathetically, carefully pondering her next words. 'And – erm – what actions were they, exactly?'

Leaving a pink lipstick smear on the rim, Mrs Nicholls sat her cup gently down on the adjacent table. She too appeared to be choosing her words.

'I left the car unlocked, on my driveway – keys in the ignition,' she replied, solemnly.

There was an assuredness to her voice as if daring the detective inspector to pull her up on the oversight – her negligence.

'Oh, my G-oodness, that is unfortunate,' pandered Michelle, catching the near blaspheme in her throat. 'Do you have your car's manual, perhaps? Its documentation?'

Thinking aloud, Michelle was uncertain where she was leading with her questions. A habit of hers, quite often she'd find herself speaking a stream of conscious thought. When it came to her chosen career, this was both a curse and a blessing.

'I kept all of that in the glove compartment.'

'Do you have a picture of it – your car? A photograph?'

Mrs Nicholls furrowed her brow in thought.

'I do, as it happens.'

With a start, Mrs Nicholls hopped up from her chair and scurried across the room. Michelle sat forward and watched with anticipation, as the elderly lady hunched herself over a sideboard beside the dining table. She appeared locked in a vigorous struggle with a reluctant drawer for several seconds before finally managing to wriggle it open. Clearly pleased that she'd won the fight over the wood, Mrs Nicholls went on to retrieve a large photo album. Returning, with a slight spring in her step, she'd already flipped to a page several leaves in. Proudly, she deposited the volume into Michelle's lap.

'Brighton, nineteen eighty-six,' she said, simply — the corners of her mouth upturning into a soft and reminiscent smile. 'Mr Nicholls was alive then, of course. He couldn't read a map, mind. Took us twice the length of time it should for us to get there.'

'Brighton?' Michelle repeated, and Mrs Nicholls nodded. 'My grandad lives there – and my parents, actually. And this, is your car?'

Michelle pointed at the vehicle in the topmost photograph.

'The very one.'

The photograph was entirely innocent and did not give Michelle even the slightest of chills. Still, she absorbed it with caution, as if it could somehow hurt her. A slightly younger Mrs Emily Nicholls sat on the bonnet of the dark-blue Renault 5 hatchback. A man, whom Michelle deduced to be the late Mr Nicholls, stood by the open car door. Ice creams in hand, they both smiled at the camera. Rolling waves upon the sea – frozen in time within the frame's background – crashed upon the stilts of the pier.

Although the vehicle appeared eerily like the one Michelle had witnessed exactly one week ago, she could not be sure. This only irritated her further, as she'd thought, if she were to see it again, she'd somehow know.

'It's a beautiful picture,' Michelle confessed, before asking. 'Did your car have any sort of *defining* features?'

'Apart from its heavy clutch control and guzzling petrol like a thirsty camel?' Mrs Nicholls sighed, as she collapsed back into the armchair. 'The cassette player was broken, and the radio's station was stuck.'

Michelle laughed.

'I mean, did you have any personal possessions in the car at the time it was stolen?'

'No, I don't suppose I did,' Mrs Nicholls considered. 'Except for our Lord and Saviour, of course!'

'I'm sorry, I don't quite follow?'

'*Jesus*,' Mrs Nicholls clarified. 'I had a little statuette of Jesus tacked onto the dashboard. He had a bobbly-head.'

'Oh!' Michelle exclaimed, finding herself only a tad surprised by the revelation.

Wracking her brains, Michelle couldn't remember to have seen a bobbly-headed Jesus. Needless-to-say, there had been a small distraction in the form of the flaming girl in the black lace dress.

'You're not in a rush, are you?' Mrs Nicholls asked, her demeanour softening further. 'I can put the fire on?'

Michelle smiled. Suddenly remembering her beverage, she quickly took a sip, welcoming the caffeine. A rich, dark roast, she imagined it to be the best Marks and Spencer had to offer.

'I have time,' Michelle replied, helping herself to a slice of Battenberg.

'I'll fetch you a side plate.'

- CHAPTER VII -

Stream of Whispers

<u>Friday 24th October 1997, 08:44am, ENGLISH CORRIDOR, GROUND FLOOR, ASHFIELD COMMUNITY SCHOOL, ASHFIELD, LONDON.</u>

Forty days since their successful shopping trip and Ally had distanced herself from Rye, as well as Fred and Zach. Her blossoming friendship with the trio had seemed to stagnate, and not flourish as all had hoped and intended. She had retreated into her shell.

Forty-one nights and Rye's sleep pattern had levelled out, until it was virtually back to how it should be. Just like ripples upon a lake, the effect from whatever causing factor had been responsible for the upset had diminished little by little.

With no further odd occurrences – voices, beating hearts or otherwise – day-to-day life for Rye had resumed. Even the song that evaded identification had all but disappeared from her thoughts. She instead looked forward. Halloween was fast approaching and, with it, her birthday.

As she'd been born on the thirty-first of October, it was an annual event that Rye Turpin's peers would poke fun, whilst Zach branded the fact, 'awesome.' Rye could not remember the last time she'd ever had a birthday party. This year, however – her sixteenth – and she would see to it that this changed. A small gathering with an exclusive guest list – that's all Rye wanted – and there was one guest in particular that she'd been aching to invite. She just had to pluck up the courage to do so.

'"Hi, Louie, what's up? See, it's my birthday, and …" – no – ahh!' Rye groaned to herself. 'That's stupid.'

She sharply exhaled. The very thought of speaking to him made her anxious.

'How about, "Hey, Louie, what're you up to next Friday?" – no – that's not right either!'

Groaning again, Rye slapped her hands down by her sides in frustration as she strode the corridor. The bell for registration had rung almost five minutes ago, and although Rye tried, her legs could not and would not work as fast as her brain. She appeared jolted and stiff.

'What I'd really like to say,' Rye sighed, 'is that, "I fancy the pants off you, and dream of the day our love story is made into a feature-length film or television series."'

It was her peculiar hybrid style of 'run-walking' that was to blame for Rye's subsequent trip and fall, as her toes caught the floor upon turning a corner. Her tattered cloth bag slipped, and her books and pens scattered. The array of objects included her diary, which uncomfortably slid a little further than anything else. It was as Rye lay sprawled, crumpled and confused, that a pair of scuffed and mud-splattered shoes appeared, a foot or so away from the tip of her nose.

Hesitantly, Rye's eyes followed the boy's body upward, absorbing each limb and segment piece-by-piece. Her gaze lingered for a split-second longer around the crotch area, but this was not-so-long as to make it obvious. This was followed by her appreciation of an athletic frame and broad shoulders. The boy's identity came as no surprise to Rye, for she had successfully recognised him by shoes alone.

Through wisps of her own hair, Rye's eyes came to rest upon Louie's beautiful face, and she smiled, sheepishly. Her situation was so clichéd that she was sure the Fates themselves had tripped her up with their thread.

'Sorry, I didn't mean to – I'm sorry – erm.'

Rye's apology – quite unfounded and unnecessary – was fumbled. Her mouth was focused on trying to form the essential sounds required for a coherent sentence, but her mind was distracted. Louie's skin; medium light-brown. Louie's hair; thick and spiralled. Louie's eyes; non-judgemental and full of wonder at the world around him.

Clambering to her feet, Rye's hands snatched uneasily at her diary as she began stuffing her possessions unlovingly back into her bag. In hindsight, she'd wish that Louie had assisted her with this, or at least helped her to her feet, but he just stood there, bemused.

'Why aren't you in registration?' Rye managed, finally finding her tongue. 'I'm usually the one who's late – so, I'm *definitely* not judging.'

Rye forced herself to meet Louie's gaze, but quickly became nervous and so looked down at the floor – then back at his face – then at her hands.

'Ain't got time for registration today, Rye,' Louie replied, with a coy smile. 'Me, Mike and Stu have got something better to do.'

'Oh, are you skiving?' she asked, bluntly, not expecting that of him.

Louie full-on smiled this time; a fantastic and heart-warming smile, that brought dimples to his cheeks.

'Skive? Me? Never.' He laughed. 'We've got band practice.'

With that, he slipped past her.

'See you later, Rye.'

'Louie!' she blurted and turned, panicked. 'Are you busy on Friday? Not, like, as in today-Friday, but next week Friday – a week today-Friday. Are you busy then?'

Rye could have mulled over exactly how to phrase the question for hours, so perhaps it was best that she just let herself organically garble. She also knew that, despite Louie's parting comment, she would not see him later. It was the final day of school before half-term, and the pair shared no further lessons.

'Birthday – it's my birthday,' Rye continued, her voice wobbly. 'I'm sixteen on Halloween, so I'm having a party. Well, not a party. It's more of a gathering, actually.'

'Sure thing, count me in!' Louie enthused. 'I'll let the guys know.'

Rye opened her mouth to protest – to express her guest list's exclusivity – but Louie was already disappearing around the corner.

'Gotta dash, Rye. I'll see you then.'

Her body a rush of hormones and adrenaline, Rye was unsure whether to consider their exchange a success. Ultimately, she supposed that a few extra guests wouldn't be the end of the world, especially if it ensured Louie's attendance.

Unfortunately for Rye, she was ignorant to just how quickly news of her gathering would gain traction. During band practice, Louie would recount their happenstance to Stu, and in doing so, would set in motion an inevitable chain of discussion.

*

'House party?' Sabrina attempted to whisper to Stu, during the second period.

A louder than average girl, she struggled with volume.

*

'Yeah, apparently her uptight sister is totally cool with it,' Sabrina later commented to Tony, as they bundled out of class a half-hour later.

*

'Wicked, a house party!' squealed Tiff, as Tony propositioned her to be his date during morning break. 'But you've got to be joking, mate. In your *dreams.*'

*

'Her parents won't be home,' Tiff excitedly informed Eva during the third period.

Tiffany Beckett's only prior communication with Rye Turpin had been when she'd asked to borrow a rubber, two years prior.

'Aren't they dead?' asked Eva.

Tiff shrugged, as their professeur, Madame Le Gars, then screeched.

'*Tais-toi et arrête de parler!*'

*

'I think they're dead,' Holly replied, as Eva asked her the very same question at lunch.

'Pinch a dick. Rye – *a party*? I don't think so,' stung Trinity, as she overheard their discussion in the queue for the canteen.

'Sounds legit,' confirmed Moya, through a blank expression and nasal drone.

'What, 'cause you heard it from Finn?' laughed Lyssa. 'That boy could shit in a pitta, call it a kebab, and you'd eat it.'

Unappreciative of Lyssa's crass words, Moya closed her eyes and projected a warning shot of throaty laughter. Her heavily made-up lids fluttering open, she proceeded to look down her pierced nose at her friend.

'Sounds legit,' Lyssa conceded.

'Well, if everyone is going, it'd be rude not to wish Rye happy birthday in person,' spoke Trinity, her smile sadistic and thin. 'Oi, Jamie!'

Eight people behind them, Jamie Stonem poked his head out from the queue.

'Can you score us some free booze from the shop for next Friday?' Trinity asked. 'Proper stuff, not like that nail-varnish-remover-*shite* from last time.'

'For the banging party next Friday?' Jamie hollered back, and Trinity nodded. 'Yeah, no worries. If you help me carry it, we can nab some snacks 'n' all!'

Jamie, whose father owned an off-licence, was an expert in nicking stock and flogging it at a hiked price; a true entrepreneur in the making.

It was miraculous, if not intentional, that the undercurrent of chatter surrounding her birthday did not find its way back to Rye before the end of the day.

❧

<u>Friday 24th October 1997, 23:57pm, TURPIN RESIDENCE, 32 KYNASTON GARDENS, ASHFIELD, LONDON.</u>

Snug within her bed and deep in slumber, Rye was skimming stones across the lake in Sullen Woods. Her dream-self was completely nude, but this was of no concern.

Though brightly lit, there was no sun in the sky. The dreamscape stark; Rye's peripheral vision faded into bright, hazy nothingness. There was no breeze, yet the leaves on the shrubs close by swayed as if caught by one, as a faint, unidentifiable tune carried itself.

'Oh, *Rye* …' softly sang a familiar voice into her sleeping ear.

Undeterred by the disembodied speech that echoed around, Rye slowly stood. Unable to fight the pull of the distant rhythm, she began wading into the lake. And the waters welcomed her. Not a single ripple lapped at Rye's calves. Instead, the liquid absorbed the addition of her body, much like a fly to nectar.

'Must make us, pretty girl,' the voice cooed again, gleeful in encouragement. 'Make us act and make you cold.'

Trance-like, Rye continued in her pursuit of the music's source, as the water around her grew deeper. With each step, her surroundings grew dimmer.

'Little girl, wants to see us,' the voice panted, louder.

As a grotesque talon wrapped itself around Rye's corporeal throat, the action was mirrored unto her dream-self. She was yanked backwards.

Rye awoke with a jolt and sharp intake of breath, causing her to retch, which in turn instigated a full-on coughing fit. It felt as if the whole world had dropped out from beneath her. Her bedsheets were sodden – a mixture of sweat and urine. The subject of her dream, and the reason for her waking; Rye could not remember.

❧ 🖑 ❧

<u>Saturday 25th October 1997, 18:27pm, TURPIN RESIDENCE, 32 KYNASTON GARDENS, ASHFIELD, LONDON.</u>

Under a pile of cushions, a duvet and two blankest, Rye lay across all three seats of the sitting room sofa. She'd been there since the early hours, since waking with a migraine, runny nose and a throat full of phlegm. Pris had aided with the clean-up, but only under the condition from her sister that she never mentioned the bed-wetting incident ever again.

Over twelve hours later, Rye did not feel any better. Her body was weak, and her temperature continued to soar, though she felt cold. Appetite lost; she could only poke at the chicken nuggets on her plate with her fork.

'… all this heavy rain travelling across from the west, towards the capital,' spoke the petite weather presenter, with gusto, from the television. 'Quite a bit of lightning, and exceptional gusts over the southern part of the country – up to seventy-five miles per hour. Flood warnings are in force from the Environment Agency …'

'I'm thinking of going out with Trish next Friday,' Pris interrupted the report, coolly. 'You don't mind, do you?'

'Huh?' responded Rye.

'I said,' Pris began, standing, 'you don't mind if I go out next Friday, do you?'

Rye raised her brow, eyes bulging.

'Are you kidding? *Next* Friday? As in, *Halloween*?'

'Yes, Halloween,' Pris confirmed, seemingly unaware of the date's significance. 'I finish work early and there's a themed night at the bar. Thought I'd take your advice and socialise for a change.'

'Well, you don't need my permission,' Rye stung, thrusting her plate angrily into Pris's crotch. 'And besides, it's not like you'll have anything better to do. I'm glad you're finally paying attention to me,' she seethed, glaring, as her sister carried her uneaten dinner through to the kitchen, 'as opposed to taking me for granted!'

'Good!' Pris hollered back.

'GOOD!'

Rye angrily blew her nose into a tissue before delicately lowering her head down to a pillow. She decided at that moment that Pris would have to realise her error in her own time. Hypersensitive yet obstinate – a not-so-unusual combination of characteristics for a younger sibling – Rye would refrain from reminding her sister of her birthday. The fact that Halloween was, and had always been, *her* birthday, was so blindingly obvious that it wasn't worth mentioning, if only to see how long it took for Rye to receive an apology.

'I might invite Fred and Zach over on Friday then! *You* don't mind, do you?'

'Yeah, why not?' Pris shouted, approvingly, from the kitchen. 'You could order a takeaway? Make an occasion of it!'

Rye rolled her eyes.

'Make *what* an occasion?!'

'*Halloween*, of course,' Pris clarified as she returned to the sitting room, drying her hands on her jeans. 'I'll tell you what, I get paid that day, too – I'll leave a twenty out. Anyway – gotta go. Can't be late for work.'

Donning her coat, Pris wrapped a scarf around her neck and leant in to give her sister a kiss. After hesitation, it was planted atop Rye's greasy crown.

'Alright, alright,' muttered Rye, pushing Pris away.

A downpour and blustery winds could be heard from outside as Pris opened the front door to leave. The temperature dropped and Rye buried herself deeper into the sofa. Aided by the wind, the door then slammed with such force that the entire house shook.

'… Mr Richard Simkins changed his plea to guilty in Magistrates' Court today. Sentencing is due to take place at Wood Green Crown Court on Monday the first of December. He's been charged with the embezzlement of over fifty—'

Using the remote, Rye switched off the television. Rolling onto her back, she let out a slow and steady sigh. Her gaze was drawn to the long shelf above the picture rail that ran the length of the enlarged room, all the way to the French doors at the rear. Upon this shelf sat Cousin Veronica's collection of nearly fifty china dolls. Rye had already spent most of the day staring at each of them in turn. Whilst some were surely antique, others were much newer. Rye hated them all, but not because they unnerved her. She just felt disdain at their impassive faces.

'Screw this,' Rye rasped.

Throwing the covers aside, she swung her legs off the sofa and tentatively stood, her body aching and chilly. She staggered out of the sitting room and stomped upstairs. Once in her room, Rye snottily fumbled through cardboard boxes, in search of something to wear for her birthday.

It is a truth known to everyone that Halloween serves as an excuse to showcase beauty. A costume could be poorly executed, unimaginative or unoriginal, yet so long as the person looked beautiful, it didn't seem to matter. And Rye wanted to look beautiful.

After a ten-minute search, Rye folded to the floor, exhausted. Nothing she owned was suitable. Nothing was beautiful. For a moment, she contemplated raiding Beryl's

Bargains, but that was before she spied Pris's bedroom across the landing. Its door had been left open. Rye had never been allowed to borrow any of her sister's clothes before, but she was scorned and spurred on by anger.

Her body sapped of energy, Rye crawled out onto the landing and pulled herself upright using the bannisters. She padded barefoot across the carpet through to the master bedroom and slid open the door to the wardrobe. The air inside was damp and its staleness hit her nose. Without care, Rye then began to rummage.

As she'd feared, every item of clothing upon the hangers wasn't suitable either. A collection of garish suit dresses and blazers, all belonged to Veronica. Mostly animal print or made of shiny fabric, so hideous was the selection that even their cousin had left them behind. Pris's few clothes were neatly folded atop the shoes at the bottom. Rye carefully sifted through them, and any hope she had left waned.

It was in a final effort that Rye climbed onto the lowest shelf. Feeling faint, but with an objective in mind, she stretched up onto tiptoe. The highest shelf was thick with dust and all but empty, except for one, large, cardboard box at the back. Gasping, Rye buckled under its unimpressive weight as she lifted it down to the floor. She wiped its lid with the sleeve of her pyjamas and in doing so revealed a date adorning its surface, in spindly black ink. It read: '1973'.

Curious, Rye removed the lid. Stored within was a beautiful white dress. Its condition pristine, it looked no different as to how it would have twenty-four years prior. Essentially a time-capsule; Rye doubted the box had ever been opened since the day it had been packed away. The dress smelt musty, but that was to be forgiven – nothing that a good airing wouldn't fix. Long, floaty, and with a cinched waist, it was a gem of a discovery. And Rye already had her suspensions as to its provenance.

Puffing and snivelling, Rye set about changing. The process took a great deal longer than it should, but the payoff was worth the pain. Admiring herself in the mirror, she girlishly twirled. Stiffly, she curtsied to an invisible crowd. Rye stood a picture of perfection, reminiscent of Kate Bush in the video for 'Wuthering Heights'. For the first time in her life, Rye looked, and felt, every inch a woman.

It was then – upon the umpteenth twirl – that Rye caught sight of a small card left behind inside the box. Dizzy, she knelt to inspect it.

'"Miss Jean Holloway, one hundred and twenty-nine pounds",' Rye read, aloud.

This confirmed it; this had been her mother's wedding dress.

Revealing her bare legs and knickers, Rye lovingly drew the dress's skirts up to her face. She took a deep sniff and her nostrils spluttered. There was no smell of her mother – or at least, not one that Rye would have recognised.

Several minutes of successful rummaging then ensued, wherein Rye managed to accessorise the dress with a pair of complementing silver heels – courtesy of Pris – and a selected piece of Cousin Veronica's costume jewellery. Pouting, she clipped her frosted hair in place with a bejewelled butterfly clip.

Louie was sure to be pleasantly surprised by this kind of vintage beauty, Rye thought, as her heart thumped in anticipation. Boasting a shy and altogether seductive smile, she hoisted the dress's skirts once more.

'Humpf,' she sounded, peering down at her legs. 'They're better than yours, *bitch*.'

With Trinity's derogatory comment regarding her pins flared up within her, Rye turned on her heels. Defiant, yet shaky, she strode out of her sister's room, in the pair of shoes that were one size too big for her. Certain Pris would object to all of this, Rye decided that she needn't ever know.

CHAPTER VIII

The House on the Corner

<u>Friday 31st October 1997, 19:42pm, ASHFIELD, LONDON.</u>
'Do you think we should have called Rye, to warn her?' asked Fred.

'I'm not sure, you know?' Zach mused. 'I mean, she must *know* everyone's coming.'

'Hmmm,' replied Fred, sceptically, and Zach pulled a face.

Both knew full-well that Rye was in the dark with regards to the numbers her birthday would attract. In fact, Zach had actively avoided telling her, not that he had seen her since she'd caught her cold, but he selfishly wanted a party – a proper party – and he'd convinced himself that Rye did too.

'I wonder if Ally's coming?' Zach voiced, mind wandering.

'Probably not,' Fred dismissed.

Together, the pair briskly strode, their breath clouding on the cold air as they conversed. Out of the alleyway, they turned left onto Dragnell Lane, where youngsters ran joyfully about the street accompanied by flagging adults. It was the driest evening in weeks and the trick-or-treaters were taking full advantage of the conditions.

'I just hope Pris doesn't lose her rag over the amount of peop-owW!'

His sentence cut prematurely short, Fred limped up and over the curb. Toes throbbing, he swore loudly and shot daggers at the chunk of masonry that had abetted his trip.

'*They* ought to be careful,' he bemoaned, and gestured in the direction of the overexcited children. 'Running about like that, they might trip over and hurt themselves.'

'Oh, cheer up, misery guts. They're just enjoying the spooky festivities. I'll tell you what wouldn't hurt – you making an effort! It's Halloween – it's *Rye's* birthday – and you look just the same as you do every other day.'

Silently, Fred side-eyed his friend's Day of the Dead-themed face paint, feeling envious of the little confidence it took to pull it off. Zach's execution was dodgy, and he'd enthusiastically overcomplicated the design, but the overall effect wasn't bad.

'I don't like dressing up,' Fred sighed.

Zach was ignorant, but Fred had spent much longer in front of the mirror. For over two hours he had tamed and coiffed his hair. He'd changed his outfit a multitude of times and even carefully applied his mother's concealer to three angry pimples.

Another twenty minutes passed before Fred and Zach arrived at the end of the cul-de-sac where Rye lived. Staring up at her house, they ground to a halt by the front gate, feeling guilty. Multi-coloured lights flashed to illuminate the shadows of countless people dancing. Even from outside, the music could be heard.

'Uh-oh,' Fred whispered. 'That's not good.'

He turned to face his friend.

'*Unexpected.* That's the word we're going with, mate – *unexpected*,' spoke Zach, as his mouth upturned into a mischievous grin.

'You're awful,' Fred disapproved.

'It's not like you told her either,' Zach defended. 'And besides, you're only sixteen once.'

At that moment, the front door of number 32 opened and a flustered-looking Rye poked out her head.

'*Help me*,' she mouthed.

<u>Friday 31ˢᵗ October 1997, 20:09pm, TURPIN RESIDENCE, 32 KYNASTON GARDENS, ASHFIELD, LONDON.</u>

Blonde hair unkempt, Rosalind Pretty spun about in the corner of the sitting room by the French windows, her pink shirtdress flapping out around. Inadvertently, she'd cleared a space all to herself by knocking everyone else out of the way with her angel wings. Ethereally caught up in the music, Ros was thoroughly enjoying herself. Despite having not touched a single drop of alcohol, she appeared drunk.

Ally stood in the room's opposite corner. Clothed in her midnight-blue minidress, she spoke only occasionally to a hockey-masked Tony, who'd proclaimed himself DJ upon arrival. Since connecting his amp and CD-changer, the music had tripled in volume. He fought off a vamped Moya for song choices, although she was currently winning, as Spice Girls' 'Who Do You Think You Are' blasted out. Walls vibrating; the framed photographs of Cousin Veronica's Pekingese were being knocked askew.

It was with horror that Rye surveyed the evolving scene from the room's threshold, as a cloud of suspicious smelling smoke drifted lazily inside from the back patio.

'Zach, Pris is gonna see the fag butts!' she stressed, clawing at her bodice. 'I thought it was OK at first, when Tony and Jake turned up, with Tiff and that lot.' She lowered her voice to a whisper. 'But I had to take a toilet break – 'cause I've been peeing almost uncontrollably, *all* week – and when I came back down, there were more people, and I could hardly ask them to leave – and—'

Zach shrugged.

'Rye, I'm gonna be honest, she'll probably notice more than just the fag butts.'

He thrust her a beer from his rucksack and Fred scowled. Zach looked pleadingly back. Rye took one final panoramic of the unfolding chaos before taking the can. Opening it, she proceeded to take a deep swig. Coughing and spluttering, almost immediately, some of her hair slipped out from its carefully pinned state. Rye had never tasted beer before.

'Zach, I don't think getting Rye drunk will make Pris any less Pris-*ed*,' Fred warned. 'And don't tell me it's medicinal.'

'What?!' Zach shouted over the noise, pretending not to hear.

Fred repeated himself, only for Zach to back away in the direction of Tony, Moya and Ally.

'Never mind,' Fred muttered. 'Rye, you look beautiful.'

Thanking him, she wiped her snotty nose on a scrunched piece of toilet paper she'd stuffed down her bra. Fred didn't want to be a spoilsport, but he felt genuinely concerned for Rye. She was still clearly unwell.

The next hour and a half progressed steadily, aided by copious amounts of free-flowing booze that had been unwittingly donated by Jamie Stonem's father. Rye, having been presented with her birthday gifts from Zach and Fred, had calmed somewhat also. Upon Zach's bestowal of his old alphanumeric pager, she'd literally jumped for joy, thereby overshadowing Fred's present of a mixed cassette tape.

Tony had finally regained control of the music selection and Blur was his current band of choice. Before then, Zach had played 'Love Shack' by The B-52's, which he'd also performed with jubilation and an exaggerated voice – both male and female vocals. Intent on impressing Ally, he must have succeeded on some level, for he now had her number stored in his own brand-new pager.

As Zach took Rye's hand, persuading her dance, Fred stood awkwardly on the sidelines. They were his best friends, yet he could not get swept up in the atmosphere as they could, as they laughed together, with Rye staggering about in Pris's heels. Fred had consumed some alcohol, but it would require much more for him to lower his defences and forfeit his inhibitions. And so, he decided to leave them to it.

For lack of direction, Fred shuffled back over to Ally and Tony. Much like himself, Ally appeared uninterested by the whole spectacle. Leaning against the wall, she'd helped herself to a book from the shelf and was aimlessly leafing through it. The conversation that ensued between them was equally disjointed, as it was forced. Fred made every effort to instigate dialogue, but Ally barely looked up from the copy of *Secrets of Jerusalem*.

Generic questions and comments such as, 'Like the music?', 'It's busier than I thought,' or 'What're you drinking?' were met only with short responses. In the end, Fred gave up. Perching on the end of the sofa, he gave in to the fact that he just wasn't enjoying himself. The only reason he was still present was out of moral obligation.

Her sickness quashed by alcohol, Rye downed her fifth beer to the applause of her peers. She lowered it from her face, wide-eyed, and after a short pause wherein she swallowed, let out a fully-fledged burp.

Embarrassed, yet pleased by the look of sheer awe on Zach's face, Rye giggled. Once more, he held out his hand to her, smiling, and she took it gladly, allowing him to lead her confidently out of the sitting room and through to the kitchen. Fred trailed behind.

Squeezing past Moya in the hallway, Fred gasped before diverting his eyes. At first glance, the girl's seemingly innocent embrace with her ex-boyfriend, Finn, was just that. Upon second glance, and it became apparent that Finn's hand had slithered down and under her skirt, where it moved, quickly and rhythmically. His face fearful, Fred clicked the kitchen door shut after him.

'What're you wanting to drink next then?' Zach asked.

With an extended arm and hovering hand, Rye scanned the kitchen counters with curious enthusiasm. She then encircled the central table – a mass of bottles and sticky playing cards. Those who sat around were partaking in a drinking game. Finally, Rye plucked a bottle of vodka out from the clutter.

'This!' she declared.

Inviting protests, Rye assumed the vodka belonged to the group, but she was unconcerned by their displeasure, for she could not put a single name to any of their faces. This was her home – her party – and so she unscrewed the bottle's cap and sploshed a generous measure into a glass tumbler. Zach held up his hands to silence the room.

'This is the birthday girl!' he clarified. 'Guys, simmer down, yeah?'

The loud protests subsided into murmurs.

'I *am* the birthday girl,' Rye reconfirmed, proudly, toasting herself.

'Vodka?!' Zach exclaimed, suddenly catching sight of the bottle's label as Rye replaced it on the table. 'Really? You should probably add some mixer—'

'Yeah, probably,' Rye cut across him. Throwing back her head, several more strands of hair broke free from their clip. 'You know what, this drinking thing ain't half bad, is it? Not *really*. I mean, I've never before – but *this* – this ain't bad.'

Rye hiccupped and Zach eyed her, warily. He swayed, then steadied himself against the counter.

'We thought that, like – thought your party – might be cancelled,' slurred a heavily bosomed witch from a chair. 'Because you were sick. But Trinity – she told everyone – it was all good.'

The witch let out a shallow belch. Spittle flew, and the rest of her group dropped their straws into their shared washing-up bowl, disappointed.

'Trinity told you?' Rye questioned.

The witch nodded.

Internally raging, Rye saw only red. She'd yet to spot Trinity in amongst the attendees, though as Moya was present it seemed only certain. Rye's anger had little time to brew, however, as she was placated by the sudden appearance of Louie. As those around him dissipated, he was left alone in the threshold to the garden, toking from a rolled cigarette. Rye's heart skipped a beat and, aided by her alcohol consumption, she gave in to impulse. Drink in hand, she clunked her way across the kitchen. Zach took hold of Fred's arm, as the latter went to follow.

'I think it's best we leave them to it, don't you?' he advised, moving to pour himself a glass of tap water.

Dressed in American football garb, complete with shoulder pads and zombified face, Louie's form took up most of the doorway. Rye casually slipped herself into the small gap that remained. Without saying a word, he smiled and offered out his fag to her. Within that instant, Rye lost all her new-found confidence.

'No – no, it's alright. I – I don't smoke,' she stuttered. 'Glad you like it, though.'

Horrified and repentant of her initial drunken confidence, Rye cast her eyes down to the patio's collection of jack-o'-lanterns, repeating her choice of words over in her mind.

'I'll have a drag,' announced a cool voice.

Rye turned to see who'd spoken, though she needn't have, for the tone was easily recognisable. All but painted into a red vinyl dress, Trinity had appeared as if from nowhere. A pair of battery-powered devil's horns sat atop her glossy, crimped mane and lit up in flashes. Her customary hooped earrings omnipresent, they were so large that Rye imagined trying to throw a tennis ball through them, only to miss.

Just as before, Louie held out his cigarette. Obliging, Trinity expertly raised it to her pursed lips. She took a deep, long pull, before seductively exhaling. Her darkened lids flicked up to unblinkingly meet Louie's gaze, as the smoke rolled up over his face. Rye grimaced.

'Seriously, that girl needs to take five and go sit on a bag of frozen peas,' Ally whispered to Zach.

Having only then entered the kitchen, she'd arrived just in time to spectate.

'Here, have some of my wine, in trade,' Trinity cooed.

Handing back the diminishing stub, she held out her glass.

'Thanks, but I don't really—'

'I don't really think a toke of a cigarette necessitates a trade deal, Trin,' Rye stung, surprising herself with her sheer gutsiness, let alone coherency.

'That's because you're unilateral, Rye. *Me?* I'm a free market.'

Zach and Ally both choked back laughter and Trinity shot them a venomous glare, as Louie took that second's opportunity to squeeze himself between the two girls and into the kitchen.

Head tilted menacingly to one side, Trinity looked Rye up and down.

'What have you come as, Rye? Bride of Frankenstein?'

'It's *my* birthday,' Rye insisted. 'I've come as the birthday girl.'

Trinity tutted, wrinkling her nose.

'It's sparkling rosé,' she then declared, holding out her glass to Rye. 'Try it.'

Rye rolled her eyes and returned to her friends. And she would have escaped the room entirely if it hadn't been for Zach and Ally physically blocking her. Without explanation, their actions could easily have been misconstrued, but Rye knew them – well, Zach at least – to only have her best interests at heart. In her own home, if nowhere else, she should stand her ground.

Snake-hips slinking, Trinity slithered her way across the kitchen in pursuit of Louie. Her excessively high heels tapping upon the linoleum, all background conversation ceased, as all eyes became glued to her.

It was either by accident, or on purpose, that Trinity's toe then clipped a chair leg – although one was more likely. Rye watched in slow, blurred motion as Trinity's ankle gave way to a fall. Staggering forward, the entire contents of her glass was poured forth – airborne – to smatter across Rye's gown. Trinity continued her dramatic lurch, right into Louie's unsuspecting arms.

Rye could only muster a succession of short breathy sounds as she held out her arms, aghast. Dyeing the dress's white satin, the pink liquid quickly bled to leave large streaks down Rye's skirts. She wheezed – bordering on hyperventilating – as the room collectively held its breath.

'Tr-Trin-Trinity,' Rye stammered, resisting the urge to cry, before then forcing the full capacity of her lungs out through her throat. 'What have you done?!'

Zach, Louie and a few others opened their mouths, though not one succeeded in speaking. They could only exchange looks.

'Oh, my God,' Trinity cackled, as she set her empty glass down on the table. 'You look just like *Carrie*!'

'That was my mother's wedding dress!' Rye wailed, just as the speakers in the sitting room were cut.

Music absent; ringing stung the ears of all those present. There was vacuous silence, pierced only by Trinity, who didn't even try to stifle her laughter. With her back to the door, Rye did not notice her sister's entrance as others did.

'Rye,' began Pris, calmly. 'Could you please tell me what the *hell* is going on?'

Slowly, Rye turned to face her elder sibling. Full of dread, deflated and stained, she stood humiliated – the remnants of her ego crushed, as she looked timidly up at Pris.

'The house – it's a mess! What are all these people doing here?!'

Stood inside the kitchen doorway, Pris visibly shook. Several party guests – cautious, yet non-too subtle – slid past her and into the hallway to make their exits. And Pris, unable to tear her eyes from Rye, let them leave without question. Far less dolled up than her sister and dressed in a work polo shirt, she, by comparison, had never looked younger. Disgust written all over her face, she screwed up her nose at the smell of marijuana emanating from the back garden. A gut-wrenching realisation then crashed over her.

'What are you wearing?' Pris whispered. 'Please, tell me you didn't.'

Rye's jaw dropped, aquiver. She had no response that wouldn't disappoint. Moya and Finn, accompanied now by a cat-costumed Lyssa, skulked in the hallway's background. Out of sight from Pris, they soundlessly fell about laughing. Rye could see them, however, and she hated them for it.

'I let you keep the photo of them in your diary – our *only* photo,' Pris wept. 'And this is how you repay me? This is how you respect their memory – our *mother's* memory? The happiest day of her life, and it's nothing but a costume to you!'

'Pris, I'm—' Rye fought, through the onset of tears.

'And your face,' Pris continued, callously. 'You look just like her.'

Index finger pointedly directed at Trinity, Pris succeeded in wiping the smug look off her face, at least.

'Do you not care about me at all?' Rye strained, her voice cracking as she diverted the confrontation to a tangent.

'I just said, I let you keep the photograph—'

'You'll never replace her,' Rye interrupted.

Her body shuddering under the weight of teenage angst, the unattractive sound of Rye's whimpering carried through the steadily emptying house.

'Rye, that's a bit harsh,' Fred whispered, as Pris responded:

'You can't even remember her—'

'No!' Rye rebuked her friend, her voice growing stronger. 'I'm never perfect enough for her. Everything I ever do is either too much, or – or too little! It's always – *never* tidy enough, or *never* on time – never good enough! But when it comes to the important stuff – the stuff that *actually* matters – I'm completely invisible!'

Pris opened her mouth, but Rye beat her to speaking.

'And, no! I didn't ask you about the party, because you would've said—'

'Well, what did you think I was going to say when I found out, Rye?!' Pris yelled, flinging her arms out to the surrounding mess. 'Did you think I wouldn't notice?!'

Rye, straight-up ignoring this fair point, ploughed forth. Whilst riled, her proximity to her crush seemed irrelevant. But Louie put distance between them.

'You said you were going out tonight! *Tonight* – on the night of my birthday! I was born on Halloween, Pris! It's hardly easy to forget! It's been the same date for the last sixteen years!'

Tears poured down Rye's cheeks. Uncontrollable and hot, they stung her face.

'Well, I—'

'You know what? I don't even care, you've ruined it! You've ruined it.'

As Rye clutched both hands to her chest, Trinity reached for her wine bottle. She was about to pour herself another drink when Rye snatched it from her talon-like grasp and slammed it down with such force that it frothed up through the neck. A rosé volcano; it flooded the table with bubbles. The liquid proceeded to drip down onto the floor from all four sides.

As she ran from the house, Rye collected her cloth bag from off the peg in the hallway, unaware of the small box that sat discarded to the side of the front step. Left by Pris, the birthday cake inside was iced with 'Rye, 16 Today'.

The party's remaining guests and Pris had all been left speechless in the kitchen, and that's where they stayed. All except one, that was. Well-practiced at jogging in her knee-high boots, Ally chased after Rye. A little over halfway down the road and she succeeded in catching up with her classmate, who'd slowed to a fast walk.

'And where do you think you're off to?' she asked, drawing level.

Rye ignored her. Face steely and determined, she kept her eyes front.

'I see,' Ally continued, matching the pace. 'No purpose or direction, I can relate.'

Still, Rye ignored her.

'Why don't you come back to mine?' Ally proposed. 'Though, you don't have to,' she hastened.

Rye stopped dead. Chest heaving, she slowly turned to face her. Appearing to digest the option, she looked right through Ally.

'OK,' Rye then whispered. 'Where do you live?'

'Guess you'll see when you get there,' Ally replied, setting off to lead.

Their walk across town took far longer than it should have, due to Rye's extreme intoxication and ill-fitting footwear – a challenging combination, for even the most practised of women.

Ally silently judged her. She harshly deemed the birthday girl inexperienced. Inexperienced in drinking. Inexperienced in dressing herself. And inexperienced in life. Inexperienced in communication? Well, she could hardly judge Rye for that.

Trundling along behind, Rye would stop every so often to retch a hot stream of undigested fluid into the gutter. If she had been sober, perhaps she would have realised their journey eastwards, across the dual carriageway and over to the 'bad side' of town. Known as Ashfield Highway, the area had experienced far more affluence during the decades prior but had since suffered hard degradation and rocketing crime rates. In a fate unfortunate as to have befallen many pockets of London that were traditionally working-class, squatters and drug-dealers had now taken over. Nowadays, these pockets were no longer friendly nor safe. Even when sober, Rye did not know Ashfield Highway well.

Down dark and dingy streets lined with sacks of long-festering rubbish, the pair walked one after the other. Lampposts flickered as unseen sirens whirred. The gardens here, though much smaller, were in an even worse state than Rye's own. A still night so far; the mist that seemed commonplace this autumn was fast turning to fog.

Ally finally came to a halt in front of what – in Ashfield Highway – could only be described as an unremarkable house. On the corner of two streets, 42 Friar Street was an end of terrace and built of dull grey brick. Its windows were clad in rusted metal sheets that had been haphazardly fixed onto the exterior façade. Large and heavy padlocks acted as both a deterrent and an obstacle to any would-be intruders.

Rye looked upon the house through blurred vision.

'You live here?' she asked, incredulously.

It was Ally who then chose to ignore her. Under a flap of metal that had revealed its underside unfastened from the brick-work, she proceeded to clamber through a broken window to the left of the door. Despite her minidress, Ally climbed capably. With little other option, Rye attempted to copy. Ungraceful; she fell flat on her face to the floor inside.

Ally navigated the pitch-black interior with ease. Only someone who had been there many times before could have tackled the labyrinth without halt or falter. Rye, by contrast, resorted to feeling her way along the walls. Following the sounds of Ally's footsteps, she was directed through the kitchen and hallway to the sitting room, where it was ever-so-slightly less dark. Shafts of light penetrated the gaps between the metal-clad windows and half-ashen curtains.

As Rye squinted, Ally set about the room lighting a collection of stubby candles that dotted the floor and mantelpiece.

Their flames seemed only to strengthen the damp and musty odour. Her surroundings illuminated in chunks, Rye absorbed the graffitied genitalia and tags that adorned the hearth's tiles and crumbling plaster. Other than a dirty and dank mattress, and a lowly wooden stool, the room was devoid of any other furniture. All litter had been shunted into one corner.

'Sit down then,' Ally gestured to the stool, as she herself fell back onto the mattress.

Tentatively, Rye took a somewhat shaky perch. Though she tried, she could not hide her uneasiness, and any attempt to do so was – like everything else – hindered by the considerable amount of alcohol in her bloodstream. It did not help either that the floorboards were uneven.

'Erm, Ally,' Rye slurred, clocking the girl's school uniform that was hung on a hanger from the picture rail. 'How the *hell* are you living here?'

Ally looked off in a daze towards the opposite wall. Slowly, her eyes came into focus upon an empty sandwich packet in amongst the rubbish.

'It's a long story,' she said. 'You see, I found a ticket.'

- CHAPTER IX -

Sullen Woods

<u>Friday 31st October 1997, 22:47pm, 42 FRIAR STREET, ASH-FIELD HIGHWAY, LONDON.</u>

'Where're your parents?' Rye asked, not awaiting a full explanation to her previous question. Slumping forwards on the stool with her lips languidly pouted, she looked upon Ally as if she was an exhibit. No matter how truly innocent her curiosity, her manner was rude.

'Where're yours?' Ally quipped.

She did not want to appear rude either, but neither did she want this conversation tonight – this interrogation. And although Ally was sure her bizarre circumstances would absolutely have begged questions – anyone with a mind would wonder – she'd just hoped Rye would have quickly passed out. Ally, however, had severely underestimated the power of Rye's enquiring mind to overcome inebriation.

Elbows rested on her knees, her head on balled fists, Rye sniped back.

'Mine are *dead*. Where are yours?' she repeated.

Casting reflections of orange fires in the eyes of both girls, the candles flickered in an absent wind. Ally shrugged.

'Could be dead,' she replied, straight-faced.

Not quite as drunk as her blonde counterpart, Ally could still feel the alcohol slide from one side of her face to the other when shifting her weight. Warming her, the sensation only fuelled temper's fire.

'I'm not sure,' Ally continued. 'I've been in foster care for as long as I can remember.'

Only a half-truth, this supplement of information was not an outright lie. Long before Mick, before Barcelona and her horrendous escape thereof, Ally had indeed been in foster care as a child, and she had no memories that pre-dated this time. What of her birth parents? Ally could pass them in the street and be none-the-wiser.

'And now you're here? How? Why?' Rye asked.

'Look, you don't have to be here. I thought I was doing you a favour. Why don't you just … go to sleep?'

'I'm not tired,' responded Rye, assuredly. 'How can you even be living on your own? I mean you're – *we're* – only sixteen?'

'And you just *assume* that I'm sixteen?'

For a moment, Rye's face softened. She opened her mouth to speak, only to close it again. This action was repeated before she then cried:

'What do you mean?!'

Ally took to her feet. Advancing, she looked imposingly down upon the birthday girl.

'Shut up, Rye. Just shut up,' she pleaded. "We can talk in the morning. Why don't you *just* go to sleep?!"

Exhausted, Ally was as much flustered as she was infuriated, yet her hostile movement only intensified the ensuing exchange. Rye too jumped to her feet, arms folding defiantly across her stained chest.

'No.'

For a further ten seconds, the two girls stood staring at each other, their respective hearts pumping adrenaline, but it was Rye who broke her stance first. She looked down at Ally's worn leather boots, before looking back up, with large and sad eyes.

'How come you came to Ashfield Community then? Given the choice, I don't think I'd attend school if I didn't have to.'

'Get out.'

'But, I—'

'Just get out!' Ally bellowed.

For the second time that evening, Rye felt herself well up with tears. Just as before, her sadness was only made worse by the feeling that she'd brought it on herself. Turning on her heels, she walked obediently from the sitting room.

Shoulders tensed, but immediately regretful, Ally listened as her classmate made her fumbled departure through the kitchen window. It sounded as if Rye had again fallen through it, onto concrete this time, but Ally did not move to check.

'Because I'm lonely,' she whispered to herself, in answer to the final question Rye had put to her.

Mere minutes later, neither would fully remember their conversation and how hastily it had escalated.

∾✑∿

<u>Saturday 1st November 1997, 00:01am, DRAGNELL LANE, ASHFIELD, LONDON.</u>

The clock had just struck midnight as the heavens opened to yet another downpour, welcoming in November. The ensuing wind and rain tore the remaining dead leaves from off the trees and pummelled the roofs of houses and cars.

A pair of hands clad in leather gloves reached down to the gutter to lift a slimy chunk of masonry from a quickly forming puddle. This was carried a few doors down the road before it was dumped, with great effort, into a yellow skip. The trio of bricks had left scuff marks upon her gloves, but, as with her shoes, Michelle thought these too could be fixed by a black marker.

Wiping her hands clean on her suit's trousers, Michelle then turned on the spot and jogged over to the nearest front porch for shelter. With the lights inside the property switched off, there was a slim chance that its occupants were still awake at this hour.

Hunched, Michelle drew her raincoat's large hood up over her head. She cut a solemn silhouette.

Shuddering, Michelle placed a cigarette between cracked lips. It took several attempts to light; her lighter's mechanism was temperamental, and her thumb calloused beneath her glove. When she'd finally succeeded, she threw the cheap plastic out onto the pavement. There was a fine against littering – a fine enforced by people such as her good self – but Michelle couldn't care less, for the action gave her relief. It was a small relief to the pent-up angst that'd been growing inside of her for the past seven weeks and two days, but a relief, nonetheless.

Not the first evening Michelle had returned to Dragnell Lane; it was, however, the first she'd returned with heightened expectation. Tonight, was Halloween – a night when the veil between worlds was supposedly thinned – and if what she had seen was ever to repeat itself, it would be tonight, surely? A new moon, rather than full, Michelle had still checked its cycle as part of her investigation's branching research, despite feeling silly for doing so. She took a drag and watched the exhaled smoke dispel amongst the precipitation.

Each of Michelle's visits to Dragnell Lane had followed near the same pattern. First, she would slowly retrace her steps from the alleyway and across to the opposite pavement. Then she'd walk the length of the street several times – both sides – peering into car windows. Before leaving, Michelle would pick up the very same chunk of masonry and hurl it the width of a car space, through an invisible window and into the gutter. Michelle considered the masonry evidence, but not wanting to remove it from context, she was reluctant to take it back to her flat. Only sometimes would she replace it atop the skip's debris.

Michelle chain-smoked another four cigarettes in total over the next quarter of an hour – lit by matches. Her fifth spiralled smoke with its descent, as it came to rest with a soft hiss.

'Hmm, hmhm, hm, hm, hmhm-hmmm …' she began to hum as she placed a sixth. 'Hm, hmm, hm, hm, hm, hmm, hm-hm.'

The joyful tune – the origin of which escaped her – juxtaposed to the miserable onslaught of rain and carried Michelle back to her own car. Apparently, there wasn't to be any ghosts tonight after all, a thinned veil or not.

❧

<u>Saturday 1st November 1997, 00:17am, SULLEN WOODS, ASHFIELD, LONDON.</u>

Her demeanour serene, Rye sat curled on the muddied ground, in her usual spot beneath the old oak tree. She had trudged along the slippery track that led down to the lake's edge – her sanctuary – daring the events that had led to her avoidance of it to repeat. Purposely, she was tempting the claws of fate with the naivety of youth. Make-up smudged across her face; Rye was sodden. Her mother's dress now bore speckles of dirt in amongst the pink.

'Hmm … hmhm … hm, hm,' she quietly hummed, off-key. 'Hmhm … hmmm …'

Warm air from inside her lungs billowed out through her mouth as Rye sighed. She stroked her cloth bag with one hand, whilst scrawling across a dampened page of her diary with the other. Her words jagged, Rye would surely not remember writing them upon re-reading, although they were pondering what Louie would say to comfort her, if he was her boyfriend. Swaying, she concluded her jumbled sentence by stabbing a full-stop that tore through at least three sheets.

'Hmm … hmhm …'

A series of five beeps fired out in jovial melody from inside her bag and Rye jolted upright. Realising the noise emanated from her newly gifted pager, she hurried to see who it was that'd messaged. Through squinted eyes, Rye read the text that scrolled across the screen:

'Hope ur OK. Ally mssgd. She says u ran out on her. Shes on her way back to urs. Come back! Evry1 is worried. Zach.'

With a single finger, Rye stifled the stream of snot protruding from her left nostril before wiping it the length of a bare arm. A single tear, lost in the precipitation that beaded there, trickled down her pale cheek. She chose not to reply to Zach, out of arguably deserving punishment, and carelessly dropped her pager to the ground.

Rye looked out across the water. Her gaze blurry, at first, she thought this to be the reason why it'd lost its reflective sheen. Upon refocusing, however, it became apparent that it had in fact turned flat and solid, like polished black marble. The leaves and branches that had been floating there, now suspended, were trapped like flies in amber.

Within the space of those few seconds, the wind and rain that had kept movement throughout the trees died completely. Branches creaked to a standstill as the drier strands of Rye's blonde hair fluttered down to stick. Everything was still. Everything was silent. Everything was dead. Unnatural; the altered landscape that came to surround Rye resembled that of a studio backdrop. Fog rolled out across the lake from the opposite bank.

Shoes sliding upon the stone-ridden mud, Rye apprehensively stood. Her fear mounting, she turned around and around, picking out shapes from the shadows. Her imagination gave them figures and forms. Then, it hit her.

An invisible force – powerful and insistent – smashed into Rye's torso. The feeling was non-too dissimilar to how she'd imagine it felt to be hit by a car. Pushed backward, Rye was not pushed over but instead thrust upwards. Her feet no longer able to touch the ground, she was pinned against the old oak, arms bent back to near breaking point.

The tree's rough bark acted like sandpaper against the back of her mother's dress and Rye could feel the splinters nicking and tearing at the fabric, as she steadily rose higher, and higher. It was as if her ankles had been strapped together, for despite her best efforts, she could not separate them.

After rising at least twenty feet, Rye came to rest, with her body held between the tree's middling branches. She remained stiff, with her arms pulled perpendicular to her torso, causing her rapidly heaving chest to protrude outward. It was impossible to pinpoint exactly where upon Rye's body the force had gripped, for its exertion was uniform.

Nauseated and dizzy, Rye struggled to process her new vantage point. As she regained awareness, she noticed a particularly gnarly and crooked off-shoot of a branch to her right begin to quiver. Gentle at first, its shuddering movement quickly grew in intensity until it snapped clean off – broken by an unseen hand. Detached, it remained static for all of a split-second before flying past Rye's nose, straight for the ground. Her eyes glued open in horror, she was unable to close them, even if she had wanted to.

Displaying a mass much higher than it could possibly possess, like that of iron, the stick collided with the mud with a force that was far greater than gravity. It was then dragged, heavily, across the ground, past Rye's cloth bag, to a patch of earth that was siltier in composition. The branch stood itself vertical, upright on-end – impossibly, yet perfectly so. The stick began to twitch at its highest-end – its opposite remaining completely still in the wet sludge – and Rye gulped. Then followed the heavy-handed flicking of the stick's whole – messy and laborious. Stroke by ridged stroke, it began to scratch away at the dirt in juvenile, blocky lettering.

Rye was beginning to hyperventilate. Pained and tran-sfixed by the spectacle below her, she had no choice but to watch as the first letter was completed.

'A'.

If this message was intended to be obvious – as it surely must have been – whoever or whatever it was had certainly succeeded in capturing her undivided attention. They needn't have gone to such extreme measures if it was not to prevent her from fleeing. Rye breathed shallow and fast, as the stick continued to swish itself about in the dirt.

'N'.

Mere feet away from where the stick was etching, Rye's pager vibrated. Flashing, it beeped out the notification of another message received. In her current predicament, it was impossible to read.

'O'.
'C'.

❧

Saturday 1st November 1997, 00:26am, MICHELLE DAVEY'S RESIDENCE, FLAT 1, 179A LONDON ROAD, ASHFIELD, LONDON.

Michelle sat alone in her flat's sitting room. Tiffany's 'I Think We're Alone Now' blared out from an old cassette tape as a muted rerun of *The X-Files* played out across the television. The remnants of her dinner – a microwave curry and a bumper pack of Jaffa Cakes – were strewn across the coffee table, amongst sheets of crumpled paper.

Michelle had always considered herself more of a Scully than a Mulder when it came to the supernatural. But as she watched Eugene Victor Tooms break into the former's apartment through an air vent, Michelle's eyes were drawn to her flat's own. She'd been wrong, and she knew that now. Some believers, like Mulder, she thought, could dedicate their entire lives to searching, hunting and hoping for an encounter such as hers. She hadn't searched, hunted or hoped, however. Michelle had stumbled, and the subsequent fall had been a great one. An ordeal; it had lodged itself within her brain like a parasite.

Nursing a glass of red, Michelle clasped it close to her bosom, as if it were a baby. Tucked between her sofa's cushions, the bottle was close to hand. Another – a Sauvignon blanc – was left cooling in the fridge. The pair had cost the reasonable sum of £3.95, courtesy of Stonem's off-licence. The quality was dubious, but the convenience satisfied impulse.

Excavating a fresh pack of fags from the table, Michelle brushed several balls of paper from its surface onto the floor. Her further attempts at drawing the enigmatic 'clawed-hand' bottle; she had repurposed one as a coaster. The owner of the off-licence hadn't recognised its description either, though he'd seemed rather preoccupied re-checking his stock count.

As for the identity of the girl in the black lace dress, Michelle had been toying with calling in a favour from a police sketch artist. A facial composite would most likely not be of any use, however, for the only time she could ever clearly see the girl's face was within her unconscious. All in all, Michelle had made no progress in the weeks since her meeting with Mrs Nicholls.

Cigarette lit, Michelle held it between her lips as she vigorously massaged her temples. She downed the rest of her glass and stood. Everywhere she turned she seemed up against a brick wall, and so Michelle mirrored this thought with action. Tying her dark hair up into a messy bun, she rounded the coffee table and walked right up to her sitting room's own. The framed poster that used to hang there had been removed weeks ago; the space left transformed into a makeshift investigation board. A map of Ashfield, with Dragnell Lane highlighted, was at its centre, surrounded by Michelle's best sketches, a copy of Mrs Nicholls' holiday photograph and annotations. The pins holding all in place had been pushed directly into the woodchip. Overall, the effort was severely lacking in detail.

Although she felt exhausted, Michelle would fight sleep for as long as she could. For weeks now, she'd been suffering nightmares – not that she could remember them at all upon waking.

*

Pris's strappy heels slid off Rye's feet and fell to the ground with a squelch. The stick flicked out its last, angry letter, then snapped into three as it bent, twisting in upon itself.

'H'.

The message was complete: 'ANOCH.' But what did it mean?

The grasp that held Rye aloft gradually slackened and she began to slip. She gasped, as her spine was scraped back down against the trunk of the old oak. Jarred and jolted; her release was neither smooth nor consistent.

Five feet or so before reaching the tree's base, the force that guided her descent disappeared completely, and Rye fell. Legs buckling at the knees upon impact, her skirts lifted up to surround her face, blinding her, until she managed to fight them off. This was the only point during the whole ordeal Rye screamed; her emanation short and shrill.

Far more shaken than she had ever been throughout her entire life, Rye fought to stand upright. She snatched up her bag and diary before tearing off into the woodland and the pitch-black of All Hallows' morn.

A solitary and lowly figure – another girl – watched Rye flee the lakeside. Bloated and blackened by the long-term effect of the waters, this girl stood knee-deep in the lake, approximately half a dozen feet from the bank. Her expression of dismay, her lower – much larger and asymmetrical – lip jutted out from her face to exaggerate a downturned smile. Her eyes, mottled by decay, acted as a window to the murky depths within, much like the lake's surface, which had returned to normal.

CHAPTER X

Male-AL10

<u>Saturday 1st November 1997, 00:47am, TURPIN RESIDENCE, 32 KYNASTON GARDENS, ASHFIELD, LONDON.</u>
'It's alright,' Pris quietly reassured herself. 'Rye will be just fine.'

She spoke the words slowly, and with conviction, but they did little to convince.

Squirting a generous amount of washing-up liquid into the sink, Pris set about filling it with hot water. She pressed play upon the cassette player and unashamedly turned up the volume of Ace of Base's 'Don't Turn Around'. Already mid-song, the unsympathetic upbeat track blasted, full of hiss and audible static.

Not wanting to cause outright offence to Zach, Fred and Ally, Pris's action was a statement, nonetheless. She was somewhat appreciative of their efforts in tidying the house but still blamed them in part. By now, she simply had nothing left to say and wanted them to leave. Her thoughts elsewhere, Pris ran her fingers through the stream of water.

'Fuck!' she exclaimed, and instantly recoiled.

Proceeding to flap her hand, Pris turned this way and that, in search of something – anything – that would soothe the sudden scalding. In seconds, she fixated on the freezer. Opening its door, she buried her injured hand deep in amongst the contents of the top shelf. Leaning her body's weight against the unit, she closed her eyes, breathing out another swear.

Once numb, she slammed the freezer door closed – yet it bounced, unseen to her – and strode back over to the tap. She turned it off, then pressed the eject button on the cassette player without even stopping the track. Fired up, Pris marched through to the sitting room.

'Alright,' she announced. 'Hope you've all had a good time. Don't feel as though you have to stay.'

*

Rye had not expected anything to follow her — not that she could have predicted any of that evening's turn of events — but she could feel it in the wind. On the very edge of catching up with her, the presence howled with ethereal, outstretched and grappling arms. How far would it follow her? What was it? And what did it want?

Grit embedded; the soles of Rye's feet were shredded from running. Her back caned and shot with pain. But she could see her home now. It shone like a beacon. A safe refuge? Rye hoped and prayed so — prayed that the company of others would somehow dispel that which had latched onto her.

*

Her words as stern as her posture, whatever had remained of Pris's patience had evaporated with her hand's burning. She cared for her sister, deeply — of course — but she kept her worry and fear hidden. This was her character. She stood, arms folded and with her sore digits wrapped in the sleeve of her sweatshirt. Pris intended to go out and look for Rye, just as soon as the other three had left.

'I'm really sorry—' Fred began.

Pris tutted and kissed her teeth.

Fred had already apologised profusely on behalf of everyone, but each time he did so, he only felt guiltier. The feeling weighed disproportionately upon him.

'Well, we can hardly leave *her* here, can we?' spoke Zach, nodding to the sofa.

Fast asleep, Rosalind Pretty lay across all three seats, a crocheted blanket draped over her. Stone-cold sober, she had been the first to pass out and despite multiple attempts, no-one had since been able to wake the sleeping blonde. Feathery angel wings still strapped to her back, they gently rose and fell with every breath.

'She's not doing any harm,' Pris admitted, dismissively. 'But come morning, she's out first thing.'

'I think we should go look for her,' said Fred, steering the subject back to Rye.

'You didn't see the state she was in,' replied Ally, haughtily.

Her arms folded also, Ally too felt guilt for Rye's unknown whereabouts but could brush the feeling off easier than most. Secretly, she still deemed the birthday girl worthy of a reality check. But her seeming dismissal for their friend's safety invited backlash from Zach. However great his growing affection was for Ally, it paled when compared to the loyalty he held for Rye.

'I think we saw enough, actually,' he snapped.

Quick to her own defence, Ally turned on him.

'I was just saying, that maybe she's best left—'

'Is that why you let her wander off?'

'I didn't see any of you follow her!' Ally retorted.

Her words – a truth – cut deep, and Zach's face visibly bore their infliction. Silence, lasting around ten seconds and thick with tension, followed, broken only by Pris, who then broke down.

'Well, now she's gone, and we have no idea where,' she whimpered. 'We're completely in the dark!'

As if on cue, the sitting room's lights extinguished themselves with a click and a tinkling sound, and the entire house was plunged into darkness.

White spots burned brightly on the back of each of their retinas, with Zach's glowing face paint providing the only point of reference. The darkness did not last long, however – with disorientation lasting slightly longer – for as suddenly as the bulbs had gone out, they rattled back into life, revealing all four of their faces looking up at the ceiling. A loud bang emanated from the hallway – the slamming of the front door – and simultaneously all turned their heads in the direction.

'Rye's home!' Fred smiled, enthusiastically, attempting to defuse rising tensions with the news they'd all been waiting for.

All the lights throughout the property continued to flicker as Pris led the group out into the hallway. As correctly assumed by Fred, Rye was indeed home. She was slumped on the mat, one leg extended, the other's knee bent upwards to her chin. Her arms splayed, attempted to cover as much of the door's surface as possible. Shoeless and breathless, little cuts laced Rye's ankles and calves. The blood thinly smeared her pale skin, as if she'd been a painting dropped into water.

'Rye, what – what the hell?' Zach managed.

Fish-like, Rye repeatedly opened and closed her mouth as she struggled to speak – to explain what she had experienced and borne witness to. Like in a nightmare, her bodily functions when most critically required, could not keep pace with her thoughts.

'I – I went to the woods,' Rye forced her speech. 'To – to the lake.'

'Did you run home?' asked Ally, needing clarification of the blatantly obvious.

The tables had turned, and it was now her that compulsively needed answers.

Grunting, Rye profusely nodded.

'Rye, has someone hurt you?' Pris asked, her tone serious.

'Who's hurt you?' Zach pushed.

'I – I – I was just sitting there, and – and then – I …'

Unable to continue, Rye began to sob. Her nose was streaming snot again, but she didn't dare remove her arms from position to wipe it. Pris made a movement to approach her sister.

Boom!

The front door lurched in its frame, sending shafts of usually undisturbed dust shooting out from between its seams. Pris froze as it proceeded to judder and grind, wood against wood. An original from when the house was built, the door was hardly the sturdiest.

'R-Rye,' Zach stuttered, as Fred and Ally both backed away. 'Who's that?'

'Who's out there?' Pris pressured with greater urgency.

Rye opened her mouth to whisper:

'*A-noch.*'

There was a moment's pause.

'Who's Anoch?' asked Zach.

Rye gave no answer.

'We – we should – slide the chain across,' Fred stammered, looking to Pris for approval.

She nodded and looked expectantly at Zach, who also nodded – unhappy, but determined that he should be the one to undertake the action. Moving closer to Rye, Zach made his approach slowly and cautiously. He could not make out any shadow behind the door's glass. With every thud, a wave of reverberation was sent pulsing through Rye's body, causing her hair and chest to waver. Both she and Zach locked eyes as he reached out with his right hand, arm steady.

Ally retreated further away from them all and the front door. Agitated, she clawed at the sides of her face, inadvertently squashing her mouth into the shape of a small circle.

'No, it can't be.' She quaked, her hard veneer wearing thin. 'It – it's impossible – how could they know where to find me?'

Her whispers went unnoticed to all but Fred, who was closest. He watched as Ally disappeared through the threshold to the kitchen – as she pulled at her hair.

His fingertips mere inches from the bronze chain, Zach felt dizzy and nauseous – a feeling made worse by the flashing of lights overhead that quickened as he reached closer. Then, just before contact could be made, the door gave way with a sudden and almighty boom. The last image anyone saw before the house was plunged into darkness once more, was the front door being ripped clean from off its hinges.

Lifted upward, Rye was thrown to one side – as was Zach. Pushed against the wall, the door slammed into Rye's back, sandwiching her in position for a heartbeat, before she came falling back down to the floor with it. The sound of footsteps – thudding upon the carpet – were then audible, as if someone or something had run through to the sitting room.

Breathing heavily, Ally steadied herself with the kitchen counter. Convinced that the intruder was a member of Mick's gang, she was already playing out all the methods in her mind by which they would torture her in retribution.

The silence that ensued seemed to last forever, as everyone – isolated, yet so close to one another – could do little but wait with bated breath. The sitting room's clock ticked, counting the extended seconds that passed by, as its metronome seemed to slow. As everyone's vision began adjusting to the dark, the quiet was cut by a soft and sliding, then clicking sound.

The noise had come from behind Ally. Startled, she smacked her head into the kitchen cabinets above and loudly swore. This was quickly succeeded, not by Pris's cassette, but perhaps the radio? More than double the player's previous volume, Lesley Gore's 'It's My Party', burst into life to assault everyone's eardrums. Blinking, Ally manically spun around, trying to deduce whether she was alone in the kitchen.

Rye scrambled out from beneath the front door. Scared she strongly took to her feet nonetheless. Moistened air whistled through the open void where the door had stood only moments ago, splattering rogue raindrops onto the hallway carpet. As the interior of her home remained shrouded in darkness, the only vague source of light was provided by the deep-yellow glow from the lamppost outside. Rye was a silhouette upon its backdrop.

Ally followed the player's electrical lead to the tile and violently ripped the plug from out its socket. The music continued to play, tinnier than ever.

With a clatter, Ally pulled open the nearest drawer and grabbed hold of the first utensil she found – a ladle – in the hope it could be used as a weapon. Fumbling further, all she could feel was a selection of spatulas, wooden spoons and a rolling pin. In haste, she moved onto the second drawer, but to no avail – only an egg whisk and what felt like a chopping board. Not wanting to waste any further time, Ally returned to the first. Certainly, a knife would have been preferable, but given her impeded vision, a rolling pin her weapon would be. Like a club, she grasped it tightly in her left hand and returned to the hallway. But forgetting the small step up, Ally tripped.

It was as Ally collided with Pris's back that the bulbs buzzed into full brightness. Fixtures shuddering, the filaments sparked, as they struggled to process the abnormal surge of power forced through their connections.

As Pris turned, it was out of self-preservation that she snatched the rolling pin from Ally. Both screamed, and Pris, without processing Ally's identity, gave the girl a sharp shove in the ribs, thrusting her into the kitchen again.

Having witnessed this minor altercation from his position crouched beside the cupboard under the stairs, Zach took the opportunity of returned visual clarity to take hold of Rye's wrist and pull her over to himself and Fred.

Maternal instinct taking over, Pris strode through to the sitting room, brandishing the rolling pin from side to side as she turned the corner. The other four followed after. Zach and Rye first, then Fred. Ally trailed in last, both hands clasped to her ears. Except for Ros, apparently still unconscious, the sitting room appeared empty. Instinctively, Rye drew Pris's free arm in front of her torso, interlacing her fingers with her sister's.

Zach was the first to notice – the others not long after – that one of the lights in this room was swinging. A result of no visible force; its cable pulled taut to its circle bracketed epicentre, as if someone was hanging from it. Still flickering, the bare bulb sparked, throwing out random bursts of light and blankets of shadow.

As its movement grew in velocity, the rest of the house gained its own phenomenal intensity. Crockery rattled in cabinets as the walls began to tremble and shake. The framed photographs of Cousin Veronica's Pekingese, which had only an hour ago been realigned by Pris, were knocked askew once more. Some frames fell to the floor, their glass breaking upon impact.

On the shelf above the picture rail, several china dolls slumped. Clinging onto their perch, their eyelids blinked to a close. Drawers throughout all the rooms were then angrily spat from their units. Spraying their contents with reckless abandon, their sounds resembled gunshots over that of the kitchen's player. Nearing its final chorus, the song's volume cranked, prompting both Zach and Fred to join Ally in clamping their hands firmly to their ears.

'Fucking, hell!' Zach shouted, taking it upon himself to vocalise the group's consensus. Though his vocal cords strained, he may as well have mouthed the words.

Arm falling limp by her side, Pris dropped the rolling pin to the floor. Her jaw dropping also, she backed up several paces, yanking Rye with her, for the heads of each china doll had – one-by-one – turned to face them. The nearest and first to face was female. Sewn into a black lace dress, its long auburn hair was drilled into ringlets. Its facial porcelain, now malleable, stretched high up its cheeks into a devilish smirk. With a sharp movement, it opened its eyes.

Fred, turning, rushed for the sitting room door. Discovering it to be closed – sealed shut and impossible to open – he fought with the knob. Even when aided by Zach, it failed to budge.

As the remainder of the dolls rubbed their eyes, awakening from their former life of inactivity, the original to manifest blinked. In doing so, it revealed a change in eye colour from light brown to black. Her petite grin widened further. She then winked and her head exploded.

This action triggered a chain reaction. As if each doll was stuffed with its own cherry bomb, they all detonated. Their order random and timing intermittent, each shattered into miniscule fragments. Delicate limbs and fragile faces were all torn from beautifully upholstered bodies without remorse. As the final doll exploded, so did the bulb above them. And as the dust settled, the cassette player squeaked, fizzling, before popping.

In the stillness that came after, Pris, Zach, Fred and Ally cowered, as Rye's body stiffened. A cold sensation flowed down her spine and like liquid metal, galvanised itself to the bone. The last thought Rye would remember having, was the fear that she too would explode, just like one of Cousin Veronica's china dolls. The voice that then spoke from Rye's mouth chilled them all. Gruff and short, it was not-so-much angered but laboured.

'Nice. Nice – to – talk.'

Immediately, Pris turned to her sister.

'Rye?' she asked, timidly, heart plummeting. 'You're not … Rye, are you?'

'Dear, Lord,' uttered Zach.

Taking hold of Rye's shoulders, he didn't think twice before attempting to shake his friend – to shake some sort of life into her, or rather, out of her. But Rye did not move. She remained statue-like. The only effect Zach's fingers had was on that of Rye's clothing – which ruffled – and skin – which rippled – upon her frame.

'Who are you?!' demanded Pris.

'Me? I – am – an – atheist.'

Each word barked by Rye was akin to a cough.

'Get out! Get out of my sister!'

Despite her best efforts, Pris was unable to break free from Rye's strong and icy grip. Awkwardly twisting, she angled herself to meet an empty stare. Drained of their beautiful blue, her sister's eyes appeared dead.

'I – am – Male-AL10,' replied Rye, cryptically. 'What's – your – name?'

Pris let out a terrific howl. Watching Rye's familiar form speak a stranger's words – with a stranger's voice – was too much for her to handle. Mourning, she was convinced that her younger sibling was already dead.

'What do you want?' dared Zach.

Holding Rye's skirts, he along with Pris, formed a trio. Both unable to speak, Fred and Ally remained behind. His back flush against the door, Fred continued to twist its knob in anguish.

'I – don't – want – to – presume – anything,' Rye sneered, succeeded by an abrupt cackle of laughter.

All of a sudden, Fred whipped his hand away from the doorknob. He had felt something warm and sticky trickle down onto his knuckles. Mouth agape, he staggered past the others into the centre of the sitting room. All around them, the pink and stripy paper had become bruised and seeping – bleeding. Pulsating; the walls seemed to have taken on the form of living flesh. Some areas thick, others watery, further patches began to percolate. It was as if the room had become an organ, and they were all trapped inside. A long stream of viscous fluid fell to the floor in a stringy gloop beside Fred, and he shrieked – reaching a pitch he thought no longer possible since puberty.

Trying his best to ignore this latest development – feeling little could shock him further – Zach remained on a mission and kept his focus on Rye. Unblinking and his voice unwavering, he ventured another question.

'Who's Anoch?'

For the first time since being overcome, Rye moved. Tilting her head to look Zach in the face at eye level, she smiled. Though only slight, the action had been immediate and enough to startle Zach, who jumped back.

'Who – is – Anoch?' Rye mocked. 'Who – is – Anoch? Anoch! Anoch! Anoch!'

Zach flinched.

'Anoch! Anoch!'

Having worked itself up into a frenzy, whatever had Rye then relaxed into a duller tone once more.

'And – which – are – you? Weird? Wonderful? Or – ordinary? Good – question. I – should – leave – soon.'

These last words unexpected, all prayed they were true. Unrepentant in their individual desires, all four prayed to God that this horrific bane would cease. For there will always come a time in the lives of even the most devote of atheists that they will become so desperate as to pray.

'Oh – but – wait.'

Ally's eyes darted over to Fred, who met her gaze only briefly before looking at Pris, whose head was in a constant swivel between Zach and her sister.

Rye's birthday cake, which had been innocuously sitting upon the dining table since being taken in, then spontaneously com-busted, taking them all by surprise. Self-contained, the fireball made quick work of the icing and sponge, and within moments all that remained was a smoking, charred mass of lava.

'Goldilocks – is – hiding – herself!' barked Rye, stealing back attention. 'Anoch's – toys – now.'

A sonic-like boom then rocked number 32, as all the windows – and all the glass throughout the property, in fact –

instantaneously shattered. With force, shards were propelled outward to hurtle down upon the shrubbery out front, and the patio and pumpkins out back. Inside the house, everything from the television to the oven door was obliterated. As the noise dissipated into nothingness, Rye limply fell to the carpet amongst the dolls' fragmented corpses. Pris – pulled down with her sister – collapsed beside her.

This final cataclysm seemingly brought an end to the night's oddities. The walls and ceiling no longer dripped blood and had returned to normal, as if nothing peculiar had ever befallen them. The rain had also ceased, but the breeze remained, causing the sitting room's curtains to billow out into the night. Still somehow undisturbed, Ros lay peaceful, only to roll over in her sleep. Angelically, she folded her hands under her right cheek.

'Rye!' Zach exclaimed, quickly kneeling.

'Oh, my God,' breathed Fred.

'Rye?!' beseeched Pris also – shaking her sister. 'Rye!'

'Check – check her pulse!' instructed Fred.

END OF ACT ONE.

ACT II

CHAPTER XI

Heavy & Weighted Words

<u>Saturday 1st November 1997, 19:12pm, BATEMAN RESIDENCE, 52 BELLAMY AVENUE, ASHFIELD, LONDON.</u>
'Fred? I'm talking to you. Honestly,' Caroline Bateman scolded her son, through a half-chewed mouthful. 'I blame your friend, Rye, and that new girl – whatever her name is. Bad influences – the pair of them. Sarah was telling me all about it this afternoon. Said that Rye's sister wasn't too impressed with her antics last night. Fancy, inviting the entire year group 'round like that for a jolly old knees-up, without so much as a warning. Well, I never.'

Caroline paused only momentarily, just long enough to swallow.

'There wasn't any alcohol, was there? Freddums?' she asked, attempting to sound nonchalant.

'No, Mum,' Fred retorted, angrily, stabbing haplessly at his own dinner. 'I've told you already, the house was drier than a nun's—'

'Alright, alright! No need to get all flipperty with me. I'm only concerned.'

Caroline proceeded to daintily dab her mouth with a napkin, careful so as not to smudge her lipstick any more than it was already. She centred herself before speaking again.

'Why can't the rest of you all take a leaf out of Zach's book? Now, there's a level-headed young man.'

'Mum, what are you even talking about?' Fred shot back, attacking his mother's blind-sidedness with malice. 'Zach was more to blame than any of us!'

Taken aback by the wrath she had invited, Caroline folded her napkin and turned to face her husband. Tilting her head to one side, she tutted loudly, as a cue for reaffirmation.

Her prompt went unnoticed, however, for Stan Bateman remained silent, as always. Face hidden behind the *Daily Mail*, he was completely unaware of all the conversation going on around him. Caroline would surely have something to say about his ignorance of her later, but would first withhold any explanation of her mood, pending an initial apology.

'I'm just saying, that all this late-night partying malarkey stems from Rye,' Caroline persisted, and Fred rolled his eyes. 'It was irresponsible what she did last night. And you, Freddums, are easily led – too quiet to speak up for yourself. And I'm just saying that, maybe, if you found your voice, you wouldn't get bullied?'

Fred slammed his fist down so hard that the entire table shook.

'Mum, I don't get bullied!'

'He doesn't get bullied because he's quiet,' Mollie then spoke up, innocently. 'He gets bullied because he's g—'

'Shut up, Mollie!' Fred bellowed.

He may have been scared witless last night, yet that was an entirely different fear to the one that filled him when imagining how Mollie would have finished her sentence.

'Frederick! Don't shout at the dinner table!' Caroline screeched. 'Or you'll have no Viennetta.'

Breathing heavily, she snatched the newspaper out from in front of her husband's face – leaving Stan dumbstruck. Mollie, unlike the other three members of her family, quickly recovered from the hostile situation that she herself had ignited. The next to speak, she asked:

'What meat goes into Spag Bol?'

'Gerbil!' Fred spat, grotesquely.

Despite his stomach's protests, Fred swallowed down his last mouthful. Chair juddering – threatening to fall – as he rose from it, he then flounced from the kitchen. Caroline objected, but she was interrupted by Stan, finally breaking silence, to ask for seconds. He was a far braver man than Fred, for Caroline had overcomplicated the simple recipe, altering it almost beyond recognition.

Stomping up the stairs, Fred slammed his bedroom door and growled. Seeking refuge in the familiar comfort of his bed, he dived beneath its covers. Burying his face, he cocooned himself, yet immediately felt robbed. His bed no longer felt safe. He pulled the duvet up around his head and inhaled the scent from his pillows. Everything smelt as it should, but Fred did not feel the same.

It was beyond him why Zach spoke so openly to his own mother, when he always strove to keep as much from his parents as possible. By comparison, Zach had always been closer to Sarah – most likely a consequence of his absent father. All that aside, Fred found it doubtful that Sarah knew the true extent of the last night's activities.

Lost in thought, Fred's head was a pool of confusion. The inability to make sense and process – this feeling was not new to him. What he had witnessed sat in the pit of his stomach as an unbelievable ache; the cherry atop the helpless pile that he stored up there, to churn over late at night, alone and in the dark.

Yawning a hearty yawn, Fred's eyes streamed warm tears. He wouldn't brush his teeth tonight. In fact, he wouldn't even clamber out of bed to pee – despite his body's agonies. There he lay, and there he'd stay.

*

The light from the landing clicked on, shining a low shaft under Fred's bedroom door and across his messy floor. One-by-one his family ascended the stairs. Mollie first – against all her wishes – his mother second, and finally his father. Unable to sleep, Fred stared into the light's shaft until it was extinguished.

Two and a half hours later, the landing light switched back on, as Caroline Bateman tiptoed down the stairs to check that her husband had been capable of double-locking the front door. Although Stan had yet to ever fail in his task, Caroline's exercise was undertaken nightly.

Why don't you slide the chain across as well? Fred thought, acerbically, to himself, thinking back to the night before.

☙✋❧

<u>Sunday 2nd November 1997, 08:13am, ASHFIELD POLICE STATION, ASHFIELD, LONDON.</u>

Michelle was late for work. A day usually considered one of rest for most, Sunday was just the same as any other for those employed in law enforcement or the emergency services. Having been absent yesterday, Michelle was suffering the second morning of a hangover.

Wearing Friday's blouse, she trudged through the station's dated reception area. She entered the inner offices and marched over to the wall where her timecard was housed. Unashamedly, she scrawled a time nearly forty-five minutes earlier than was true, then made a beeline for the canteen.

Michelle prodded the option for a large black Americano and watched listlessly as the machine sputtered and whirred into action. Reluctantly it spat out a plastic cup and, with a hollow squirt, filled it to the brim. It would surely taste of dishwater, but it was caffeine all-the-same. Extracting her beverage, Michelle exited the canteen and turned the corridor that led to her office.

Thankfully – for the time being, at least – Kevin Gunn was nowhere to be seen. Their office door was unlocked, however, and so she assumed him to be close by. Michelle sat down, heavily, dropping her handbag under her desk as she did so.

One day absent from the job and her inbox had exploded with emails. Their number stalled her machine as they loaded before her in chunks. Agonised by the thought of sifting through them, Michelle slapped her forehead and sank her face down level with the desk.

'Morning, Michelle.'

Michelle did not look up, for she knew who had spoken.

'Morning,' she grumbled back.

'Hungover?' Kevin probed.

Michelle's head shot straight back up again.

'No,' she replied, sharply.

Michelle hated that Kevin had asked that. She was hungover, but why did he feel the need to say it? Why did anyone, ever? Was it really that obvious?

Waltzing over to his own desk, Kevin appeared smug. He was clearly pleased about something, which only deepened Michelle's discomfort. Casually, he reclined upon his desk and stretched out his legs to cross his feet. His trousers rode six inches up his ankles to reveal bright pink socks – hardly dress code.

'You've seemed distracted recently,' Kevin smirked. '*Distant.* I believe it's been affecting your work ethic.'

Michelle raised an eyebrow.

'Excuse me?'

Kevin paused, if only to savour his next sentence.

'That's why Malcolm thought someone … a little more focused … should take up some of your slack.'

'Slack? What slack?' Michelle seethed, practically vibrating. 'Need I remind you that it was me who collated the entirety of the CPS report, not to mention practically carried the case since its inception.'

'But you didn't attend court,' Kevin smiled, revealing pearly whites.

'No, I didn't.'

'But you said you would, and that's exactly the slack Malcolm's referring to.'

'It wasn't necessary for me to attend. Not with you there,' Michelle consigned. 'And I did warn you. But who is Malcolm exactly? If you're referring to Malcolm Goodfellow, I think you'll find he's our DCI. On what planet are you on a first-name basis?'

'Since I'm his golden boy.'

Kevin reached out to lean back upon his desk with his left hand, but missed, causing him to fall off sideways. Standing, he regained composure.

'Self-proclaimed title, is it?' Michelle fumed, standing also. 'My God, you're such a male chauvinist pig, you know that?'

Displaying no fear, Kevin boldly approached his colleague.

'Woah, Michelle. Hold up, slow down,' he coaxed, raising both hands. 'You're throwing some pretty weighty words around. It's no secret you're not on top form. And if there's a reason – a personal matter, that's preventing you from working to the best of your ability – it's nothing to get your back up about. DCI just thought it wise his 'Top Gunn' was piloting from here on out.'

With this, Kevin clicked his fingers, pointed and winked.

'You're a tosser,' Michelle spat.

Kevin laughed.

'Neeeooowww! Better duck and cover,' he cajoled. 'Zzzooom, here comes another weighty word.'

Leaving Michelle speechless, Kevin proceeded to prance around the office. She had no idea what he was doing, and she wasn't the only one.

'Jesus Christ, you auditioning for the ballet?'

Caught off guard, Kevin ceased mid-prance, as both he and Michelle turned to their office door.

'This place isn't a crèche, Kev,' Shaz continued, berating. 'If you want somewhere to play aeroplane games, there's a preschool just around the corner.'

The fact that Kevin Gunn outranked Sharon Knight would never stop her from speaking her mind. A detective sergeant, five years fresh out of college, and she was quickly proving a force to be reckoned with. Warm-hearted but feisty, she was a woman Wales would be proud to have produced. As Kevin opened his mouth to respond, it took but one look from the dyed red-head to make him reconsider.

'I'm – I'm just going to,' Kevin stuttered, before tapping his watch. 'I've got somewhere to be.'

His ego dented, he departed their company. Shaz stared after him.

'These came for you yesterday.'

Shaz breezed forward. Approaching Michelle's desk, she held out a trio of letters.

'Thanks,' Michelle smiled, weakly, taking them. 'And thanks, for what you said to Kevin. He's a—'

'Dickhead? Yeah, I know,' affirmed Shaz, and the pair chuckled. 'You've got to ignore him, Michelle. Just because he's in cahoots with the DCI, doesn't give him a free pass to be a total asshole.'

'What do you mean, "in cahoots"?'

Shaz looked sheepish. The expression did not suit.

'Well,' she deliberated, 'there've been rumblings.'

'Rumblings?'

'Rumours, really,' Shaz tried to backtrack. 'You know this place – upstanding establishment – it's really no different to any other office. Like being back at school.'

'Shaz,' Michelle appealed. 'What rumours?'

'I think it's probably best you speak with the DCI directly,' Shaz advised.

'I will. And it's probably best you get on.'

Shaz nodded her understanding and left the room without another word. Michelle harboured no ill-thought towards her, as such, as she knew Shaz was not one to partake in gossip. However, Michelle's pride had taken a real battering that morning already, and she just wasn't sure if it could handle much more.

Fighting the urge to cry, Michelle returned to her emails. In search of a distraction, one provided just that, though not the welcome kind she'd hoped for. It was from DCI Goodfellow, entitled: 'Monday 3rd November Meeting'.

Michelle opened it:

'Dear DI Davey,

I am writing to inform that you are required to attend a disciplinary meeting on Monday 3rd November at 11:00 am, which is to be held in my office.

At this meeting, the matter of your attendance will be addressed. You are entitled, if you wish, to be accompanied by another colleague or Police Federation representative.

Yours sincerely,
DCI M Goodfellow
Metropolitan Police Force (Ashfield)'

Michelle's jaw dropped. She had expected such a conversation to be inevitable at some point, but seeing it written down – and so formally – still presented itself as a shock. As she double-clicked the email's attachment, it was to Michelle's utmost horror that she found it summarised all her recent occasions of lateness, culminating in yesterday's absence:

'Thursday 11th September 1997 – Arrived at 10:40am. Forty minutes late. No explanation or advance warning given. Time was not made up.

Wednesday 17th September 1997 – Arrived 16:12pm. Two hours and twelve minutes late. Explanation given: 'I'm really sorry – I had an emergency dentist's appointment.'

Tuesday 21st October 1997 – Left work at 17:30pm. One hour early. Explanation given: 'I have a doctor's appointment.' No advance warning given. Time was not made up.

Saturday 25th October 1997 – With regards to, 'Richard of York,' did not attend court, as expected.

Saturday 1st November 1997 – complete absence. No explanation or advance warning given.'

Michelle growled, leaping from her seat. Angrily, she rushed over to Kevin's desk and roughly pulled open the bottom drawer. She removed the hip flask stashed there – between ring binders – and unscrewed its cap to take a deep swig. Burning the back of her throat, she gasped to savour the warm, tingling sensation.

Michelle then fished a small bottle of pills from out of her blazer's inside pocket. She swallowed two down, dry, then another four with a mouthful of brandy, ignoring the labelled instructions upon her prescription: 'Take ONE tablet daily. Not to be mixed with alcohol'.

'Bastard!' she declared and kicked the drawer shut with her foot.

Kevin's pencil pot rocked before tipping over.

⚜

<u>Monday 3rd November 1997, 10:40am, ART ROOM 1, GROUND FLOOR, ASHFIELD COMMUNITY SCHOOL, ASHFIELD, LONDON.</u>

Period two, Monday morning, and Rye sat at the back of her Art lesson. With an entire desk to herself, it was one of the few classes that she had separate from Zach and Fred. Ally, however, was present. Herself at the very front, had actively avoided Rye.

For the first time in weeks, Rye had been on time for school that day. She had the morning's attended assembly, as well as the first period. Far from intentional, her punctuality had instead resulted directly from her lack of sleep since Friday. Wide awake? Not-so-much. She had been uncontrollably yawning throughout.

Rye looked down at her oil pastel piece. Hideous; it bore the portrait of one of Veronica's china dolls. Complete with auburn ringlets, black lace dress and black eyes, it leered from off its sheet. Ironically, Rye had previously been stuck for ideas regarding her topic: 'FEAR.' Chalked up within the centre of a class brainstorm, the word now bore deep into her soul. There it was written – white on black. Other pupils didn't know the meaning of the word, she thought. Selecting the black pastel once more, Rye set about adding further darkness to the doll's eyes.

Despite their high ceilings, the Art rooms of Ashfield Community always appeared dingy. The windows, although large, were dwarfed by the nearby Main Hall and never caught the sun. Rye felt dwarfed also, and so pressed down harder with her oil pastel. Head low, she glanced forwards at Ally, picking her classmate out from between the hunched forms of the other students. Everyone was unusually silent. Rye pressed harder still. Ally – much like herself – appeared consumed by her art, and this angered her.

Snap!

The sound of Rye's pastel breaking clean in two echoed throughout the room, prompting a handful of students to turn. Uneasily shrugging off her own disruption, she replaced the pastel's parts back within their tin.

The bell rang for morning break. Without instruction Rye's fellow pupils begun readily stuffing their pencil cases back within their bags. Deliberately avoiding Rye's gaze, Ally made a beeline for the door.

Rye threw her stationery – loose – into her own bag. The lead in her pencils would surely break, but so be it. Eager in her pursuit – the straps of Rye's bag caught the chair leg. She pulled it, ripping them free. So be it. With force, she then pushed herself through the stream of departing pupils.

'Excuse me, pardon me, coming through,' she excused, before shouting, 'Ally!'

Unhearing, or ignoring, Rye's cries, Ally did not turn.

Within touching distance, Rye – out of desperation – reached out and grabbed hold of Ally's arm, jolting the girl backwards and spinning her around. Quickly turning on her, Ally pinned Rye up against the wall, partially crushing the cardboard artworks stapled to it.

'OK,' Ally spoke through gritted teeth. '*OK.* We can talk – but not here. Someplace quiet.'

*

A dry and chilly day with only a slight wind, it was as if nature itself had taken relief in the wake of Rye's birthday. A weight had been lifted from the world, since transferred to the shoulders of all those present at her possession. As Rye and Ally snuck out of the school's gates, the former still trembled from being manhandled and allowed herself to follow the lead along the path through to the churchyard.

Careful in choosing their spot, Ally and Rye took up position opposite each other, atop two lichen-covered stone sarcophagi situated at the base of the nave. Rye deliberately chose the higher seat, for if the two were about to exchange verbal blows – as they mostly certainly would – she wanted the higher ground, even if the advantage was negligible. Once settled, both girls locked eyes, prepared for battle.

'Friday night. Halloween – my birthday,' Rye served, her body tense.

'Like I'd ever forget,' Ally replied.

'You left pretty quickly,' Rye commented. 'Not that I remember, what with being out cold and all. Left without saying goodbye – so I was told.'

Outstared, Ally looked down to the ground. Aggressively, she began kicking a tuft of grass with the toe of her right boot. She said nothing, and so Rye decided to change tact.

'I can't even begin to … comprehend what we saw – what happened.'

Ally shook her head, but totally in agreement.

'That was some proper *Exorcist* shit you pulled there. Never – *ever* – have I seen anything like it. Fucking, mental.'

'Yeah, fuck-fucking mental,' Rye stuttered, choosing to swear for the simple reason that Ally just had.

'I'd never even thought – or given much thought – to ghosts before.'

'Is that what you think it was? A ghost?'

Anxious to gain Ally's perspective, Rye – despite everything – still felt ridiculous asking such a question.

'Maybe, I don't know, a poltergeist? Not gonna lie, Rye, but what else could it have been? Hardly ordered entertainment for your Halloween party.'

'Well, for starters, it wasn't a Halloween party, it was my birthday party, but, like, whatever.'

Rye angrily took to staring at the ground also. Her irrelevant irritation was only short-lived, however. She breathed her next words between dry lips, for she had licked them until scabby.

'I can't sleep.'

'Can't say I'm surprised,' Ally replied, curtly. 'If I'd been talking gibberish – unknowingly channelling a gruff, masculine—'

'So, you've been able to sleep, have you?' Rye interrupted.

Ally shrugged.

'I keep hearing the voice,' she said in meek surrender, and Rye appeared horrified. 'In my head – I keep hearing the voice – in my head, when I'm trying to sleep.'

Silently, Rye was pleased Ally had finally admitted something.

'How's Pris?'

'Who's Mick?'

Ally, clearly taken aback by the curveball, swallowed.

'I'm sorry?' she asked, physically withdrawing.

'*Mick*. You said his name right before my front door was torn down. You thought it was him – that he'd come for you, or something. Fred told me,' Rye clarified, before twisting her voice into a very bad attempt at a Scottish accent. 'It's impossible – he's found me! It's Mick – how can it be—'

Ally held up her hands in protest.

'OK – OK. Mick was – is – an ex of mine. That's all.'

Ally's explanation was followed by a moment's awkward silence, which threatened to fester if it wasn't for Rye's persistence.

'That can't be all,' she sighed, wholly unconvinced.

'It's hardly relevant, considering.'

'Hardly relevant?' Rye fired back. 'Hell went down, and if this Mick guy is in any way responsible—'

'He wasn't – he couldn't have been. It's not exactly his style—'

'Well, someone's responsible.'

'I think the word you're looking for is, "something".'

Rye tutted and raised her eyebrows, as a sudden gust of wind whipped up the soggy leaves between them.

'What are you trying to say?' Ally demanded, uncomfortable with Rye's implications. 'That Halloween – oh, I'm sorry – *your birthday* – was somehow my fault?'

'Not just Friday night. The heart beating too.'

'The heart?! Again, how – may I ask – was that my fault?'

'The common denominator is you.'

'Common denominator? How? How did you come to that conclusion? You were present on both occasions as well, unless I'm mistaken?'

Ally's body flooded with warmth, aggravated by needles of angered pain. She was reaching the end of her tether, but Rye was far from done. Quick to respond, the young blonde's brain had yet to connect properly with her mouth, and so she garbled.

'You just show up – with clearly a lot of baggage – or lack of. You're unwilling to share – about your past. So, excuse me – I have questions!'

'What happened on Friday was not my fault,' Ally seethed. 'Whatever entered your house – *your* body – followed *you* home. You brought it back with you. That wasn't me, *Goldilocks*!'

Disgust and distrust lacing her features, Ally screwed up her face.

'What are you even doing here, Ally? In Ashfield? Why are you here? How did you get here?'

Although deliberately ignoring the accusatory jibe, it had not escaped Rye that there'd in fact been two other blondes present in her sitting room, during her possession.

'That's none of your—'

'Tell me!' Rye shouted, standing.

'By train, OK? I took the train!' Ally bellowed.

Rye flinched as a bird took flight from the top of the church's steeple. Cawing loudly, it flapped – disgruntled – across to the school building opposite.

'I took the train,' Ally repeated, much quieter.

'Train?'

Ally sighed as she pulled her blazer tighter around herself.

'I *found* the train ticket. I found it in my sandwiches whilst at Liverpool Street Station.'

'What?'

'You heard,' Ally replied, side-eyeing. 'And sit down. You look ridiculous.'

Rye ignored the demand of her. Silently, she vowed to never sit again, if it meant only infuriating her classmate further.

'You "found" it? Tell me, Ally, did you even know where you were going?'

'I've never known where I was going.'

Her eyes welling up, Ally sat, a lost and lonely girl. Traffic along the high street could be heard – muffled though it was, upon the breeze. But this sound was not enough to comfortably fill the void.

'So, this Mick. Were you running from him?'

Defeated, Ally threw up her hands.

'Yes! Yes, I was. I lived with him – in Spain. He wasn't very accommodating, and so I stole some of his money to make my getaway, and, well – you know the rest.'

'You "stole"?' Rye repeated the word. Disbelievingly, she inhaled – much like a disapproving mother, or Pris, would. 'How much?'

'Enough to get by.'

Rye sat back down. At last, the pair were getting to know each other.

'Pris wants to call an exorcist,' Rye breathed.

She loosened her tie and opened her collar.

'I don't fucking blame her, Rye. The whole fucking thing was insane, and now, according to "Male-AL10", at least, we're like Anorak's "toys now" – or whatever,' Ally air quoted. 'You've got to admit that all sounds pretty damn ominous. I'd just count myself lucky, if I were you, that you don't remember saying any of that shit. You don't, do you?'

Rye hugged herself. The scratches on her upper body still stung. The bruises and grazes that were visible upon her calves had sparked concerns from two teachers that morning already.

'Anoch,' Rye whispered, before coughing. 'I – he – "Male-AL10" … would have said "Anoch". And no, I don't remember.'

With anger's fire dissipated, Rye shivered. She had feared speaking the name aloud, for somehow inciting it. But as she thought, however, Rye now came to accept that in order to understand her classmate further, she too would have to share. She took a deep breath — as if she were about to dive into water, as opposed to a conversation — and started from the beginning.

Rye narrated to Ally all that she had heard whilst alone in Sullen Woods on the evening of the second of September, as well as all she'd seen the night of her birthday. And afterwards, long after the bell had tolled for the third period, Ally would ask:

'Are we still friends?'

'Were we even before?' Rye would reply.

CHAPTER XII

Ars Goetia

<u>Monday 3rd November 1997, 10:59am, ASHFIELD POLICE STATION, ASHFIELD, LONDON.</u>

Slowly, the minutes until Michelle's disciplinary meeting ticked by. She wished it had been first thing; it would all have been over and done with by now.

11:00am – her computer deemed it time.

Swiftly, Michelle locked her workstation and walked the two doors down from her own office to that of her DCI's. Smartly, she rapped upon the door and it opened almost immediately. Sat behind his desk, DCI Goodfellow looked up from a stack of papers. He shifted them to one side before awkwardly smiling.

'Good morning, Michelle. Come in – take a seat.'

He gestured to the trio in front of him.

Entering the room, it had yet to cross Michelle's mind as to how the door had opened, until she went to close it and came face-to-face with Harriet Frost. The ageing, skeletal manager of Human Resources scuttled out from behind, causing Michelle to jump back.

'Harriett will be joining us for the duration of the meeting,' DCI Goodfellow clarified. 'She'll be notetaker.'

Michelle nodded her understanding, catching a glimpse of her own name upon the file that Harriett carried back with her and over to the desk. She followed, settling on the central pew opposite her superior. Bespectacled and bird-like, Harriett sat hunched, to DCI Goodfellow's left.

This office was not unlike Michelle's own, in so much as, that it too was dated. Its dark furniture – sun-bleached – reflected the aggressive strip-lighting. Far too bright; it forced consciousness down upon Michelle, whose yellowed skin near-equalled that of the desk's veneer.

Then began the briefing of disciplinary procedures – the required recite of mundane spiel. All the while, Harriett incessantly tapped her pen against her pad.

'Now that's out of the way,' said DCI Goodfellow, suddenly. 'How's your day been so far?'

Michelle forced a pained smile.

'So far, so good.' She nodded, slowly, and DCI Goodfellow reciprocated by mirroring the action. 'I was on time.'

With the admission, Michelle descended into fake, characteristically nasal laughter. Her DCI did not look impressed, however, and so she coughed, to clear her throat. Regretful; Michelle diverted her eyes' stare to the coffee-stained carpet.

'Well, we're both aware why you've been asked to attend this meeting today,' DCI Goodfellow finally spoke, and Michelle muttered an apology. 'I've got a print-out here,' he continued, sliding across a single sheet. 'It's a hard copy of the attachment I sent with the email – for your own records.'

Taking it, Michelle pretended to skim read.

'DI Gunn has mentioned that he's finding your partnership ... *challenging* at present. He says that you appear distracted – unfocused – and unwilling to co-operate. And I have to say, he's not without grounds.'

Her superior had dived right in now. Any attempt to soften the accusations he presented with tone was ineffective, and Michelle was pissed.

'Of course, he'd have said that, wouldn't he?' she bit back. 'He's never liked working with me, let alone ever liked me. If there was a problem with my attendance, how can you have spoken with Kevin before speaking with me?'

DCI Goodfellow's moustache twitched. While taken aback by Michelle's outrage, he remained calm and professional.

'I'm sorry to hear you feel that way, Michelle. DI Gunn approached me, and we were only trying to gather all the facts, before—'

'"Facts"?' Michelle spewed. 'The only thing you'll get from Kevin Gunn is hyperbole bullshit!'

She had not intended on swearing – in fact, before the meeting, she could never have imagined doing so – but talk of the tangerine misogynist had riled her beyond the point of no return. Leaning forward in her chair, Michelle shook with rage.

'I didn't mean to … *agitate* you, Detective Inspector,' DCI Goodfellow replied. His bushy eyebrows raised, he folded his arms, authoritatively. 'May I remind you that this is a *formal* meeting?'

Michelle's tongue twisted uneasily within her mouth, as Harriett Frost scribbled down notes at lightning speed.

'Sorry, I just wouldn't take Kevin's word as gospel, if I were you. He's hardly impartial.'

'I don't, but your time-keeping and attendance do both speak volumes on their own. Is there any particular reason for this that we should be made aware of? Personal hardships? Family problems? Any stresses?'

Rendered speechless by the direct nature of this question, Michelle feared detailing her recent visit to her doctor. That she'd been prescribed both sleeping pills and anti-depressants would hardly aid her case for promotion, that was, if she hadn't kissed goodbye to that dream since walking through the door to her superior's office – since receiving the email, even. Like a stone thrown into water, Michelle felt herself sinking.

'I like to think of myself as firm, but fair,' DCI Goodfellow continued.

Taking Michelle's silence as a rebuttal, he nodded to Harriett, who – in flipping her notepad to a clean page – began writing much shorter sentences, at a significantly slower speed. This action, Michelle thought, implied a decision had long since already been made.

'I think you'd benefit from taking your career back to its bare-bones.'

'What – what do you mean? What does that mean, "bare-bones"?'

Overcome, Michelle's lips trembled. Her head wrung.

'In other words, allowing yourself to relive some experiences that will hopefully make you appreciate how far you've managed to progress in your policing career thus far,' DCI Goodfellow explained.

It took all of Michelle's willpower to stop the tears that pooled from pouring down her cheeks. She took to staring at the wall's clock above her superior's desk. Simply a point of concentration, its time was irrelevant.

'Demoted?' Michelle asked.

'Not demoted – you'll retain your rank. But starting today, you will be re-assigned to detective constable duties, on a temporary basis. Think of it as a learning exercise. This is your first warning in as many years as I can remember, after all.'

'What about all my open cases? All those I share with—'

Harriett Frost stabbed an overemphasised full-stop upon her pad. Evidently, there was no leeway for negotiation.

'I wouldn't worry about them for now,' DCI Goodfellow insisted. 'DI Gunn seems to have a firm grasp of the reins.'

'I suppose he does,' Michelle whispered.

With that, she stood and firmly shook her superior's hand. Ignoring Harriett, as she herself had been ignored, Michelle departed the office with as much grace and poise as she could muster. In truth, she appeared stiff.

<u>Monday 3ʳᵈ November 1997, 12:49pm, ENGLISH CORRIDOR, GROUND FLOOR, ASHFIELD COMMUNITY SCHOOL, ASHFIELD, LONDON.</u>

'So, why isn't Ally joining us, exactly?' Fred asked, himself reluctant.

'She's decided to sit this part out,' Rye huffed, leading their charge down the corridor. 'I think she's reached her limit with all this for one day.'

'Reached her limit with you more like,' Zach jested.

'Yes, probably,' Rye conceded.

By way of silent, noted conversation, Rye had abridged her – somewhat heated – discussion with Ally to the other two during the fourth period. She had not disclosed every detail, however. The catalyst for Ally's fleeing of Barcelona, for example, had not been shared. Some things, she thought, were best left private.

Rye swung open the door to the library. As expected, the room was virtually empty – not even a librarian greeted them. Yet the trio of computers at its far end were all currently occupied.

'What do we do now?' Rye asked, her face falling.

'Leave this to me,' replied Zach.

*

As he confidently led Rye and Fred across the library, a book – itself upside down – was lowered from in front of a face. Sitting alone, whoever held it watched closely as the trio passed by, before sliding across to the adjacent seat, in an effort to obtain a better view.

*

Targeting the youngest of the computers' users, Zach tapped the boy on the shoulder.

'Year Sevens can't use computers at lunchtime,' he lied.

'I'm Year Eight,' the freckled red-head replied.

'Same thing,' Zach dismissed.

'But I booked the slot – see?'

The boy pointed up at the sheet tacked to the board.

'Please, could we just use the computer for five minutes,' Rye pleaded. 'It's a matter of life and death.'

She was growing more panicked by the minute. Not having a computer at home, Rye had banked on the school's resources to aid her in time of need.

'I'm sorry, I can't help you,' the young boy replied, pitilessly. 'You shouldn't have left your homework to the last minute, should you?'

Leaving Rye speechless – itself, quite a feat – he turned back to the screen.

'What's your name?' Zach asked, kneeling beside him.

'Shaun,' the boy answered, his eyes unwavering.

'What you working on there, Shaun?' Zach pried.

Shaun ignored this question, and so Zach reached over and decidedly turned the monitor towards him.

'History essay, hmmm?' he mused, reading the title. '"Henry VIII and his Wives." Well, let's see – reckon I could help you out with that one.'

'Please, don't—'

'Divorced, beheaded, died. Divorced, beheaded, survived,' Zach ploughed onward. 'Catherine of Aragon – past her prime. Anne Boleyn – clever, but not clever enough. Jane Seymour – supposed love of his life. Anne of Cleaves – airbrushed, ousted, but lived out her days in luxury. Catherine Howard – very unlucky. Catherine Parr – a helluva lot luckier.'

'Henry got fat,' Fred chimed in.

'Whole range of medical problems,' Rye lamented.

'*Dead*,' Zach concluded.

Annoyed by their persistence, Shaun was sure to save his document before addressing them again.

'You're not going to leave me alone, are you?' he squeaked.

'No,' confirmed Zach.

Ejecting his floppy disc, Shaun snatched at it before standing. Dramatically, he threw his rucksack over his shoulder and scuttled off, silent.

Pleased by their result, Zach went to collect two extra chairs. As he turned, the group's watcher was quick to re-lift their book, as to ensure their presence remained undetected. By the time Zach returned, Rye had already logged herself onto the computer.

'Where're you gonna start?' Fred asked, taking a chair.

Rye responded by opening an internet connection.

'If only Chris MacNeil had had the World Wide Web at her disposal,' sighed Zach.

Rye would admit that her plan was by no means sophisticated, but in her opinion – at this stage – complicating their investigation with books made no sense. Looking up, 'Anoch' anywhere other than the web would likely be time-consuming, if not impossible, considering the school library's subject matter.

After a painful few minutes, a connection was made, and Rye typed into the AltaVista search bar. Transfixed, she hit enter. The computer was – as always – slow to respond, but after several, further seconds, her results were displayed.

'That wasn't very difficult – *first hit*,' Rye whispered.

It was a tight squeeze having three around one computer, but Rye had to whisper so that the other two students – an older boy and girl – seated at the other workstations, did not hear. Any pride she felt from her initial success was quickly soured, however, by reading the page's title: 'Miscellaneous Spirits and Unthinkables.' She continued to read, aloud.

'"In the late fifteenth century, a group of Spanish peasants claimed to have suffered attacks on their villagers and livestock; first manifesting in illness, the attacks escalated in ferociousness, until many of the villagers' animals had been slaughtered. The assault culminated in the deaths of two local children. Hearts torn from their chests, their deaths became attributed to the demon,

Anoch. The demon's given name derives from the Spanish "Anoche", translating directly as "last night" – in a reference to their fear of the night before.'"

Pausing for breath, Rye sniffed into a tissue. Her nose was streaming again.

'A *demon*?' repeated Zach – disbelieving, yet not necessarily surprised by the revelation. '"Hearts torn"?' he questioned, with greater angst.

'What else does it say?' Fred pressed.

Rye plugged her nostril with the tissue, letting it un-attractively dangle.

'"Exact location … unknown … a devoutly Catholic community … children's eviscerated bodies were cremated." There's not much else.'

Struggling to process the mental imagery, Fred buried his face in his hands. Unlike Zach, he had never enjoyed horror as a genre – much preferring romantic comedies and musicals whenever they fought over films to watch. *Tales from the Crypt* had left its mark on him from a young age, and now it felt as if they were starring in their very own instalment, which terrified him.

'You'd have thought Ally would've known that,' said Zach, suddenly.

'Known what?' Rye asked.

'Anoch – or rather – *Anoche*. You said it was Spanish.'

'To be fair, she probably didn't think it relevant,' Rye mumbled, through chewed lips. 'A single word like that – removed from context. She probably wouldn't have even recognised it, considering the voice I spoke it in.'

'Anoch!' barked Zach, all of a sudden, rasping.

Both Rye and Fred thwacked him in the torso, as the other two students turned to shoot them withering glares.

'Don't joke, Zach,' Rye scolded, emphasising her words with further hits. 'How can you joke about something like this?'

'I wasn't joking,' Zach protested, as he pushed Rye off him. 'I was just *demon*-strating – ow!'

'I can't believe you're defending her,' whispered Fred. 'After she just left us all like that. You could have been dead.'

'I haven't forgotten,' replied Rye, dryly. 'But it's definitely worth asking her. Hang on – there's a link at the bottom of this page.'

Hurriedly, she dragged the reluctant mouse across its scuffed pad to click, and the screen flicked to a predominantly black and red page, headed, 'The Lesser Key of Solomon'. The trio huddled closer to each silently read through its opening paragraph:

'The Lesser Key of Solomon, otherwise known as the Clavicula Salomonis Regis or Lemegeton, is an anonymous grimoire, comprised of several books, focused on demonology. It was first amassed in the mid-seventeenth century, utilising materials from the centuries before. The demons' names (listed below) are taken from the Ars Goetia – the Lesser Key's first book.'

Having beaten the other two to the paragraph's end, Fred's face dropped. Ten, long seconds later, and Rye finished next. Both she and Fred took to looking at Zach, expectantly, as he – tongue held between his teeth – then slowly nodded. On cue, Rye scrolled the page downward.

'"Under Satan, there are seventy-two demons of notable importance",' Rye read aloud. '"Having all proven themselves worthy of status, they were each given titles, such as King, Duke, President, Prince, Mar – Marq—"'

'Marquis,' Fred interrupted, correctly.

Fretfully fiddling with his tie, he ultimately took the unprecedented action of loosening it.

'Right – that,' said Rye, squirming. '"And under each of these demons, respectively, are ten knights, who instruct five lords. Under each lord are five generals. Each general, commands three hundred and seventy soldiers."'

Unable to fathom even middling sums, Rye screwed up her face, as Fred delved into his rucksack for a calculator. Moments later, he held the screen up for all to see.

'Six million, six hundred, and sixty thousand,' he whispered.

'Makes sense,' Zach gulped.

Silence enveloped them as Rye's mind sped through many thoughts in quick succession. All interwoven and jumbled, they could, however, be summarised: First, she was mystified as to how Fred could have calculated the number so quickly; second, she realised she was not breathing, and so resumed doing so; third, she thought of her long-dead parents, and how she was in no rush to join them; fourth, tiredness; fifth, the night of her birthday, and the sound of the first china doll exploding.

'Well, Anoch is just one, isn't he?' Rye tried her best to reassure.

Deflated, she reverted to staring at the screen.

'That's hardly a comfort, Rye,' Fred admitted, uncomfortably shifting.

Rye went to print the webpage before clicking a further link, which instigated a document download.

'What else does the Ars Goetia cover, exactly?' Zach asked. 'Doesn't have a handy appendix with the Vatican's contact details, I suppose?'

'Well,' Rye began, 'this says, it was purportedly written by King Solomon himself, in which he mostly describes particular demons' attributes – how they could be controlled – even contained. The Ars Goetia provides a kind of self-help manual to serve against them.'

'Controlled, contained – I'm a fan of both words.' Fred laughed, nervously.

'No such luck with the containment, I'm afraid,' replied Rye, and Fred's face fell once more. 'At least, not without

Solomon's bronze vessel-ly thingy – and that's been lost for thousands of years, apparently.'

'Control?' asked Fred.

'Maybe,' replied Rye.

'So, let's cut to the chase,' said Zach, slapping the desk. 'Is there anything on how to destroy a demon?'

'The only thing I can see … is something on how to entrap a *person* possessed by an evil spirit – could've done with that last week…'

Printing two copies of the lengthy, downloaded document, Rye suddenly remembered her previous print. She regretted leaving it unclaimed for so long, and so wasting no further time, bounded over to the front desk. Thankfully, it was still unmanned, and Rye rounded it. Impatient; she waited for the last of her pages to rattle through their presses.

But upon collecting their research, Rye flicked through the wad, confused – her initial print-out was missing. After a pause, wherein she second-guessed herself, she finally placed blame upon the mechanics of ancient technologies and deemed a re-print inessential. *'Six million, six hundred, and sixty thousand,'* she thought – it was hardly a number easily forgotten.

Upon returning to Fred and Zach, Rye removed her diary from her cloth bag, folding one copy of the Ars Goetia within.

'What now?' Fred sighed.

'We talk to Ally,' Rye affirmed.

ა❦ა

<u>Monday 3rd November 1997, 13:19pm, MAIN HALL, GROUND FLOOR, ASHFIELD COMMUNITY SCHOOL, ASHFIELD, LONDON.</u>

Ashfield Community's Main Hall only dated back to the mid-nineteen twenties, but its interior had been constructed in an overt mock-Tudor style. Dark wood panels clad the lower walls, with the space above white-washed – now, turned yellow. Beams and flying buttresses adorned the high ceiling – beautiful, but completely unnecessary. An anomalous extension, it had been built by way of a grant, donated by the widow of an ex-pupil who had died in the Great War.

It was within the Main Hall that Rye, Fred and Zach found Ally, at the end of a long table with only a plate of food for company. Piled high with generous helpings, she had cared not to separate the beans, mashed potato and pizza from one another. Wrapped in napkins, four parcels stuck out from her blazer's pockets.

'Anoch.'

Rye bombarded Ally with the single word.

At first, Ally choked, then she smiled – a half-amused, half-irritated smile. Looking up at the trio, she found their stance adorable.

'Yes?' she replied, wiping her mouth clean.

'What does it mean?' Rye fired.

Ally flipped her dark hair over a shoulder. Unsure of what was being asked of her, she settled on responding to Rye's question with another. She shouldn't have, but Ally thoroughly enjoyed making it difficult for Rye, for the girl asked too many questions.

'What do you mean, "what does it mean"?'

'What do you mean, "what do you mean, what does it –"' huh?'

Easily tongue-tied, Rye floundered, and Ally sniggered.

'It's Spanish,' Fred interjected. '*Anoch* is a Spanish word.'

Ally turned up her nose.

'*Anoch* is a Spanish word?' she repeated, sceptically.

Fred nodded, as Rye silently fumed.

'One hundred percent *Espagnol*,' Zach confirmed, eyeing Ally's plate in awe.

'Anoch? Ano – do you mean, *Anoche*?' Ally laughed, and all three nodded. 'Yes, Anoche would be a Spanish word, if you pronounced it properly. *Anoche, Ah-noh-cheh, Ah—*'

'We get it,' interrupted Fred. Not appreciating her superiority, the strength of Ally's character made him uneasy. 'It means "the night before".'

'I know it does,' replied Ally.

'But you didn't realise that's what it meant when I said it the night of my birthday?' Rye probed.

'No, of course not. How could I?' Ally flung out her arms as to emphasise the ridiculousness of any suggestion otherwise. 'Whatever was possessing you, pronounced it just as stupidly as Fred did. And are we actually using that word, "possessed"? Is that what we're calling it?'

Fred opened his mouth to protest that he was anything close to stupid, but Zach beat him to speaking.

'If the shoe fits.'

'Better than hers did,' Ally jibed.

'I believe you,' Rye insisted, surprising even herself with certainty and ignorance of insult. 'And I'd prefer if we didn't call it anything at all.'

'Isn't that a turn out for the books?' Ally laughed. 'Hallelujah! Rye Turpin is satisfied with an answer – at long last! What's the significance of it being Spanish anyway? Except for you jumping to the conclusion that *I* am, in some way, responsible?'

'We searched the web,' replied Rye. 'Here.'

She thrust the second copy of her print-out forward.

'Thanks, I think,' said Ally. Taking the pages, she stuffed them into a blazer's pocket, amongst the food parcels. 'I'll read them later.'

Gobsmacked by the complete disregard for the information presented, Rye took to the bench opposite.

'Why aren't you reading them now?' she asked.

'Well, we don't know that anything else is going to happen – not for sure—'

'My point exactly!' implored Rye.

'There's more to a horror film than just its first act,' Zach chipped in. 'If anything, the second only follows with worsening scenarios, wherein the protagonists have yet to master the needs necessary to deal with them. Which is why—'

'You should read them *now*,' Rye hammered.

Zach and Fred nodded enthusiastically, but Ally shrugged.

'You've certainly changed your tune from this morning, that's all I can say,' Rye huffed. 'I just don't understand. You were terrified earlier – we're *all* terrified. We should all be doing as much as we can to understand what happened – to prepare ourselves for what could happen next. You can't just ignore it all. Maybe you'd feel differently if it was you that had been—'

'Talking incessantly?' Ally laughed.

'Talking gibberish,' Rye corrected.

'Maybe,' Ally admitted. 'But, maybe not. Listen, our conversation this morning got me thinking, and if anything at all, it's given me an epiphany. You've got to live for now, Rye – live for the moment. You could wake up tomorrow, choking to death on your own vomit, cursing the fact that you'd never really lived.'

'Erm,' Rye began. 'I don't *really* get your point, and I don't think I can relate to it, *so* …'

Ally's eyes twinkled. She loved how Rye so unknowingly invited these ripostes.

'I wouldn't be so sure after Halloween,' she smirked.

'So, you suggest we do, what? Nothing?' Rye shot back.

'Me?' Ally questioned, loading a chunk onto her fork. 'I suggest we party.'

Proceeding to stuff her mouth to full capacity, Ally ignored – or at least, pretended to ignore – the look of confusion that was now shared between the others in the wake of her unexpected suggestion.

'You what?' blurted Fred.

'That is, quite possibly, the worst suggestion you could've made,' agreed Rye.

- CHAPTER XIII -

Under the Arms of Strangers

<u>Friday 7th November 1997, 20:30pm, ASHFIELD HIGHWAY, LONDON.</u>

Darkness suffocated North London, only intermittently broken by fireworks, set off by those celebrating Guy Fawkes Night two days late. A parade of persons – primarily teens – navigated the streets in streams. Joining in confluence, all were headed to a large abandoned warehouse on the De Mandeville industrial estate. Although its venue was rudimentary, the event held there still required tickets and their low cost had ensured a sell-out.

Within the stream, Zach and Ally led Rye and Fred, with a dozen feet or so separating the pairs. A mere four days since their harsh exchange of words, all had – for the most part – been forgiven, albeit not forgotten. As Zach had easily succumbed to Ally's charms, regarding her suggestion, it was he who'd obtained the group's fraudulent – photocopied – tickets. Rye and Fred had succumbed to peer pressure.

But Rye could not deny she felt far safer away from home at present. For Pris was due to work the bar that evening, and neither sister was yet keen on the idea of spending a night alone. That was why Rye had lied and said she was to stay over at Zach's. All would be well, so long as Pris didn't call to check up on her.

Wanting to erase all reminders that she could from the night of Rye's birthday, Pris had swept and vacuumed their home's every nook and cranny. All shattered bulbs and kitchen wares had been replaced – sans the oven door. The windows were due a repairman next week, but, as a temporary measure, had been patched with cardboard and tape. A new television was out of the question.

Despite her early leanings towards exorcism, Pris – like Ally – had proven eager to brush the information on Anoch aside. Becoming hostile when the subject was broached, she expressed the desire never to speak of it again. All that said, and although she was petty, Rye felt relief in Ally having so far been proven correct. Nothing further had reared its ugly head since her birthday, and this had left all involved feeling hopeful. Sure, Rye was still not sleeping as she should, but this had once again become the norm.

A chain-link fence funnelled the amassed crowd to the gated entrance. Separate from the rabble and separated from their friends, a select few individuals stood bent-double and puking – their night over before it had even begun.

The gaggle slowly filtered, and Zach, Ally, Rye and Fred were shunted forward, where they were met by a large, spikey-haired man, whose leathery skin was covered in blurred tattoos. The name across his right forearm read 'Rich', mirrored by 'Vicky' on the other, which was rendered near illegible by the presence of a black X. Rich – for that most certainly was his name – held out a hand for their tickets, without greeting. Zach reciprocated by passing them over.

'Nah – ain't genuine, mate,' Rich dismissed, handing them back. 'Next!'

All it'd taken to ascertain their inauthenticity was a simple shine from his torch onto the back of the first paper slip.

'What do you mean?' Zach protested, saddened.

'They ain't genuine tickets, *mate*,' Rich repeated, gruffer than before. 'There's no UV – they're fake.'

Rich turned his attention to the couple behind.

'That's a new low, even for us,' Fred admitted, hiding contentment. 'Ah, well, can't say we didn't try. Let's head back to Zach's.'

Rye, inclined to agree, steered a disheartened Zach away from the bouncer. Allowing her to guide him out of the throng, he kicked a discarded beer can, and partly crushing it, inadvertently sprayed the tarmac with booze.

'That's so shit!' he bemoaned. 'Our tickets looked no different to everyone else's! Tony and Jake had the same ones, and they got in – I saw them!'

Walking fast, Zach followed the chain-link away from the gate, without thought to his direction. He kicked another can and this one sent a stream of alcohol to shoot up the inside leg of his jeans.

'That's the point of UV – you can't see the difference, idiot,' Ally joked, catching up with him.

Her tone was light, and she meant no harm, but perhaps it would have been better if she'd said nothing at all. Sidling up beside him, she ventured a hug but was pushed off.

'You don't have to be so cheerful about it,' Zach snapped.

He gave the fence an almighty kick, and Ally's eyes widened. With a tilt of her head, she made a gesture. Distorted and stretched, the chain-link had left a gap just high enough to crawl under.

'What?' Zach breathed.

Ignorant as he turned to it, he ran a hand through his black hair.

'What?' Zach repeated, taking a second glance. 'I don't get it,' he groaned, preceding a third, prolonged and final look. 'Oh,' he beamed.

❧🌵❧

Friday 7th November 1997, 20:32pm, ASHFIELD POLICE STATION, ASHFIELD, LONDON.

One of only five others whom Michelle could count from her newly designated desk, the station was unusually quiet for a Friday evening. Peering over the partition, she lifted her coffee to take a sip.

Michelle recoiled and instantly spat it back out – by way of a spurt and trickle. The liquid had turned stone-cold and so she dropped the near-full plastic cup into the bin. She readjusted her messy bun with a sigh.

Far from being committed to the task at hand, Michelle's stack of curfew forms had decreased little in size since she'd begun filing them. Mundane – it altogether bored her to the point of insanity. A freshly brewed caffeinated beverage … that would surely increase productivity. Or a cigarette. Settling on the former, a uniformed Michelle stood and made her way across to the canteen.

*

Always the gentleman, Fred gave no thought to Ally's thighs as she wriggled under the fence. For Ally, this scenario was all too familiar, as she thought back to that day in early September. At least, this time, however, the stakes were lower and the fun factor far greater. Excitedly, she followed in Zach's wake, crawling quickly in the hope of not drawing much attention.

After Ally, Fred ushered Rye through next, before he then too – reluctantly, as he did not want to stain his jeans – manoeuvred under. With the crowd thick on the other side, only a few made comments, with some suggesting that their own friends do the same. Buried deep within the gaggle, Trinity, Moya and Lyssa had arrived early. They'd swindled their own, legitimate tickets – at an inflated cost – and once inside, had wasted no time in getting down to their favourite pastime – gossiping.

'I heard Sophie's here,' Trinity was spouting. 'She escaped from rehab – *again*. I'm telling you, she's only doing it for attention. Apparently, the bouncer made one comment about her scars, and she just ran past him in tears.'

Clutching a lit cigarette between her manicured fingers, Moya cackled.

'What a total sket,' she branded. 'Girl needs to stay locked up. I ain't seen her since that day I told her she looked like a Kinder egg toy.'

'Oh, she's an absolute psycho,' Lyssa agreed. 'Complete Looney Tunes.'

Joined by Moya, Trinity fell about laughing. Lyssa followed suit. Apprehensive at first, she gained confidence from the reaction her comment had sparked.

Her laughter punctuated by shivers, goosebumps covered Trinity's cleavage. Squashed upwards, everything was held firm by tape and her favourite sequined boob tube. Moya had opted for the somewhat more conservative choice of a skin-tight leopard-print minidress. Lyssa sported an eye-catching, neon-yellow number. Suspiciously similar to the one found in Beryl's Bargains, she would never admit to her friends where she'd bought it. Slightly removed from the trio and silent was Liam. And he was utterly bored by the conversation.

'So, Moya,' began Trinity, slyly, 'what's the deal with you and Finn? Are you guys, like, officially back together again now, or what?'

'Yeah,' Lyssa chimed in, enthusiastically. 'Is he here tonight? I heard he was coming. Is he your date?'

Moya fluttered her darkened lids and fluffed out her volumised hair with clawed fingers. Several overdramatised seconds later, and she tongue-popped.

'Yes, we're officially a couple.' She grinned.

'I knew it!' exclaimed Trinity, clapping her hands together.

'Called it,' agreed Lyssa.

'The term "Power Couple" is thrown around so often nowadays,' began Moya, 'And I'm not saying we're the new Brandon and Kelly, but—'

'Oi, Freddums, bringing up the rear!' interrupted Liam. 'Good to get the practice in, mate.'

Unknowingly, Zach had led his group straight into the lion's den. The scathing taunt from Liam their first warning; it was now too late for him to change their trajectory.

'Don't you look dapper,' Liam praised, his eyes wide with mock sincerity.

Moving uncomfortably close into Fred, he proceeded to fondle the hem of his victim's flannel shirt, whilst staring into his eyes with false adoration.

'Shouldn't you be at home wanking off to *Gladiators*?' Liam asked.

Stunned into silence, Fred didn't want to correct him that *Gladiators* in fact aired Saturday evenings. He looked pleadingly from one friend to the next. The first to snap, Ally opened her mouth, ready to throw out a fiery retort, only to be cut off.

'Rye!' beamed Louie, bounding over. 'Your face — it's lacking paint,' he pondered, his smile fading. 'Nah, we can't be having that.'

Taking her by the arm, Louie half-led, half-dragged an awestruck Rye away from the situation that he'd unwittingly broken up. Looking back over her shoulder, Rye mouthed an instruction for her friends to follow. Ally shot Liam a disdainful glare before tearing through his grasp of Fred's shirt.

'Didn't realise you were his girlfriend,' Liam scoffed.

'You're not a big man, you know that?' Ally sneered. 'You're just a little boy, without anyone in his life who truly cares. I've seen it all before.'

Amid weakly formulated and delayed insults, Ally took Fred by the wrist to march him through the crowd.

'What she said,' said Zach, simply.

Shrugging, he grimaced, then darted after the others.

*

Having almost finished her new coffee already, Michelle swirled its unappetising dregs. She was debating another, though her body craved something stronger.

Hoping that by fulfilling one craving she could dull another, Michelle reached inside a blazer's pocket for her pouch of tobacco. Roll-ups were not her preference, but she'd taken to smoking them, in an attempt to curb her increasingly expensive habit.

*

Her hair in plaited pigtails, a double-denimed Rye stood frozen. Her face felt electric to Louie's touch, and whilst she longed for the contact to last forever, she simultaneously wished he'd desist. Like a deer in headlights, she had watched him paint, as sweat trickled from her underarms. Since being pulled aside, she'd been unable to emit anything beyond a mumble. With his tongue protruding, Louie retracted his hands from Rye's face.

'Ah, yes,' he concluded, surveying his artistry. 'Much better.'

Rye's mouth pulled itself into an aching smile.

'Alright – catch you guys inside.' Louie smiled back, and gently squeezed her shoulder.

As he bounded over to re-join his own group, Louie was welcomed back with laughter and joviality. Having waited for him, they were soon drawn into the swathes entering the warehouse.

'He drew a heart,' Fred gushed.

'He never,' Rye gaped, disbelieving.

'He sure did,' Fred affirmed, secretly jealous.

Rye's real heart performed somersaults within her chest. She raised her fingers to her cheek, hoping somehow to translate the wet and wobbly neon outline by touch. Fred batted her hand away.

'Careful – you'll smudge it,' he warned.

Giving no thought to Louie's actions, Zach and Ally were themselves swift to follow him into the warehouse. From a distance, Trinity had paid attention throughout, and she seethed.

'Shall we go in?' Rye asked, euphoric.

'If we must,' Fred grumbled.

'Hey,' Rye mused, as the pair joined the throng. 'I wonder if they'll play my song. For the life of me, I still haven't figured out what it is yet.'

'Doubtful,' Fred sighed, as their ears were met with an onslaught of alt-rock.

*

'Hmm, hmhm, hm, hm, hmhm-hmmm,' Michelle hummed. 'Hm, hmm, hm, hm, hm, hmm, hm-hm.'

She slid her notepad out from her bag and once more allowed herself to become distracted. Flicking out another sketch of the 'clawed-hand' bottle, Michelle's skills had seen some improvement since her first attempt nearly two months ago. She sat back and moved her hand away, to survey her latest, and—

Splosh.

As she'd knocked over her mug, the remaining coffee spilled out across the desk.

'Piss-flaps!' Michelle exclaimed.

She ripped her drawing free and attempted to soak up the spillage with it. The paper turned brown but absorbed little and so Michelle watched as the liquid pooled. She then stood. It would seem no-one had heard – or at least, had taken any notice of – her predicament.

*

At the back of the crowd, it was to everyone's surprise that Fred found himself dancing with Rye, as a local band played and sang:

In a blissful state; I float,
A stripped-back dreamboat,
That's sinking,
Taken, as I'm given,
An answer to life's meaning.

Kissing your scars, I bandage your wounds,
For no-one else, but because you're brood-ing!
Ignore the hate; it only adds to confu-sion,
Intrusion; it's time,
and you're mine for the choos-ing!
You're my morning star,
And I always knew you were!'

Since entering the warehouse, Rye had been unable to spy Louie, and she craned her neck often. Zach had wandered off, to flit from one group to the next. And as for Ally, she was busy grinding up against a man at least twice her age. Utilising every limb and muscle, she popped, locked and dropped – much to the stranger's apparent satisfaction. Rye and Fred could only assume Zach had yet to see, for if he had, he most certainly would've had something to say – if not to Ally, but to them.

'What happens when the music stops, and the power drops from your
heart?
You're right back at the star-t, the star-t!
Now the music's stopped, and the power's dropped from your heart,
You're all torn apa-rt, torn apa-rt!

Slit open my soul (like blood),
And let the truth flow (in water),
Slit open my soul (like blood),
And let the truth flow (in water).'

Rye took hold of Fred's hand and lifted it high in the air. He reciprocated by pirouetting under. Both giggled, then embraced in a platonic cuddle.

'I love you!' Fred shouted, pulling away from her.

The shape of his mouth overemphasised the words, for neither could really hear. That's why, when Rye replied, she shouted directly into his earhole.

'I love you, too!'

Spinning themselves around and around, Rye and Fred absorbed their surroundings, in all its grimy splendour. A large platform constructed from wooden pallets and oil drums had been erected at the warehouse's furthest end. Upon this, the female-fronted band worked their magic. Dimly lit; fairy lights and lanterns had transformed the industrial space into a dreamscape. The venue was a church, and the singer a preacher, and all basked in the deliverance of the electronic, cult anthem. In awe, both Rye and Fred secretly felt very cool at their presence therein.

'Overcome, capsized; I've sunk,
A dreaming half-drunk,
That's diving,
Taken, for God's spoken,
An offering that's token.

Repenting your sins, I bandage your wounds,
For no-one else, but because you're brood-ing!
Ignore the hate; it only adds to confu-sion,
Intrusion; it's time,
and I'm thine for the choos-ing!
You're my morning star,
And you always, always were!

What happens when the music stops, and the power drops from your heart?
You're right back at the star-t, the star-t!
Now the music's stopped, and the power's dropped from your heart,
You're all torn apa-rt, torn apa-rt!'

As the guitarist riffed solo, a large, circular void opened around Ally and her dance partner. The crowd retreated further and further back until the pressure of those behind meant they could retract no more. And so all collapsed back inward, in monumental fashion. Leaping forward, several men threw themselves about, uncaring as to whoever was in their proximity; flailing and bouncing, they flung.

'Slit open my soul (like blood),
And let the truth flow (in water),
Slit open my soul (like blood),
And let the truth flow (in water).
Slit open my soul (like blood),
And let the truth flow (in water),
Slit open my soul (like blood),
And let the truth flow (in water).'

With Ally inadvertently finding herself in the mosh pit's centre, a rowdy-ginger foolishly elbowed her in the face. Bare and sweaty, the man's chest missed the tip of her upturned nose by a mere inch. Unaware of his actions, the man turned – screaming out the lyrics to pre-chorus – as Ally drew up her knee, in aim for his backside. He staggered upon collision, and headbutting the girl in front, sent both of their drinks flying.

Where Rye and Fred recoiled, three men pointed. Dispersed throughout the crowd, these men then all altered trajectory, to approach. Each with their sights set on Ally, they didn't care who else stood in their way. Mischievously, the band broke down their track to its outro, by dropping layers of meticulously interwoven, digital sounds.

'I need some air!' Fred shouted and Rye nodded in agreement.

At that moment, Ally tapped Fred on the shoulder and motioned to the door.

The singer rasped, to then whisper:

Just let me float…
Let me float,
In a tank of dreams and ecstasy,
May become the death of me,
An organic burst…
Fireworks of thought,
Capsized and sunk,
Drag my name through the mud…
Purified antagonist,
Drive a dagger through this chest,
Montagues and Capulets can capitulate…
Selfishness won't satisfy a conclusive new beginning…'

*

Bursting through the door to the toilets, Michelle hurried over to the paper towel dispenser, but to no avail, for it was empty. Unnecessarily dismayed, she refused the urge to cry – sniffing her tears back up inside – and instead headed for the nearest cubicle.

Michelle grappled for the toilet roll. Metal teeth scratched at her knuckles, yet she struggled to find the paper's end. Seconds passed and all she achieved was a tiny, torn and shredded strip.

Michelle sank to the cubicle's floor. Near-defeated, she groaned, realising that an entire roll was placed atop the toilet's tank. It sat, taunting her.

*

Having located Zach outside, the foursome stood in a square, laughing and joking. For the first time since the absorption of Ally into their group, each now truly felt at ease within the newfound dynamic.

'So, this one time – in Berlin – I befriended this artist guy – not really sure how, 'cause I can't speak German – but, I digress,' spoke Ally, in an anecdote. 'He was some sort of "conceptual artist" – or so he claimed – and he said, that if I was looking to make some easy money, then I could come work for him at this club night he ran. Anyway, it was some proper dingy, underground place. Graffiti – *all* over the walls – none of the toilets had doors, looked like it had rats – you know the kind of place—'

'Oh, yeah,' Zach enthused, completely unable to relate.

Fred looked to Rye, whose expression mirrored his own.

'Turned out, right – get this – that there was a room at the back of the club, where men paid to be spanked—'

'*Spanked?*' repeated the other three in unison, and with varying degrees of repulsion.

'Yeah, spanked,' repeated Ally, dismissively.

She reached out to a stranger's bottom, and for a second, all feared Ally was about to provide a demonstration, but she instead plucked the pack of cigarettes right out of their back pocket.

'So, what happened next?' asked Zach, eager.

Passing Ally his lighter, he watched as she lit a straight.

'Well, it was all very tasteful,' Ally defended, and Zach nodded, ardently. 'Lovely bunch of gals too, and they had the most handsome bouncer – *gay*—'

After falling a little, Zach's face then perked up, as Fred's twitched.

'And he'd throw anyone out who tried it on.'

'How long did you—' began Zach.

'Work there?' Ally interrupted. 'Put it this way, I was known as Frau Fraika Fich-Dich for about three months. Went down in the club's history as their most successful performer – had my own dressing room.'

As Ally took a puff upon her cigarette, a hand dug its fingers deep into her shoulder. Mid-exhale, she was forced to turn, blowing a plume of smoke directly into the face of whoever had handled her.

'Dearest Alexis, did you miss me?'

As the smoke cleared, it took Ally's smile with it. In a crinkled suit and dirtied overcoat, her ex-boyfriend, Michael Bennet, cut an unintimidating figure. Skinny as a rake, he could only really be described as blandsome; tall, dark and boring. Crossing his arms, Mick signalled to his two henchmen – one on either side of him – by way of a singular nod.

The altogether larger of his accomplices – a black man, with biceps the size of Ally's head – made a grab for her, but she ducked his clutches. Upon making a second attempt, Ally fell backwards into Zach's arms, and the henchman whacked the man from whom Ally had stolen the cigarettes in the small of his back.

In reaction to being thumped, the stranger turned, revealing himself as a forty-something-year-old biker, with a vast array of facial piercings. Not taking kindly to his unprovoked beating, he proceeded to plough a fist into the face of Mick's henchman, and a scuffle unfolded. Despite being tackled to the tarmac, the biker's mohawk continued to defy gravity.

Regaining balance, Ally pivoted before tunnelling through the crowd. Stooping, she scurried under the arms of strangers.

Mick's other associate – a shorter, balder and fatter, white man – then lunged at Rye with both arms, who instinctively leapt backwards, only to fall into Trinity, who had been stood nearby. Like cards – comically so, even – Trinity then folded into Moya, who in turn brought down Lyssa. Carelessly, Rye used all three girls as support in standing. Trinity even supplied a beneficial shove, but only out of disgust.

Mick stood on tiptoes. Yet, he could not pick Ally out from the swathes.

'Get back here, Alexis! You can't run!' he hollered above the crowd, before punching his more muscular henchman in a shoulder. 'Don't get distracted!'

His lackey – now embroiled in a full-on fight with the biker – kicked his opponent in the stomach.

Utilising the opportunity, Zach guided Rye and Fred away from Mick and back towards the chain-link fence. Themselves in a chain, manoeuvred around a pack of girls in pink tutus, only to run into a gabbling group of grunger girls – thick eyeliner, Doc Martens and dip dye. Still, Zach pushed forwards, pulling his friends along with him. Though unseen by them, Ally was close by. Running, *again* – she was good at that. Brown locks bouncing; cold sweat covered her brow.

'Stop that girl!' Mick could be heard shouting, having caught a glimpse. 'She's a thief!'

Attempting to sound above his class, Michael Bennett had ditched his true cockney accent now. He pointed in the direction of his fleeing ex, before he too then disappeared into the masses, as heads turned.

'I'm not surprised,' Trinity tutted, to Moya's and Lyssa's tittered agreement.

Out of the gated entrance, Ally ran past Rich – the tattooed bouncer – and past the stragglers still hoping to gain entry. She could just be seen disappearing around the corner as Zach, Rye and Fred emerged from beside the warehouse.

Sprinting the entire length of another two streets, Ally's boots stomped the uneven petrol-smeared paving. Past bargain stores, corner shops and the Salvation Army. Past an old scraggly woman dressed in a nightie and holding a pool cue. Past a homeless man, trying to extract the absent heat from within a doorway.

Diverging down a random alleyway, Ally's soles skidded upon the damp cobbles, as she slowed to a fast walk. Shadowy; the alleyway's end was further obscured by steam from an extractor fan. Ten seconds or so later, and the sound of multiple footsteps could be heard approaching from behind. Not choosing to look back, Ally sped up.

'Ally!' Zach shouted.

Running to catch up, he grabbed her by the shoulder, whirling her around to face him. She raised her fists; her face was fury. Exhausted and wheezing, Fred and Rye ground to a halt behind. Bent-double, with hands upon their knees, both clutched stitches.

'Who – were – they?' Rye managed, breathlessly.

'Yeah, Ally, who the fuck are they?' Zach stressed. 'Who were those men?'

Distressed, Ally turned from him and continued up the alleyway.

'It doesn't matter,' she replied, her teeth gritted and body shuddering.

'Ally!' Zach pressured – himself stood still.

Surrendering, Ally kicked an abandoned washing machine before turning again.

'That man is Mick,' she clarified, her voice desperate.

Rye's mouth fell open.

'*Mick*?' she repeated. 'As in the guy you stole money from. You said he was dead?!'

'Mick, as in the guy's name you screamed before running out on us all at Halloween? You stole from *him*?' Zach questioned. 'Mr wannabe Bond villain?!'

Her face pale and expressionless, Ally said nothing.

'How *much* money, exactly?' Zach pressured, only for Ally to look down to the cobbles. 'Ally?!'

'Ten grand,' she clarified, frankly, and totally unrepentant.

'*Ten grand*?!' blurted Zach and Fred, together.

'I have no idea how he could have found me, he—'

'You seem pretty clued up on all this,' Zach turned on Rye. '"You said he was dead." That's what you said.'

Dripping water filled the silence that followed, as Rye thought carefully about what to say next.

'She told me he was dead – I didn't think it mattered. It was her business – her *personal* business.'

'I *thought* he was dead!' screamed Ally.

She turned to stride down the alleyway.

'Well, you got that wrong, didn't you?!' Zach shouted.

All three jogged to catch up with her.

'*You* have ten grand?' asked Fred.

Together, they all walked in step.

'Not anymore,' Ally admitted – keeping her face forward. 'If I still did, I'd feel significantly better than I do now.'

'Who has it now?' Zach asked.

'Some man. A random man. A man whose bonus probably exceeds the amount that was even in that briefcase,' Ally growled.

'Why did you take Mick's money?' enquired Fred further.

'Because!' Ally shouted back, abruptly stopping and squaring up to him. 'Because, he doesn't deserve it! He deserves nothing but – but pain – and suffering! He deserves to die – and he should have!'

Taking hold of Fred, Ally shook him.

'I had – to get – away!'

Zach pulled Ally from off his friend.

'And what a good job of it you made,' he stung. 'He followed you from whatever-the-hell it was you ran from.'

Ally now turned to him.

'That's why we should keep moving, Zach,' she pleaded. 'Come on – now! We're – we're wasting time.'

The sounds of new footsteps fast-approaching suddenly echoed off the pavement adjacent to the alleyway. All four exchanged terrified looks before breaking into a sprint. Rye still clutched her side.

Just how Mick had found her? Ally could not be sure. But she'd known him to have taken out bounties before – or, used location trackers. And it was this thought that led to her loosening her watch before throwing it to the ground.

Friday 7th November 1997, 22:36pm, DE MANDEVILLE INDUSTRIAL ESTATE, ASHFIELD HIGHWAY, LONDON. 'Can you see anything?' Rye asked, whispering.

Sprawled out next to Zach, her stomach flat to the tarmac, Rye's question was directed forward, to Ally and Fred.

'I can see plenty,' Zach mused.

Himself inches from Ally's behind, her dress had risen to reveal more thigh than she'd care to know, and so Rye smacked him – hard – across the shoulder. Zach yelped, seemingly unaware of having shared his private thoughts aloud.

'Not the time, Zach,' she scolded.

He opened his mouth to respond, but Ally shushed them both.

They all saw a shadow – seemingly that of a large dog – flash past the side of the lorry under which they'd hidden. Its silhouette temporarily eclipsed the half-moon's light. However, not human; all breathed a sigh of relief.

'How long are we all supposed to sit here, playing hide-and-bloody-seek?' Zach asked, shivering. With a cramp in his right leg, he'd long since lost patience with the whole escapade.

Having escaped the alleyway with only seconds to spare, the foursome had doubled back to the De Mandeville industrial estate, with the aim of throwing off their pursuers. Since then – for the past hour or more – they had been lying low.

'He's got a point,' Fred whispered. 'Surely they've given up by now. And, I'm cold. And it's really hard not to hit my head on the – ouch!'

There was a muffled thud, as Fred's head collided with the pipe above him.

'Oh, would you, please, just, shut up,' Ally hissed.

Slowly, she edged her way out from under. Although Ally would not admit it, she too was cold, and keen to get moving once more. But as her head and shoulders came up as level, a strong hand clamped down – firm – around her neck. Wrenched out, she was dragged upright. The others, shocked by the unexpected appearance of another, scrambled out after her.

'OK, let's try this again,' spoke an aggravated voice.

It was Mick. With Ally held in a headlock, he brandished a gun, and as he released its safety – with a decisive click – she whimpered. Ally had lost face; lost all hope and chutzpah.

'No!' Rye shouted.

Impulsively, she dived forwards in a futile attempt at rescue, but the henchman of herculean build – to Mick's right – restrained her in a half-second before she could even get close. Zach jumped onto the man's back, as Rye was forced to her knees.

In all the commotion, Fred reached out for Ally's hand. On touching, he found hers to be cold and quaking. But their contact was brief, for Mick's second crony lifted Fred off the ground. All seven players were now locked in a scuffle.

Mick yanked upwards upon Ally's neck and her resistance lessened. A smile spread like a disease across his face.

'I'm sorry that it had to come to this, Alexis,' he said, aiming the gun's barrel at her temple, as she closed her eyes. 'Truly, I am. Tell me where the money is, or I swear, I'll do to you what I did to that little manwhore of yours.'

Her facial features trembling, Ally dribbled but remained silent.

'No answer? Fine,' Mick continued. 'Just one final question. How exactly did you lock me in that room, huh? Before you die, I want to know.'

With Fred pinned to the ground and Zach in a headlock now also, only Rye could see Ally, as the girl forced a whispered reply:

'I ... did-n't.'

'You're a liar, Alexis – always were,' Mick dismissed. 'And to think, I took you in out of the goodness of my—'

His face instantly drained of colour, Mick's sentence was cut short by a moist and squelching, slicing sound. His grasp on Ally loosened, and she fell at his feet.

Gasping for breath, Ally looked up at the man whom she despised – their eyes locking, just for a moment, before Mick looked down at his own torso. Ally followed his gaze.

A set of five claws gripped at Mick's suited chest. Having penetrated him from behind, they had pierced his back and run him through. Slowly, the hooked nails contracted to close in and around the area of his heart. The organ was pulled back. Mick's breath rasped; his final exhalation condensing as a cloud, as crimson blood spluttered from his mouth to a splatter.

A gaping void was all that was left where Mick's heart once sat. His harsh features contorted, Mick's final look was that of horrific pain and shock, as he fell to his knees and the icy tarmac beside Ally. Head tilted to one side; his eyes glazed over.

CHAPTER XIV

Alexis Monaghan

Sunday 31st August 1997, 18:14pm, EL POCO SOL, LAS RAMBLAS, BARCELONA, CATALONIA, SPAIN.

The shot glasses hit the bar one after the other:

Smack.

Smack.

Smack.

Ally gasped, only to then chuckle at the head rush. Flailing her arms, she gestured to Rogerio to pass her a lemon slice from the bowl. Other than the two of them, the bar was empty.

'I don' know why you wid him,' Rogerio spoke, passionately and in broken English. 'You clever, Ally – clever girl. Mick, he is mon'ster – *ladrón – estúpido hijo de puta.*' He spat.

Ally clicked her fingers – an action only a friend could excuse – and Rogerio obliged by passing across the entire bowl of lemon segments. She took them eagerly and proceeded to chase her tequila. After sucking on a slice, she shook the salt cellar directly into her open mouth.

'Another, please,' Ally smiled, sweetly.

As Rogerio turned to dutifully fulfil her order, he too couldn't help but crack a smile. He found Ally endearing. A lost soul, unsure of her place in the world – he could relate. He also appreciated that Ally preferred her spirits neat, for contrary to the tacky neon sign that flashed above him, his father's bar – El Poco Sol – no longer sold cocktails. Rogerio had in fact never made a cocktail in his life, unless you were to count sangria.

'Rogerio, I've told you before,' Ally croaked, before coughing to clear her throat. 'Mick looks after me. I love him, and he loves me—'

She burped. Although pungent, it was shallow and quiet, and by no means loud enough as to alert Rogerio to its expulsion.

'It's as simple as that,' Ally concluded, limply waving her hand to disperse the smell.

'If he relly loved you, he wouldn' make you do dose … things.' Rogerio shook his head as he slid Ally another shot. '*Amour verdadero?* No!'

He'd had this conversation with Ally at least a hundred times before, and each time it would play out exactly the same, as he knew it would.

'It's for our survival, Rogerio. It's a cruel, hard world out there. We've all got to make sacrifices.'

Ally spoke with assuredness and strength, yet – for some reason – did not bring herself to look at him. She instead busied herself by stacking the collection of empty shot glasses.

'And whad sac-fice does Mick give? Huh?' Rogerio pushed.

He'd never met him, but Rogerio had heard more than enough of Mick over the past six months to harbour a passionate opinion.

Downing her latest shot with a grimace, Ally ignored the question and Rogerio huffed. Exasperated, he retrieved what was left of the tequila bottle from behind the bar and poured himself a shot also. Unlike Ally, he downed it without any reaction.

For Rogerio, there was no mystery why Mick found Ally attractive. Other than her physical attributes, there was just something about her unadulterated feistiness. She had a fire about her; an aura that was hard to come by in someone of her age. Rogerio scratched his head as he thought this – tousling dark, thick hair. Barely a man, he was not much older than Ally, though he appeared younger. His inability to grow facial hair left his cheeks as bare as the day he was born.

'You saying thad all this is … he say for you?'

'I'm not a whore,' replied Ally, sharply.

Unblinking, she raised an eyebrow, as Rogerio opened his mouth to protest.

'Ignore me,' Ally retracted, throwing up her arms. 'I know that's not what you meant. I … I don't find our situation easy, but that's what this is for.'

She held the tequila bottle aloft in emphasis before taking a swig from it. Upon swallowing, she again gasped from its initial burn.

'Dutch courage,' Ally breathed. 'And besides, it's not going to be this way forever. Mick says that when we've got enough money, we'll go away – get out of Barcelona – for good. A fresh—'

'A fresh star'!' Rogerio interrupted. 'I know, Ally. I know.'

It was now his turn to not meet Ally's face, as he took to staring at the small television behind her. Attached to the end of a pole that protruded down from the ceiling, images of Duran Duran – singing upon a yacht – flashed across its screen. The latest developments on the death of the Princess of Wales, scrolled along the bottom. The nostalgic track – its volume dulled – served as good a metaphor as any for El Poco Sol. An ex-pat's haven during the eighties, the bar had been neglected in the years since. Random trinkets – now thick with dust – littered every surface, and the once bright posters that adorned the dark wood-clad walls appeared faded.

Rogerio sighed. He had far bigger dreams than managing his father's failing business; dreams he'd all too happily share with Ally. If only she'd ever ask.

'Ah, Ally, clever girl, Ally,' Rogerio lamented, pouring himself another shot. 'You de'serve better than thad – thad, *Fagana*.'

Necking the tequila, he slammed the glass to the bar.

'*Fagana*?' Ally enquired – dubious as to translation.

'*Fagana*,' he repeated. 'Oliver Tweest?'

Much to Rogerio's annoyance, Ally doubled up laughing.

'Fagin!' she corrected, between giggles. 'You mean, *Fagin.*'

Rogerio hid his embarrassment by loading the glasses into the dishwasher.

'You de'serve, better man,' he reiterated, simply.

Rogerio, himself tanned, athletic and goodhearted was by far the better choice in a suitor. Anyone could see it. Anyone, but Ally. Clueless, she had never truly appreciated how deep his feelings for her ran. She considered them friends – good friends – but nothing more. Someone with whom she'd share banter – confide in, from time to time. That was all. Checking her watch for the time, Ally jumped up from her stool in a fright.

'Oh, shit – I've gotta go! Mick hates it when I'm late.'

Removing her designer sunglasses from atop her head, Ally brushed her hair back behind her ears, before repositioning them upon the tip of her nose. Seductively, she peered at Rogerio from over their rim.

'*Muchos Besitos*,' she purred, in faux-husky tones.

Ally puckered her lips to blow a kiss – a kiss that Rogerio pretended to catch and pocket – then dramatically flung her hair over a shoulder. She flounced out of the bar, controlling her steps as best as she could. The alcohol had certainly achieved its desired effect; her senses were numbed.

❧

Sunday 31st August 1997, 20:02pm, MICHAEL BENNETT'S VILLA, MONTJUIC, BARCELONA, CATALONIA, SPAIN.
The front door to the villa clicked shut as the client let himself out. He'd been the usual type – a middle-aged family man, away on business. A man whose heady habits were kept secret from those nearest and dearest to him. Having awaited the door's sound, Ally

glided down the stairs. Wrapped in nothing but a bedsheet, her feet softly padded the bare treads.

However grand in scale, Mick's villa had seen better days. Once lavish, it had become dilapidated – crying out for the right sort of love and attention. Boasting numerous period Gaudi-inspired features, it remained nevertheless an architectural gem. An example of such was the staircase that Ally descended. Large, sweeping and fluid, it clung to all four walls of the entrance hall.

The villa itself clung to the steepest slope of Montjuic, south-west of the city, and its rear gave sharply away to a cliff-face. During daylight hours, brilliant views of the Mediterranean could be seen from almost all windows. At night, there was nothing to detract from the monstrous port that dwarfed the cliff's base, for it flooded with an industrial glare.

At the stairs' bottom, Ally commenced her search for Mick. The ground floor was mostly open-plan, and so he shouldn't have been hard to find. The few walls that did divide living areas were crumbling, and – in places – Ally could see between their exposed wooden slats to the rooms behind. Mick cared not for necessary repairs and renovations. He instead preferred to surround himself with beautiful things, such as artworks, artefacts and expensive suits. Materialistic – possessive – Mick's most prized possession was in fact Alexis Monaghan herself.

As Ally turned the corner to the solarium, she was able to spot her boyfriend. He majestically reclined upon one of the comfy leathers, his body splayed out like a dog on a hot patio. He patted the seat to his left.

Ally strode over and took up position next to him, as instructed. Instinctively, she snuggled back into his wiry frame. With her left hand, she dropped a small baggie of cocaine to the coffee table – her payment for the last hour. His gaunt face stretching into a yawn, Mick wrapped an arm around her.

'I can't relax,' he breathed, in a way he perceived as alluring. 'I need a massage.'

'Ask Solanki for a massage,' Ally joked, slyly, leaning away from him.

'You massage me?' Mick asked, though this was more of an order.

Expectant, he unbuckled his belt and unzipped his fly.

Tired – her head woollen – Ally did not particularly want to satisfy him but felt an obligation. She did not want to upset the man whom she loved.

*

Minutes later, Mick zipped back up his trousers and kissed Ally tenderly on the forehead. She wiped her hand on the bed sheet that was still wrapped around her naked body.

'Ally, you love me, don't you?'

As he pulled her close, Mick playfully twisted her hair around his fingers. But she retracted from his touch, to look him dead in the eyes. It was unlike him to ask for reassurance, and she was affronted by the question.

'Of course, I do – dearly,' Ally confirmed. 'Why are you asking me that?'

Mick forced his arm back around her, and together they slid down the sofa.

'And I love you,' Mick reciprocated. 'It's just—'

'It's just, what?'

Ally slung her legs over Mick's lap and clasped his free hand to her tattooed wrist. He appeared hesitant – a quality, again, that Ally was not used to seeing in him.

'It's just that Terry has heard talks, and an opportunity has presented itself. It's a job, but it's a big one. I'm just hoping that you'll be up to it.'

Terry – like Solanki, and herself – was another of Mick's permanent house guests. An addict, he was an informant and crucial to their business. Paid in gear, he was kept much like a pet. Ally did her best to avoid him.

'How big, exactly?' Ally asked.

'Bigger than usual,' began Mick, slowly, before spouting fast-paced reassurance. 'It'll secure our future – the future we've always dreamed of. This will be the deal that'll get us out of here – out of Barcelona – forever. A top geezer – mega-rich – and his two colleagues – they'll be in town tomorrow evening. They're prepared to pay a big price—'

Horrified at the prospect of more than one man, Ally's jaw dropped. This was new territory for her. Mick let go of her wrist and raised his hand.

'I promise that you'll be safe, Ally – I love you! I wouldn't let anyone hurt you, and you'll have Solanki and Den here as back-up – just in case. Nothing bad will happen, I promise.'

Ally's head having fallen, Mick lifted it by the chin, to kiss her on the forehead once more. Unsure, Ally, however, nodded her acknowledgement. Still, she did not consider herself a prostitute; they each had their roles to play. She simply considered herself a cog in the wheel that ensured their survival, and their future.

*

The next evening, Ally sat upright in bed under luxurious purple sheets. She could not settle. To her left, a bottle of tequila – two-thirds full – stood on the bedside table. Having come straight from El Poco Sol, she had been cagey regarding the details of her night's plans to Rogerio. Yet he had been shrewd to observe the shift from her usual demeanour. Distant, Ally had appeared impassive – her persona remarkably quiet. Details withheld from him, Rogerio had still done his best – as always – to talk Ally out of whatever she was about to do. And after an hour's discussion, a compromise was reached, but that compromise was a bottle to go, and on the house.

The door to the bedroom opened, and in came Mick.

'My love, they're here,' he said.

Generally, Mick being tall and gangling was unimposing, but from her current position, Ally found their difference in height unsettling. Baby-faced and with his hair waxed into curtains, Mick looked more like a boy band member than he did a drug-dealer, but his face bore an unhealthy pallor – a pallor that even the Mediterranean sun could not fix. Overcome by expectation, Ally nodded, and Mick held the door open wider.

One-by-one, not three – not even four – but five businessmen then entered the bedroom, each with a strong swagger. In shock, Ally pulled the sheets higher up her torso, as one man – the youngest, and most enthusiastic – was already removing his jacket and tie. The short conversation that ensued was brisk and business-like.

'You've got the gear?' Mick directed to the eldest.

'Two and a half kilos of Charlie. Weighed it myself,' the man replied.

'Have fun, boys,' said Mick, his voice cold, as he received the brick of cocaine. 'And remember, if she screams – it's all part of the act. She likes it rough.'

Assured as he was with speaking, Mick did not have the courage to look at Ally. Appearing downcast, he backed out of the room and slammed the door. Ally leapt up but could already hear the key turning in the lock. Left with only her arms to conceal her naked chest, she stood, rooted to the spot and shaking all over.

The youngest man was the first to drop his trousers. He didn't even step out of them before lunging.

🌵

Tuesday 2nd September 1997, 22:44pm, EL POCO SOL, LAS RAMBLAS, BARCELONA, CATALONIA, SPAIN.

'Ally – Ally, please don' cry. Oh, sweet, *belleza!*'

On the customer side of the bar, Rogerio sat beside her. Not soon after the Scottish brunette's arrival and the sign upon the pub's door had been flipped to 'cerrado'. As she'd arrived distraught, Rogerio had repeatedly tried to hug Ally – in an attempt to calm and soothe – but each time, she'd violently rebuffed him. Four hours later and two empty tequila bottles stood before them. The pair each had their own glass tumbler.

'I'm not crying!' Ally sobbed, indignantly – her eyes red and puffy.

'Jus'd tell me truth – *please*,' Rogerio implored – for he'd still not heard it. 'Whad haz Mick done now – huh? Deed he hur' you, Ally?'

'He lied to me!' Ally cried.

She wiped her tears upon the sleeve of her white blouse and hocked trickles of snot back up her nostrils. Her hand unsteady, she reached out for her tumbler and downed the last of the neat spirit, displaying no reaction to its burn this time.

'Whadever he has done – he won' ged away wid eet!' Rogerio declared.

He slammed a clenched fist onto the bar, causing the glassware to shudder. Ally didn't even flinch.

'Don't worry. He won't,' Ally whispered, before raising her voice and slamming her fists down also. '*Voy a romper el puto cuello del hombre! Amour verdadero?* Fuck him!'

Her body stiff, she took to her feet. The pain from her waist down was so great, even vast quantities of alcohol had failed to numb it. Ally steadied herself against the bar; focussing her eyes upon her empty tumbler. Such was the degree of rage that she levelled at it, she felt that it might shatter from her look alone. Ally would have hurled it across the bar right there and then, if she hadn't had wanted to spare her friend the clean-up. She headed for the door.

'Ally!' Rogerio shouted after her, standing also. 'Where you go? Ally?!'

Knowing he'd have to accompany her, Rogerio began scanning the bar for his keys. The door to El Poco Sol slammed – its closed sign swinging – and his search grew frantic.

Tuesday 2nd September 1997, 22:50pm, <u>COMETELO TODO CAFETERÍA, LAS RAMBLAS, BARCELONA, CATALONIA, SPAIN.</u>

Across the road from El Poco Sol, a man sat alone by the window of a late-night café. From in front of his face, he lowered a newspaper – *20 Minutos*. A Nigerian man, Ally knew him well, and he watched as she exited the bar opposite.

Lifting his spiked coffee to his lips, the pages of the newspaper fell limp to the table. The coffee ordered had been black, but Solanki had added the brandy himself. Chuckling at the thought of Mick's displeasure, he toasted this, for he anticipated what it would mean.

Tuesday 2nd September 1997, 23:33pm, <u>MICHAEL BENNETT'S VILLA, MONTJUIC, BARCELONA, CATALONIA, SPAIN.</u>

Ally took a cab to the summit of Montjuic, but without any money with which to pay, had argued with the driver. She took the steps leading up to the villa two at a time, thinking over her confrontation. And as she entered, Ally tried her best to remain calm but spoke strongly.

'Mick, we need to talk.'

Sat at the head of their glass-topped dining table, Mick was midway through counting money from out of a black leather briefcase. The notes crisp, each was worth five-hundred pesetas. Beside the briefcase was an uncapped bottle of absinthe – short and stout, with a rectangular base. Ally felt sick just looking it. *The Devil's Hand*, she deemed the drink aptly named, for there it was in front of her, counting the cash that she had the bruises to show for.

'Not now, Alexis. I'm counting the prize,' Mick slurred. 'Got a good price for it too – you should be proud.'

Without even looking at her, he took a glug of the green spirit – laced with sugar.

'You lied to me.'

Ally stated the words.

Mick remained silent and shunted a stack of banknotes down the table. He turned his attention back to the briefcase and began counting out another. His lack of concern was all it took to open the floodgates to Ally's tirade. Any fear she may have had for him was far outweighed by feelings of betrayal.

'Look at me,' she whispered – he did not. 'Look at me!'

Spittle flew from the corners of Ally's mouth, as she then marched over to slap the notes from out of Mick's fists.

'How could you let them do that to me?! Humiliate me! Degrade me!' she screamed – shaking him by the shoulders. 'You said you'd never let anyone hurt me! You—'

'This isn't about me!' spat Mick. 'This is about *you* – what *you've* done!'

He grabbed Ally by the wrists and turning on her, stood, pushing her off him. Her legs uneasy, Ally tottered back a few paces. Mick's bloodshot eyes flashed violently in the dimmed light.

The front door softly clicked closed – Ally had not heard it open. This was followed by thudding footsteps across the hallway. Neither Ally nor Mick broke eye contact from the other to look.

'What are you talking about?' Ally hissed.

'You think I don't know?' Mick seethed. 'You think I don't know what you and that – that – *barman* have been up to? Behind my back!'

Ally turned at the sound of something heavy being dropped – like a colossal sack of potatoes – under the archway behind. Rage dying, it felt as if her heart had been ripped from out of her chest, for on the floor – out cold and sprawled – was Rogerio. Stripped naked from the waist up, his toned physique was covered in welts and bruises. The harsh beating he'd received had been quick to sprout them.

Den laughed – a short chortle, that ended abruptly after a daggered stare from Mick. A large, bald man, Den had more fat than muscle. What he lacked in strength, however, was more than compensated for in temper. Beside Den stood Solanki, his arms folded and smirking. Built like a brick shithouse – a far sturdier one than in which they all lived – he towered over everyone in the room, Mick included.

Ally darted to kneel beside Rogerio.

'You've killed him!' she squealed.

'Not yet,' Solanki boomed.

Den let out another short burst of laughter.

'You're fucking him – aren't you?' Mick snarled.

After checking Rogerio's neck for a pulse – with relief she discovered there was one – Ally stood once more. Striding back over to Mick, she proceeded to plead appeal directly into his face.

'I'm not – I *wasn't* – he's my friend!'

Ally was disgusted by the allegation. Rogerio was her friend, and it was only now that she realised him to have been her only one.

'You belong to me, Alexis – you're mine! Do you hear me? No-one else's!'

Ally backed away slowly.

'Please – Mick. *Micky*, please – just let him go! Rogerio didn't do anything. I haven't done anything – I swear!'

Ally manoeuvred herself around the glass-topped table.

'Bet you were having a right ol' joke behind my back. Weren't you?!' Mick roared, and Ally flinched. 'Weren't you?!'

As Mick began to follow, both encircled the table.

'Micky – *please*.' Ally beseeched. 'I don't underst—'

'WHORE!'

His lips downturned in revulsion, Mick spewed the label with vigour, his torso heaving. In one swift motion, he swept his crystal-cut glass from the table, which flew to shatter beside Ally's head, smattering the stucco with bright green.

'I promise you – I didn't do anything!' Ally begged – tensed yet truthful. 'Micky – *please*! Micky, I didn't do anything!'

'I thought you'd learnt not to tell lies since you came here – since I took you in! Do I need to beat it out of you? Filthy habit – filthy girl!'

Having encircled the table by a full three-hundred and sixty degrees, Mick took the unexpected action of coolly replacing the banknotes back within their case. Closing it, he exhaled slowly, as he secured the clasps.

'Leave us,' he instructed, to Den and Solanki. 'And take him with you. Shoot him in the head, bag him, weigh him, and drop him off the cliff.'

Ally shrieked in protest and made a sharp movement towards Rogerio, but Mick was too fast. Catching her, he yanked at her blouse and pulled at her hair.

As ordered, Den and Solanki proceeded to haul Rogerio's unconscious body out of the room, and out of sight. Ally trembled, hot tears streaming down her cheeks, as she wept in a struggle.

'You need to be taught a lesson,' Mick stated, solemnly, shaking his head, as if it were his job – and a chore – to educate her.

But breaking free, Ally dashed back around the table. Mick gave chase. She'd turned a corner, when he – quick as a cat – altered direction, cutting her off before she could reach the hallway. Turning again and Ally's foot caught a chair leg. She stumbled forwards, tripping over her own feet, before falling spectacularly down to the boards.

At first, Mick did not lower himself down to her level. Instead, he stood over her and stared. As Ally rolled herself onto her back, she was now – as he'd always felt – beneath him. Time seemed to slow to a standstill.

Ally's watch broken; its face was cracked right down the middle. Buttons ripped open; her white blouse hung loosely from a single shoulder, revealing her black bra strap. Shrouded in the elongated shadow cast by Mick's height, her body quivered. Seconds passed, as no movement was made by either person. Ally's chest rapidly rose and fell, as her eyes swivelled back and forth within their sockets.

Then, with outstretched arms, Mick sprang at her.

Ally squealed and began writhing, attempting to evade capture, as he grappled for her wrists. Her free arm flailed, but failed to hit him, for Mick batted it away. She snatched at his ankles but could not reach. She tried to kick him, but he restrained her.

Having gained a firm enough grip of her, Mick turned, dragging Ally across the floor by her arms. She screamed; the angle at which he pulled felt enough to break her. She kicked and dug her heels – anything to try and slow their progression. But this achieved nothing beyond the odd scuff and squeak upon the boards. Splinters and shards of broken glass gouged at Ally's thighs.

As she sped past a chair, she clamped her feet around its leg, only for Mick to pull it along with them – a few feet or so – before Ally relinquished her hold. Her feet fought for a table leg next, but all she did was shunt it. The table nudged an inch, causing the absinthe bottle to rock and fall from off the glass-top. Failing to break, Ally yelped, as the green splattered itself across her face and blouse.

Mick slung the briefcase over his shoulder, as he continued to drag Ally – like a doll – by a singular hand. Even with one arm free, Ally could not gather enough momentum to land a proper punch.

All through the hallway and up the stairs, she was hauled; each step causing her body to flop and thud. The first door at the top of the stairs – Terry's bedroom – was their destination. Purposely, Mick had not selected their own, for it was far too proper for his intentions. Ally was flung to the foot of the single bed, and supporting herself by its rusty frame, she staggered to her feet. All of Mick's next actions were met with resistance. Ally struggled, until all she could do was cry.

Wednesday 3rd September 1997, 04:51am, MICHAEL BENNETT'S VILLA, MONTJUIC, BARCELONA, CATALONIA, SPAIN.

Ally's eyelids flickered open. Gasping and wheezing, she was crushed by the weight of the man passed out on top of her. Using both her hands and all her remaining strength, she rolled Mick's naked body over on the mattress. His hand fell limp to unconsciously cup her breast. Disgusted, Ally slapped it away.

Out of bed, she faltered across the room, her legs weak. Purposely slow, Ally retrieved her strewn clothing as silently as she could. She stepped into her skirt, arms shaking, and slid her boots on over bare feet. Her blouse was peeping out from under Mick's backside and after some hesitation, Ally whipped it out from under him with bated breath. Mick rolled over once more – this time onto his face. He did not stir and instead started snoring. Ally exhaled a juddered sigh of relief. Not wanting to waste any more time in dressing, she draped her blouse over a shoulder and headed straight for the door.

Ally had already reached for the knob before she took the decision to turn back. There had been no forethought as to what she did next.

Kneeling, Ally reached her arms far under the bed's frame. The briefcase made a scratching sound upon the gritty floor as she pulled it towards her. Though it contained only paper money, its volume was such that it was still heavy. It was now or never – make or break.

Halfway back to the door, Mick spluttered, and Ally froze. She listened intently as his spluttering turned into choking; he was coughing up vomit. The noises emitted only affirmed that he was still face down on the mattress. And as Mick's breathing became laboured, Ally's grip tightened on the briefcase's handle. She did not turn; she would not aid him.

Ally left the bedroom, leaving the door ajar. Her glossy hair dishevelled and her top half nude, she softly descended the stairs. The sun had only just kissed the horizon and the birds outside were tweeting the arrival of a new day. A singular shaft of light shone through from Terry's bedroom to the stairwell, to illuminate dusty air.

As if pulled by an invisible hand, the bedroom door then slowly creaked and clicked shut. Even more slowly, the locking mechanism squeaked into life – its internal bolt sliding defiantly across. The rusting hole glinted menacingly in the half-light. Its key had been lost for years.

- CHAPTER XV -

Warehouse 16

<u>Friday 7th November 1997, 22:42pm, WAREHOUSE 16, DE MANDEVILLE INDUSTRIAL ESTATE, ASHFIELD HIGH-WAY, LONDON.</u>

Three plots down from the illegal gathering, Warehouse 16 had been the home to a packing firm for over fifty years. Only recently closed, its primary use was now storage. A rusting graveyard; abandoned forklifts and machinery from the past half-century had been crammed within its shell, serving a ghostly foreshadowing of Ashfield's declining industry. Its large doors – unlocked – had conveniently been left ajar, and the group – headed by Ally – slid neatly inside. All except for Den, who had to laboriously squeeze. The doors were too heavy to open further, or indeed close.

From over her shoulder, Ally had taken one final look at Mick before they'd all made a break for it. There had been little time, but she had not thought to retrieve his gun. Skidding upon the oil-streaked concrete, Ally was the first of the six to reach the warehouse's opposite wall, running full pelt.

'There's no way out!' she cried.

'We're trapped,' reiterated Fred.

'You've gone and boxed us righ' in!' Den chided.

'I never asked you to follow us,' Ally snapped, squaring up to him.

'What the hell was that thing?' asked Solanki – an open question to the room, and one they were all thinking.

There was group silence as each looked blankly – and shiftily – from one person to the next. Den jolted his face closer to Ally's and he smirked at the fright he'd caused her.

'Hope you're still laughing when that thing cuts out your cholesterol-ridden heart, yer fat bastard,' she raged.

Her eyes darting around their dark and shadowy metal prison, Rye spotted a discarded scalpel atop an oil drum. She dashed for it, snatching it up.

'What you gonna do with that?' Zach asked, unimpressed.

Rye swung the blade in a demonstration. She quickly realised, however, as Zach had, that it stood little chance against a creature that could tear the heart out of a gangster, and so pocketed it.

'I don't know about you, but my money's on them,' Zach whispered, subtly nodding in the direction of Den and Solanki, as both loaded their respective magazines.

With the full cartridges slotted back into their casings, Ally stared at them with a look of disgust. With a click, Solanki pulled back his gun's slider and kissed the barrel.

'Are you scared?' she asked him, venomously. 'You gonna shoot it in the head, like you did Rogerio?'

'Take a wild guess,' Solanki replied, dryly.

'Why didn't you shoot it before? Is it because you're scared?'

Marching right on up to him, Ally bravely took hold of Solanki's gun arm to wrestle – for no reason other than to be taken seriously. In less than a second, he easily wrenched himself free of her grasp.

'You are scared,' Ally taunted, looking up at his face. 'I can see it in your eyes. What's the matter? That creature not defenceless enough for you?'

'You know, Alexis, there's a multitude of ways in which you could die tonight, and that – out there – is just one.'

Ally held Solanki's gaze – his eyes bulbous – for several seconds before choosing her next word.

'*Sn-ap*,' she enunciated.

With a loud thwack, Solanki smacked Ally across the face with the barrel of his pistol. Her head knocked to one side, she whipped it back, and hocking snot, spat a viscous globule directly into Solanki's face. It collided with his cheek, just below his left eye.

All, having intently watched the pair's exchange, suddenly turned their attention to the warehouse's doors. Like a fox scavenging for food, the creature's scampering could be heard from outside.

The nearest to her, Rye took hold of Fred's arm, and the two of them took cover behind a row of forklifts. Zach had to physically drag Ally away from Solanki and was the only reason eye contact was broken between them.

As Zach and Ally crouched behind a stack of wooden pallets, only Solanki and Den remained in the warehouse's centre. Despite their intimidating builds, without Mick, they were simply the brawn with trigger fingers for brains. The muscle, without any common sense.

Peeping out from their hiding places, the others could just make out the creature's shadow as it slipped between the large doors. It had nimbly stood upright upon hind legs to navigate the gap but continued on all fours, for a slow and steadied approach. Its eyes – slits of burnt orange – shone out like lasers. Unblinkingly, they penetrated the void between them. A few feathers scattered across its hide; the creature's silhouette was comparable to that of a half-plucked chicken.

Giving little thought unto herself at that moment, Ally willed the creature to rip the hearts out from both Den and Solanki – poetic justice, for what she had felt when they'd dumped Rogerio's unconscious body to the floor of the villa.

Stalking at an ambled pace, the creature appeared unperturbed as Mick's henchmen lifted their weapons. Together, they squeezed the triggers in unison, but no shots were fired. Instead, the magazines from both their guns flew out from their cases, to clatter tremendously upon the concrete. They shuddered and bounced, unexplainably haemorrhaging bullets of their own accord, that rattled to roll out in all directions. Confused and scared, Solanki and Den looked to each other for an explanation. Neither had one.

'Let us play game,' the creature declared, gleefully.

Distinctive; Rye instantly recognised the voice. It was the same she'd heard within Sullen Woods, two months prior.

Closing the gap, the creature took to its hind legs once more. It was no taller than five feet, and with its front legs – or arms – being of disproportionate size, its claws dragged on the floor.

'Let us see,' the creature sang. 'Hide-and-seek!'

Visibly shaking – presumably too afraid to move – neither Solanki nor Den ran.

'Found one!' the creature declared in a voluminous croak.

From behind the forklift and wooden pallets, the school friends watched as the creature plunged a set of long talons up and into Solanki's chest. They could just about hear his gasps for breath before he tumbled – crashing to the floor – atop the pistols' components. Much louder in his whimpering, Den dropped his weapon's useless casing beside his lifeless partner, and as fast as his fat legs could carry him, bolted for the door. His rounded form could be seen making an escape, all very much to the creature's disinterest.

'Bored of game,' the creature sighed, through a rasp.

It proceeded to throw Solanki's heart at a nearby oil drum. Bouncing off it – much like a squash ball – it ricocheted out of sight with a squelch.

'I spy – better game!'

At this declaration, Fred repeatedly elbowed Rye in the ribs, before frantically waving his hands in front of her face. He had given no thought to the neon face paint until now, and so spat into his palms, to vigorously scrub Rye's cheeks clean. Unsuccessful; Fred only managed to smear Louie's wonkily-drawn heart.

Horrified, he proceeded to facepalm her, and she slapped her own hands down upon his. Together they parted fingers – in scissor motion – to bestow back unto Rye her vision.

'I spy, with my little eye,' the creature began, and the lights within the warehouse flickered into reluctant life to undermine all efforts. 'Something beginning with B.'

Rye gulped as Fred's hands slipped out from under hers.

'Blondie!'

Professed squeal and the abomination was back on all fours to charge. Making a beeline for Rye, it ploughed through three oil drums, sending them flying and their contents glugging. The creature dived through the compartment of the forklift behind which she and Fred crouched, but it had not realised – nor anticipated – that its opposite door was closed, and so collided with it.

Rye and Fred fell back against the wall. Mere inches from them, the creature's dark-grey and blotchy flesh pressed up against the glass, gurning slobbering jaws and gnashing snaggle-teeth. Skeletal; it appeared almost bird-like, except for its goblin-esque head, which was covered in open sores and lesions. Its elongated nose squashed upwards, the creature attempted to swipe at Rye from behind the pane. Its mouth snapped like a turtle, as it struggled, pawing at its prey with its talons, which still bore a bloodied sheen.

Ally's gut was clenching. Slouched upon the floor beside Zach, her suffering was going quite unnoticed by him, however, as he eyed up the pistols' remnants. Silently, he was debating whether he had enough time and skill to piece one together and fire it. A member of the Ashfield Archery Club; Zach was a good shot.

Gripping Zach's football shirt, Ally then retched, and the warehouse appeared to spin. One hundred and eighty degrees; floor, ceiling, machinery and creature all blurred, as the four teenagers all seemingly remained static. Defying gravity, Ally's stream of vomit plumed out of her mouth like a geyser. It shot upward, but up was down. They remained crouched, but upon the cold, corrugated ceiling. The floor was above them.

Softly flowing out above her, Ally's hair stood on end. With every tilt of her head, it moved only slightly. She felt horrid, but there was no sensation of physically being upside down. She covered her hot lips with sweaty palms and coughed out a swear.

Fred apprehensively crawled across the ceiling towards the base of the nearest light fixture. Like Ally's hair, the chain that suspended its large shaded bulb stretched vertically upwards, itself taut. It swayed – swung – as Fred took hold, causing a beam of light to dart across the floor overhead.

Free from the forklift and the creature jumped up and down upon its hind legs, bemused. Though eager, there was nothing it could do – dozens of feet separated them.

It appeared that only the group's bodies were immune to the earth's gravitational pull. Everything else surrounding them – their clothes, possessions and accessories included – was not. Loose change – a fifty pence piece and shrapnel – came shooting out of Zach's trouser pockets, to rise and rain. Rye's necklace, dangling to brush against her nose, was quickly wound around her bra strap.

'I hope this isn't asbestos!' Zach hollered with nervous laughter.

He rapped the roof with his knuckles.

'Sure, like that's the worst of our problems!' Fred garbled – his flannel shirt flapping up around him.

With her eyes, Rye traced Fred's arms to the rusting base of the light's fixture. As with Maths, she was not particularly gifted in Physics either, and that was within natural permits. But seeing the effects of their altered state, she had forged a plan.

'Fred!' she shouted. 'Catch!'

Rye threw the scalpel she had pocketed earlier. Exerting enough force to counter gravity, her aim was on target. Fred instinctively relinquished his grasp upon the light's chain, just as the scalpel had begun to curve upwards to the floor. He caught it, himself remaining glued to the ceiling, much to his surprise and relief.

Rye gestured to the light's fixture and Fred, correctly interpreting her almost unrecognisable motions, began tinkering at its base. It didn't take long for the light and its chain to hurtle, rising to the floor with an almighty smash – near atop the creature. Its large bulb shattered; sparks scattered to ignite the oil-sploshed concrete. Flames caught the drums not long after, and an enormous fireball erupted down from the floor above them. The creature was engulfed within seconds.

Plumes of billowing smoke spilled out as a hazy sea around the crouched forms of Ally, Zach, Fred and Rye. There was no hope if they were to fall back down to earth now, but the roof was rapidly heating.

ঌ✋ଽ

Friday 7th November 1997, 22:53pm, A10 NORTHBOUND, ASHFIELD HIGHWAY, LONDON.

The call had come through much to Michelle's appreciation. A fire – possible arson – was not a matter to be taken lightly but served as a means nonetheless to distract her from increasing anxiety.

The blaze had taken hold of an old warehouse on the De Mandeville industrial estate, attracting the attention of nearby partygoers. Location considered, the witnesses were surely attending an illegal gathering, which would require an even longer call out for herself and the other officers. Again, for this, Michelle was glad.

'Alpha Delta one-four, Alpha Delta one-four,' crackled the police car's radio. 'This is Alpha Delta one-seven, over.'

'Alpha Delta one-seven, Alpha Delta one-seven,' Michelle leaned in, to reply. 'This is Alpha Delta one-four. Go ahead, over.'

'Alpha Delta one-four, we've taken a wrong turn. The fire appears to be on the North-East of the complex, over.'

'Alpha Delta one-four, I'll head to the North-East of the complex. Received, out.'

Alone in the police car, Michelle shunted the gearstick into fifth, sirens blaring. Paperwork abandoned; her night was about to get a whole much more interesting.

*

Zach led the crawl towards one of the roof's skylights. Easily breaking its single pane, he closed his eyes to shield his face from the fragments. He inhaled thrice – filling his lungs with sweet oxygen – before taking a fourth and much deeper breath. Taking the risk – for he had no choice otherwise – Zach then lowered himself through the skylight's opening. An infinite and bottomless chasm sprinkled with stars; the inky-black sky stretched out forever.

Immediately, Zach experienced an odd, twisting sensation, as he was flipped the right way up once more. It was as if the warehouse's roof itself was the centre of this strange gravitational field, and it pulled them all to it, no matter which side they were on.

Once all four were free, each shimmied to the roof's edge. Their knees and palms scorched against its metal. Quickly, but carefully, they descended a drainpipe to the tarmac below. Mick's eviscerated carcass still lay discarded beside the lorry, right where they had left it.

After helping Fred – the last of the four down – Zach ushered the others towards the gates of the car park. Flashing lights and sirens could already be seen and heard from across the far side of the complex. Zach took one last look back at the raging flames, disorientated, but somewhat in awe. They reflected in his eyes, burning deep into his consciousness for all of a few seconds before he coughed. He wiped his hands upon his jeans, composed himself, and turned to hasten after his friends.

Upon turning, however, Zach found himself locking eyes with those of a woman, and he froze. Aged forty or so – by his guess – she appeared tired and flustered. Dressed in full police constable uniform, her fluorescent jacket was emblazoned with the shield of the Metropolitan Police. The woman opened her mouth, and Zach – in fear that she was about to alert others to his presence – pleadingly pressed a forefinger to his lips.

'Sssssssh,' he begged.

Against protocol, Michelle Davey silently pardoned him. She nodded her head slowly in acceptance but did not understand why she had given into him. Although it was preposterous, Michelle felt a connection with him. Zach edged away before breaking into a run. He did not look back.

Michelle's torch beams caught on Mick's lifeless body. Recoiling, she dry-heaved. She had seen many bodies before, but the shock still caught her off guard. Immediately, Michelle regretted having let the boy go, but looking around, Zach had long since disappeared.

*

Badly burnt and blistered, the creature limped past the fence behind, as Michelle crouched beside Mick's corpse, speaking into her radio. Weakened and in pain, the creature staggered to then hook its talons around the links in the fence. It sniffed; the action of great effort.

'*Another,*' it rasped.

CHAPTER XVI

Weird, Wonderful & Ordinary

<u>Sunday 9th November 1997, 23:06pm, LEITH RESIDENCE, 7 BROOK STREET, ASHFIELD, LONDON.</u>
Despite the collection of darts already clustered at the board's centre, Zach's latest throw had managed to squeeze itself in amongst them; *bullseye*. Still, he sighed, and laid back upon his bed.

Demons, poltergeists et al, Zach had seen them all in almost every horror film ever made. On some level, he'd even believed in their existence, but seeing was altogether different to believing. He was unnerved – of course – but couldn't say he was shocked. If anything, his close encounter with the long arm of the law had shaken him a great deal more. A reckless, and at times easily led, young man, Zach was always close to trouble in some way or another. Yet he had never – until two days ago – faced off against the police before.

Throwing his right arm out to his side, Zach blindly felt about the floor for his school bag. Successfully, he hooked it and hurled it onto the bed. He sat up and unzipped its main compartment to rifle through textbooks, wrappers and loose doodles, until he'd found what he was searching for – a half-empty pack of cigarettes and a porno magazine.

With an item in each hand, Zach weighed up his options. He settled on the Marlborough Lights and so dropped the magazine. An occasional – usually, only social – smoker, Zach had acquired the pack through trading his dessert on Wednesday lunchtime. The brand was not his usual choice, but he wasn't well-versed enough in the habit to have yet developed a true preference.

Kneeling on his mattress, Zach snapped open the skylight that was set into the slanted ceiling of his loft room and surveyed the view of Ashfield through its crack. Appearing still, the sounds of buses and police sirens could nonetheless be heard. The latter filled him with dread. Removing a lighter from the cigarettes' carton, Zach lit the straight placed between his lips. He coughed but quickly settled into the sensation of the smoke hitting the back of his throat.

Zach's mind raced. Raced over Rye's birthday celebrations. Raced over their encounter with Mick and his henchmen and their guns. Raced over the warehouse blaze. And the creature. Raced over the police constable and how she'd spared him. Raced over Alexis Monaghan. She had been the reason that they'd ended up on the ceiling, and Zach knew it. What a colourful and chequered past Ally had – having lived far more years in her few than many could claim in an entire lifetime. This didn't quell Zach's feelings towards her – in fact, quite the contrary. It made her even more appealing.

∾✋∾

<u>Sunday 9th November 1997, 23:09pm, TURPIN RESIDENCE, 32 KYNASTON GARDENS, ASHFIELD, LONDON.</u>
Ally's snores were 'loud and masculine', as Rye had just described them in her diary. Angrily, she prodded her.

'Oi, shut up,' Rye hissed.

As Ally rolled over, she proceeded to drool, and her snores became muffled.

The pair had shared a single mattress since Friday, with Rye having informed her sister that Ally would be staying with them for an undetermined period. Used to having Fred and Zach – boys at that – over for sometimes days at a time, Pris did not overly question this arrangement, as she placed trust in those with whom her sister shared a friendship – birthday shenanigans aside. This was one thing that Rye would give her credit for.

For all of yesterday, Ally had remained in bed, incapacitated and groggy. Today – still weak – and she'd finally succumbed to reading the pages from the Ars Goetia. By the afternoon, Ally had gotten up only by Rye's insistence, and it was together that they'd collected her few possessions from 42 Friar Street.

Tonight, unable to sleep, Rye confided in her diary.

'I thought it best not to tell Pris,' she had written, referencing the warehouse fire and their meeting of Anoch – all present had agreed that was the identity of the creature. *'She's still not dealt with my birthday, not that I have. But … whenever I watch a horror film, I always yell at the screen when characters aren't clear with one another – when they don't overtly share every nugget of information they come across, or every fright they encounter. The reality, however, as I myself have come to discover, is that the truth is a far too bitter a pill to swallow. The questions asked of such circumstance (What? How? Why? Why me? Why now?) either to others or simply oneself, are hard to ask for fear of the answer. That's why Pris would rather bury her head in the sand. Anoch is dead – burned alive. We all saw it. There's no way it could have gotten out of there alive. I will tell Pris, but there's no urgency. There are questions that I want answering first. Anoch went for me.'* Rye underlined the pronoun, twice. *'Why me? Why now?'*

❧✋❧

<u>Sunday 9th November 1997, 23:10pm, BATEMAN RESID-ENCE, 52 BELLAMY AVENUE, ASHFIELD, LONDON.</u>

Dressed in pyjama bottoms and a hoodie, Fred sat cross-legged on the chair in front of the home computer. The light from its monitor – which he'd dimmed – was the only source illuminating the sitting room.

Fred had waited over an hour since hearing his mother check the front door, before creeping downstairs. He had been unable to sleep the past two consecutive nights, and as such hadn't planned on even attempting to do so tonight.

Resilient as he was to bullies and life's challenges that his teen years were rapidly revealing, Fred did not feel brave. He wanted nothing further to do with the Ars Goetia, or Rye's very own version of *The Amityville Horror.* That Anoch had apparently met its demise was of no comfort either. He did not believe it.

The computer gave off a loud whirr as its fans sprang into action and the dial-up tone sounded. Fred shushed it as he would a person and pricked his ears, listening intently for any movement from upstairs. A minute after the machine settled and he concluded himself safe. He opened an already completed Geography essay saved upon the desktop, only to minimise it, and open a fresh webpage. The homework would serve purely as a safety net – an excuse, one super-fast click away, should Fred be caught.

He took a wine gum from out of the packet in his hoodie's pocket and placed it in his mouth to chew whilst typing 'RTC' into the search bar. The first result, then his desired category within the chat room: 'Gay and Lesbian'. Fred logged in. He did not frequent the site often but did so when feeling particularly blue, seeking a sort of solace.

'89 people online.'

Fred skim-read the first twenty or so usernames before selecting the one that most appealed to him within that moment – 'fitlondonboi26'. Fred initiated the conversation.

'Lonelyandconfused:

hey.'

Horrified by the squeaky trumpet noise that accompanied his message as it pinged into existence, he yanked the speakers' cable from its connection.

'Lonelyandconfused:

wanna chat?'

On edge once more, Fred popped another three wine gums as he awaited the reply with a racing heart.

fitlondonboi26:

hey,

yh ofc,

whats ur name?

Lonelyandconfused:

Liam,

yours?'

Fred never chose the same pseudonym, and it was for reasons he could not explain that he'd chosen this name upon this occasion.

fitlondonboi26:

miles,

asl?

Lonelyandconfused:

16 london.'

Fred lied again, adding more than three months onto his true age. This was still two years below the legal age of consent for homosexual males.

fitlondonboi26:

26 tottenham here,

where bouts in london?

Lonelyandconfused:

croydon.'

Whilst still within the M25, Fred had deliberately chosen a location as far south from Tottenham as he could think of. He had zero intention of meeting 'Miles' – that was not the purpose of this exercise. And as Fred himself so often lied within the online community, he had come to expect nothing else in return.

fitlondonboi26:

ah shame mate,

we could have had fun ;)'

Fred stuffed a fistful of sweets into his mouth. Miles' presumption filled him with mild anger.

'Lonelyandconfused:
does my age bother you?
fitlondonboi26:
nope.'

The stranger's age was of no concern to Fred either, for as already established, he would never meet him. Ever.

'fitlondonboi26:
what u wanna chat bout?
Lonelyandconfused:
I dunno,
just had a crap day I suppose,
I'm feeling down is all.
Fitlondonboi26:
ah shit dude. Why so bad?
Lonelyandconfused:
just home stuff…
and school stuff…
and other stuff…
Fitlondonboi26:
What other stuff?'

Fred grimaced. Usually, he was all too happy to anonymously spill his guts. But there was no way he was about to unload the gruesomely specific details of Mick's evisceration, the warehouse fire or Anoch, to a total stranger.

'Lonelyandconfused:
just stuff.'

*

Zach stubbed his half-smoked fag out on the roof's tile and let the butt roll to the gutter. He closed the skylight then hugged his upper body; the night's air had been cold.

At a loss of what to do next, Zach surveyed his bedroom. His possessions mostly comprised of VHS tapes. Recorded from the television, they lined his shelves. All were carefully labelled and ordered. The remnants of his Halloween make-up – encrusted in its pallet – lay forgotten atop a pile of comics. His prized bow and quiver were propped in a corner.

Zach lay back on his bed again. Above his head was a wonky shelf – that he himself had erected – and it held half a dozen Ashfield Archery Club trophies. Tacked onto the slanted ceiling was a poster of Rose McGowan in *The Doom Generation*, and a trio of glow-in-the-dark stars. The latter made him think of Ally once more.

Zach's hand reached for the porno magazine. He'd downplayed his interest whilst Tony passed it around the changing room but had been eager to stuff it into his own bag the second his friend's back was turned.

Zach turned to a random page. A voluptuous blonde – bare-chested and brassy – posed beside a mantelpiece in nothing more than a pair of stockings. She clasped a feather duster. In a caption, 'Lucy' shared her insight:

'I, for one, will be sad to say goodbye to the old fifty pence piece. Sure, my purse will be lighter, but it'll feel like I'll have less money.'

Zach wriggled his boxers down to his ankles. Oh, how he hoped he wouldn't die a virgin. As per horror movie lore, he was no doubt in a better position if he remained. This was real life, however. *Scream* had only deconstructed the genre the year before, and as far as tropes went, the only one that concerned him was how the antagonist always comes back.

*

The tissue missed the bin, but Zach wasn't bothered. He'd pick it up later. Rolling to one side, he hung off the bed and peered across to his shelves.

What to watch? *The Evil Dead, The Evil Dead II, The Exorcist,* (entire trilogy), *Halloween,* (choice of every instalment from the original through to *The Revenge of Michael Myers*), *The Hills Have Eyes Part II, A Nightmare on Elm Street,* (or its sequels *Freddy's Revenge* or *The Dream Child*), the *Poltergeist* series or *The Shining,* amongst others.

Zach's mother was working her usual Sunday night shift at the twenty-four-hour supermarket, which meant he had free reign of the television and no-one to remind him it was a school night. Not that his mother would be overly fussed if she were in — the few rules she encouraged were not enforced with any severity.

Zach reached for *The Exorcist.* What with Rye's unintentional impression of Linda Blair last week, he considered a re-watch to be nothing other than revision. Either that, or *Child's Play.*

*

It was harder to write whilst wearing gloves and Rye did not appreciate the challenge. Tent-like, she had pulled the patch-work quilt up over her head. The house was still without windows and was freezing. Her breath clouded as she wrote on:

'Zach said he came face-to-face with a police officer as we escaped the warehouse, but she let him go! Just like that! It doesn't make any sense. I just pray to God that there's nothing left behind that could incriminate, or somehow lead back to us.'

*

If he hadn't been fumbling with the remote's batteries, Zach would have turned on the video player already, but in doing so, would have missed the current news report. Catching a glimpse of the blurry images broadcast, however, he dropped everything.

Shot from what Zach assumed to be a helicopter, flames leapt, and smoke plumed high into the night's sky from an industrial warehouse. Frightfully familiar, the voiceover confirmed his fears.

'The Metropolitan Police are appealing for witnesses over Friday's warehouse fire in Ashfield, North London. At this stage, the cause of the fire is undetermined, although arson is suspected. Two bodies have so far been recovered from the scene, the first having been identified as 23-year-old Michael Bennett.'

Zach flinched as a mugshot of Ally's former lover appeared on the screen. Looking several years younger than the other night, Mick was yet more dishevelled and sullen.

'According to our sources, Mr Bennett's heart had been removed from his chest and was discovered several feet away from his body at the crime scene, prompting a murder investigation. We can confirm that Mr Bennett was known to the authorities for a history of drug convictions and petty theft, and that police suspect his death as resultant from gang-on-gang related crime. The second body of an – of yet – unidentified male, was recovered from the debris inside the warehouse yesterday afternoon. CCTV footage shows four suspects fleeing the scene—'

The screen switched to a grainy black and white still and Zach's head fell forward – his mouth agape. As the image zoomed into the background of a car park, four silhouettes were distinguishable. Depicted mid-stride, with their backs to the camera, Zach realised them as belonging to himself and his friends. Ally – limping – was propped up by Rye and Fred. Zach knew this from memory, but the image's quality was poor enough that even he was unsure exactly whose silhouette was whose.

'—Residents of the local area have expressed concerns in recent years over the rising number of gang-on-gang related incidents such as this. I'm Shona Simpson; News at Eleven.'

*

fitlondonboi26:

life can be tuf sumtimes,

don't be down,

Im sure ur a handsome young lad.

Lonelyandconfused:

sometimes I think I am.

fitlondonboi26:

send me a pic and ill tell u how handsome u are.'

Fred looked into the lens of the webcam before replying.

'Lonelyandconfused:

sorry. I don't have a webcam.

fitlondonboi26:

ah that sucks.

Lonelyandconfused:

can I ask you something?

fitlondonboi26: sure.

Lonelyandconfused:

how did you tell your family you were gay?

Fitlondonboi26:

ah you aint come out yet…

thats tuf dude.

Lonelyandconfused:

I'm scared my parents will like … disown me or something.

fitlondonboi26:

dont worry about it mate,

life is tuf enough as it is,

dont let it get you down.

Lonelyandconfused:

I just feel so alone.

fitlondonboi26:

talk to a friend,

send me a dick pic?'

Fred screwed up his face as a series of pictures followed – each popping into the chat at speed and in varying degrees of pixelated clarity. Photographs upon photographs of nude men – none two alike – each proudly displayed their anatomy. Fred typed his response between the stream.

'Lonelyandconfused:

none of these is you.

fitlondonboi26:

(picture)

(picture)

yh they r.

(picture)

Lonelyandconfused:

so you can change your ethnicity? Or is that just the lighting?

fitlondonboi26:

they not all me ofc.

r u touching urself?'

Fred angrily closed their dialog, loading his last wine gum into his mouth as he did so. It turned out some people were not as like-minded as he'd hoped.

Fred stared at the chatroom's logo at the top of the screen: 'Random Teen Chat'. The slogan beneath read 'Weird, Wonderful and Ordinary' in a basic typeface. 'Miles' had not been a teen. Maybe he hadn't even really been twenty-six, but he'd definitely been weird.

'Weird, Wonderful and Ordinary.'

The tagline struck a chord within Fred. Why did it speak to him? It spoke to him because it had, in fact, been *spoken* to him – to all of them. The voice Rye had spoken with had said those exact words on Halloween—

'And which are you? Weird? Wonderful? Or ordinary?'

As Fred repeated the words back to himself, a chill spread down his spine. Clicking into the chatroom's search bar, he then paused. What else had the voice said? None of it had made any sense, but Fred was beginning to piece it together.

'Male-AL10,' he whispered.

It had to be a username. And sure enough, after Fred typed it in and hit enter, the result was revealed – not that he was happy about it. Selecting the profile displayed, it read:

'Username: Male-AL10

Gender: Male

Age: 27

Five words to describe yourself:

1. Sporty   2. Spontaneous   3. Creative   4. Empathetic   5. Supercalifragilisticexpialidocious

Interests: Disney films are a guilty pleasure of mine. Footie (Oi, oi! :P) Arsenal fan since I was a young lad. Reading (I don't read a load, but the books I do read, I read over and over and over…). Dickens is my favourite author. Gym. Swimming. Keeping fit in general. I also like being lazy – nothing better than a night in, in front of the telly with a pizza!

About me: I'm single and have been unlucky in love. Had my heart broken before but I'm hopeful. I'm a lost soul and would like to meet someone similar for good times, so that we can make new memories, together.

Orientation: Heterosexual.

Religion: I am an atheist.

Last login: 24/07/1997.'

Horror-struck, Fred screenshot the page before turning on the printer beneath the computer with his toe. It lurched into life – startling him. He shushed it.

- CHAPTER XVII -

A.M.

<u>Monday 10th November 1997, 10:02am, ASHFIELD POLICE STATION, ASHFIELD, LONDON.</u>

Three days since the Warehouse 16 blaze and Ashfield Police Station was still rife with talk of Michael Bennett's homicide. For a London borough on the capital's periphery, it was a far more brutal attack than their usual BOCU's standards. The case was now firmly in the hands of CID and out of Michelle Davey's.

Michelle had flung her handbag under her desk and turned on her PC, but it wasn't until after she'd returned from the canteen with a coffee that she'd noticed it: a scrap of paper sitting neatly folded beside her keyboard.

Confused, Michelle picked it up with one hand whilst setting her coffee down with the other. It was then that the lights overhead flickered, but it was an average day, and their behaviour was bypassed with little to no comment by anyone.

'What the …?' Michelle voiced, to no-one's attention other than her own, as she turned the paper over in her palm.

She quietly sat before carefully unpicking the tiny scrap. Flattened out against the desk, it revealed a message, with the few words written cursive and flowing. The ink was a dark pink:

'A.M. 1 Beggar's Hollow,
Say: Elyon, Shaddai, Yahweh, Elohim.'

'Shaz,' Michelle began, lifting her head to speak over the desk's partition. 'Do you know what this is?'

Aside from being a fierce DS, Sharon Knight was, as Michelle described, 'an observer'. A trait not uncommon within their profession, Shaz, however, possessed a very keen eye and noticed many things that others did not.

Taking a gulp of coffee, Shaz looked up at the mention of her name.

'Do I know what, *what* is?'

This was not a promising response.

'Looks like an address,' Michelle mused. 'At least, I think it's an address. It was just left here, on my desk.'

'No idea, love,' Shaz replied, unhelpfully – her Welsh accent strong. 'Scott hasn't been around with the letters yet. What's that to?'

And with that, Shaz stood to lean over.

'No,' Michelle hastened – suddenly keen on keeping the note to herself. 'It's alright, actually – I remember what it is. I wrote it.'

She rolled her eyes at her own excuse. It was just as limp, as it was detrimental, to her compos mentis façade.

'*You* wrote it?' replied Shaz, sceptically, though she sat back down.

'Mm-hmm,' Michelle nodded.

Michelle wished she could say more – provide an explanation for her absent-mindedness – but she could not think on her feet, as she used to. Thankfully, Shaz had her own work to contend with and so questioned her no further.

Opening her computer's mapping software, Michelle proceeded to type '1 Beggar's Hollow' into its search bar and hit enter. Impatiently, she watched the hourglass rotate over and over.

'Did you mean: Beggar's Hollow, Ashfield, London, AF2?'

Eager; she clicked the suggested correction. Apart from the address, Michelle could only translate one other of the note's words – 'Yahweh.' Recalling her secondary school lessons, she knew it to be the personal name of God. Those of Jewish faith held it in such reverence that they dared not even speak it.

'Oh, for God's sake!'

Caught off guard, Michelle jolted at Shaz's exclamation. Panicked, she peered over the divide; Shaz had spilt her coffee all over herself, desk and paperwork. The mishap – a daily occurrence within any office – was indeed irritating, and one to which Michelle could easily relate, but she did not wish to assist in the clean-up. Instead, she sunk back lower into her chair.

With Beggar's Hollow pinpointed on the map as a stretch of country lane, Michelle knew its location. Cutting through Sullen Woods, she had driven along it many times – on her way to Mrs Nicholls' nearly two months prior, in fact – although she'd never registered the road's name. As far as Michelle could recall, there had been no indication of any properties there.

Nonetheless, Michelle consigned the route to memory. Glancing across to the clock opposite, it read a little before quarter past ten. She locked her workstation.

Michelle was unsure whether 'A.M.' referred to the time of day at which she should visit the address or whether the abbreviation was the initials to a name, but if the former, then she hadn't a moment to lose.

Only DI Kevin Gunn took any notice as Michelle slipped out of the office. He shouted after her, but she did not hear.

*

There she was; the road sign confirmed it. Indicating left, Michelle turned onto Beggar's Hollow. Her journey had been short, lasting around fifteen minutes, but would have been even quicker had it not been for the set of temporary lights installed on the high street.

Beggar's Hollow was narrow. A winding road, it appeared totally devoid of traffic. Driving its length and not a soul could be seen – nor building, house or property. There was only thick woodland – so thick, that hardly any sunlight could penetrate. With no signs of life, the only sign Michelle saw was at the road's end junction. To her left was the village of Crowthorne. To her right, the town of Hatfield.

Her hands clammy on the wheel, Michelle was only now starting to doubt the note's credibility. The cruel likelihood was that Kevin had planted it, to distract and mislead her, before alerting DCI Goodfellow to her absence. She breathed deeply; it was time to turn back. Her foot heavy on the gas, and without looking, Michelle's Mini lurched forwards with an almighty roar.

A large truck zipped past the front of Michelle's bonnet just as she slammed the breaks. Honking – the noise fading fast with its speed – the passing truck missed her car by a hare's whisker.

Michelle's first thought – amongst the shock – was for a cigarette. Shakily, she lit a pre-rolled one, mentally chastising herself for her error.

Hyperventilating a little, Michelle stalled twice whilst trying to manoeuvre herself out from the road's centre. A quick U-turn, however, and she was back driving along Beggar's Hollow. Again, there was nothing out of the ordinary. Michelle drove slowly – steadily – cranking the radio up louder for comfort – New Order's 'True Faith'.

Then, a glint.

From out of the corner of Michelle's vision, a shaft of light quickly expanded to blind her. Fighting to see, she pulled over beside the ditch that ran parallel to the road. As the radio continued to play, she squinted through the trees. But there was nothing to see. Even the light had faded.

Michelle felt overcome – a feeling she could not explain, but one that was becoming all too common. Just as she'd felt compelled to help the girl in the black lace dress, as she'd felt allowing the boy to flee the warehouse fire, Michelle felt drawn into Sullen Woods. Exiting her Mini, she slammed the door to lock and before she knew it, was traipsing through nettles and brambles.

With no destination in mind, Michelle walked until her toe clipped a brick. Itself seemingly randomly placed, she knelt to inspect it. The brick was old. Weathered; its corners had become rounded. Upon its uppermost side, the word '*Elyon*' had been carved. Gauged deep, the lettering was imperfect, as if scratched by a key. Michelle recited the word aloud.

'"Elyon".'

No sooner than she had, Michelle found herself back at her newly designated desk within Ashfield Police Station; the mapping software's hourglass rotating. Only the reflection of the brick remained – miniscule and shrinking – upon her pupils. She hadn't even blinked, or, at least, was not conscious of doing so.

'Oh, for God's sake!' exclaimed Shaz, and Michelle jolted.

Peering over the partition between them, Michelle could see that Shaz had spilt her coffee, but she already knew this – she had seen it all before. Shaz, continuing to swear, slid her bin out from under her desk to catch the streaming brew.

Michelle collapsed back into her chair. The time on the clock opposite read a little before quarter past ten.

❧❦☙

<u>Monday 10th November 1997, 10:12am, ASHFIELD POLICE STATION, ASHFIELD, LONDON.</u>

Eyes trailing down past her computer's monitor, where the location of Beggar's Hollow was pin-pointed, Michelle picked up the tiny scrap of paper from beside her keyboard. She stood – just as she had before – although this time shaking in the extreme. Silent, yet determined, she left the office without a word – just as she had before.

'Michelle!' Kevin shouted after her. 'Michelle!'

*

A fifteen-minute drive – only delayed by the set of temporary lights installed on the high street. This was all very familiar. Driving faster than she had done, Michelle did not drive the length of Beggar's Hollow this time. Instead, she pulled over in the exact same spot as she had previously – only her beige Mini was facing the opposite direction.

'We're going back an entire decade with our next track,' spoke the radio station's presenter. 'Released in 1987, New Order's, True Faith, peaked at number four—'

Michelle did not close her car's door – the action was superfluous to her burning desire. Jogging through the undergrowth, she let the brambles tug and tear and the nettles sting. As she was looking for the brick, it did not clip her toe. Half-hidden by a tuft of grass, she found it just as she'd hoped. Michelle knelt.

'*Elyon*,' she spoke, wiping the brick clean.

Nothing happened – not that Michelle knew what to expect. Looking around, she reached into her trench coat's pocket to retrieve the note. She unfurled it to read:

'"Elyon, Shaddai, Yahweh, Elohim".'

Michelle took a presumptive step forward; a building was revealed. Where there had been trees, there were no more. As if focusing a lens, the property appeared like a mirage to then impose upon everything surrounding it. Three storeys high, the Georgian townhouse was out place – out of time, even. Old in style, it yet appeared new in construction. A set of five steps led up to a central doorway. Covered by a porch, its pediment was held up by pillars. The house's number – number one – had been gracefully daubed upon a glazed tile beside its door, confirming the address. With all its curtains drawn, the dappled autumn sun was blocked from entering by heavy crimson velvet.

Trance-like, Michelle went to ascend the steps. Her shoes clicked imposingly on the stone. The air was still, the scene dreamlike. Not even a leaf – of which there were few – rustled.

Michelle dared not blink. Her eyes watered as she fought the urge, but she did not yield. She would not – if she could help it – allow this to become *Groundhog Day*. Michelle was unsure whether the action of blinking had somehow triggered her earlier time-jump, but she would not risk it.

Michelle licked her lips in anticipation. She took one last drag from her rolled cigarette, disposing of it over her shoulder, and with stiff fingers reached for the eagle-shaped knocker. She rapped its brass thrice.

Waiting, Michelle retreated down a step. Then another, and another. In hushed tones, she berated herself for her silliness. She was a detective inspector – by rank, at least – why should she possibly be so anxious?

The front door was swiftly opened by an elderly gentleman with a large nose and thinning hair.

'Hello,' Michelle blurted. 'What am I doing here?'

The old man smiled, and Michelle suddenly felt intrusive. It seemed likely that she'd pulled him away from an armchair in front of the television.

'My name is Mr Magnus, but you can call me Albe. I've been expecting you.'

His reply was matter-of-fact.

'I was just here,' Michelle spoke, plainly.

'It's interesting that you should say that, my dear. You may have been.'

The man spoke with an air of unashamed enjoyment, his blue eyes twinkling with youthfulness, within an otherwise ancient face. He then bounced back to open the door wide with a sweeping movement.

Cautious, yet throwing caution to the wind, Michelle bowled over the threshold, keeping the man in her sight all-the-while and sizing him up as best as she could. He was at least eighty years of age and dressed in a smart red shirt and tie that matched the shade of the curtains. If need be, Michelle thought, she could defend herself against him. She just wouldn't accept any brew or refreshment offered to her – as was a rookie error.

Michelle hovered in the hallway as Mr Magnus closed the door. It made no sound. She would not turn her back on him, but the desire to blink was becoming overwhelming. The elderly gentleman took off down the hallway at an extraordinary pace – a jovial hop to his step. Uneasily following behind, Michelle slid down after him, in his shadow.

Though not endless, the hallway was more a corridor. Elongated, narrow and paradoxical in length, its proportions seemed impossible for the building's dimensions. On their upper halves, the walls were papered beautifully in deep maroon, its pattern reminiscent of a William Morris design. Their bottom halves – in keeping with the floor – were clad in dark wood panelling that was varnished and gleaming.

There were at least fifty doors, each identical, that led off from the hallway on either side, and one final door right at its end. There were no windows, and without electric lighting, the hallway was instead lit solely by wall-mounted candelabras. The wax from them had collected generously to form inch-thick crusts.

The fifth door along, on the right, and Michelle was ushered through. She backed inside – uncomfortably so – as Mr Magnus shut the door behind them. As with the front door, there'd been no squeak, not even the slightest creak.

As Mr Magnus passed her, Michelle turned with him, and her jaw dropped. She blinked, but the sight remained. Preposterously sized; not only was it not possible for this room to exist within the Georgian property, but there was no way for it to even exist off the hallway from which Michelle had entered. Like the hallway, its length was of incredible distance. And the height was immense. Storeys of books, all accessible by ladders and walkways, reached up and up. Volumes and tomes littered every surface, of which there were many – tables, sideboards, cabinets of curiosities. If Michelle had been able to see properly in the candlelight, she would have seen books piled down from the ceiling also, where they were unnaturally held there.

'Welcome to the Library!' Mr Magnus declared.

Arms spread with pride, the old man fell back into the comfort of an old leather armchair. Michelle gawked at him.

'Well, don't just stand there, gawking,' Mr Magnus reprimanded. 'Come in, take a seat, settle down.'

'I don't – this doesn't – how – but – where are we?' Michelle spluttered.

'This is *the* Library,' Mr Magnus reaffirmed – perplexed, his brow furrowed. 'Did I not say that already? You'll have to excuse me, I'm getting rather old.'

'No, you did say that already.'

'Then why are you making me repeat myself? Come in, take a seat, settle down.'

Whether out of confusion, or lack of any real reason not to do so, Michelle did as was instructed and perched on the armchair opposite Mr Magnus. With many feet between them, she was still not far from the door – she could still escape, if necessary.

For a moment, both sat in silence. The old man straightened his tie and Michelle took her eyes off him – just for a moment or two – to read the few book titles nearest to her. *Mediums and Clairvoyants: A History of the Gift; The Origin of Species* – the copy appeared incredibly old and fragile. Possibly a first edition, it was surely rare and definitely priceless. *Ars Goetia, The King James Bible, Demonology* – a hefty tome, it gave off a bad vibe. *The Bunney-Fluff's Moving Day* – a Ladybird book, that probably provided a spot of light reading, amongst the heavier materials.

'You're wondering what you're doing here, aren't you?' asked Mr Magnus.

He had spoken kindly, but it was clear from his demeanour that he intended to steer the conversation.

'Yes, that is really the first question that comes to mind,' Michelle agreed – ungluing her sweaty palms from the leather. 'And I'll be the one asking them, thank you. What – what am I doing here?'

Mr Magnus shook his head and smiled. This irritated her.

'Let us not turn this into an interrogation, Miss Davey,' Mr Magnus replied, with a sigh. 'Why is it always the persistent types?'

This question, in no doubt reference to her, was not directed to anyone. Michelle, too, shook her head slowly, but confused.

'Would you care for a coffee? A Bourbon, perhaps?' Mr Magnus continued. 'And I mean the biscuit, not the whiskey – so don't get excited.'

He eyed her warily as he said this, almost judgingly so.

'No, thank—' began Michelle, remembering her vow to not accept beverages from strangers, before asking, 'How do you know my name?'

Mr Magnus smiled from ear-to-ear.

'I know the names of all of your kind, my dear. Well, most.'

'My kind? What does that mean, my "kind"?'

Promptly, Mr Magnus removed himself from his armchair to leap across the room. Michelle instinctively tensed. He bypassed her, however, moving towards a desk a few dozen feet away. For a man of such a great age, he was surprisingly spritely.

'Think of me as your go-between!' Mr Magnus hollered. 'Your line manager, if you will.'

Bounding back over to her, a biscuit tin in hand, he proceeded to shake it enthusiastically under Michelle's nose. She pushed it away.

'Line manager? Line manager to what?'

Not accepting her declination, Mr Magnus shook the open tin ever closer.

'I'm your guide.'

Once again, Michelle pushed the tin away. The biscuits inside rattling; they were fast turning into crumbs.

'My "kind"? My "guide"? Stop evading the question, please.'

'I am your advisor. Part-time Agony Aunt.'

Mr Magnus shook the tin one more time, and Michelle slammed a fist into its side to send it flying across the room. Its contents rained down in amongst the stacks.

'Stop it, damn it! Stop – stop, all this,' Michelle exclaimed – waving her hands about in annoyance. 'Stop it and answer my questions like a normal person. For the love of God.'

Appearing unperturbed by her outburst, Mr Magnus sprang back over to his own chair. He produced a Bourbon from his trouser pocket and crunched upon it before continuing.

'You're special, Miss Davey,' he spoke – his mouth full. 'Though I do hate that word, "special" – it implies something more than what it is. *Different,* is perhaps a more appropriate word. For everyone is special in the eyes of—'

'So, you're what?' Michelle interrupted. 'Like a spirit guide or something? My Dumbledore to your Harry? Bond's M? Gandalf? Professor X? Mr Miyagi? Glinda? The fucking Cigarette Smoking Man? What? How do I know that you're not just some figment of my imagination? Something I've fished out the bottom of a bottle?' Michelle paused for breath. 'Excuse me, Obi-Wan Kanobi, but you're not my only hope, so please, don't act like it.'

'All very good references, Miss Davey. Really, they are some good choices,' Mr Magnus gushed, clapping his hands together before clasping them into prayer. 'I am not your only hope. Others have fared – and are faring – just fine without me, but the very fact that you even suggest that I, could be, just a figment of your imagination, all but confirms that you could benefit from my guidance. I am a truth-seeker, Miss Davey. A philosopher, if I may be so bold as to claim such—'

'Mr Magnus, I—'

'Please, call me, Albe,' Mr Magnus implored. 'Did I not say that already? You'll have to excuse me, I'm getting rather old.'

He suddenly jumped up again, and Michelle stood also – to mirror him. She had no qualms in restraining this pensioner if he became hostile. Darting past and around her chair, Mr Magnus slid himself between its back and the bookshelf behind. Michelle swivelled on the spot, as to keep him in eyesight – backing away all-the-while, until her legs hit the cushions of Mr Magnus's armchair. She toppled into it.

From her new position, Michelle watched as Mr Magnus wheeled the ladder, that was attached to the bookshelf, towards him.

'Now, I do have something very special for you to look after,' Mr Magnus explained, as he sprung up the ladder. 'I'm entrusting you with it, so it's incredibly important that you do not lose it.'

Remaining silent, for she was still infuriated by him, Michelle suddenly caught sight of another book. This one, *Secrets of Jerusalem*, had been stuffed between the cushioned seat and right arm of Mr Magnus's chair. She stole a look back up at the strange man before pulling it free. Far too preoccupied in his quest to notice, he was busy pulling book after book from a shelf and throwing them to the floor.

Michelle opened the book's cover and flipped through its pages with her thumb, right through to the flyleaf. Nothing out of the ordinary; the volume appeared as any other academic text. A photograph of the author – Dr Jean Holloway – was displayed on the inside of its jacket. Bespectacled, beaming and blonde, the woman was young, with slight features and a thin mouth.

Michelle could hear Mr Magnus begin his descent and so crammed the book back between the leather. She tried to appear casual as he returned.

'A little something for you to deliver to Miss Turpin,' he announced. 'She's flagging rather behind – as were you, until only *moments* ago! But I can sense she's a slow learner; she may need some assistance in that department. Poor girl, Miss Turpin, everything considered.'

And with that, Mr Magnus held out his cupped, bony hands to her.

'It's a stone.' Michelle replied, flatly – puzzled.

'Yes, I suppose it is.'

Sounding impatient, Mr Magnus requested that Michelle take the stone from him by shaking it, much like he had done the biscuit tin, but she refused – she first wanted answers. Growing tired of her stubbornness, Mr Magnus dropped the stone within her lap and took a seat upon the chair in which Michelle had initially sat.

'So, is it just a stone?' Michelle asked.

Cautiously, she picked it up. Flat, black and circular; it fit within her palm, almost perfectly. She turned it over in her hands. Cold; it seemed entirely ordinary. Mr Magnus sucked his teeth and scratched his chin.

'It doesn't belong to you, does it, Miss Davey? It belongs to Miss Turpin.'

'No, I suppose it doesn't,' Michelle replied, meekly. 'But what does it do? Does it *do* anything?'

'To be frank, Miss Davey, that is none of your—'

'Yet, you expect me to deliver it to this … Miss Turpin? Whoever the hell she is.'

'Alas, even if I were to tell you, I doubt you would understand, let alone remember. It is powerful, my dear, you can be sure of that.'

Mr Magnus spoke with such certainty, that it was easy to understand why Michelle mistook it for arrogance. She sat forward in the chair.

'But it's just a stone? How can a stone be powerful?'

'What makes you so sure that it's "just a stone"?'

Michelle sighed.

'Because …' she began, before giving up on the argument. 'Who is this Miss Turpin anyway? Do I know her? Why can't you give it to her yourself? You still haven't told me who you are! Wh—'

'My name is Mr Mag—'

'Yes – yes – I know that! But I can call you, Albe! And, yes, you have told me that before, ancient buffoon!' Michelle exploded. 'I've had it just about up to here.'

Still holding onto the stone, Michelle stood, before continuing.

'I've seen things. Things I can't explain. I've not been able to eat – or sleep. I've had to drink myself to sleep for nights on end, because every time I close my eyes, I have nightmares – not that I can ever remember them. I'm smoking again. I'm on medication. I've been demoted – or, close to it! Now, you're going to tell me everything you know – or – or – I'm going to arrest you!'

All of a sudden, Mr Magnus began violently coughing. He looked pained and a small part of Michelle felt regret for her tirade.

'Arrest me?' he spluttered, wheezing.

Unwavering, Michelle fought through his coughing fit.

'I won't be lied to, Mr Magnus, nor do I appreciate being left in the dark, and if you have some explanation for all of this, I need – no, I deserve – to know.'

Whacking his back with a clenched fist, Mr Magnus finally surrendered.

'Patience is a virtue, Miss Davey. I would have explained it all to you, and over a nice mug of coffee at that. Although it is always preferred that you come to the realisation in your own time.'

He sighed. 'We all have our parts to play, be sure of that. We are just cogs in the wheel.'

Michelle opened her mouth to again protest his riddles, but Mr Magnus held a hand aloft to silence her.

'You, Miss Davey, are – let's opt for the technical term – a Spiritist!'

- CHAPTER XVIII -

You Like That, Don't You?

<u>Monday 10th November 1997, 15:52pm, BELLAMY AVENUE, ASHFIELD, LONDON.</u>

'Oi! Gay boy!'

Fred turned to see who had shouted. Obviously meant as derogatory, he'd disappointed himself by even reacting to the address. To his horror, it was Liam Pritchard – he must have followed Fred all the way from school, just waiting for the right time to pounce. Having been acknowledged, Liam sped up. Still, he walked with an unearned swagger.

Turning away, Fred quickened his pace also. He was nearly home and did not want to give his enemy the satisfaction of seeing him run. But before long, they were parallel. Fred swallowed.

'Hey, you alright?' he asked, trying to sound casual.

Fred did not care how Liam was feeling. He'd purely hoped that by being nonchalant Liam would be less of a prick – not likely. Liam produced a piece of paper from his pocket.

'What the fuck is this, Freddums?'

Fred eyed it, and him, warily. Folded into four, as neatly as Liam could have managed, none of the paper's corners quite met.

'I don't know what on earth you're talking about,' Fred answered, truthfully.

Liam pulled Fred backwards by his rucksack, jarring him to a halt. Fred then watched as he unfolded the paper, cleared his throat and recited aloud – displaying far greater confidence in presentation than he'd ever during class, despite mispronunciation.

'The Lesser Key of Solo-man, otherwise known as the Clav-ic-ula Salmon-is Reg-is, or Lemon-gate-on, is an anon-a ... anonan ... anonymon ...' Ultimately losing battle against the words, Liam gave up trying and skipped ahead to summarise: 'You and your pals are into some dark shit, Freddums.'

Fred responded only with an open mouth, and Liam laughed. Not usually one for patience, Liam had held onto the paper for a whole seven days, awaiting the perfect moment, and he was going to enjoy it.

'You're a very strange boy,' Liam grinned.

In mock jest, he slapped Fred hard on the back and drew him into a belittling embrace that lingered, uncomfortably so.

'Where did you get that?' Fred demanded, attempting to writhe free. He wanted nothing more than to deny the paper's existence.

'You're asking me? You and your pals printed it, Freddums,' Liam whispered into his ear.

'Yes, we did print it,' Fred conceded, bluntly and pulled away, his blood pressure rising. 'And so why do you have it?'

Fred snatched for the sheet, but Liam withdrew from reach. Snubbing the question put to him, Liam replied with his own.

'I mean, like, seriously, what shit is this? You trying to magic yourself a boyfriend?'

A silly and childish remark, it still produced the desired result. Fred's eyes watered as he fought off tears.

'I don't think you should joke. It's not something to be taken light—'

'*I'm* not something to be taken lightly.'

Stony-faced and serious, Liam maintained eye contact as he then slowly screwed the paper into a ball and flicked it at Fred's forehead. It bounced off, leaving Fred blinking.

'Well, if you've quite finished, I'm going home.'

Liam grabbed Fred's shoulder.

'No, you're not.'

'Yes, I am!'

Defiantly flinging Liam's hand off of him, Fred turned to march away. Everything considered, he now wished he'd accompanied Rye, Zach and Ally on their reconnaissance mission.

❧

<u>Monday 10th November 1997, 15:54pm, SULLEN WOODS, ASHFIELD, LONDON.</u>

Ally and Zach in tow, Rye led a path through the undergrowth and deep into Sullen Woods. The sun was sinking lower in the afternoon's sky and Rye quickened her pace; she had hoped to complete their mission before dusk.

'I still don't understand why Fred bailed,' Rye pondered aloud.

Breaking the silence, she'd looked over her shoulder to project her voice. They were nearing the lake, and her fear was spiking.

'He just didn't want to come,' Zach answered, from the back. 'And after Friday, who can blame him? Now that we're wanted arsonists – prime murder suspects – we'll probably all be featured on this week's *Crimewatch*.'

'Oh, I'm not worried about that,' Rye dismissed.

'What about Anoch? Are you worried about him?' Zach raised an eyebrow.

'Burned alive,' Rye squashed the topic. 'It's just that Fred had done all that research. He found "Male-AL10" on that chatroom, and now decides not to follow any of this up? I mean, why was Fred even on a chatroom in the first place?'

'Lots of people do it,' Zach replied – quick to his absent friend's defence.

'Do you?' Rye returned.

'Well, no, but—'

'I just don't understand why someone would choose to chat with random people. Fred has friends – he has *us*. Why would he choose to talk to strangers when he could just talk to us?'

Ally batted a rogue bramble away from her face, only for it to swing back and slap her around the cheek.

'Never mind Fred,' she spluttered. 'What am I doing here?'

Negotiating the pathway, Rye trampled a nettle to the earth. Readily, upon relinquish, it pinged back to sting Ally's knees, deviously targeting the strip of bare flesh between her knee-high boot and skirt. Ally cursed under her breath, but ultimately bit her tongue.

'For protection,' Rye affirmed

'For protection?' Ally repeated.

'I think we all know it was you that put us on the ceiling,' Rye commented, dryly.

As unpredictable as Ally had proven herself to be, she could not deny feeling safer within the girl's presence.

Ally said nothing.

'I know exactly why I'm here,' Zach mused.

Eyeing up Ally's long and shapely legs from behind, he was in no doubt.

For the next dozen or so footsteps, all three silently contemplated their presence and respective roles within their task. Rye, however, was the only one who went on to voice that.

'Someone or something gave me that message in the dirt,' she exhaled. 'We'd all gotten so bogged down in trying to find out *who* or *what* Anoch was that, until Fred, I'd completely overlooked the mystery of how I was given the name in the first place. *Whoever*, or *whatever* it was, was in the woods with me the night of Halloween.'

'Your birthday,' corrected Ally, rolling her eyes.

'And all this has nothing to do with Mick?' queried Zach.

Ally grimaced at the name's mention, remembering the look upon her ex-boyfriend's face as he'd met his maker.

'What makes you say that?' she asked.

'No real reason,' Zach admitted. 'But you don't think that Anoch and Mick are connected at all?'

'Oh, don't be dense,' Ally rebuked. 'The only thing connecting them was Anoch's claws. Anoch ripped Mick apart – may he rest in pieces! Mick was just a hateful leftover from my past – nothing more, nothing less.'

'Ally,' Zach began. 'You never actually explained what it was Mick did that was so awful. I mean, before trying to shoot you.'

Rye almost stumbled. She wished Zach hadn't asked the question so directly – not that she was one to lecture when it came to asking questions. Rye turned to shoot him a look as if to say, *'Quit whilst you're ahead,'* for she already knew the answer.

Ally stamped some nettles down from her path before matter-of-factly replying.

'He had my friend killed. Then, he raped me.'

*

'Why are you following me?'

Fred had repeated several variants of this question but was only met with laughter. He did not understand – Liam had no accomplice, no friend to share the joke with. What was so funny?

Three doors. Three doors down, and Fred would be home. Three doors. Three doors. With every step he took, he reminded himself of this. Two doors. Two doors. But Liam continued to trail. One door.

Turning onto his home's driveway, Fred all but ran up to the porch. He swung his rucksack off his shoulder and swiped for the pocket's zipper. The dirt within clogged under his nails as he scrambled for his keys. He groped them, momentarily, only for them to slip between his fingers.

Liam's hand tightened around Fred's right underarm. It was a cold day but sweat had managed to moisten both his shirt and blazer. Liam yanked, struggling to turn him against his will, for Fred – a stronger boy than he looked – stood steadfast.

Liam prised himself between him and the doorway. He pressed a palm flat against Fred's stomach. The action – unanticipated – was without comment and Fred froze as Liam's hand then travelled – sliding confidently downwards – past, below and under his belt. Before Fred could comprehend what was happening, Liam was fondling his genitals.

Skin against skin; Fred stood rooted to the spot. Liam had not restrained him in any way, he just could not bring himself to move. On some level, the fact that another male was intimately touching him was exhilarating, but the feeling of violation – of ownership – that feeling was overwhelming.

Liam's mouth was so close to his own that Fred could smell the tobacco on his breath. Fred worked his mind over every detail, as Liam worked his way over Fred's privates; Liam's buzz cut, his squinting eyes, and dirtied trainers. Fred wanted to move. Fred *couldn't* move – his thoughts would not connect to movement.

'You like that, don't you?'

Although a question, it had been stated as if it was a fact.

Fred's rucksack dropped to the front step. Locking eyes with Liam, he then finally endeavoured to push his hand away. Liam, however, insistently shoved further down his pants.

'Get off!' Fred yelled – his voice cracked.

He tried, but failed, to knee Liam in the crotch.

There were new voices – voices that Fred instantly recognised. His mother and sister were several houses away from them and approaching fast. Dangerously swinging her skipping rope, Mollie scampered ahead. Only missing the parked cars out of luck, she intoned some playground rhyme at the top of her lungs.

Liam gave Fred's manhood one final fondle before retracting his hand. He smirked a stomach-churning smirk as Mollie came bounding up to her brother. Fred's untucked shirt – the only indication to his violation – was easily overlooked.

'First comes love, then comes marriage, then comes a baby in a baby's carriage!' Mollie chanted.

She whipped Fred playfully – albeit painfully – with her rope.

'Mollie!' Fred roared. 'That fucking hurt!'

Clearly devastated by the reaction she had innocently triggered, Mollie's jaw fell, trembling. Both of her top front teeth were missing. Her pigtails wavered as she began to well up. Liam looked from one sibling to the other with a look of overly exaggerated dismay.

Fred's mother, finally catching up with her daughter, held her mobile away from her face to address her son. Expertly, she withdrew her own key from out of her designer handbag.

'Who's your friend, Freddums?'

'I'm Liam, Mrs B. It's so lovely to finally meet you.'

Caroline Bateman nodded, as Fred shot Mollie a quick glare, daring her to cry.

'Me and Fred were just—'

'Working on a project,' interjected Fred.

'Biology,' Liam added, with a subtle wink.

'That's right. Liam was just leaving.'

'Going OK, is it, this project?' Caroline asked, as she opened the front door.

Fred opened his mouth to ad-lib an answer. He felt obliged to lie, to lie to himself about what had happened, if only to convince himself that it hadn't.

'Mollie!' Caroline shouted, causing Fred to jump. 'Would you put those snails down! Come here, I have some wipes in my bag.'

'The project's going great,' Liam smiled, sweetly. 'Thanks for asking.'

'Yeah,' Fred hastened, flushing with colour. 'To be honest, it was kind of *forced* upon us – the last thing I needed. The subject's pretty dry and uninteresting.'

Liam laughed.

'Sorry, Sarah,' Caroline spoke into her phone again, suddenly remembering the person on its other end. 'I'll only be a minute.'

Juggling both her mobile and antibacterial wipes, she held the latter out to Mollie, who solemnly took one. True to form, Caroline breezed past Fred's comment with a self-centred soliloquy. He may as well have not responded at all.

'My day has been a right nightmare, Freddums – I was just telling Sarah. Sandra from work called to say that Lynette was under the weather, and so they needed me for Mrs Nicholls' ten o'clock – I hadn't even done my own hair by that point! How they expected me to toil over someone else's looking the way I did – I'll never know.'

What a martyr Fred's mother was. She barely worked, committing only to part-time hours at the local hair salon. Still, Caroline prattled on.

'Needless-to-say, muggins here dropped everything – gave Mrs Nicholls a nice do though. Mind you, would have been easier without Marco flitting around me all morning like a mosquito – flaming poofter. Why people like him can't just play it down, instead of shoving their lifestyle down other people's throats, I'll never—'

'I'll see you tomorrow,' Fred interrupted, speaking directly to Liam.

'Bet on it,' Liam grinned.

Infuriated by everyone and everything, Fred slid inside his warm home. He strode swiftly and silently upstairs to his room, taking no notice of his mother's 'no shoes inside the house' policy. What did it matter? Liam had just sexually assaulted him.

*

'Here's your pager,' announced Zach. Pulling it free from the gravelly mud, he flipped it over. With its back panel missing, the battery was orange with corrosion. Zach sighed. 'Well, it was a good present whilst it lasted,' he mourned. 'Was my first pager 'n' all.'

With that, he lobbed it into the lake.

Rye paced the clearing, lost in thought.

'OK, so I was sitting here,' she spoke. 'Quietly minding my own business—'

'Pissed outta yer mind more like,' said Ally. Leaning against a tree, she chewed upon a stick of gum.

Rye ceased her pacing. Growing ever more serious, she continued.

'Like I said – *quietly*. And then the lake turned black, and I was shoved up, and into, *that* tree.'

With a finger, Rye pointed to the oak against which Ally was leaning. Shifting her weight back onto the balls on her feet, Ally took a tentative glance up the trunk of the towering specimen.

'Bloody, damn hell,' voiced Zach, ceasing his skimming of stones to stare also.

Rye decisively walked up bedside Ally and to the base of the tree itself. Ally backed away.

'My shoes – *Pris's* shoes—' she held up her hands in confession '—fell off. Why aren't they here? Surely, they'd still be here?'

Rye spun around to face her friends, expecting them to offer an explanation.

'Why?' Ally countered. 'It's been ten days. They were probably carried off by a fox or something.'

Ignoring the logic, Rye began an inspection of the nearby bushes.

'Precisely, or "something",' Zach repeated, suspiciously. Like a television detective, he scratched at his chin.

'You think Anoch stole Pris's shoes?' Rye asked.

Ally groaned.

'Oh, come off it,' she berated. 'You're reading too much into everything. Not every single *shoe* is of significance.'

'OK, ignoring the shoes,' Rye relented, terminating her harassment of the shrubbery. 'Then I saw the message being spelt out in the dirt; *Anoch*. All in capitals.'

Bending to a crouch, Rye stroked the dirt. The letters had, of course, long since perished in the wind and rain. She crawled the few feet to the lake's edge and peered into its dark depths. In her pursuit of answers, Rye had done so without thinking – examining each element, singularly.

Everything appeared as it should. Twigs floated beneath a swarm of midges as a pond skater skipped. The odd branch stuck upright, firmly wedged. From out of the bank, a mass network of roots led Rye's eyes down through a thick cloud. She imagined the lake to be quite deep at its centre.

Rye blinked – or rather, she thought she must have. She could have sworn it was the lake which had done so, and not her. The sensation repeated, and it was then Rye saw it. She tilted her head as to misalign her reflection from that of a girl's face staring up from beneath the water. With long, beautifully curly, auburn hair, the girl looked not much older than herself.

Rye fell at Zach's feet, only to climb up his legs and tug at the hem of his duffle coat. He failed to move of his own accord and so Rye pulled him down to the ground beside her.

With Rye clutched to his side, Zach cast his eyes into the murkiness. Alas, he saw only their reflections beneath the midges. Ally too rallied next to them as Rye continued to mutely jab out with a forefinger. Like Zach, she too was unable to see anything other than the ordinary.

'Can't you see her?' Rye finally squealed, and Zach and Ally recoiled. 'She's right there!'

From behind her, both of Rye's friends exchanged looks.

'I can't see anyone,' Ally confirmed.

'Her face — it's right there!' Rye persisted.

Frustrated, she inched her own face ever closer to the water's surface and that of the girl's. The girl's image was so clear — so vivid — that for not even one second could Rye be in doubt.

'I — I don't like this,' Zach stuttered.

*

Having established that she was the only one able to see the girl, Rye had watched — conflicted — as the ghostly apparition had floated away into the distance from the bank. Out of desperation, and in an effort to chase her, Rye had resorted to awkwardly balancing along the trunk of a fallen tree. Slowly decaying, yet steadfast in the boggy waters, it bridged the lake's bank to its centre. This was all very much to the protestation of her friends. Zach had even tried to restrain her, but Rye had smacked him.

As she held onto one of the branches for support, it snapped, and Rye faltered. Close to slipping, she carefully knelt to rethink her strategy. Ultimately, she twisted and took to sliding along the trunk's length on her bottom.

Reaching the end of her available path, Rye paused. She shifted back onto her knees, gazing into the waters, and sure enough, the girl's image looked back at her. Slowed to a halt; the spectre seemed to have sought privacy.

'Hello?' Rye spoke, softly.

Her friends watched from the bank as she hunched. Zach shook his head.

'I think she's finally lost the plot,' he whispered to Ally.

'Definitely,' Ally whispered back.

Trying to coax a reaction, Rye stretched further and leaned lower. Overcome by sympathy and sorrow, she felt less afraid.

'Please, my name is Rye. You can talk to me – if you want?'

By the smallest of increments, Rye slipped forward, her bare knees providing little friction against the moistened bark. Her focus strong, she was unaware, however, and leant further still.

'I – I can see you. That's gotta mean something, right? They couldn't, but I can,' Rye continued, pleading. 'I was here the other week – do you recognise me? Was it you who gave me the message in the dirt? 'Cause I've – we've – met Anoch. We killed it.' The girl gave no reaction. 'But something else followed me home the night I was here. I'm not s-sure who he was, but he took my body – against my will. He … he used me somehow.' Rye sighed. 'I can feel your pain. It hurts me.'

Swoosh!

Suddenly, the girl's face and torso rose out from the water, arms outstretched. Dressed in a tattered, black lace dress, her shimmering and pallid complexion had become rotten and bloated the moment she'd crossed the waterline. The girl wrapped her lesioned arms around Rye's neck and in doing so caught her fall, which had been imminent. She turned Rye's head to one side and through puffed lips spoke into her ear.

'My name is Elizabeth.'

Despite seeing the girl holding her – touch her skin – Rye felt nothing. There was no feeling of touch, no wetness, nothing.

'Rye – Rye, are you alright?!' Zach hollered.

Both he and Ally once more exchanged looks. They'd just seen Rye's body stiffen and head turn, although she appeared alone on the fallen tree.

Desperately trying to reclaim calm, Rye fought flustered fear. Not daring to move, she forced out the necessary question.

'Wh-what – what happened to you? Who's Male-AL10?'

Before the girl was able to reply, however, a further pair of rotting arms emerged from the lake's waters to clasp either side of her torso. Both she and Rye let out blood-curdling screams.

Hearing only Rye's, Zach prepared for rescue by wriggling free of his duffle coat and blazer. Ally held him back.

Instinctively, Rye positioned her arms out in front as she was pulled from off of the tree's trunk. She was still held by the girl, and it was together they experienced the force of the third, as if being pulled by a magnet. Flailing as she hit the water, Rye collapsed atop the girl's decomposing face.

Rye could not be sure when the girl had disappeared, for she had closed her eyes, but once opened again, she was isolated. Gone was the girl and gone was whoever had pulled them. Bobbing, Rye thrashed about in panic.

'Get – get off!' Zach demanded, throwing off Ally's restrain.

Without removing his shoes, he hopped down from the bank and began wading over to his friend. Rye swam to meet him but struggled with her stroke. Even when her feet could reach the lake's floor, there was no grip to be found on the grime. As the pair met with an embrace, Rye's anguish gave way to sobs. Unable to speak, she choked; the sounds emitted comparable to those of a seal.

∿☝∿

<u>Monday 10th November 1997, 16:04pm, BEGGAR'S HOLLOW, ASHFIELD, LONDON.</u>

On the other side of the woodland, Michelle turned back to where the Georgian house had stood only moments ago. There were only trees. There was no house, no stone steps, no brass eagle knocker, no Mr Magnus, and the images of such were fast erasing themselves from her memory.

Ever so slowly, Michelle realised the scrap of paper held within her right hand, and her brow furrowed. It had been written by another:

'A.M. 1 Beggar's Hollow,
Say: Elyon, Shaddai, Yahweh, Elohim.'

What did it mean? It looked like an address. But where even am I? Michelle wondered.

'A.M. 1 Beggar's Hollow,
Say: Elyon, Shaddai, Yahweh, Elohim.'

- CHAPTER XIX -

Coincidental Synchronicity

<u>Tuesday 11th November 1997, 12:52pm, ASHFIELD TOWN LIBRARY, ASHFIELD, LONDON.</u>

Rye trotted through the grand entrance hall of Ashfield Town's public library, feeling conspicuous in her school uniform. She had removed her tie, but the effort was negligible. Checking the clock above the door to the main reading room, Rye had precisely forty-eight minutes remaining of her lunch break – she had to hurry. Like last time, Zach and Ally had offered to join her, but she had declined. They hadn't seen Elizabeth, and it was Rye that felt an obligation towards her. Elizabeth had sought privacy, and out of respect, she thought to honour that, for the time being, at least.

They had all updated Fred on the previous day's developments, but he'd seemed distant and nothing like himself at all. Rye did not think this unusual, everything considered. Fred had not offered his company.

Through the revolving doors and Rye made a beeline for the nearest computer. She made a hash of taming its swivel chair and, tripping over her cloth bag, fell into position. This invited a cough from the librarian. Rye waved a surrender before turning her attention to the login screen.

Wanting to avoid any and all conversation, Rye selected 'guest login' and typed in the number from her library card. Distributed through school, she had owned the card since age eleven but had yet to christen it. Rye could not remember the last time she had visited a public library, guessing she'd probably been a child.

'Ashfield Newspaper Archive, 1915 – present.'

The database took several attempts to open. Like the computers within Rye's school's library, this one was proving just as laggy. Overwhelmed by the number of fields and search criteria, it was beginning to dawn on Rye that she had very limited information to go on.

'First Name. Surname. Date of publication (+/-) years. Location. Journalist. Keywords. Gazette/Advertiser.'

Rye typed 'Elizabeth' into the first field and hit enter. Naturally, her attempt yielded more than two hundred and fifty entries; Rye slumped in her chair. After scanning the first few results, she clicked back. It was unlikely that Elizabeth Fox winning first place in the Middlesex inter-schools cross-country in 1967 was of any relevance.

Refining her search this time, Rye hopelessly added 'murder' into the keywords field. One hit. Fervently, she clicked the article. Ashfield Gazette, 20th January 1986, page six; 'Murdered Eliza from Haringey – Brother detained.'

Rye skim-read the article:

The brother of Eliza Morris has been taken in for questioning by the Metropolitan Police. The torso of Miss Morris was discovered in a holdall, floating in the Thames near the Isle of Dogs last Thursday. Yesterday evening, Mr Thomas Morris, 27, of Grange Avenue, Camden Town, was arrested on suspicion of her murder. The case continues.'

This story was close, but not close enough. And there was no picture.

Defeated once again, Rye replaced the word 'murder' with 'missing' in a sudden change of tactic. If her Elizabeth's death was unexplained, maybe even unknown, it was possible that she might still be listed as missing.

ঌ✋ঌ

<u>Tuesday 11th November 1997, 12:53pm, ASHFIELD POLICE STATION, ASHFIELD, LONDON.</u>

As if her new role was not tedious enough already, Michelle was reduced to tidying and filing. Sorting through old case files, she was tasked with moving them from a cabinet on one side of the office to the storeroom on the other. Monotonous and mind-numbing, Michelle could almost feel her brain cells atrophying.

There she sat, on the floor beside the cabinet, cross-legged and uncomfortable, amid stacks. For the past two hours, she'd been first categorising and alphabetising hundreds of paper sheets.

'Got you a coffee, partner.'

The voice – Kevin's – spoken into Michelle's ear, caused her to drop a carefully organised wad. Growing overly jumpy in recent months, her anxiety was only worsening. And her medication was not helping any. Most of yesterday was a blur and so she'd decided to stop taking the prescription. She intended to inform her GP of the purported side effect, if she ever got around to making another appointment.

Michelle turned.

'Sorry, I mean, *ex*-partner,' Kevin corrected himself.

He spoke politely but his smile was gross. Crouched behind her, he held a steaming mug in his hands.

'Thanks, pal,' Michelle replied, loudly, offering a reluctant smile.

All too aware that DCI Goodfellow's office was mere feet away – its door wide open – Michelle took the brew and placed it on the floor. Their superior had yet to confront her over yesterday's absence, but she considered it only a matter of time. Kevin strutted off, hands in pockets.

'*Dick-head*,' Michelle seethed.

Sceptical, she took a strong sniff of the beverage. Michelle half-expected it to be laced with poison, or at the very least some kind of laxative.

Returning to the task at hand, Michelle re-collected her dropped sheets into their cardboard folder and thrust it atop a two-feet-high pile. Staggering to her feet, she adjusted her skirt and blouse and bent down to lift the stack. Unsurprisingly, it was incredibly weighty.

Michelle expertly meandered a course between desks and colleagues. Pardoning and excusing herself appropriately, she squeezed past Scott, the post-boy, and his trolley, several DIs and Harriett Frost from Human Resources.

Approaching the door marked 'Archived Material', Michelle's arms felt as if they could give up on her. She shifted the stack further down her forearms and reached for the knob. It would not turn. Desperation mounting, Michelle tried it again – no luck. Famous amongst the station's employees as a decidedly dodgy door, no-one quite knew the knack for opening it. Muscles aching, Michelle kicked. Still, it did not budge.

It was a difficult balancing act, to be sure, and Michelle should have sat the pile down. Instead, she leant against the wood and pushed her whole body's weight against it. Simultaneously, she wrestled with the knob.

'Come *on*,' she growled. 'Piece – of – absolute – crap.'

Click.

The door relinquished its position, and Michelle tumbled through, her stack splaying out. Falling to the floor, her head collided with the corner of an overflowing box. Paper sheets fluttered gracefully down all around her.

Shaken, Michelle clambered to her feet whilst clutching her forehead. It hurt like hell, but she was still startled to see a small amount of blood on her palm. In anger, she kicked the box, denting it. Several sheets poked out of the file nearest to her and so Michelle stuffed them back inside their sleeve. Moving onto the next, she repeated the process.

*

Three hits. Rye selected the first and began scanning its content before slowing and realising that she may have found what she'd been looking for:

'Ashfield Gazette, cover,
Thursday 31ˢᵗ July 1997,
FEAR FOR ELIZABETH THACKERALL, MISSING FOR SEVEN DAYS.

Elizabeth Thackerall, 18, of Dragnell Lane, Ashfield, disappeared from her parent's home on the night of her birthday, Thursday 24ᵗʰ July. Elizabeth – Lizzie, to her friends and family – was last seen by her mother at around seven-thirty pm. It is suspected that she may have climbed out of her bedroom window after an argument. She was not seen leaving the property.

Elizabeth was last seen wearing a grey sweatshirt – an emblem of Mickey Mouse in its centre – and dark-blue jeans. Police are circulating a photo of Miss Thackerall, (opposite), in an appeal for witnesses.'

Rye's eyes tore across the screen to the badly scanned image of the girl. Unlike the article's description, Elizabeth Thackerall appeared in a tank top, behind a table in a restaurant. She was smiling. Rye wanted to convince herself that this had been the same girl from the lake, but she could not be sure. Either way, when Rye had spoken with her Elizabeth, she had been wearing a dress – or rather, the remains of – and not a sweatshirt and jeans.

Rye hastened to continue reading.

'Miss Thackerall is described as approximately 5ft 5ins, with long, curly auburn hair and light brown eyes.'

'That's more like it,' Rye whispered to herself.

'A recent graduate of St Anthony's College, Hatfield — a private school for the gifted and talented — Miss Thackerall has been described by her former Headmistress, Mrs Theobald, as "an exceptionally bright and funny girl". She had already secured herself a place at De Montford University, Leicester, to study Creative Writing — a course due to commence in October this year.

The Metropolitan Police has urged anyone with information as to Elizabeth's whereabouts to come forward, by contacting them directly on 0181 772 6467, or Crimestoppers, anonymously, on 0105 623 267.'

Quickly moving onto the second article, Rye — for lack of a better word — was hooked.

*

Inside the small, cupboard-like room, Michelle refastened a photograph of a sour-faced girl with long, black locks, back onto the respective form. 'Summer Murphy, Age: 19' was then consigned to a folder.

Working her way clockwise, systematically through the devastation, Michelle retrieved yet another photo from the floor, where it lay, upside down. The label on its reverse read, 'Elizabeth Thackerall, Age: 18.'

Michelle turned it over, intending on simply reattaching it to its form also, but then she saw the photo's subject and her mouth gaped. Hauntingly familiar, Michelle recognised the face, instantly — *instinctively*. It was the face from her dreams, or more accurately, her nightmares. It was the face from within the car in Dragnell Lane. It was the girl in the black lace dress.

Amid a dimly lit restaurant setting, the girl sat innocuously within her creased photograph, a pint of cola upon the table in front of her. In a red tank top, she appeared the air of teenage sophistication. Her face so full of expression, she looked happy —

so full of life. This bore a stark contrast to the blank dull eyes and vacant expression she displayed in Michelle's subconscious.

Michelle turned the photo back over in her hand.

'*Elizabeth Thackerall*,' she whispered.

Michelle let all the other forms fall back to the floor, allowing them to disperse in a flurry once more. Hurriedly, she read Elizabeth's coversheet, trying to absorb every detail:

'Name: Elizabeth Marie Thackerall.

Age: 18.

D.O.B.: 24/07/1979. Sex: F. Ethnicity: IC1.

Address: 23 Dragnell Lane, Ashfield, London, AN2 0SX.

Home telephone number: 0181 366 2417

Date of disappearance: Thursday 24th July 1997 (actual/ ~~*approximated*~~*)*

Time last seen: 19:30pm (~~*actual*~~*/ approximated)*

Time discovered missing: 21:30pm (~~*actual*~~*/ approximated)*

Last known whereabouts: Home address.

Description of missing person: Oval face, thin, shallow nose. Pale, with freckles concentrated towards the nose.

Height: 5ft 5ins.

Hair colour: Auburn, light brown/ginger. Tightly waved. Longer than shoulder length.

Eye colour: Light brown.

Clothing: Grey, long-sleeved sweatshirt. Large emblem of Mickey Mouse's face, face-on, in the centre. Dark-blue, boot-cut jeans.

Reported to (signature & role): DS Sharon Knight.

Reported by (signature & relationship to missing person): Ann Thackerall (mother).'

*

'Ashfield Gazette, page 3,

Tuesday 12th August 1997,

Investigation Continues for Missing Ashfield Teen.

Metropolitan police have so far drawn a blank in their investigation into the disappearance of teenager, Elizabeth Thackerall. CCTV footage has so far proven unhelpful, with every reported sighting wrongly identified.

Mr Peter Thackerall, Elizabeth's father, released the following statement yesterday afternoon, appealing for witnesses. Through tears, Mr Thackerall pleaded, "I want my Lizzie home. She needs to be home with her family. If anyone has any idea where she may be, I beg you to come forward. She's our daughter — our little girl. Just bring her home, please. Bring her back to us, safely."

The investigation continues.

The Metropolitan Police has urged anyone with information as to Elizabeth's whereabouts to come forward, by contacting them directly on 0181 772 6467, or Crimestoppers, anonymously, on 0105 623 267.'

This article, too, was accompanied by the same grainy image of the missing teen. Rye opened the final article:

'Ashfield Gazette, page 12,
Monday 25th August 1997,
Elizabeth Thackerall: Missing One Month.

A lack of new evidence has stalled the investigation into missing Ashfield teen, Elizabeth "Lizzie" Thackerall. A month after the disappearance of the 18-year-old on 24th July — her birthday — and the case is threatening to falter. Miss Thackerall was last seen at home, by her mother, on the night in question.

DS Sharon Knight, of the Metropolitan Police, has made a fresh appeal for witnesses to come forward. Anyone with any information is urged to contact Ashfield Police directly on 0181 772 6467.'

Rye was aghast; no image accompanied the article this time. Within the space of four weeks, Elizabeth Thackerall had been reduced from front-page news to a mere two-paragraph segment surrounded by advertisements.

Rye removed her diary and a pen from her bag. Past entries and etchings, she thumbed to a new leaf. It was beside a sketch of the bloated, dead Elizabeth, that she transcribed the latest article word for word, and at painstakingly slow speed.

Writing the date twenty-fourth of July upon reaching it, Rye paused. She recognised it. Why did she recognise it? She flicked to the back of her diary and the bumf of loose papers she kept there, as an appendix. Between the printed pages of the Ars Goetia, she found what she was looking for – the screengrab from, 'Random Teen Chat,' that Fred had given her yesterday. *Male-AL10.'* The profile's last login date matched perfectly to that of Elizabeth's disappearance. This had to be more than coincidence.

Looking back at the computer screen, and—

'Guest login has expired. Please contact the system administrator for support. © Copyright 1997 E.Y.E. Computer Technologies.'

Within a second, the monitor had turned black before returning to its initial screen. Frantically, Rye retyped her library card's number, but to her dismay was only met with the same message.

Taking to her feet, Rye strode across to the main desk. Thin and hunched, the twenty-something librarian sat behind – her face depressingly buried in a tattered copy of a Mills & Boon novel.

'Hello? – Hi,' Rye began, only to lower her voice. 'The computer terminated my guest login. Could you fix it, please?'

'If by "fix" you mean sign you up for an actual login, then yes, I certainly can.'

'Brilliant!' Rye beamed, enthusiastically, and the librarian aggressively pressed a finger to pursed lips. 'I mean, *brilliant,*' Rye repeated, in a whisper.

Eagerly, she slid her library card across the desk.

'You're sixteen, correct?' the librarian asked, reading Rye's birthdate.

'Yes, I'm sixteen.'

The librarian looked down at Rye from over rounded glasses, revealing prematurely formed crow's feet.

'Do you have an adult with you who can sign the terms and conditions for usage?' she asked.

'Are you kidding?' Rye exclaimed – again, louder than intended.

This only irritated the librarian further, who shook her head despairingly.

'I am most certainly *not* kidding.'

Infuriated, yet desperate, Rye attempted to wrangle.

'Can't you just, I don't know, ignore that tiny part? Just this once?'

'I have already chosen to ignore the fact that a sixteen-year-old schoolgirl is not at *school* on a Tuesday.'

Rye froze, taken aback by the truth delivered by a woman hardly a half-decade older than herself.

'OK, well, let's keep ignoring *that*,' Rye breathed. 'Do you have the hard copies of the newspapers uploaded to the archive?'

*

Michelle dashed out of the Archive Store, leaving her mess discarded. Nursing her forehead with her right hand whilst grasping Elizabeth's file and photo in other, she headed right across the office and over to Shaz. Uneasy on her feet and still slightly dazed, Michelle arrived at her colleague's desk breathless and distressed.

'Shaz,' she began. *'Elizabeth Thackerall.'*

Michelle held up the file as a further explanation and, ignoring her friend's customary beaming smile, physically injected the cardboard into the conversation before Shaz even had a chance to properly greet her.

'I'm sorry?' Shaz excused.

'Elizabeth Thackerall. Who is she?' Michelle demanded, continuing to freak her colleague with abruptness. Wheeling over a vacant chair, she plonked herself down.

'Missing teenager, eighteen. Disappeared from home, in the middle of summer. Why—'

'Why isn't this being followed up?'

'Michelle, she's an adult,' Shaz explained, looking up from the form. 'Do you know how many adults are reported missing every day in London alone?'

There ensued a short silence wherein Michelle let the question hang. She knew the answer, but it wasn't good enough.

'What happened to your head? It's—'

'She turned eighteen on the day she went missing!' Michelle interrupted. 'She's barely even an adult!'

'Sssh, Michelle. Keep your voice down, please.'

Unbothered by the plea, Michelle picked up the photo from Shaz's desk. Transfixed, she stared Elizabeth right between the eyes.

'She's an adult, Michelle, and as horrible as it is, her whereabouts are not a priority. Children are; you know that. We investigated all the leads we had, we did everything we could. Statistically, the chances are that she left home of her own accord. Her laptop, mobile and chargers were all missing. It's likely she packed a bag – took them with her.'

Shaz warily eyed her would-be superior.

'An *eighteen*-year-old female!' Michelle stressed. 'Statistically, the chances are she was lured, surely – lied to – abducted, even! Statistically – by now – she's dead! How could this—' she held the photograph up to Shaz's face '— not qualify as a priority?!'

Michelle's voice was cracking, and at such high-volume, others were beginning to crane their necks to get a better look at her. Shaz lowered her own voice.

'The last person who saw her was her mother. And they were both at each other's throats, apparently.'

'What is that supposed to prove, exactly?!'

'Well, nothing, but it infers everything. It infers that she ran off.'

'Or homicide?!' Michelle shrieked.

'There was nothing to indicate homicide. We interviewed the parents, scoured their phones, emails, all that. They checked out.'

'What about cell tower pings?' Michelle asked. 'If she took her mobile with her, had it since connected to any towers? If she'd used it—'

'Elizabeth's mobile last pinged to her home's local tower at eight twenty-three pm,' Shaz confirmed, reading the report. 'The last handshake was an explicit detachment, indicating her phone was switched off.'

'I met her once.'

Michelle rasped the words and Shaz's face changed.

'Met her? Michelle, you mean you've seen her? Since she disappeared?'

Shaz immediately set Elizabeth's file down upon her desk and looked enquiringly towards her. Several seconds passed – and loudly so – as the ticking of the station's clock pressed the urgency of her question.

'No,' Michelle lied, flatly. 'I mean, I've seen her around, from before. Before she disappeared.'

It was a bad attempt to shrug off a weighted comment.

ᔓ🖐︎ᔐ

<u>Tuesday 11th November 1997, 15:46pm, KYNASTON GARD-ENS, ASHFIELD, LONDON.</u>

With all three newspapers stuffed in their entirety inside her cloth bag, Rye recounted her findings to her friends whilst walking home that afternoon. She had stolen the articles from beneath the pointed nose of the no-nonsense librarian and unashamedly so. Upon closer inspection, the photograph of Elizabeth Thackerall was a dead ringer for the girl in the lake.

Normally the first to offer fearful comment, Fred appeared wholly disinterested – distracted, even. He had barely said a word, not that Rye had given him much chance, for she was spouting an endless stream of conscious thought. Regardless, he still declined the invite back to her house and departed their company.

'My theory,' Rye shared, as she, Zach and Ally neared the end of her cul-de-sac, 'is that Male-AL10 is the one responsible for Elizabeth's death. If we find him, her or it, we've found the killer.'

'What's all this got to do with Anoch though?' Zach asked.

'I'm still not sure about that part,' Rye admitted. 'All I know is we have one dead demon, and two spirits to date, without any idea of how they're connected, not for sure.'

'It could be anything,' Zach replied. 'A run-of-the-mill murder, a Satanic cult, a sacrifice, a Satanic-cult-sacrifice.'

'"Anoch's toys now",' Ally quoted, 'How do we know that now the demon's dead, Male-AL10 won't come back, properly—'

'We don't,' Rye interrupted. 'We can't be sure of anything – what the—'

Exiting an old, grey Ford Escort, parked outside of their home, Pris had proceeded to strangely drape herself across its bonnet, in a faux modelling pose.

'Erm, Pris-*ter*, what are you doing?' Rye asked, upon approach.

'Do you like it?' Pris replied, stroking the metal.

'Like it? What do you mean? Is it – is this yours?'

Gobsmacked, Rye could hardly believe what she was seeing and hearing.

'It sure is,' Pris nodded, proudly.

The only one with any real interest in cars, Zach began encircling the five-door with blatant envy. Judging by the plate's registration, he guessed the vehicle to be about eighteen years old. The bumper was scuffed, and it only sported a couple of noticeable dents on the bodywork.

'Is it a one-point-three or a one-point-four?' he pressed, excitedly, and Pris's face drew a blank. 'Two-point-seven, maybe? Nought-to-sixty in five-point-five, right?' he smirked, impishly, before asking, seriously. 'Can I take a look?'

'Erm, sure,' Pris shrugged, as Zach extracted the keys from her hand.

'I didn't know you were even learning,' spoke Rye.

'Does it have an engine?' asked Ally, smiling. 'Or is it a Flintstones-type deal, where your feet stick out the bottom?'

Only Zach laughed, from the driver's seat.

'Ta-dah, surprise!' Pris beamed, with a wave of jazz-hands. 'I was taking lessons in secret. I only passed last week. Rye, are you surprised?'

'Well, I'm surprised you passed – yes. Surprised you were learning and surprised we can afford it. We only got the windows and oven fixed yesterday. Where did you get the money?'

A few months ago, the prospect of Pris owning a car would have thrilled Rye, but there were now more important concerns – a replacement television, for example. Pris had also still not bought Rye a present for her sixteenth. If the only reason they'd been eating chicken nuggets for the past eight months was so that Pris could buy a clapped-out banger, Rye deemed it not worth the sacrifice.

'I was hoping you'd be proud,' said Pris, her face sinking. 'We've got the money.'

Rye scoffed, then questioned further.

'Was it expensive?'

'It wasn't, actually. Trish from the bar – you know, Trish – her boyfriend, Thierry, works up at the garage on Cat Hill. He gave me a very good deal.'

'How much?' Rye and Zach both asked in unison.

'Never you mind,' replied Pris.

Zach tapped the eldest Turpin on the shoulder. She hopped off the hood and he lifted the bonnet.

'How many minors?' he asked, cheerfully.

'Fourteen, but I passed first time. And you know what this means, Rye? No more walking to school in the rain.'

Pris gave the bumper a pat and a gentle caress. Ignoring this, Rye carelessly altered the conversation.

'Pris, yesterday, we went to the lake—'

'I don't want to hear it.'

'But—'

'We agreed you'd never to go back there again.'

'But—'

'No, Rye! I thought we decided to put this whole charade behind us?'

Nearly taking off Zach's fingers, Pris slammed the bonnet closed, by way of emphasis.

'Do you even know what "charade" means?' Rye snapped back. 'This isn't make-believe! You witnessed it! And "we" never decided anything.'

'We're not having this conversation.' Pris shook her head.

'You can't just pretend it didn't happen!' Rye shouted – her voice echoing all around the end of the cul-de-sac. 'Just like I can't pretend that the spirit that followed me home that night – the spirit that *possessed* me – probably murdered a girl named Elizabeth Thackerall, whose corpse is most likely rotting at the bottom of that lake!'

Approaching her sister, Pris took her hands in her own.

'Rye, please,' she beseeched, eyes glistening. 'It's not our place to get involved. Just move on, and let ghosts lie.'

Rye, however, was having none of it and snatched her arms away.

'Move on? That's what you've done, is it? Is it, really?! Is that why you sleep every night with the light on? Why you wake up to check the front door a bajillion times?! Why every time I try to talk to you about it, you change the subject?!'

'I don't want to talk about it anymore!' Pris screamed.

Several birds took flight from their neighbour's tree – squawking, into the twilight. Rye had not heard her sister shout like that in years – not since they were children – not even at her birthday. Trying her best to compose herself, Pris brushed strands of stray hair back behind her ears.

'Is Zach staying for dinner?' she then asked, calmly.

'Prove my point, why don't you?'

Rye spoke calmly also, yet between gritted teeth. Adopting a stoic silence, Pris simply stared at her and Rye knew that, for now, the battle was lost.

'I – erm – I actually have archery practice,' Zach spoke up.

He pulled a tight, forced smile and slung his rucksack over his shoulder.

'No, you d—' began Rye.

'There's nuggets in the freezer,' Pris declared – also with a forced smile.

'I think we'll go to the chippy,' Rye strained.

'Don't expect a lift.'

❧✋❧

<u>Tuesday 11th November 1997, 22:53pm, MICHELLE DAVEY'S RESIDENCE, FLAT 1, 179A LONDON ROAD, ASHFIELD, LONDON.</u>

Another glass of wine and four painkillers later, and Michelle was beginning to feel marginally better. Since returning home, she had spent a good few hours pondering the existence of a flat, black and circular stone, which currently sat upon her coffee table. Discovering it in her trench coat's pocket whilst searching for her door keys, it had fit almost exactly in her hand's palm. Stuck to it was a

Post-it note that read: 'FAO Miss Turpin'. Its origin? Michelle did not know. She hadn't written it.

Miss Turpin – this mysterious stranger – was the latest in a long line of enigmas that plagued Michelle's life. Another piece of the puzzle, or just a part of something else entirely? Nonetheless, the Post-it was now stuck to her sitting room's wall, devoid of any detail other than one bullet point: 'stone'.

Slowly, Michelle got up from the sofa and crossed the room to her make-shift investigation board. Piercing a drawing pin through the woodchip, she attached a photocopy of Elizabeth Thackerall's missing person's report and photograph. There it joined the Post-it, map, Mrs Nicholls' holiday snap, a multitude of sketches, (depicting the unidentified, 'clawed-hand' bottle), and a scrap of paper, (of note, 'A.M. 1 Beggar's Hollow, Say: Elyon, Shaddai, Yahweh, Elohim.')

The board's latest addition unnerved her, and it was with an unsteady hand that Michelle drew a line connecting the report to the map, where Dragnell Lane had been highlighted. Although she had highlighted Beggar's Hollow also, Michelle knew there wasn't a property along the road. She had even checked, driving there to be sure.

Eyes glazed, Michelle stood upon tiptoes as to reach the very top of the wall. In large, squeaky letters, she then wrote her chosen heading; 'The Death of Elizabeth Thackerall.'

'Hmm, hmhm … hm, hm … hmhm-hmmm,' she hummed to herself.

- CHAPTER XX -

23 Dragnell Lane

<u>Wednesday 12ᵗʰ November 1997, 10:03am, DRAGNELL LANE, ASHFIELD, LONDON.</u>

Michelle took one final toke of her rolled cigarette before flicking it to the gutter. From inside her car, opposite number 23, she'd been staring at the property for her smoke's duration. She was still unsure how she would approach the situation; what she'd say and how she'd explain herself. There was no more time for procrastination, however – Michelle was due on the job within the hour.

Exiting, then locking her Mini, Michelle strode across the street in a matter of seconds, taking note that the builder's skip had since been removed.

Michelle rang the bell – an ominous single chime. Her apprehension was irrelevant, she reminded herself. She needed answers. *Elizabeth* needed answers. The door opened a crack and a woman drew her face to the gap.

'Mrs Thackerall?' Michelle asked. 'I'm DI Michelle Davey.'

The woman nodded, confirming her identity. She then temporarily closed the door and Michelle could hear the chain being disconnected. When it opened a second time, Ann Thackerall was revealed in full. A bob of blonde hair graced her head, and although undoubtedly an expensive dye job, it was in dire need of a touch-up. Her roots were showing.

'What's happened?' Mrs Thackerall wept, clutching her pearls. 'Have you heard from Lizzie? Please, don't tell me you've found a body.'

Her gaunt face stretched as she spoke; her vocal cords strained.

'No, I'm afraid I haven't any new information,' Michelle lied as best as she could. Although it was true, she knew not where her daughter's body was. 'I'm sorry, but can I come in? I'd just like to revisit a few details.'

Mrs Thackerall flicked back her hair.

'We were told there was nothing else to be done,' she replied, haughtily.

'That may have been what you were told, but I've been assigned the case now.'

Now, this was an outright lie, and one which Michelle hoped would not come back to bite her.

Without inviting Michelle inside, Mrs Thackerall turned on her heels. Michelle entered and clicked the door closed. She hovered awkwardly in the darkened hallway of the tight and narrow terrace, as Elizabeth's mother hollered up the stairs.

'Pete! It's the Police! They've come about Lizzie!'

Michelle could hear a newspaper rustle and the sound of a mug smacking down against a surface.

'No rush! There's no news!' Mrs Thackerall shouted again, before turning back to Michelle. 'Tea? Coffee?'

'Coffee, black. No sugar.' Michelle smiled. 'Please.'

Her choice was standard; she didn't like to overcomplicate things.

'Pete!' Mrs Thackerall shouted once more. 'Could you put the kettle on, please?! A black coffee for our visitor!'

Her thin frame supported by that of the kitchen door's, she then directed Michelle with a sweeping arm through to the front room. And Michelle obliged. Painted purple, with gold furnishings, the lounge appeared garish – tacky. Despite the efforts of a clearly house-proud Mrs Thackerall, she had not wholly succeeded in achieving the aspired luxurious aesthetic.

Michelle took up position on the black leather three-seater opposite the television set into the hearth. The sofa's cushions sucked her downward – they were too squishy to be comfortable.

'You'll have to excuse the mess,' Mrs Thackerall began, as she set about yanking open the curtains. 'No-one told us you were coming.'

The room was in fact spotless.

'That's OK, I really don't mind,' Michelle spoke, softly.

Having secured the curtains by way of golden ties, Mrs Thackerall then appeared lost. She smiled, but there was no feeling behind it. Leaving a large space between them, she hesitantly sat beside Michelle.

'If we could just wait for my husband,' she croaked.

Michelle nodded, crossed her legs and looked down at her shoes. Mrs Thackerall looked away as Michelle stole another glance, and so she took the opportunity to scan the room further.

Pictures of Elizabeth lined the mantelpiece above the television, as well as the wall above the armchair to her left. At different ages, they chronicled almost every year of the only child's short lifespan, from birth to adulthood: a babe in mother's arms; a toddler at the top of a slide; a cutesy Elizabeth aged around six, her auburn hair in pigtails, grinned as she held a melting ice lolly; on her grandfather's knee at Christmas, aged around eight. Several school portraits then froze the girl in time – each one progressed in awkwardness. Dressed in a leotard, another Elizabeth clutched a certificate. And finally, the photograph Michelle recognised, of the grown young woman in a red tank top, sat in a restaurant. There were no pictures of the family altogether as a unit – no group portrait. It was obvious that Elizabeth herself had been this couple's life.

'Pete won't be long,' Mrs Thackerall finally spoke again, breaking the silence.

Michelle swallowed.

'I won't stay long. I don't want to disrupt your morning any more than is necessary.'

Crossing her own legs, Mrs Thackerall huffed. She played with her hair, then picked at her cuticles – anything, to avoid conversation and eye contact. It was another few minutes until Mr Thackerall appeared, carrying three steaming mugs. He distributed them and Michelle muttered thanks. Mrs Thackerall said nothing.

Peter Thackerall was ageing well. Not only had he been lucky enough to retain his hair and hairline into middle age, but it remained thick. He too was auburn – a rusted red. Miraculously, his face remained free of wrinkles. No lines encroached around his eyes, unlike his wife's. He perched on the arm of the unoccupied chair.

'So, what are you doing here? PC, DC, DI …?' he asked.

'*DI*. DI Michelle Davey,' Michelle clarified, confidently. 'As I told your wife, I just want to go over the timeline—'

'That's all on record,' Mr Thackerall interrupted.

'It is,' Michelle conceded.

'Then read it,' he snapped. 'Do we really have to go through this all again?'

'What were you arguing about?' Michelle asked, addressing Ann Thackerall directly. If the ensuing conversation was to be strained – at best – she thought it wise to cut to the chase. 'On the night of Elizabeth's disappearance, July twenty-fourth – her eighteenth birthday. What were you arguing about?'

Mr Thackerall scoffed.

'What's the matter, Pete? Embarrassed?' his wife spoke. 'Embarrassed at having to tell another stranger about your indiscretions? Not as embarrassed as I am, you can bet on that.'

Fighting downward suction, Michelle pulled herself to the edge of her seat. She opened her mouth to speak but was cut off.

'*He*,' Mrs Thackerall said, pointing. 'My loving husband, was having an affair.'

'Oh,' Michelle managed.

'Some young intern,' Mrs Thackerall continued – her wounds still noticeably raw. 'Legs up to her armpits, and breasts,' she choked. 'Breasts like melons—'

'Please – Ann. This isn't helping,' Peter Thackerall implored, whilst simultaneously sounding bored by the subject.

'Tell me, DI Davey, do you have any children? A boyfriend? Husband?' Mrs Thackerall asked.

'No. I – erm – I don't. I can't say I've had the time.'

'Well, my advice is, have a caesarean and invest in a push-up bra, because it turns out that men only stay interested if everything's still tight and perky.'

Michelle choked on her coffee. The truth was, that aged forty-two, she thought her window of opportunity closed. Besides, Michelle had never desired children.

'Lizzie, she – erm – she found the texts on my phone,' Peter Thackerall ploughed onward. 'She confronted me about it.'

'But your file ... it says that Lizzie had an argument with you,' Michelle nodded to Mrs Thackerall. 'It says that you slapped her. How did it escalate to that, exactly?'

Michelle was only acting confused, for she had read all the statements over and over until she'd nearly memorised them word for word. She just wanted to hear it from the horse's mouth.

'That's true,' Ann Thackerall replied. 'I did slap her. I already knew that Pete had cheated, but he'd told me the sordid affair was over, and I believed him, stupidly. When I told Lizzie that I knew of his ... past dalliances, she began yelling at me – saying that I should have left him straight away – that I should have had more respect for myself. She – she was right up in my face, and I – I slapped her.'

With the admission, Mrs Thackerall's mug began to shake. Quickly, she placed it on the side table and tucked her hands under her thighs.

'What she said – it only hurt because it was true. I should have slapped you instead.'

Her voice stronger as she said this, Ann Thackerall removed her hands from under her thighs and began stroking her white cardigan. She pursed her lips as she stared at her husband, who had turned a shade similar to his hair.

'What happened next?' Michelle pushed.

Eager to keep the pace of exchange, she swallowed another mouthful of coffee.

'Oh, for goodness' sake, we've gone over this a hundred times!' Mr Thackerall shouted.

Gesturing, he sploshed a spout from his mug. It landed upon the cream carpet and Mrs Thackerall's eyes darted to it. Clasping a hand to his scrunched forehead, Peter Thackerall took no notice. His temples were visibly throbbing.

'Lizzie ran upstairs to her bedroom,' Ann Thackerall confirmed.

Evidently, she'd chosen to ignore the stain. It was the least of her problems and paled in comparison to the one that her husband had left upon their marriage.

'You didn't follow her?' Michelle asked.

'Not right away,' Mrs Thackerall admitted. 'I wish I had. I'll always have the guilt that I didn't. I needed to calm down, and so did she. When I came up later—'

'Around half nine?' Michelle interrupted.

'Yes. She was gone.'

Mrs Thackerall buried her head in her hands.

Michelle's heart bled for the woman. She hated stringing her along – stringing them both along. Michelle was feeding a false hope, simply by visiting them.

'You have no idea where she may have gone?' Michelle probed. 'Did Elizabeth have a boyfriend? Any friends?'

'This is ridiculous!' Mr Thackerall blurted, jumping up. 'You have all this information already. I'm sorry, Ann, but I can't do this. If there's no new information on Lizzie's whereabouts, then – I'm done. We're done.'

Stomping the few paces across the lounge over to his wife, Mr Thackerall swept her mug up from the table, before snatching Michelle's out from her hands. Ann Thackerall displayed no emotion to his leaving of the room but waited before speaking.

'No boyfriend that we knew of. She did have friends but none of them know where she went, or at least, that's what they claim. She got on well with everyone.'

'It says in the report that her laptop and mobile are missing. Was there anything else missing from her room? Clothes? A bag?'

Michelle was particularly interested in the answer to this question.

'I don't think any of her clothes are missing – other than those she was wearing. I still do all of her – sorry – I still *did* … all of her washing. I think that if any of her other clothes were missing, then I'd have noticed.' Mrs Thackerall sniffed. 'As for a bag, well … this is going to sound awful, but I just don't know. Lizzie had so many things.'

Mrs Thackerall plucked a tissue from a box beside her. Rather than blowing her nose, she proceeded to slowly tear it in half.

'I guess you could say that we spoiled her,' she continued. 'As she took her laptop and mobile, then it's possible she took more things with her.' Mrs Thackerall scrunched up both halves of her tissue. 'You know, as parents, we do all we can to raise them safely – shield them from life's cruelties. And then, without even realising it, they're facing them alone. You're no longer able to protect them – they're their own person. I guess, you can't relate.'

Michelle could not.

'It's the not knowing,' Mrs Thackerall explained. 'Every day is waiting – there's no end. I pray that she's found, of course. But if she was dead, at least then we'd have closure. I'm sorry, DI

Davey – is it? I think you should go. Unfortunately, on this occasion, I think my husband is right. If you have nothing new to tell us, then it's best you leave.'

No longer able to fight the pain and anguish, Mrs Thackerall began openly sobbing and Michelle knew she had outstayed her welcome. Brushing the crinkles from her skirt, Michelle stood and slung her handbag over a shoulder.

'Thank you for your time, Mrs Thackerall.'

Unable to speak, Ann held up her hands.

'I'll keep you informed of any developments,' Michelle assured. 'I'll see myself out.'

Exiting the lounge, Michelle found herself pausing at the foot of the stairs. A collection of framed certificates – wall-mounted – led the way up to the landing. They all belonged to Elizabeth. Tentatively, she placed a foot upon the first stair; the movement was soundless.

Horse riding, gymnastics – Michelle lifted her other foot, up level with her first. Clarinet, grade seven and eight – Michelle placed a foot on the second stair and craned her neck. St Anthony's College, winning debate team, 1995. Third stair, and the tread let out a loud creak. Horrified; she quickly reversed.

Michelle let herself out in a hurry. As much as she wanted to snoop, there was no way she'd be able to.

Back beside her Mini, Michelle slumped against it in relief. Reaching inside her handbag, she extracted a bottle – not dissimilar in size and shape to the one whose identity still evaded her. With a crack, Michelle broke the vodka's seal to neck the top inch.

It was then, whilst grappling with her car keys as she juggled the bottle, that Michelle noticed a small scrap of folded paper tucked under one of her wiper's blades. Anyone else would have assumed it to be a note from a peeved neighbour, perhaps angry for taking their parking space, but Michelle suspected differently. She whipped it out.

Written in the same neat and flowing dark-pink script as the previous note, presently tacked to her sitting room's wall, it read:

'A.M. 1 Beggar's Hollow,
Say: Elyon, Shaddai, Yahweh, Elohim.'

In a flurry, Michelle consulted her watch. It was a little before half ten. She was unsure whether 'A.M.' referred to the time of day at which she should visit the non-existent address, but if that was the case, then she hadn't a moment to lose.

In a spontaneous action, Michelle poured the remainder of her vodka down the drain. She would not give herself any reason to forget.

- CHAPTER XXI -

James 1:24

<u>Monday 17th November 1997, 08:44am, SCHOOL CAR PARK, ASHFIELD COMMUNITY SCHOOL, ASHFIELD, LONDON.</u>

Michelle's head felt packed with cotton wool. For the past week, gaps had been appearing in her memory, with huge chunks failing to register anything at all. Time would jump, and so would Michelle's location with it. She would fade out of darkness, to find herself in Sullen Woods, beside a road – *Beggar's Hollow*.

Michelle had collected a total of three notes. Each was identical in the message they bore, and all were tacked to her sitting room's wall. As a consequence, she had missed many more hours of the job – entire days, even. Not going unnoticed, DCI Goodfellow had called her into another meeting the previous Friday. Facing suspension, it was clear Michelle would not regain her former role any time soon. Promotion, if it hadn't been already, was out of the question.

Michelle's fear of suspension was nothing compared to her fear of the blackouts themselves, however. Convinced she was losing her mind, she would not admit this to Occupational Health, whom her superior insisted that she meet with.

Michelle took a gulp of vodka and felt the two painkillers she swallowed along with it slide smoothly down her gullet. She realigned her face as she slipped the small bottle back within her handbag. Its glass clinked off the flat, black and circular stone kept there. Her possession of it unnerved her. She wanted to be rid of it, and only carried it so she could do just that, as soon as the opportunity presented itself. But that wasn't all. Somehow – and Michelle had no idea how – she had acquired two bulky books. Heavy in her bag, she had discovered them therein the last time she had regained awareness within Sullen Woods.

The first, and by far thicker volume, was simply entitled *Demonology*. Bound in brown leather, it would not have looked out of place in a museum. Michelle, scared to have properly studied it, found it to contain ink drawings of the most hellish abominations, along with pentacles and words in a language she could not decipher. The second, and much newer text, *Mediums and Clairvoyants: A History of the Gift*, by B.M. Haegar was still significantly dog-eared. Like the stone, Michelle hated their mere presence. Yet she dared not part with them either and kept them close as a reminder that she'd not imagined them.

'Ashfield Community School, est. 1558.'

Michelle absorbed the sign's letters – faded with the years – as she contemplated all that she had to. PC Hollings was surely already waiting for her inside.

❧

<u>Monday 17th November 1997, 08:49am, MAIN HALL, GROUND FLOOR, ASHFIELD COMMUNITY SCHOOL, ASHFIELD, LONDON.</u>

'Would you rather fight one hundred duck-sized horses, or one horse-sized duck?' Zach garbled – to anyone who would listen – as the foursome, snug within the gaggle of their year group, trotted obediently along the corridor leading to the Main Hall.

Ally's mouth twisted into a half-smile.

'I dunno, Zach. What would you rather?' she asked.

'Well, that depends,' Zach pondered. 'In an enclosed space? The one hundred duck-sized horses – hands down. Not in the wild, though. In the wild, it would have to be the horse-sized duck.'

Ally laughed, but she was the only one to do so.

'Oh, my, how privileged we are to be given chairs this morning,' observed Rye, sarcastically, upon their entering.

'But o-o-of course, Miss Turpin,' interjected Mr Bullen. 'Got to crack out the f-f-fine china for the local constabulary, s-s-so to s-speak.'

Having been out of sight behind the door, their headmaster had not been out of earshot, however, and so Rye murmured a greeting.

'Nice to know it's for the Old Bill's benefit, and not us lowly peasants,' Zach whispered to Ally.

'Not a huge fan of the Old Bill myself, if I'm honest,' Ally admitted.

'Guess not, you crooked sister,' Zach japed.

As the school friends took their seats towards the back of the hall, Michelle Davey entered at its front. She had been offered the stage, but had declined, in favour of moving the lectern to the floor. Unpacking paperwork from her handbag, Michelle was careful to keep her alcohol and strange selection of books concealed.

'You've got to be kidding me,' Zach stressed. 'Is that who I think it is?'

'I dunno, who do you think it is?' replied Rye.

Looking left and right, Zach checked for his nearest exit. Alas, a teacher stood post by each door, like prison guards during visiting hours.

'It's the policewoman bird from the warehouse,' he clarified.

Sinking further down in his chair, Zach slumped as low as he dared.

'There's a tonne of students in here,' Ally attempted to reassure him. 'She probably won't notice you in the crowd.'

She patted him on the shoulder.

'Are you even listening to yourself?' Zach hissed. 'Because you might as well have said, "pick you out of a line-up". She's a bloody police officer!'

The others simultaneously shushed him.

'Would you stop it?' stung Rye. 'She won't notice you.'

Her relationship with Pris still at a stalemate, Rye had been ill-tempered for the past six days. Having made so much progress with identifying Elizabeth Thackerall last week, she had by now exhausted all possible lines of inquiry, and this had only infuriated her further. Rye was at a loss. There was nothing left within her power to do; she wasn't a police officer.

'Oh, yeah, 'cause "good observation skills" was only listed under "desirable" on her job description,' Zach air quoted. 'Jesus – I'm panicking. Like, I'm not usually the panick-er. Why aren't you all panicking? All four of us were in that CCTV footage. Fred, why aren't you panicking? – *Panick-er.*'

'She only saw you,' replied Fred, deadpan. 'It was dark, and the image was really grainy. You couldn't see our faces.'

'Way to make me feel better, mate. Cheers.' Zach scratched his head. 'Hey, Ally, how come your mug wasn't plastered over every rag after you escaped Heathrow, huh?'

'That,' replied Ally, 'is a very good question.'

Zach huffed and upturned the collar of his blazer. Although she might not ever know for sure, Ally silently thought the answer to his question the same as why many other unexplainable things happened around her.

'G-g-good morning, Year Eleven. It's my p-p-pleasure to introduce you all today to Detective Inspector M-M-Michelle Davey, and, P-P-PC Harry Hollings, of the M-M-Metropolitan Police Force. I hope you f-f-find what they have to say m-m-most worthwhile. Over to you!'

Michelle feigned thanks as Mr Bullen handed her a bullet point list of suggested topics, stapled to a print-out of the pupils' names.

'Thank you, Mr Bullen, for that introduction,' she began. 'Today, PC Hollings and I will endeavour to cover several topics, which we hope to do so successfully and concisely within the allotted timescale. Although, I've been told we're able to overrun slightly into your first period, if necessary—' several whoops emanated from the audience '— we'll do our best to wrap up in time.'

Year Eleven's collective sigh was audible.

'Right then! Let's begin with Crime and Safety within the parameters of your School itself. Your headmaster has ever so kindly offered up a box of items that have been confiscated from your fellow pupils, since just the beginning of term.'

PC Hollings passed Michelle an inoffensive cardboard box from the stage. With great difficulty, she attempted to balance it upon the lectern.

'Is Tony's stash in there, miss?!' shouted Moya, from the third row.

Beside her newly reappointed boyfriend, Finn, Moya was sat away from Trinity and Lyssa – much to their annoyance. As Finn's hand sneakily reached around the back of her blouse, she let out a yelp and a giggle, as he succeeded in unfastening her bra.

'She's not a "miss", she's a D-D-Detective Inspector, Miss Goldsmith. And that's an inappropriate c-c-comment!'

'I'm sure that any drugs would have been handed into the police and not left lying around the school office,' continued Michelle. 'Unless, of course, any of your teachers fancied themselves a cheeky pass around, in anticipation of an Ofsted inspection!'

Michelle's joke raised smiles from the pupils, as well as select members of the teaching staff – two in particular, whose Friday night activities were a well-kept secret.

PC Hollings took a step forward.

'*That's* an inappropriate comment,' he whispered.

His face uncomfortably close to her own, Michelle flapped him away. The pus-filled pimple on his chin was grossly full to burst.

'Let's see what we *do* have in here,' Michelle announced, rummaging. 'Two craft knives—'

Demanding their return, Miss Roberts had detained her Art class for a full ten minutes into lunch, before deciding she valued her own time more than their whereabouts.

'—some disassembled pencil sharpeners—'

Their blades had been repurposed as mini-weapons, or tools of self-harm.

'—two flavoured condoms. These probably shouldn't have been confiscated, as we're all meant to be promoting *safe* sex. A bicycle's chain. Some kind of—' Michelle coughed '—whip.'

Dubiously, she lifted the thick plaited leather out, then allowed it to drop.

'Some cherry bombs, and bangers.'

Michelle suspected the latter to truly be tiny parcels of speed, but she could not be bothered to question this. Other contents included a lady's G-string, a can of spray paint and an opened pack of JPS cigarettes – only four straights remained. There had been five, until the school's receptionist had pinched one after a strained conversation with the mother of a Year Eight pupil.

Slyly, Michelle pocketed the remaining fags. She was certain PC Hollings had noticed, but ploughed forth regardless, briskly reciting policy.

*

Skilfully, Trinity hooked the straps of Ros's rucksack over the toe of her shoe and slid it back from between the legs of the chair in front.

'*Get in,*' she whispered to Lyssa.

Delving into the pink, rhinestone-covered bag with a mixture of disgust and awe, Trinity proceeded to pass Ros's Maths exercise book across to her friend. The book – much like the bag – was decorated in jewels and glitter. It smelt of perfume.

Together the pair set about copying the latest set of algebraic equations. Both were careful to miscopy the odd answer, as to ensure passing the plagiarism off as their own work.

*

Michelle wrapped the first section of her presentation as best as she could, after several off-topic questions. Running her fingers through her untidy hair, she fought off a yawn. Her brain was struggling.

Referring to the bullet point list, the next suggestion for discussion was 'Day in the life of a Police Officer'. Michelle vetoed this. She could hardly remember her own. The next was 'Career options' – all things considered, Michelle concluded herself not the best to lead a talk on that at present. Or 'Self-defence', which was a potential contender.

Indecisive, Michelle flipped to the next sheet – the list of pupils' names. That's when she saw it:

'Turpin, Rye. Female. 31/10/1981.'

No bigger in font size than the names above or below, Rye's name – *Miss Turpin's* – shone out from the page in far greater focus and clarity.

'Ma'am,' PC Hollings breathed into Michelle's ear. 'Would you like me to—'

'Self-defence,' Michelle began with a start. 'Statistically, women are more likely to suffer sexual and domestic violence. But that's not to say that men are immune – of course – because, they're not.'

Uneasy, both Ally's and Fred's eyes shot up towards the front, as each paid attention for only a split-second. They too then slunk down in their respective seats, to match Zach's level.

'With winter fast approaching and the nights drawing in, it's not safe to be walking home alone. Ashfield has its fair share of alleyways – heck, your school is right next to a graveyard! I for one wouldn't fancy staying late for choir practice at this time of y—'

Ginger hair flopping forward, PC Hollings coughed loudly just as Mr Bullen was about to interrupt, fearing Michelle was about to discourage the few choir members that there were.

'Not that I'm trying to scare you,' Michelle backtracked. 'I'd just like to make sure that you're all adequately prepared. Now, I'll need a volunteer.'

Few hands were offered up from the audience.

'No-one?' Michelle asked, blindly. 'Well, I guess I'll just have to pick someone at random. Rye Turpin!'

As she read forth the name, Michelle jabbed at the sheet with a forefinger. She looked up for the girl's reveal, heart pounding.

Rye's heart sank. Never in a million years would she have volunteered herself. Naturally, she slid down in her chair, bringing herself in line with her friends.

'Shit, I knew she'd recognise us,' Zach whispered, his mouth covered.

Growing impatient, Michelle walked out from behind the lectern.

'Come on, Miss Turpin, we haven't got all day!' she pressed.

Grabbing hold of her from under the armpit, Ally thrust Rye upwards.

'Don't go!' Zach hissed.

He pulled at Rye's skirt.

'She has to go,' Ally hissed back.

Michelle watched as a blonde girl, of average height, shuffled out from the back row and into the aisle. Slowly, Rye

Turpin made her way up to the front of the Main Hall. Michelle perceived her a natural beauty; cautious and doe-eyed.

'No need to be shy,' PC Hollings offered.

Nervously, Rye looked from one officer to the next. If the detective inspector did indeed recognise her – or her friends – she was doing a good job at hiding it. She took Rye by the shoulders, and physically led her over to the space beside the lectern.

'Stand with your legs shoulder-width apart,' Michelle instructed.

Michelle's discovery of Miss Turpin had given her a new-found energy – the much-needed spark to ignite the vodka in her belly. She was about to relinquish ownership of the stone, and her mind – as well as her handbag – would soon be slightly lighter for it.

'This might be the only time you get asked to do this whilst in school,' Michelle continued, 'but you might want to hoist your skirt up a bit higher.'

Rye obliged as the audience whooped and whistled. Catching a glimpse of Louie, she blushed. Mr Bullen looked mildly alarmed.

'The Metropolitan Police obviously does not condone violence, but self-defence – if executed properly – is sometimes necessary. Now, can anyone guess the advantage of taking this stance?'

Michelle signalled to Rye with both arms, then pointed to a boy in the front row.

'Offers more balance and stability?' answered Tony.

Michelle nodded and clapped her hands together.

'Bingo! You're far less likely to lose your balance and fall over. That should be your go-to stance,' she confirmed. 'Walking home in the dark, it's recommended to carry your keys between your fingers – like this.' Michelle demonstrated. 'They become an instant weapon to strike the eyes, throat or neck. If you're able to see your attacker coming, then the other most obvious thing to do, is knee them where it hurts – righ' in the coin purse!'

Michelle chuckled at her own impromptu choice of phrase – it was the most 'Essex' she'd sounded in years. She then made a movement to jokingly demonstrate this unto PC Hollings.

'Don't worry, Harry,' Michelle reassured him, as he reached down to protect his family jewels. 'I'm not actually going to knee you in the testicles.'

The hall erupted with laughter. Even Rye cracked a smile, but it was fleeting, as for over the course of the next five minutes, her body was continuingly repositioned by the detective inspector, as if she'd been a mannequin.

*

The school bell rang for the first period, inviting a groan from Year Eleven.

'Sorry guys, we're out of time!' Michelle shouted, over the chatter. 'We're going to have to leave it there! I'm DI Michelle Davey and this—' she pointed to PC Hollings '—is my assistant. I'm just sorry that we couldn't have found him a sparkly leotard.'

PC Hollings buried his head in his hands. And as chairs were scraped back against the hardwood floor, Mr Bullen pranced over to Michelle.

'But y-y-you're welcome to c-continue. W-we've told the s-staff that—'

'We're done,' Michelle replied, shutting him down.

'I'd be more than happy to give a short talk—' began PC Hollings.

'I guess we could always get Miss Turpin here to actually kick you in the balls, if you *really* wanted to run on a little longer,' Michelle whispered, aggressively. 'If any of you have any questions, feel free to come over and speak with Harry here! He's more than happy to answer them for you! Andrew, you might want to hand these out to the children before they escape.'

She thrust the headmaster a plastic bag full of rape alarms.

Intent on re-joining her friends as quickly as possible, Rye started to walk away. Michelle, however, reached out to clasp her wrist.

'Not-so-fast. I'd like a word with you.'

Rye gulped.

At the back of the hall, Zach threw up his arms as they watched the detective inspector lead their friend up the steps to the stage and behind its curtain.

'She knows!' he gestured, horrified.

'Please, you're being overdramatic,' Ally scolded him. 'There's no solid evidence tying us to the fire. At least, nothing that would stand up in court.'

'Maybe we don't all share your confidence, *Princess Caraboo*,' Zach shot back.

*

Behind the curtain, the stage was a mess. Milk pails were stacked onto lunch trollies that had been transformed into farmer's carts, and racks of costumes had been packed up against a backdrop of rolling hills. Creepy papier-mâché carnival masks were strung up on lines, drying from an Art lesson the day prior. At the very back of the stage, ModRoc had been applied to a chicken-wire base to create a village well. A metal bucket was suspended over its centre.

Slapping Michelle's wrist away, Rye finally managed to wriggle free.

'What are you—'

'I have something for you,' Michelle interrupted.

With no further explanation, she delved into her handbag to extract the stone. She offered it out, but Rye – sceptical – did not take it.

'It's yours. Take it,' Michelle insisted.

She attempted to push and prise the stone into Rye's clenched fist.

'What do you mean it's mine? It's – it's a stone,' Rye observed. 'You look scared of it.'

Michelle groaned.

'Yes, *obviously*, it's a stone, and it's *yours*.'

Michelle pulled Rye's fingers apart, pressing the cold, flat stone into her palm.

'I don't—'

'I've had it far too long – take it. *Please*.'

Forcibly, Michelle closed Rye's fingers around it. For a few seconds – before releasing her grip – she held the schoolgirl's hand in her own, and the two locked eyes.

'Where did you get it?' Rye asked.

'That's the part … I can't recall. And please, don't ask me why, because I can't explain that either. All I know is, it's meant for you.'

Michelle looked pleadingly at her.

'OK, well, I'm not sure what you want me to do with it.'

Rye turned the black stone over. Though wary, she felt an unexplainable affinity with it – a familiarity. Its shiny and smooth surface grew warm to her touch. It fit her palm, perfectly.

'Use it as a paperweight, keep it as a pet rock, throw it away for all I care.'

*

Sight unseen; the scorched and cracked talon of a certain hellish creature reached out from its hiding place. Anoch's body ached, and the demon had to support itself by clasping onto the rim of the well from wherein it was concealed. It had paid the price for over-excitement – for the second time – with blood and broken bones and was under strict instruction to only intervene if necessary. Although temporarily weakened, nothing would distract Anoch from its mission. The demon would continue to watch, and report to its master. Anoch would serve, always.

*

'Why are you scared of it?' Rye repeated her earlier statement as a question.

'I … just haven't been feeling myself lately.'

Michelle felt hot. Her armpits were sticky. Without thinking, she reached back inside her handbag to remove the bottle of vodka. Uncapping it, she proceeded to take a deep gulp.

'Oh, my God,' Rye spluttered. 'I don't think you should— '

'Probably not,' Michelle admitted. 'Look – Miss Turpin – *Rye* – I've … I've seen things – things I can't explain.'

'"Seen things"? What sort of things?'

Holding her vodka at an angle that threatened to empty it over the stage, Michelle's arms began to shake.

'Rye – tell me,' she breathed, in hushed tones. 'Do you know of a girl named—'

Clank.

Clang!

Clatter!

The noises, emanating from the back of the stage, startled the pair, and both abruptly turned. A milk pail that had been balanced upon the rim of the well had fallen with an almighty commotion; bouncing to then roll.

'Ma'am, I need your help with something.'

Michelle and Rye turned once more, as the voice spoke.

PC Hollings appeared flustered.

'I'll be there in a minute, Harry,' Michelle dismissed, clawing at her chest with her free hand. 'I'm just finishing up with Miss Turpin.'

'Have – are you drinking?!' he suddenly exclaimed, his eyes wandering.

'No,' Michelle replied, looking down at the bottle also. 'Not at all. This – this isn't mine.'

'It's mine,' Rye piped up, and Michelle opened her mouth to object. 'She confiscated it from me. She was just giving me a lecture about … alcoholism – and how important it is to … seek help.'

'Ah, I see,' PC Hollings replied, sternly. 'Best you take heed of her warning.'

'I will – definitely.'

Rye dryly swallowed, and PC Hollings nodded his acceptance.

'There's a girl down here who'd like some information on the workings of CID. They're very specific questions, actually.' He stretched a weary smile. 'And you'd be much better at answering them than myself.'

Having endured as much as he could take, Harry gladly held the curtain aside for his superior. Reluctantly, Michelle moved forwards to duck through it. Pointedly, she dropped the bottle of vodka back within her bag.

'*Confiscated,*' she confirmed.

'Wait!' Rye pleaded – herself reaching for the arm of the officer this time. 'What if I need to speak with you again?'

She did not know why this might be but considered it wise to ask.

'You know where to find me,' Michelle offered. 'Ashfield Police Station. I'm there … most days.'

After Michelle, Rye too exited stage right, followed then by PC Hollings, and the curtain fell to kiss the floor.

'I've definitely found, *another,*' Anoch rasped to itself, head rising from inside the well. 'Oh, how master will be pleased with me. Anoch will be redeemed!'

Like a barber's blade across flesh, the demon's serrated tongue slicked over an ulcerated pallet with sleek ease and loathing.

'Anoch will be baptised in the blood of the heathen! Make beads from their vertebrae, and fashion their shoulder blades into paddles! Anoch will dine at the table of the Last Supper, and be crowned—'

Clang!

Anoch's head came crashing back down to earth – quite literally – for the demon had gotten carried away, and to an extent that it had quite forgotten the hefty metal bucket that hung suspended above its cranium. The demon's dreams of grandeur reverberated around its skull.

*

The piercing screech of rape alarms filled the rest of the school day, as students threw them about classrooms like grenades. Liam made a jibe to Fred during their shared sixth period – Drama – about him 'being vulnerable to penis' – whatever that was supposed to mean.

- CHAPTER XXII -

Suspension & Invitation

<u>Friday 21st November 1997, 11:01am, DCI GOODFELLOW'S OFFICE, ASHFIELD POLICE STATION, ASHFIELD, LONDON.</u>
Michelle knocked upon her superior's door and waited for the ominous 'Enter!'

The morning after her given assembly at Ashfield Community, she had received the fateful email requesting a meeting and had dwelt upon it for the next three days. There had been no attachment to the email this time – no timeline of attendance and absences. That said, the meeting's purpose was no mystery.

Two out of these past three days, Michelle had remained sober. Valiantly, she had fought her urges, but on day three – last night – she had cracked, with anxiety carrying her to Stonem's off-licence. And today, on the day of reckoning, that meant Michelle was hungover.

'DI Davey,' spoke Malcolm Goodfellow, looking up from the file on his desk. 'Please, take a seat.'

Michelle clocked that her DCI had not used her first name when addressing her this time. Cautiously, she sat. At the very top of the thick wad between them, she could read: 'OFFICER RECORD: DAVEY, MICHELLE CONSTANCE.'

Michelle's heart thumped against her ribcage. She could still taste the spirits on her tongue.

'I think we both know why you're here,' DCI Goodfellow continued.

He folded his arms across the record.

Michelle looked across to Harriett, who was once again present. She was already scribbling notes with speed – her loose, scraggly grey hair shuddering.

'DI Davey, this can't continue.'

Michelle crossed her own arms against her chest to conceal her damp armpits. She had showered that morning – her first in days – but could again smell her sweat. She now regretted ditching her blazer last minute, but she was so hot.

'I know, it won't – I promise,' she replied, awkwardly wiping her brow, whilst ensuring her pits remained clamped. 'I'm going to prioritise my career – completely – one hundred percent, from now on.'

Within that moment, Michelle convinced herself that she was able to ditch the booze. She had never had a problem with alcohol before and thought she could end this habit just as quickly as she'd started it. She would forget all about Elizabeth. At this stage, however, Michelle was not even sure what had occurred first – her dependence, or the girl's apparition.

'Unfortunately, it's too late for empty promises.' DCI Goodfellow sighed.

Michelle sat forward in her seat. She was shaking.

'It's not an empty promise. I prom– I swear it!'

'Wednesday the twelfth of November. Saturday the fifteenth of November. You failed to show up for work. Monday the tenth of November – you disappeared soon after you'd signed in. On the Wednesday, we attempted to call you *six* times. You didn't even answer your phone.'

'*Seven*,' Harriett interrupted, her eyes narrowing over the top of her bifocals. 'Seven times.'

She ceased scrawls just long enough to sternly point her pen in Michelle's direction. Oh, how Michelle could have swung for her!

'Seven times!' DCI Goodfellow repeated.

Michelle sat further forwards in her chair, bringing herself ever closer to her superior, before she feared he might smell the vodka on her breath, and so retracted.

'But, sir, I've been – I haven't been myself.'

'I'm aware you've been struggling,' he replied. 'Believe me, it hasn't gone unnoticed.'

He sighed again. Michelle shivered.

'If you're referring to the presentation I gave at the school, then I'll apologise to Harry—'

'I'm referring to your visit to the Thackerall's last week.'

Michelle's eyes widened. Beads of sweat were forming on her forehead.

'How do you know—'

'Mr Thackerall called into the station to make a complaint. He wanted some explanation as to why – after being told the investigation into their daughter's disappearance was benched – an officer by your name had shown up – unannounced – to drag it all back up again! He wanted answers – answers that I could not give. What on earth were you thinking?'

His voice raised, DCI Goodfellow had not quite shouted, for he had restrained himself, but his posture had become rigid.

'I was following a hunch.'

'*A hunch*?! Michelle!'

Abruptly, DCI Goodfellow wheeled back his chair, stood, and turned to face the window behind. Michelle had never been the recipient of his temper before, and it saddened as well as scared her, but she felt too queasy to even flinch.

'That's not how we work, and you know it,' he continued, peering out between the blinds. 'The case was *inactive*. If you had a hunch, you should have liaised with the necessary officer before even thinking about arranging a meeting.' He groaned. 'I don't know what's happened to you. You're a good officer – or, at least, you were. Up until two months ago, you were the golden girl, front-runner for promotion without even a blemish on her record. I'm at a loss. Harriett had organised for you to visit Occupational Health, but you never showed. We can't help you, if you're not willing to help yourself.'

Harriett tutted and shook her head.

'I'm – sorry,' Michelle garbled.

DCI Goodfellow turned to face her.

'You're suspended. A date has been set for your hearing. Friday the fifth of December – two weeks from today.'

'I'm really sorry that I've let you down,' Michelle wept, tears running down her cheeks. 'This profession is my life. I swear to you that I'm going to sort myself out … I *will*.'

Defeated, Michelle got up to leave the room. She had no excuse for her actions; she could not even explain her absences.

'Michelle,' spoke her superior. 'You'll need to hand over your badge.'

�❦�

<u>Friday 21ˢᵗ November 1997, 12:30pm, MAIN HALL, GROUND FLOOR, ASHFIELD COMMUNITY SCHOOL, ASHFIELD, LONDON.</u>

'What do you think we're doing here?' Zach asked.

'Absolutely no idea,' replied Rye.

Without explanation, both had been called out by name during the fourth period – English – and instructed to make their way to the Main Hall. Upon their entering thereof, it was near empty, except for a small but very loud collection of pupils gathered in front of the stage. A solitary dinner lady – unappreciative of the rabble – was set about assembling the tables for lunch. Sat atop the stage, their headmaster ushered Zach and Rye forwards with a wave of his hand.

'Ah, Mr Leith, and M-Miss Turpin!' he declared. 'I've s-s-seen yours around here s-s-somewhere – ah, yes!'

Thumbing through a pile, Mr Bullen then handed them each an envelope. Sealed, they bore their names and year group upon stickers. Looking from the envelopes to each other, Zach shrugged, and they both proceeded to open them. Rye removed a cardboard slip, to read the message typed upon it:

> *'Dear Miss Rye Turpin,*
> *Congratulations on being awarded the Year 11 prize for:*
> *Art – 'FEAR' project.*
> *As such you are invited to attend the prize-giving ceremony at 19:30pm on Sunday 30th November, in the Main Hall. Please find enclosed your three tickets; for yourself and two guests. If additional tickets are required, or if you are unable to attend the ceremony, please speak with Lorraine Pickering in Main Reception.*
> *Please use your prize to purchase a book of your choice. You will be required to bring this book with you to the ceremony, so that it can be presented by our guest speaker.*
> *Ashfield Community School'*

Stapled to the reverse of the message, along with the tickets, was a gift voucher for the bookstore in town, up to the value of twenty pounds.

'Sports Personality of the Year!' exclaimed Zach. 'That's crazy. I know I'm taking P.E. as an option, but I'm not even on any of the school teams. I suppose, I did win the Archery County Championships over summer. Mr Bullen must really be pushing the extra-curricular aspect. Either way, a book voucher's cool – not that I read much. Rye, do you read?'

Rye shook her head. She was still in shock over her own prize and, if truth be told, a little chuffed. She had won something; for the first time in her life.

Slowly backing away from the crowd, Rye hit something solid. She had backed right into another student and trodden heavily upon their toes with her heels. Rye spun around, and they were revealed as non-other than Louie – his face scrunched up in discomfort.

'Hi,' he whimpered, forcing a smile.

'S-sorry!' Rye whimpered also, before quickly turning to grab Zach by the arm. 'Come on, Zach, we've gotta go.'

Zach took one look at Louie, murmured a greeting, and walked straight for the door. Rye went to follow, but in doing so unintentionally engaged in an awkward side-step shuffle with her crush. Mirroring each other's movements, they both swayed.

'Can I ask you something?' Louie finally asked, breaking the stand-off, and Rye nodded. 'What did you win your prize for?'

Her mind suddenly a blank, Rye's brain ceased to function. The answer to the question was easy, yet she couldn't summon a single word into existence. Louie grinned. Rye took note that his teeth were perfect.

'Mine's for Music,' he offered, holding up his invite.

'Art – I got mine for Art. That was my prize. That was the subject.'

Hating her own garbling, Rye looked over to see where Zach was. Stood by the door, he brazenly typed away on his pager. His abandonment of her only fuelled her nervousness.

'They liked my Fear project,' Rye precisely expanded.

'Oh, right, yeah. The creepy doll – I remember.'

Louie combed his fingers through his hair. And Rye appreciated every detail – his fingernails and jawline, even the small mole located just below his left ear. Being able to engage every aspect of his physical appearance at such proximity was a rare and satisfying treat.

'I'll see you later then,' Rye spouted.

'Rye, wait! That wasn't my question.'

Rye pivoted. Her shoes squeaked noisily upon the varnished parquet.

'It wasn't?'

'Are you free this weekend?' Louie asked. He too now sounded nervous. 'And by weekend, I mean Sunday. At around half six? I've got two tickets to see *Titanic,* and none of the guys want to see it with me.'

'Ummm-errr…'

Rye wanted to scream yes but could only manage noise. *You've got to live for now, Rye – live for the moment.'* She repeated Ally's advice over in her head. Then, like an actor preparing for stage, she gulped and lowered her shoulders.

'I thought that wasn't out 'til January?' she questioned. 'It only debuted at the Tokyo Film Festival the other week – I saw it in the paper.'

'My brother, Sam, he works at the ABC down Southbury. He gave me a couple of spare tickets for an advance screening,' he confirmed. 'Is that a yes?'

Overemphasising her coyness – not that this was needed – Rye plunged her hands into her blazer's pockets, eyelids fluttering. The act was an emulation of Ally. Her fingers closed around the flat black stone. Though she and her friends had written the detective inspector off as a crazy drunk, Rye had still not brought herself to throw the stone away. She stroked at its surface, pretending to mull over her reply.

'Yes,' Rye finally spoke. 'I'll see you then.'

'And I'll meet you there,' Louie squeezed in, before she could vanish.

Rye nodded. She dared not participate in further conversation with him at present. That Louie had just asked her on a date was enough to risk disjointed sentences again. He had just asked her on a date? That is what had happened, wasn't it? Rye was already beginning to think that she'd imagined it.

Re-joining Zach, Rye impulsively took one last look behind her, hoping to catch a sneak peek of Louie's rounded bottom. He was still looking at her. Unperturbed, as she turned the corner, Rye punched the air. She couldn't wait to tell Fred.

Friday 21st November 1997, 15:22pm, BOYS' CHANGING ROOM, ASHFIELD COMMUNITY SCHOOL, ASHFIELD, LONDON.

'Fred, where you been, mate?' Zach asked, stuffing his rugby top into his bag, as his friend approached. 'Tony said Liam was causing some real problems over on your pitch. Said the dickhead was getting right up in your face. What happened?'

Fred pulled his top off over his head, dropped it to the bench, and reached for his school shirt. He didn't say anything, but Zach noted that his eyes were red and puffy.

'Look, Fred, if Liam tries anything again, I'll—'

Zach proceeded to whack his dirty boots on the bench, inadvertently splattering chunks of mud over both their rucksacks.

'I've got your back,' he confirmed.

Still, Fred said nothing. Silently, he wiped his bag clean of the mud with his top. After buttoning his shirt, he then sat to roll down and remove his socks.

Zach sat beside him. Slipping on his school shoes over his own sports socks, he couldn't be bothered to change completely – it was the final period, after all.

'What did Mr Shaw say then, eh? He couldn't have just ignored—'

'Mr Shaw dragged us both into Mr Bullen's office for a "chat".'

Fred paused momentarily from changing to air quote the word.

'And?' Zach pressured. 'What did Mr Bullen say?'

Pulling his tie down from the peg, Zach accidentally whipped Fred on the shoulder. His friend flinched, and Zach hastened an apology, before tying it around his collar.

'Mr Bullen asked Liam whether he picked on me because I'm "effeminate",' Fred responded, dryly.

He stood and pulled down his shorts as Zach gawked, open-mouthed.

'He said what?' Zach gasped.

'He asked Liam whether he picked on me because I'm "e-e-effeminate",' Fred repeated, deadpan, pulling up his trousers. He left his shirt untucked as he fastened his buckle. 'I'm gay, Zach.'

'Oh, I know you're gay, Fred, mate. But Mr Bullen should never 'ave said—'

'You know I'm gay?'

Fred whispered, as to be sure the few students that remained wouldn't hear him. Like a deer in headlights, he was caught off guard by Zach's revelation, and now needed clarification.

'Is it because I'm effeminate?' he asked, fearful.

'Oh, don't be an idiot! Course you're not. Not that it would matter. I've known you since the day we both popped out our mothers' vaginas! I just, noticed things, you know?' Zach shrugged.

However vulgar his phrasing, Zach was correct. They shared the same birthday; their mothers had met in the hospital during delivery. And he was wholly unshaken by Fred's truth. Zach continued in dressing himself – pushing his arms through the sleeves of his blazer.

'How long have you known?' asked Fred.

Having bottled up his emotions for so long, he didn't know how to react to this anticlimactic confession.

'Always.' Zach nodded, affirming. 'So, what happened to Liam?

'Well, after laughing … a lot, he was suspended, and given a Sunday detention. He's only been bloody drafted into helping with the prize-giving ceremony, ain't he.'

'Good! Serves the little shit right. And remember—'

Zach clenched a fist and punched his left palm.

'Eh?' He smiled and prodded Fred with a finger until his friend reciprocated with a smile of his own. 'We missed you at lunch again today. Have you spoken to Rye yet? She was very excited to tell you about her date!'

Friday 21st November 1997, 23:44pm, MICHELLE DAVEY'S RESIDENCE, FLAT 1, 179A LONDON ROAD, ASHFIELD, LONDON.

The cool air from the fridge hit Michelle's face and she squinted to focus her vision. Leaning too far forwards, she staggered and smacked her forehead on the top shelf. It hurt, but the pain was mostly dulled by alcohol. In time, it would no doubt form a lovely bruise.

Unable to find what she was looking for, Michelle swore, and slammed the door closed. There was no wine left in the fridge, but that was OK; she had suspected as such. Moving on, Michelle could have bet there was a bottle of vodka somewhere in the kitchen – or a bottle of red, maybe? She had only bought three bottles of wine yesterday and did not remember drinking them all. Michelle had every intention of embracing sobriety tomorrow.

Turning her attention to the kitchen cupboards, Michelle started high and worked her way low, ransacking one shelf after another. Angrily, she discarded boxes of cereal, packets of pasta and tins, as she swept them all from storage onto the countertops.

'Arrrrrgggggghhhhhhh!' she screamed.

In her drunken frenzy, Michelle had even checked under the sink, in amongst the bleach and lemon cleanser, just to be sure.

She marched into her sitting room and dived to the floor – so quick that it emulated a military exercise. Two empty bottles of wine were under the coffee table, but that was OK; she'd thought that to be the case. That left one more to be found. Michelle checked behind the television, behind the sofa, under the sofa, the windowsill, but there was still no sign. Exasperated, she pulled at her hair before dramatically turning back to the kitchen, intent on inflicting another raid. It was then that she caught sight of the third bottle. Innocently, it stood propped beside a bottle of vodka – both empty – and half-hidden by the sofa's cushions. Michelle had finished it, mere minutes ago – she remembered now.

'Arrrrrgggggggghh!' Michelle screamed again – her voice breaking before it had reached the desired pitch. 'It's OK,' she reassured herself, and grappled for her purse from off the coffee table.

She clawed for it, but missed, only to knock over a vase of long-dead flowers. Falling to the carpet, it spilt brown water but did not break. It was of no concern.

'I'll just … pop to *Stonem's*,' she exhaled.

Michelle stumbled around the coffee table and next reached for her mobile that lay on the sofa. The device was not essential for her trip to the off-licence, but she felt naked without it. Earlier, Michelle had misplaced it for whole twenty minutes – an act that had, in and of itself, invited a separate search of her kitchen, bedroom, sitting room and handbag, whilst having been in her pocket all along.

Distracted by her mobile's flashing light, Michelle perched on the sofa, her head swaying. After three failed attempts, she unlocked its keypad. There was a message from Shaz:

Hi Michelle. Hope you're doing OK …? I heard about what happened earlier. Remember I'm here for a chat if ever you need it. S x, 23:11pm.'

Michelle re-read the text three times.

'*Eleven*? How can it be gone eleven?!' she shouted.

Stonem's closed every night at eleven, precisely. It was the only off-licence for several roads and was Michelle's only readily available source of alcohol. For a minute, she weighed her car keys up in a hand, but ultimately thought better of it. As pissed as she may be, Michelle knew better than to attempt driving to the twenty-four-hour supermarket. She groaned, slapping the cushions in a tantrum.

'THIS IS YOUR FAULT!'

Michelle leapt from the sofa, stepping onto and over her coffee table.

'YOU'VE DONE THIS!'

She tore the map of Ashfield away from the wall, pulling the woodchip and plaster away with it also. Ripping it in half, she let the two halves flutter.

'I'VE LOST MY JOB, BECAUSE OF YOU!'

Throat strained, Michelle scratched at her collection of drawings, tearing some free and tearing holes in others.

'I'M DRUNK, BECAUSE OF, *YOU*!'

Her words were perfectly matched by her movements as she dragged down Elizabeth's missing person's report, Mrs Nicholls' holiday photograph and notes. Eventually, all Michelle was left with was the photograph of Elizabeth Thackerall, sat behind the restaurant's table. The teen beamed, unshaken by the suspended officer's outrage. Michelle lifted a hand to the picture. Anger dissipating, she began to cry hot, searing tears. Tenderly, she stroked Elizabeth's face.

'I don't know how to help you,' Michelle choked. 'I don't think I can,' she admitted, sliding down the wall in a slump.

*

Michelle rolled over and retched. Chunks of vomit spilled out of her mouth and over her chin. She coughed and wiped away the webbing that connected her lips to the sitting room carpet.

Having woken mid-nightmare, she was shaking and scared. If her head wasn't so groggy, Michelle might just have remembered what the nightmare had been this time.

❧ ✋ ☙

<u>Sunday 23rd November 1997, 22:13pm, ABC CINEMA, SOUTHBURY ROAD, ASHFIELD, LONDON.</u>

Over forty-eight hours since Louie had asked Rye to the cinema, and he waited for her outside its toilets.

'Well, what did you think?' he pressed, as she exited.

Rye had been desperate to pee ever since the Titanic had impacted that 'berg and had held her legs tightly crossed throughout the remainder of the film. She would have left the screen to relieve herself, if it hadn't been for Louie holding her hand. Rye had not interrupted the connection, fearing it might not have returned. Overall, the film left her melancholy; the haunting melodies making her reflective and sad.

'I think, there was definitely room for them both on that door.'

'I reckon that'll be a topic of controversy for years to come,' chuckled Louie.

'But, yeah, I liked it,' Rye clarified. 'Bit long though.'

'Yeah, I suppose it was. You were a proper trooper at holding your wee in 'til the end – I could feel you shuffling about.'

Louie laughed as Rye's eyes widened.

'I didn't wanna miss a second – I was hooked,' she lied.

'Line and sinker, right?'

'Ah, "sinker".' Rye smiled – her face melting with a beautiful glow. 'I see what you did there.'

Louie smiled back, and with that, the pair headed out towards the box office. Halfway down the corridor, Louie took hold of Rye's hand once more. She'd hoped that he might, but the action still came as a surprise. As he interlaced his fingers with her own, Rye could almost feel her heart pass up through her throat and out of her open mouth. If she were a cartoon, she would have exhaled butterflies. Approaching the exit, Louie paused and turned to her.

'I've had such a great time, it'd be a shame to cut it short – not short, 'cause that film was *long*. But we've hardly had a chance to talk. That's the problem with going to the cinema for a date.'

There it was; Rye's confirmation. Not that it was needed, but hearing Louie say it sent Rye's hormones into overdrive.

'I know this pub – The King's Head,' Louie continued. 'It's pretty close. If we hurry, we can make last orders. Let me buy you a drink. They never ask for—'

'Louie,' Rye began – her mouth speaking before her head realised it was rude to interrupt, 'I'd love to, but it's a school night … and Pris … we're not exactly seeing eye-to-eye at the moment. I'd feel guilty testing her patience.'

Rye sighed. As wondrous as her time with Louie had been, she was still eager for it to end. Being near the boy – conversing with him – was proving increasingly difficult.

'That's fair,' Louie conceded, although he appeared saddened. 'I wouldn't wanna be the one to blame if you two had another argument.'

'We're *always* having arguments.'

'Let me walk you home then.'

'I thought you – don't you live the complete opposite direction?' Rye asked, frowning.

'Yeah …' Louie trailed off. 'But I'm your date, and it's the gentlemanly thing to do.' He smiled, laughed, then smiled again.

*

Even in her anticipation to return home, Rye would have preferred to walk the longer route, via the roads. Instead, Louie had persisted in his suggestion of the quicker – and substantially darker – alternative, through the playing fields behind the cinema. They had stood by the spiked gates debating this for well over a minute before Louie took Rye's hand again and gallantly vowed to protect her against anything that may lurk within.

'But I'd really prefer not to,' said Rye.

'Come on, Rye. Don't be a wuss. It'll be over before you know it.'

Rye felt only slightly reassured by Louie's presence and touch. She considered him naïve to the strange dangers that walked this earth – unlike herself – but was too embarrassed to argue further.

Their path was long, straight and wide, lit only by dispersed lampposts – their yellow light minimal. Rows of bare, leafless trees flanked either side. By the light of day, they'd have easily seen the path's end. At night, however, it was a walk into the unknown.

After exhausting all discussion regarding the film, Rye thought their conversation might falter – she was wrong. Louie kept the pace and flow of exchange with interesting topics that kept her mind at – relative – ease from their surroundings. She had learnt all about Louie's older brother, Sam, who they'd briefly spoken with at the box office, prior to the film's start.

Sam had left Ashfield Community a few years earlier and Rye thought she could vaguely remember him. A sporty lad, he looked similar to Louie, albeit shorter. Their mother was very judgmental of Sam's decision to not attend university and disapproved highly of his life's apparent lack of direction. Louie wanted to pursue a career in music; an aspiration that too invited a backlash.

Rye spoke mostly of her friends, for the subject brought her confidence and comfort. Careful as to what exactly she shared, her exclusion of certain details sat well with her; for the first time in a while, Rye was beginning to feel like a normal sixteen-year-old. Her worries and obsessive thoughts over Elizabeth Thackerall were being replaced by a pleasant, warm and tingling sensation.

Louie began talking about the band he was planning to form with Stu, and Rye retracted her free hand from out of her jacket's pocket. She had, until then, been fondling the stone therein. Rye chose to embrace the distraction from it, which was most welcome. Louie could not only play the saxophone but guitar and piano also. He hoped Jake would teach him the drums soon.

Louie asked Rye about her parents, and she answered his questions more openly than she had done in years. She had never found the subject easy – having only ever briefed the bare facts even to Ally. But to Louie, during their walk, Rye divulged her innermost feelings. She did not shy away from her dislike of Cousin Veronica and Harry either, going into expletive-ridden detail of their draconian rule and subsequent abandonment of them. It was at this point that Rye had felt herself well up, but Louie squeezed her hand, and her mind settled. She lived an entire lifetime within that one moment, wherein they made love a thousand times, were married, shared holidays and children. Just as Jack had been Rose's, Rye considered Louie her soulmate.

*

A pair of eyes – slits of burnt orange – glistened in the darkness and watched as Rye and Louie passed beneath the tree within which the demon was hidden. Anoch was healing, but was not quite at full strength, yet. Vehemently, it stripped the bark from off the tree's branch.

*

By the time the pair reached the top of Rye's cul-de-sac, a little over half an hour had passed since they'd left the cinema. It should have been less, but both simultaneously slowed from a walk to an amble as they reached their destination. Neither wanted their chat to end. They stopped, and Louie turned to face Rye, taking hold of her other hand as he did so. He leant in to kiss her, and she let him.

It was Rye's first kiss, and the world stood still as their tongues clumsily navigated each other's mouths – wet and sloppy. After ten seconds, both withdrew, beaming.

Louie looked to the floor, embarrassed; he knew his kissing skills were far from perfect. Rye, having nothing to compare it to, thought kisses could get no better.

'Thank you for a wonderful evening,' she smiled, sweetly.

'No, thank you,' said Louie, holding onto her hands. 'I was wondering, if my brother came by some more free tickets, whether you'd want to go to the cinema with me again? I mean, it doesn't have to be free, I'd pay—'

'I love you – I'd love you to! Shit. *I'd love to.*'

Rye's love-addled brain, and the sense of security Louie had unknowingly lured her into, had ruined the connectivity between her mind and mouth. Needless-to-say, she was utterly mortified.

'I better head off,' said Louie. 'It's late.'

He cleared his throat and suddenly let go of Rye's hands. He checked his watch, but the act was superfluous.

'I'll see you at school, tomorrow?' Rye asked.

Somewhere between a grunt and a hum, Louie sounded his agreement. Rye had never heard a noise quite like it before.

Then Louie was gone. Taking off without so much as a proper goodbye, he left Rye on a metaphorical precipice off of which she wished to fall and be swallowed up. Heart crushed, she berated herself for her tongue's slip. Rye stood alone and watched as Louie's departing form grew smaller.

ৡ✋ও

<u>Monday 24th November 1997, 03:31am, TURPIN RESIDENCE, 32 KYNASTON GARDENS, ASHFIELD, LONDON.</u>
Sleeping later that night, Rye was back within Sullen Woods. Sat beneath the old oak tree, she was nude and completely alone, the

lake reaching out before her like a sea. The haziness of the dreamscape prevented her from seeing its opposite bank.

Without a thought as to what she was doing, Rye flung a stone across the water's surface. It bounced thrice before sinking. Head tilted to one side; her loose blonde hair tumbled over bare shoulders. There was no breeze, yet the leaves on the shrubs close by swayed as if caught by one. A faint, unidentifiable tune, carried itself unto her ears.

Looking down at her palm and Rye discovered another stone laid placed upon it. It was flat and black, and almost perfectly circular. It fit, perfectly. As before, Rye drew back her arm and skimmed it. Like her previous throw, it hopped thrice and sank in the exact same spot. Not a second after it had and Rye felt a weight back within her hand. The same stone had manifested itself.

Rye stood and walked towards the water's edge. She could not feel the ground beneath her feet. Drawing back her right arm for the third time, Rye launched the stone across the water. It bounced thrice and sunk.

Rye took one step forward and the water caressed her toes. The lake invited her in, and she had no choice but to oblige. A watcher within her own body; Rye had no control over her actions.

One step after another, Rye was drawn onwards. The water had no temperature and welcomed her as she walked in to then wade. Rye turned her hands against the body of water as she did so. With each step, the scene of the lake grew dimmer and dimmer. Her eyes dipped below the surface and all was dark.

Beneath the water's level, Rye could breathe, but no air bubbled out from her nostrils. She could hear the music clearer and it grew louder as her feet followed the steep, downward decline of the lake's floor. Innately, Rye recognised the tune, and she hummed along in time.

'Hmm, hmhm … hm, hm … hmhm-hmmm.'

From the bank, the waters had appeared clean and crystal-like, but with each further step became dirtied by murky clouds. Weeds and plants flapped against her calves, but Rye could not feel them.

'Hm, hmm…hm, hm, hm, hmm…hm-hm.'

Rye could recognise the song now. Gargled and slowed as it was, she knew it: Sheena Easton's '9 to 5 (Morning Train)'. Whereas before she had thought to be following its source, it seemed to be coming up from behind her. Instinctively, Rye turned, and the volume of the record soared.

Behind a smeared and speckled pane of glass, a girl's face bobbed – puffy, bloated and open-eyed. The girl was dead. The girl was Elizabeth Thackerall.

Rye screamed.

*

'Rye! Rye, wake up! *Jesus Christ.*'

Rye took a sharp intake of breath as she jolted upright in bed. The movement meant that Ally was forced to dodge her, for risk of being head-butted. Gasping, Rye clawed at the patchwork quilt. Ally knelt up beside her.

'Sssh,' Ally cooed, attempting to soothe her. 'Calm – you're OK – you're alright.' She felt Rye's forehead with the back of her hand. 'Christ, you're burning up. Here, have some water.'

From the mattress, Ally reached out across the bedroom floor to present Rye with a glass. Rye batted it away, dismissively.

'No! No – I don't … I don't want any,' Rye managed.

Ally replaced the glass, mildly irritated.

'I saw Elizabeth,' Rye wept, pulling at her eyelids.

'You what?' Ally questioned, sharply.

'I saw … I saw Elizabeth. She was in the lake – *dead.* She was dead – just like before. Oh, Ally, I don't know how to help her. I don't know what else I can do! It's like she knew I'd given up on her. But I don't know what else I can do! I don't know how to solve a murder! We're not the police! We're – I'm, just—'

'Erm, Rye,' Ally interrupted, cautiously.
'What?!' Rye wailed, as Ally grimaced.
'I think you've wet the bed.'

END OF ACT TWO.

ACT III

- CHAPTER XXIII -

Look Up

<u>Monday 24th November 1997, 07:04am, TURPIN RESIDENCE, 32 KYNASTON GARDENS, ASHFIELD, LONDON.</u>
'Ashfield Police Station, Louise Brenner speaking.'

From her position behind the sitting room door, Rye kept one eye pressed to the crack in case Pris was to descend the stairs. Cordless phone held rigidly to her ear; she fiddled with her vest's neckline.

'Is – erm – is DI Davey there to speak to at all?' Rye asked.

'DI Michelle Davey?'

'Yes,' Rye confirmed.

'I'm afraid DI Davey is unavailable. Is there something I can help you with?'

'Do you know when she'll next be free?'

'I'm afraid I don't, no. She's on long-term leave.'

'Is there another number I can reach her on? I *really* need to speak with Detective … Inspector … Davey,' Rye pressured, beginning to weep.

'Can I ask who's speaking, please?'

On the other end of the line, all that Louise Brenner heard in answer to her question was a disconnect, followed by a recording that advised 'the other caller has cleared', as Rye hung up the phone.

Immediately after, Rye had looked up Michelle Davey in the phone book; she had not been listed. Elizabeth Thackerall's parents had been, but she'd not called them.

That afternoon, Rye emailed St Anthony's College, posing as a journalist. And on her walk home from school, she pilfered Sheena Easton's debut album, 'Take My Time', from the local record store.

In the days proceeding, Rye received no reply to her email, and went back to visit the lake every day after school, where she would listen to the same first track from the cassette's second side over and over – pausing her Walkman to rewind. Beside her, Zach and Ally would play cards by torchlight. Alas, despite Rye's persistence, the only place she could see Elizabeth Thackerall was in her nightmares. The missing teen was rotting beneath the lake, and there was seemingly nothing to be done. Whilst knowing the location of the body, Rye could hardly make a report to the police – how would she explain herself? She contemplated visiting St Anthony's in person, or perhaps Elizabeth's parents – but what would she say?

Each night, Ally covered their shared mattress in towels as Rye's wetting of the bed continued. No-one found her incontinence more embarrassing than Rye herself, but she could not help it, no matter what she tried, and Pris was beginning to grow suspicious over her repeated use of the washing machine.

As Rye slept, Ally would study the printed pages of the Ars Goetia in the hope of finding something – anything – of use. She had not shown any evidence of abnormal abilities since the warehouse fire but seemed far keener on researching Anoch and Solomon's spells than any of her friends. Rye, though curious, did not see this as a priority.

⁌✋⁍

<u>Sunday 30th November 1997, 19:14pm, SCHOOL CAR PARK, ASHFIELD COMMUNITY SCHOOL, ASHFIELD, LONDON.</u>
Between the pair of them, Rye and Zach had managed to invite Pris, Ally and Fred, along to the prize-giving ceremony. Zach's

mother, unable to swap shifts at the supermarket, could not attend. Pris had driven them all to school in her new car. She had stalled four times and insisted on travelling at twenty miles per hour, but the journey was made safely.

'There we go, right on time,' Pris beamed, as she fixed the handbrake and turned to face her sister.

Her parking was wonky – at least she was proud.

'We're just lucky the school doesn't issue parking tickets,' replied Rye.

Without another word spoken by anyone, the group exited the car and headed for the school's main entrance.

*

Sat behind a table positioned to the side of the corridor, outside of the Main Hall, Liam Pritchard glowered. He appeared uncomfortable and sullen – sulking. And spending an entire evening with his shirt tucked into his trousers was proving a personal challenge. Perhaps placing the boy on display to collect tickets from pupils, parents and governors, was not one of Mr Bullen's smartest moves.

'Good evening,' Liam managed, reciting a memorised script.

Fred stood silent as his nemesis begrudgingly shoved an order of proceedings into his hand. Their physical contact was only fleeting, but Liam had essentially stroked the back of his hand, and Fred snatched it away, seething.

'The ceremony starts in ten minutes,' Liam confirmed, through a wicked smile.

Ally bit her tongue until after Pris, Rye and Fred had disappeared through to the Main Hall. She was oblivious to the true extent of the boys' tensions but had no fear in dismissing Liam's forced niceties.

'You can fuck right off,' she spat.

Instantly riled, Liam angrily took to his feet – with such force that his chair overturned. It fell with a clatter to the parquet floor. He pushed up his shirt sleeves and clenched his fists.

'What are you gonna do?' Zach goaded. 'Hit her?'

'Come get me,' Ally whispered, leaning in, before gliding back through the doorway. Zach followed.

At that moment, Ros strode grandly up to Liam's table. Not waiting to be handed a programme, she helped herself to one.

'You're uglier when you're angry,' she observed.

*

After perusing the aisles for several minutes, Rye was grateful when Mr Bullen had then directed her to her allocated seat. She thanked him, then proceeded to tiptoe through the narrow gap. As she approached her name card, however, Rye's eyes widened – the place to her left had been labelled as 'Louie Morgan'.

Rye craned her neck over the assembling crowd. Maybe Louie had decided not to attend? She could only hope. Both had tried to ignore each other since their date exactly one week ago, and every circumstantial encounter since had been laced with underlying awkwardness.

In a second's thought, Rye picked up Louie's name card with the intention of switching it with another. She reached out to grab the next one along, and Ros almost sat down upon her hand.

Frantic, Rye turned upon the spot. All the seats surrounding her were fast being taken up by her peers. Even Zach was too many rows back – there was no way she could now escape and persuade him to switch. Perhaps that was for the best; she was bound to mess up some specific order anyway.

Rye finally dropped Louie's name card back down and sat, defeated. She smoothed out her hair and breathed deeply, trying to appear nonchalant, despite all her fears.

Towards the back of the hall, between Pris and Ally, Fred stared miserably into his order of proceedings. Face buried, he had been looking at it for several minutes but had yet to read a word. Still reeling from his encounter with Liam, Fred was questioning why he'd even agreed to attend.

'Aw, they ain't 'alf done the place up nice,' spoke Pris.

She nodded to the stage. It had been lined with planters of plastic flowers. The dusty, red velvet curtains behind, remained drawn.

'Ah, I'm so proud of my little sis. In all my years here, I never won a prize,' she continued, before turning and speaking directly to Ally. 'Zach looked happy; what did you say to him?'

Their blossoming romance hadn't gone unnoticed to her.

Ally laughed, blushing.

'I only complimented his aftershave. I think his ego exploded in his pants.'

Pris's face soured at her lodger's vulgarity.

ঌ✣ঌ

<u>Sunday 30th November 1997, 19:25pm, SCIENCE ROOM 6, SCIENCE BLOCK, FIRST-FLOOR, ASHFIELD COMMUNITY SCHOOL, ASHFIELD, LONDON.</u>

'Well, Miss Fry, I'm afraid I'll have to leave you with the task in hand. The ceremony starts—' Mr Vincent consulted his watch '— in five minutes.'

'How shall I ever manage without your supervision,' Trinity derided.

'Oh, my child. Would you like me to go over it again?'

Trinity leaned over the desk and tapped the pile of exercise books with a forefinger. She spoke like a toddler.

'So, let me get this straight – the named stickers go on the front – *here* – right?'

'Yes, yes – just on the front, here,' Mr Vincent huffed. 'Right in the middle, like this. Then you look up the name on the list, and code it with a circle in the colour of the corresponding teaching set.'

'A *circle*?'

Chewing her gum loudly, Trinity faked confusion.

'Yes, Miss Fry, a circle. I'll tell you what, you can leave that part out if it becomes too complicated. Now, there're two hundred or so of these exercise books for you to get through—'

Trinity groaned and kissed her teeth.

'Maybe next time, Miss Fry, you'll think twice before tearing out another pupil's earrings,' Mr Vincent reprimanded. 'And you shouldn't be chewing. God knows how many break times I've wasted scraping the stuff off the underside of your desk. Maybe that's something you could do next time.'

Mr Vincent produced a tartan handkerchief from his corduroy trousers' pocket and held it out. Trinity spat a large globule of saliva-covered gum into his palm. She made a faux-apology and watched as her teacher clomped out of the lab. He could be heard walking the entire length of the corridor, but it wasn't until the door slammed at its opposite end that Trinity dismissively knocked over the nearest stack of books with the back of her hand.

Popping another strip of gum between her jaws, Trinity chewed, pondering the task ahead. Concluding it beneath her, she fished a Tamagotchi from out of her blazer.

*

Louie had taken his seat just in time, as the lights dimmed. And as the high-ranking teachers, guest speaker and governors then all ascended the steps to the stage – in a morbidly slow procession – he gave them a mock-salute. Louie and Rye avoided eye contact, but had exchanged fraught greetings, for in such close confinement, neither could ignore each other's presence completely. Louie had appeared just as rattled as she had by their chance seating arrangements.

After the initial applause subsided, the evening was kicked into full swing as two pupils belted out a rendition of The Foundations' 'Build Me Up Buttercup'. The duet, performed by

Elaine Burgess – a black girl, with one serious set of pipes – and Douglas McGuiness – a skinny, white beanpole of a boy – had almost all the crowd singing along.

A seated Mr Bullen could be seen enthusiastically tapping his feet, as Douglas slid and shuffled his own around the stage in front of him. The pupil was relishing his time in the limelight and swung his microphone around and around. This was much to the horror of Miss Devoil, the Music teacher, who was doing her best to conduct the school orchestra.

The room was hot, and Rye could already feel sweat forming on her brow. Each word sang by her peers only increased her discomfort, for her heart was already broken, and every lyrics' plea to the contrary was bittersweet. Rye risked a sideways glance at Louie; he seemed to be enjoying the performance.

Minutes later and the crowd, including Rye and Louie, took to their feet to applaud and whoop. Mr Bullen shook his students' hands, slapped Douglas McGuiness on the back, then signalled them off stage. He approached the lectern and microphone and cleared his throat. The crowd re-seated in dribs and drabs, as pupils competed against one another for the last clap.

'G-g-good evening,' Mr Bullen stuttered.

His hands shook and so he grasped either side of the lectern. He'd spent all day hidden away in his office practising his speech, but the large audience – as expected – only exacerbated his chronic anxiety.

'W-w-we h-have invited you all h-here t-t-tonight to c-c-celebrate the m-many achievements accomplished by the p-p-pupils here at Ashfield Community, within the last academic y-year.'

In the grips of stage fright, Mr Bullen skipped several lines of his speech, that within that moment he deemed unnecessary.

'I think y-y-you'll all agree it's b-been a f-f-fantastic y-year for both p-pupils and t-t-teachers alike, with p-p-progress being made in the classroom as w-well as out on the s-sports field.'

Members of the audience – pupils, teachers and parents – collectively sighed. At such painfully slow presentation, they would be lucky to make it home by midnight.

Mr Bullen coughed as a baby's penetrating cry screeched out from within the depths of his audience. This newborn had no qualms in sharing exactly how they were feeling. Mr Bullen coughed again, and his mortarboard slid slightly down his forehead.

'It is with g-g-great honour that I now w-welcome unto to you all, our g-g-guest s-speaker for the evening, Detective Chief Inspector Malcolm Goodfellow. Er – erm – an old b-boy of the s-s-school, Malcolm left Ashfield Community in – and I h-hope he doesn't mind me s-s-saying – nineteen fifty-nine.'

DCI Goodfellow held up his hands in surrender and a couple of ageing dads in the audience chuckled. This gave Mr Bullen the extra boost he needed to close his first contribution with only minimal stuttering.

'He has s-s-since gone on to achieve g-great things within the Metropolitan Police Force. Having ascended through the ranks, Malcolm now p-p-plays a vital p-part in our community's s-safety and wellbeing. Please give a hand for, Malcolm Goodfellow!'

On cue, DCI Goodfellow rose from his chair and strode over to the headmaster. The pair firmly shook hands.

'Y-y-yes. Not too b-bad, Andrew,' Mr Bullen reassured himself, as soon as he was out of the microphone's reach.

'Thank you, Andrew,' spoke DCI Goodfellow. Adjusting the microphone, he waited for the applause to diminish. 'Firstly, I'd like to say what a pleasure it is to be invited back after all these years, to celebrate the achievements of the pupils here at Ashfield Community. When I was a pupil here, which was – as Andrew has already divulged – longer ago than I care to remember—'

The same dads that chuckled before did so again. Rye chanced another look at Louie, to see if his reaction was the same as hers. Head in hands, he emitted a low groan. Rye stifled a laugh.

'I was the quiet kid, who always sat at the back of the classroom, feeling ignored. The one called out for being a "boffin" or a "nerd",' Malcolm Goodfellow continued. 'If I could give only one piece of advice to all you students here before me, it would be: be proud of your achievements and academia. If you are ever singled out negatively by your peers, be proud of those titles, because it is nothing to be ashamed of. Your school years are only the very beginning. You each have the reins of your own future – even if it doesn't always appear that way.'

Rye rolled up her order of proceedings into a tube and looked through it, up towards the large clock above the stage. Louie sniggered, and she blushed.

'Your headmaster has been liaising with myself, to allow the police force to play a more active role within the day-to-day life of Ashfield Community. One promising outcome of these discussions has been the decision to launch an anti-bullying campaign.'

Rye yawned, and Fred rolled his eyes.

'It is through the continued dedication of your staff, such as Mr Bullen …'

*

Trinity lit her fag off a Bunsen Burner – for her own sheer amusement, as she had always wanted to do so. Hoisting open one of the windows, she blew smoke out into the freezing night.

'Fucking boffins,' she snarled.

The Science block, separated from the school's main building, looked out and over the Main Hall opposite. Trinity could see the light of the ceremony taking place through its windows, and it disgusted her. Dejected, she rested her head against the window's frame, inhaling her cigarette in quick short bursts.

The smoke from her latest exhale had barely passed her lips when a thunderous clatter – like the sound of dropped kitchen pans – caused her to drop the cigarette through the open window.

Composing herself from the initial fright, Trinity slid the window closed, giving her straight a final dismal glance. Its dog-end glowed, still visible against the dark tarmac. Turning, she marched towards the lab's door, intent on investigating.

It was then she heard a scream – a gut-wrenching howl – and Trinity stopped dead in her tracks – the hairs on the back of her neck on end. The air was colder than it was before – even colder than outside – and Trinity could see her breath. It misted before her eyes.

Clang.

Trinity stiffened. The noise had been much quieter this time. She watched as a metal bin rolled past the open door like a tumbleweed.

Cautiously, Trinity resumed her approach. Only the lights at the back of the lab were switched on, which shrouded its front – chalkboard, teacher's desk and doorway – in a half-light.

'Hello?' she stammered

There was no reply. Instead, black smoke began drifting through the doorway; thin and wispy at first, then thicker, as it spread out across the floor. Still, Trinity advanced. Slow and steady, she swallowed her fear. A few feet from the threshold and she cleared her throat.

'Who's there? Don't think you're scaring me, 'cause you're not, alright?!'

Her words were far from convincing.

Trinity poked her head out of the room. The strange smoke was already beginning to dissipate, but the air remained chilled. She looked to her right – not a soul to be seen. Only the metal bin revolved lazily about the floor, amongst scrunched paper, drink cans and crisp packets.

The sound of a door slamming echoed down the corridor and Trinity's gaze shot to her left. Adjacent to the lab she was in, it had been the door to the teacher's storeroom, and it was slammed from within. Just past this, Trinity saw what she thought to be a large dog or wolf. Its hazy silhouette was slipping and sliding, as it tried to find a grip on the floor.

Trinity took a single step backwards into the safety of the lab. Quibbling over how much courage she truly possessed, she then slammed the door and flicked the latch to lock.

*

Rye was relieved to sit back down. She had come extremely close to tripping up the stage's steps and into DCI Goodfellow's crotch – whose hand she'd been required to shake before being reunited with her chosen book. Rye hadn't needed to look to know it was Pris who'd been responsible for the extra loud whoop she had received.

Wanting instant distraction as Mr Bullen began prattling on about sports results, Rye opened her book. 'Categories of Ghosts and Apparitions' – the title was considered an odd choice by many, including DCI Goodfellow, who had made a comment. But it was the most avant-garde choice that Rye thought she could get away with.

Stuck into the book's fly-leaf was a short inscription, beneath the school's shield of the blue fleur-de-lis:

'Ashfield Community School
Rye Turpin
has been awarded the prize for Art in Year 11
… I think you should look up.
No, really. Look up …'

'What the …'
Rye immediately did as the inscription said.

'*Look up*' – look up, *where?* She peered across to Louie's book. Open in his lap, she could read its inscription, and her suspicions were affirmed; the extra lines of advice given unto her were unique. Rye shuffled uneasily in her seat. She strained for an improved look at the stage.

'Pssst, Rye,' whispered Louie. 'What's up? You need the can? I've been bursting for the past half-hour.'

Rye snapped the cover of her book shut.

'Yeah,' she replied, distracted.

Turning, Rye attempted to catch Zach's eye. Alas, he was completely zoned out from overwhelming boredom.

*

Something large and heavy repeatedly slammed itself into the Biology room door. Its lock would surely not last much longer. The creature's shadow was visible through the frosted glass; if it wasn't for the wire set between the panes, it would have shattered. The creature – whatever it was – had first tried and failed to ram the door to the storeroom adjacent. Trinity had heard it.

Through all the commotion and her flinching, Trinity did not hear or notice the interlinking door, that connected her room to the storeroom, open.

Out of panic, Trinity picked up a stool and threw it at the lab's door. It impacted and fell with a bang yet did nothing to deter. Backing further, Trinity knocked over another stool. Shocked and incensed, she kicked it to one side, and turned, anxious for a way to escape—

Trinity did not see her attackers. Multiple hands grabbed at her body, face and shoulders. She couldn't scream, could barely breathe, as a cloth was tightened around her eyes, nose and mouth. It smelt awful. Painfully, her arms were forced back.

Something solid collided with the back of Trinity's knees, buckling her legs out from under her. She blindly fell in a tangled mess. Dazed, but kicking, she was dragged by her arms across the floor.

With one final push, Trinity fell backwards into what felt like a stack of plastic boxes. The hands that held her down released, and she heard another door slam and a key turn to lock. Disorientated, she fought the blindfold from off her face – it felt like a tea towel. She remained unable to see, however. Pitch black suffocated her sight.

Trinity attempted to stand but whacked her head almost immediately on what she assumed to be a shelf. Yelping, she crumpled, and a stream of pens rained down upon her skull. This confirmed it; she had been bungled into Mr Vincent's stationery cupboard.

Rubbing her scalp, Trinity controlled her breathing as best as she could and shifted her weight forwards. Hushed voices could be heard beyond the cupboard. Muffled as they were, she could not distinguish gender or the content of what was being said. It did not help that their talking was interspersed by the rhythmic thumping of the creature.

Trinity pressed her ear against the cupboard's door and heard one almighty bang. She lurched with an automatic reflex. Hitting her head on the metal shelving, Trinity was knocked out cold.

*

'… and I t-think that all the t-t-teaching s-s-staff deserve a round of applause for their c-c-continued efforts to provide f-fantastic opportunities for our p-p-pupils both inside, and outside, of the c-c-classroom.'

Mr Bullen gestured to the crowd for a standing ovation and they necessitated.

'And f-f-finally, in recognition of Detective Chief Inspector M-Malcolm Goodfellow f-for his—'

'Fire! Look – up there! Fire!'

An elderly gentleman – likely a pupil's grandfather – dressed in an ancient suit, had not retaken his seat as the rest of the crowd had done after the applause. He stood quivering, with the forefinger of his right hand pointed shakily aloft.

One-by-one, and in quick succession, members of the crowd also stood to extend their necks in the direction of the high windows. DCI Goodfellow, as well as several members of the governing board, then leapt from their seats to descend the stage, running to get a better-angled view.

Chaos ensued.

Rye dropped her book to the floor. It fell open, disregarded. She clambered onto her chair and stood upon it, tiptoed. Within the Science block opposite, flames shot across one of the rooms.

Rye quickly spun around, the only one to now look in the opposite direction. She was unable to pick her friends out from the endless rows of students and parents.

'Sorry! Excuse me.'

Rye pardoned herself as she used Louie's shoulders for support in dismount. Proceeding to tread upon her book prize, she ignored his confusion at her extreme descent into a frenzy.

In a desperate flurry, Rye pushed the chairs to her front forwards and into the backs of pupils' knees. She then rudely shoved Ros out into the aisle, so that she herself could get past.

Rye could see her friends and sister now. Zach, Fred and Ally had also managed to free themselves from their rows, and she caught a glimpse as they ducked out through the back set of doors into the corridor. Pris had somehow become marooned in a sea of chairs that caged her in.

In a sudden rush of fear and sweat, Rye dropped her blazer from off her shoulders. It fell and was soon trampled. With both hands, she pushed a suited father back into his row and fought her way over to the exit.

'Rye! Where are you going?!' Pris hollered after her.

The eldest Turpin began to climb over the obstacles that separated them, but in a tight skirt, this was no easy task. Rye ignored her. Ponytail and school tie swinging, she slipped out in pursuit. No-one other than Pris and Louie had noticed Rye and her friends depart.

She met the trio in the corridor, with Zach pulling at her arm and forcing her into a stumbled, full-force pelt. Fred was still massaging his left arm from where Ally had dragged him out of his seat.

Zach and Ally ground to a stop at the corridor's end, outside of the school's Main Reception. This allowed Rye and Fred to catch up over the short distance.

'Is this how – it's gonna be – from now on? Something weird happens – and we have to – investigate?' Fred panted, flustered.

'My prize told me to "look up"!' Rye blurted – desperate to share the discovery.

All four friends stood in a square as the ensuing conversation unfolded rapidly, with tensions running high.

'What are you talking about?' demanded Ally.

'Someone must have been trying to warn me of the fire!' Rye declared. 'The inscription in my book … it told me to "look up"!'

'I'm sorry, but I don't understand why we're all gunning it to the stairs when all we're probably going to find is Anoch, or something just as horrible. Why aren't we running in the opposite direction?' Fred gestured violently.

'Anoch is dead,' Rye stated, coldly.

'Is he really though?' Ally asked – her eyes crazed. 'None of us actually saw a body.'

'He's dead, Ally!' Rye's voice shook. 'Anoch is dead – it has to be. Oh, God, I hope it's dead.'

'I still don't know *why* we're *running* towards the danger!' Fred shouted, only to have his friends shush him. The chances of him being heard over the growing racket emanating from the hall were slim, however, and he didn't take kindly to their rebukes.

'It's Trinity,' Zach whispered. 'She got detention for ripping out Sabrina's earrings in Biology last week. She's up there, now – alone.'

'Leave her there?' suggested Fred, shrugging his shoulders. 'Where's Liam anyway? She's his girlfr-ouch!'

Zach walloped his friend around the shoulder.

'Fred, mate. The girl makes my pubic hair curl as much as the next guy, but we have – *here* – possibly the only person who could scare off a—' Zach lowered his voice further '— *demon*.'

'If that's even what it is!' cried Rye. 'Anoch is dead!'

She was desperately trying to convince herself of something that she had only moments before taken as fact.

'So, this all rests on my shoulders?' asked Ally.

Though she knew the question to be rhetorical, Ally still felt the need to ask. She did not yet understand – nor fully realise – the true extent of her abilities and had no faith whatsoever in using them.

There was a slight pause before Zach then answered, by turning and racing up the stairs. Rye and Fred were quick to follow.

'Brilliant,' Ally growled to herself, sighing. 'I bet it's a tramp ... I *hope* it's a tramp.'

She too then hastened after them.

Zach had already passed through the double doors onto the bridge by the time Rye, Fred and Ally had reached the first floor. The doors – one set at either end – swung wildly as they each passed through them, threatening to hit the next.

The Science corridor was shrouded in darkness. The only sound was that of their feet squeaking upon the lino as they ran. Almost bypassing the Biology room completely, Zach slid to a halt.

'Run faster!' Ally yelled, as she overtook Fred and Rye.

An expert at running by now – even in her minidress – Ally rallied up beside Zach. Both Fred and Rye skidded into her back.

The door to Mr Vincent's lab had been ripped clean from off its hinges. Split in two, its remnants littered the floor. Jets of flame emanated from gas taps, shooting out at waist height. And Trinity was nowhere to be seen.

Zach entered first. Striding in, he panned the scene. A stool had been jammed under the stationery cupboard's handle and the room's central window had been shattered from the inside.

Looking to their right, and the foursome saw the adjoining door – leading through to the storeroom – slowly click shut. Its sound was inaudible over that of the ignited gas. Zach and Ally went straight for it.

'No!' screamed Rye. 'Splitting up only works when more than one person is useful! Don't be *stupid* – we're sticking together!'

Rye had no desire to find out what lurked within the adjacent room – a loud commotion could already be heard from within, as objects were thrown and furniture scraped the floor. Rye did not want to be separated from Ally but would follow her no further.

'Just don't open that door!' Ally instructed, pointing to the stationery cupboard. 'We'll be right back.'

Begrudgingly, Rye and Fred watched as Zach and Ally disappeared into the storeroom, just as the sounds within ceased. Wasting no further time, they then set about the lab, turning off the gas taps one-by-one. They did not notice the fire extinguisher by the foot of one of the desks.

*

Entering the storeroom, Zach and Ally only managed to catch a glimpse of a person slip back into the corridor. What had been left behind was a state; smashed glass and thrown equipment. Two desks and a chest of drawers had been pulled out from against the wall. It was as if the intruder had tried to put as many obstacles as they could between them.

Ally took hold of Zach's clammy hand and together they traversed the wreckage. It was not difficult to do so, though it may have been quicker if they'd not held hands, or indeed simply backtracked through the lab. But soon enough, the pair stumbled out into the corridor and were hot in pursuit.

Not one, but three shadows – all human – were forty, maybe fifty, feet ahead of them. Unidentifiable; they appeared to be two girls and a boy and were just about to pass through the double doors onto the bridge.

Ally and Zach burst into a sprint – hands still clasped. Their similar speeds meant that their joint decision to remain connected did little now to hinder their progress.

Slamming their torsos into the first set of double doors – still swinging – Zach and Ally followed the mysterious trio out across the bridge. The impact hurt, and Zach filled his head with thoughts of Colossus – the *X-Men* hero he'd chosen to channel. Ally on the other hand wasn't thinking anything at all – she wouldn't allow herself to. She appeared fearless, but her true feelings were of weakness, self-doubt and terror.

Bang!

Zach and Ally collided with the second set of double doors, finding themselves again at the top of the stairs. The staircase itself was large. Constructed around the shape of a square, it left a wide void whereby one could easily spy on the ground floor. Many pupils utilised this layout to spit on each other during lessons' changeover. Ally let go of Zach's hand to lean over the railing. No intruders; but DCI Goodfellow and Mr Bullen were ascending, and fast.

'*Ally*,' Zach urged.

With seconds to spare, he grabbed her, pulling her away and through another set of double doors. The pair flattened themselves against the wall on the other side, as Zach held out a hand to steady the doors' swing. Cautiously, Ally tilted her head to peer through the vertical slit of glass set within the wood.

'They're heading straight for the Biology room,' she breathed. 'What about Rye and—'

Elbowed in her side by Zach, Ally was cut off mid-sentence. He nodded towards the opposite end of the long staff corridor. Like the Science block, this too was gloomy and darkened, and only the silhouettes of the three intruders could be seen. Cornered – at a dead-end – they stood hunched and talking, loudly.

*

Rye and Fred navigated the maze of flame quickly. Upon turning off the final two taps, both re-joined by the broken window to look out. Shimmering fragments could be seen on the tarmac below.

'What are you two doing up here?'

The voice that had spoken was stern.

Rye and Fred whirled around to see who had addressed them – it was DCI Malcolm Goodfellow. Mr Bullen stood beside him, slumped and wheezing in the doorframe, and backed by several members of senior management.

'They've run down the staff corridor!' Pamela Stoker, Chair of Governors, shouted, skidding to a stop behind the group.

*

'I don't know how to make it work!' Zach and Ally could hear one say.

'She's going to get us!' said another.

Their voices sounded familiar.

Slowly, one of the intruders turned to stare right at them. Still, Zach and Ally could not make out a face.

'Do you reckon you could knock her out or something, before—' the intruder began.

Several things then happened at once. One of the shadowy figures pulled the other two through the door to Mr

Bullen's office, before slamming it closed, just as the line of chairs opposite were sent flying through the air. Their legs impaled the door, as well as the wall, embedding themselves several inches into the plaster. The chair that had pierced Mr Bullen's office door was speared up to its seat.

Ally knew herself to be the one responsible for this apparent telekinetic activity; the sickness in her gut told her so.

Wispy black smoke trailed out from under the office door.

'There they are! Just like I said!'

Zach and Ally jumped; both turned to see who had spoken.

Pamela Stoker – Chair of Governors – stood with an extended accusatory arm and pointed finger. Mr Bullen and DCI Goodfellow were on either side of her.

- CHAPTER XXIV -

The Pentacles of Solomon

<u>Monday 1st December 1997, 15:26pm, ST BOTOLPH'S CHURCH, ASHFIELD, LONDON.</u>

School gossip was rampant with what had purportedly happened at the prize-giving ceremony. Teachers tried in vain to dispel the circulating rumours of gunmen, but the 'bullet holes' Ally's chairs left behind in the plaster only fuelled speculation. It had taken the school caretaker hours to dislodge, even chisel free, the seven seemingly hammered into the wall.

Mr Bullen had decided that rather than fill the holes, they would instead be covered by the installation of a new display board. His office also received a new door. In time the rumours would cease as students forgot. It would take Mr Bullen longer to forget, however. In all his thirty-one years of teaching, he had never seen anything quite like it.

Rye, Fred, Zach and Ally were all let off with only a lunchtime detention, simply for wandering the school corridors – unsupervised – during a time of crisis. Their watertight alibi of having all been present within the Main Hall when the fire had started meant they were pardoned of all other accusations Pamela Stoker had thrown at them. For Rye and Zach, it was a novelty to have received both a prize and a detention within the space of one hour.

Rye had provided scarce detail when questioned by her sister about her decision to flee the hall, other than her futile excuse of wanting 'to get closer to the action'. Pris was sceptical but did not push the subject. She was just relieved that Rye was safe.

Trinity had been found – unconscious – in Mr Vincent's stationery cupboard, not long after the fire brigade had arrived. Although rightly rattled, she had milked her incarceration for it all it was worth, insisting on a doctor.

The day after the prize-giving, and in the shadow of their school, Rye, Fred, Zach and Ally all sat cross-legged upon the cold tiled floor of St Botolph's vestibule. It was the only place Rye could think of that was close by, but also out of earshot from teachers and family, or general members of the public. Two pews – piled high with hymn books – flanked the two stone walls and an ornately carved cupboard stood tall in a corner. In hope of finding sanctuary deeper within the church, Rye did try the door to the nave, but it was locked.

'What are we all doing here then?'

Fred was the first to ask, having been ambushed – along with the others – the moment he'd been released from the final period. Rye hadn't allowed any of them to question her until they'd settled.

'Because of this,' replied Rye.

She cast the stone into the group's centre. Its flat surface – no longer ordinary-looking – bore an etched and intricate design. A tiny pattern within a small circle, within an equally as small square, was encased by a double – much larger – circle that reached right up to the edge. Miniscule writings and glyphs, in a language impossible to read, were inscribed all over and around. The level of artistry required to fit such detail into a space no more than three inches in diameter was masterful.

Zach loosened his scarf before picking up the stone for examination.

'How long has it looked like this?' he asked.

'Since at least last period,' informed Rye.

Zach passed the stone to his left.

'It's a pentacle,' said Ally. 'One of Solomon's. There're dozens of them. I've been reading up on them for the past few weeks.'

'Well, what does it mean? What does it do? Does it do anything?' Rye asked.

Calves bare against the tile; she shivered and drew up her knees to hug them.

'I'm not sure,' Ally mused.

The others watched as she produced two – inch-thick – piles of print from inside her briefcase.

'Just give me a minute,' she said, beginning to flick.

Rye recognised one of the piles instantly. The flowery border of its title page confirmed it to be the Ars Goetia. She did not recognise the other but assumed it to be another one of Solomon's texts that Ally had printed during her spout of independent research.

'I've had it with all of this!' Rye suddenly exclaimed – startling the other three. 'I can't keep doing this! *We* can't keep doing this! We need answers, and we need them now.'

As usual, Rye had many questions, but their formation in her mind was now of exponential proportion. There were too many unanswered for her to cope with, and it frustrated her to no end.

Ally took a deep breath.

'Well, I might actually have something that could help with *that*.'

Extracting a selected page, Ally then passed it across. Rye took it, open-minded as to any suggestion that would give her the answers she yearned for. The page had been highlighted and its top-most right corner folded down.

'"The Fifth Pentacle of Jupiter",' Rye read, slowly.

The figure accompanying the subheading was similar to that now upon the stone. It too had double concentric circles on its outermost edge, as well as scattered writings and symbols, but the design at the pentacle's centre was altogether different. A six-pointed star; it had been extended sideways by the addition of two diamonds on either side. Rye proceeded to read aloud the paragraph beneath.

'"As I was among the captives by the river of Chebar, the heavens were opened, and I saw visions of Elohim".' She scrunched up her face. 'What does that mean?'

Ally ceased her continued search just long enough to meet Rye's eyes.

'It's a quote from the Book of Ezekiel.'

Rye flung her arms out to her sides and vigorously shook her head. Her mouth stretched wide with a sarcastic smile.

'From the Bible,' Ally confirmed, momentarily lifting her head again.

Rye nodded, and Ally busied herself once more — scattering pages all around, as her search became more manic.

'Anyway, it's just a quote. That pentacle—' Ally pointed blindly at the paper held in Rye's hands '— the Fifth of Jupiter — was supposedly on Jacob's person as he ascended the ladder to heaven. It's invoked in ritual for visions.'

'I don't want to ascend to heaven, thank you very much. At least, not any time soon,' Rye hastened.

She flapped the page under Ally's nose, in a prompt for her to take it back. But Ally batted it away and so Zach took it instead.

'It won't *make you* ascend to heaven,' Ally spoke, as if it was obvious. 'It's just supposed to give you some sort of enlightenment — clarity — revelation. *Answers*. I figured we could use it to give you yours — *ours* — all of ours. At this stage, knowledge is our most powerful tool.'

'Alright, *Mystic Meg*, what about protecting ourselves?' Zach asked. 'Or mind control? If we're talking in the realms of visions, then that's not totally out of the question, right? Sure, you have a few magic tricks up your sleeve, but if Anoch attacks again then—'

'Anoch's dead, Zach,' Rye shot back. 'We should be concentrating on Elizabeth.'

'Controlling a demon would take practice, as well as lengthy exposure – not something I'm keen on. And I'm sure would be beyond my capabilities.'

'Would, we all, please, stop talking about—' began Rye.

'The only problem,' Ally continued, 'is that we can't perform the vision ritual anytime soon. It calls for the blood of the Avem, slaughtered on the night of a New Moon.'

'What on earth does that mean?' Rye asked.

'I looked it up in the school library—'

'Internet?' interjected Zach, jokingly.

Ally took her eyes off what appeared to be an index page to look at him.

'No,' she cooed. 'Latin Dictionary, actually. *Avem* means bird.'

'That's disgusting!' Rye protested, clasping her hands to her mouth. 'What bird?'

'Mr Tumnus,' said Ally, suddenly dropping her wad of pages to the floor. She had finally found the stone's pentacle within the writings of Solomon and had pieced something together.

'What? You can't be serious?' cried Rye – distraught at the very thought. 'We can't *kill* Mr Vincent's pet budgie!'

Rye looked to Zach, then Fred for assurance. They provided none. Zach simply picked up the page from the top of the pile Ally had dropped. Fred just gazed at the floor, tracing the pattern on the tile with a finger.

'Think about it, I think we already—' began Ally.

'Couldn't we just trap a pigeon?' suggested Rye – brainstorming any alternative.

'Trap a pigeon?' Zach repeated. 'That's gonna be easier said than done.'

'Just lay some breadcrumbs, and – and tea towel it!' expanded Rye.

Enthusiastically, she demonstrated catching a pigeon with an invisible cloth.

'I think—' Ally attempted to speak again.

'Like I said,' interrupted Zach, 'a lot easier *said* than *done*.'

Rye tapped her fingernails on the tile and gritted her teeth.

'Ignoring the bird then,' she said, 'when's the next New Moon anyway? Not that I'm condoning animal cruelty.'

'Not for another month,' Ally hissed. 'The last one was yester—'

'I can't wait another month!' protested Rye.

'That's what I've been trying to say!' Ally shouted, and both Rye and Zach flinched. 'I don't think you have to. This pentacle—' she held up the stone '—it's the Fifth Pentacle of the Sun. It allows for temporal displacement of physical beings.'

Rye and Zach looked at her, confused.

'Time travel,' Ally confirmed. 'Or, at least, that's what Solomon says it's for. And he should know, seeing as he devised the bloody thing.'

'What are you trying to say, exactly?' asked Rye.

'I think what she's trying to say is that she thinks we've already used it to somehow go back in time to yesterday evening. She thinks that *we*—' Zach waved his hands around like a magician '—were the intruders.'

'Thank you!'

Ally threw up her hands, exasperated, but relieved. Zach winked at her.

'You think, that we all went – *will go* – back in time, to kill Mr Tumnus?' Rye spoke, slowly. 'I'm not killing Mr Tumnus.'

'I'll do it.' Ally shrugged.

Having inadvertently enabled, then witnessed the death of Solanki, the prospect of killing a budgie did not greatly faze her.

'Couldn't have been a gerbil,' Fred croaked, surprising everyone by speaking. 'Has the bird even gone missing?'

'Come to think of it,' Zach mused, scratching his chin, 'I didn't see him in the storeroom yesterday.'

Rye gasped and pointed a finger at Ally.

'I can't believe you killed Mr Tumnus!' she shrieked.

'*I* haven't done it yet!' Ally snapped. 'Give me a break. All I know is that we can't keep doing this – you said it yourself. We need answers, and *this*—' she jabbed at the stone '—is the way to get them.'

'Agreed,' said Zach.

Nodding his head affirmatively, he then turned to Rye.

Rye hesitated at first, thinking her response over in her mind before committing. The idea of Mr Tumnus' demise was not a pretty one, but if it ultimately lay the mystery of Elizabeth Thackerall's death to rest, then she deemed the sacrifice necessary. Besides, if Ally was right, then it had already been done anyway.

'Agreed,' she confirmed, and looked over at Fred.

His face was pale, and his mouth quivered as he spoke, but his eyes were angry.

'So, you're planning on doing a spell, with this stone, so you can kill Mr Vincent's pet bird, all so you can do *another* spell?'

'*Yes*,' the others all replied in unison.

'Count me out.'

'We need five people for the vision ritual to work,' replied Ally, severely. 'So, we're counting you *in*.'

'Nope – not doing it.' Fred reaffirmed.

*

From its hiding place within the cupboard in the vestibule, Anoch silently laughed to itself. The demon found it amusing listening to the human's discussions and was the only reason it had not attacked them already. They were novices trying to make sense of things they did not understand, and they would never get to understand them if Anoch succeeded in killing Rye Turpin. The demon found it funny – predictable even – that without even realising it, they had sought solace in a house of God to make crisis talks.

Dumb-looking; its long nose pressed up against the wood, the demon strained its pointed ears, as its widened – saucer-like – eyes blinked. Anoch's profile was strikingly similar to Roald Dahl's Grand High Witch.

*

'Well, there are four of us already,' spoke Zach. 'Who do we get as a fifth?'

'I'm not—' began Fred.

'Ah, well, you see,' Ally spoke over him. 'We need five to conduct the ritual, but Rye you'll have to be in its centre. We'll need another two people to sit with Zach, Fred and I, on the outside of the pentacle.'

Fred ardently shook his head, as Ally addressed only the other two.

'I can ask Pris,' Rye suggested, before backtracking. 'Wait, why am I sitting in the centre of the pentacle?'

Zach furrowed his brow.

'How on earth are you going to convince Pris to join?' he asked, incredulously.

'Because you're the person with the most questions that need answering,' Ally responded to Rye.

Rye nodded slowly as she processed this, then turned to answer Zach.

'I don't know – shock tactics or something? Explain to her what danger we've been enduring the last few months.'

*

Anoch sharpened its talons upon its rough hide. There was no way that the demon would disappoint its master again. Now fully healed, Anoch vowed to rip the heart from out the blonde sixteen-year-old before she could solve the mystery of Elizabeth Thackerall's murder.

Anoch would take great pleasure in killing the police-woman also, if only its master allowed. At present, Michelle Davey was only a hindrance unto herself, and not yet a threat to their mission statement. Anoch had been disallowed any further unnecessary killings.

*

'That means we're still a person short,' Ally mused.

'No, it doesn't!' Fred shouted.

'Why don't you ask that policewoman?' Zach asked Rye. 'She did give you the stone after all.'

'I told you, she's on long-term leave, apparently, and I have no idea where she lives. Besides, she didn't want anything more to do with the stone, and I'm guessing she'd want even less to do with it now it's magically covered itself in millennia-old graffiti. She didn't even know where it came from.'

'And you believe her?' Ally questioned.

'She's a copper, ain't she?' Zach offered, futilely. 'And she didn't arrest me—'

'Exactly!' Ally retorted. 'And arresting you is something she definitely should have done as a police officer. We need answers? Well, until we have them, the only people we can trust are each other. Which means we still need another pers—'

'I'm not doing it!' Fred shouted.

Louder than before, his voice boomed and echoed around the tiny vestibule. Even Anoch jumped.

'I don't understand any of you!' he continued. 'You don't trust the policewoman, but you're willing to trust – and use – a stone that she gave you to travel back in time? Are you even listening to how crazy that sounds! That's if it even works.'

'After everything you've seen over the last two months, you're willing to bet it won't?' asked Ally, coldly.

'Begs the same question!' Fred shouted. 'How can you be sure that you can trust this?'

'Because we've already done it!' Ally shouted back.

'That doesn't mean that it's safe!' Fred implored.

No-one replied, for no-one could guarantee he was wrong. Fred looked at each friend in turn, daring them to challenge him. Still, no-one said a word and so he asked, calmly:

'How does it even work?'

Ally inhaled deeply before replying.

'The text says that the Fifth Pentacle of the Sun must be etched upon a sacred stone — *eso*!' Presenting the stone with the Spanish equivalent of *'voila!'*, she proceeded to wave her hands mystically over it.

'Which means?' asked Fred.

'That it's been blessed by a saint,' replied Ally.

Fred rolled his eyes and stood up to leave.

Ally picked up the stone and ran a forefinger over its intricate markings.

'"And thee must fill thy heart, and thy head, with thoughts of the time and place",' she recited.

Rye reached out and felt the etching upon the stone also.

'That doesn't sound very technical,' she mused. 'Are we just supposed to sit and stare at it?'

'"He shall give his angels charge over thee, to keep thee in all thy ways".'

Subconsciously, Zach began to stroke Ally's knee as she read. She did not object to him doing so; in fact, she quite liked it.

Fred passed by the cupboard on his way to the outer door, where he then paused to take one final look back at his friends. He agreed that answers were needed but did not agree with their method. There was sure to be another way — not that he knew what that was — but if they weren't even willing to consider other options, then he did not care to stay.

*

Now was the time. Anoch had let the humans talk for too long. Too much time had already been wasted in relishing the build-up — a key flaw of all beings that were truly evil but lacking any real intelligence. As Anoch reminisced over the injuries sustained at their hand, its joviality was quickly replaced by anger. They had all hurt it and made the demon's mission personal. All four would now die, even if it meant inciting the wrath of its master.

*

'"They shall bear thee up in thy hands".'

Ally finished reading just as Anoch burst out from within the cupboard. In one swift movement, the demon wrapped a talon around Rye's right shoulder, as they both – along with Ally and Zach – were engulfed by a plume of black smoke that gushed thickly out from the centre of the stone's pentacle. The smoke readily filled the vestibule as all four beings were then folded into the stone, as if they'd been made of paper.

Fred hardly had time to process Anoch's presence, for the demon had disappeared just as quickly as it had appeared. His eyes – wide with horror – darted all around the vestibule. Loose paper sheets flew about in a wind. He was alone. Even the stone had vanished. Suddenly, the door to the nave squeaked open and Fred fell back into the door behind. A short blonde emerged, dressed in school uniform.

'Oh, it's you,' spoke Ros, sounding surprised. 'I thought I heard a noise. Frederick, what's all this mess?'

'I – erm – I dropped Ally's briefcase,' Fred breathed – his heart racing. 'Ros, what – what are you doing here?'

'I'm setting up for choir practice,' she replied – sizing up the boy.

'What are you doing afterwards?' Still leaning against the door, Fred thought his body was unable to support itself.

'Visiting a friend around half seven, then … nothing. Why?'

Fred took a drawn-out breath, disbelieving of what he was about to say.

'We're a person short of … a project.'

❧

<u>Monday 1st December 1997, 19:21pm, THE KING'S HEAD PUBLIC HOUSE, ASHFIELD, LONDON.</u>

After her suspension, Michelle had tried her best to remain sober. Tried and failed. For the past seven days, she hadn't seen a soul other than those she'd crossed paths with on her way to Stonem's off-licence. But today, after receiving another text from Sharon Knight, Michelle had decided to take up the offer of an evening's pub quiz – not that she was in the mood. However, Michelle had an ulterior motive. She would make a point of only drinking non-alcoholic beverages, in the hope that word would get back to her DCI.

Having found Sharon and Gary towards the back of The King's Head, Michelle had sat silently for what she knew to be precisely twenty-one minutes. Their drab talk was boring her to death, and she willed for it to be eight o'clock so the quiz could finally commence. Chain-smoking, Michelle enviously eyed up Shaz's gin and tonic.

'Ah, the wife would not approve of this,' Gary chuckled.

He rubbed his hands together as the waitress presented him with an all-day breakfast. Michelle could hear his rounded belly rumbling.

'The cholesterol?' asked Shaz, sounding concerned.

'No, no.' Gary chuckled again, squeezing a generous amount of brown sauce over his plateful. 'Well, maybe. It's because she's already made a shepherd's pie.'

'Ah, no, really?' Shaz laughed and brushed her red hair behind her ears. 'What are you going to do?'

'Eat that too o' course.' Gary grinned, lifting his pint to his lips.

Michelle stared dreamily as he proceeded to gulp the amber liquid. She was angry with the pair of them. Sure, she'd not actually given up drinking, Michelle knew this, but they didn't. And the more she thought about it, the more she was hurt – hurt by their audacity at even inviting her to a pub. Shaz had bought Michelle an orange juice before she'd even arrived — did they not trust her to order for herself?

'I'm going to the toilet,' Michelle announced.

Stubbing out her cigarette, she got up to leave the table. Gary looked to Shaz, shrugging. Shaz shook her head, despairingly.

Flouncing across the bar, Michelle angrily swung open the panelled door to the toilets, letting it slam behind her. Her head still pounded in the aftermath of yet another blackout that afternoon and she winced at its sound.

The King's Head was an old pub, in dire need of refurbishment. This was no better demonstrated than by the state of the unisex toilets. Filthy; they stunk strongly of urine.

Choosing the first cubicle, Michelle locked it before pulling her jeans down to her ankles. Heavily, she took a throne. Two flies buzzed around her head and she flapped them away as she relieved her bladder into the bowl.

Michelle reached out and pulled two squares of paper from the dispenser, reading the words that had been scrawled upon it in permanent marker:

'Liam sucks gay cock.'

A detailed picture of an enormous phallus accompanied the untidy writing. Michelle screwed up her face in disgust and reached under to dry herself. It was then she saw another scrawl. This one was not on the dispenser, or the walls of the cubicle, however — it was on her own thigh. Written in biro upon her stubbly skin, it read:

'You're writing this in the bathroom of Albertus Magnus's house. You need to remember. Next time, remember. Next time bring your Dictaphone. You will only remember BEING HERE WHILST

YOU'RE HERE. It's a precaution – so the demons can't find him. DON'T be scared by this message.'

The word 'don't' had been underlined twice. But Michelle *was* scared. As implied, the writing was her own; she must have written it herself but could not recall doing so. 'Demons' – Michelle had a book entitled *Demonology*. It was sat within her handbag back at the table at this very moment.

Michelle re-read the message again, and again. Then she stood, pulling her knickers and jeans up with her. She did not re-tuck her blouse, nor did she flush the toilet or even wash her hands, because for the first time since the book's manifestation, Michelle was itching to leaf through it.

*

'Speak of the Devil! We were just wondering if you'd fallen in,' Gary joked, as Michelle strode over to their table.

He retracted his hand from her handbag, where it was now placed upon the seat of her chair. Michelle had left it slung over its back.

'Why're you touching my bag?' she demanded.

Immediately, Gary was taken aback.

'This girl – a schoolgirl. She just knocked it off,' he replied, defensively. 'I probably should have asked if she was with her fam—'

'What girl? Where?'

Michelle spun around on the spot, attempting to pick out anyone within the filling bar who was dressed in school uniform.

'I dunno, just a girl – a blonde girl,' said Gary.

He looked to Shaz for support.

'Where is she now?' Michelle pushed.

'I don't know, I think she was leaving – *listen*,' spoke Shaz, standing. She placed a calming hand on Michelle's forearm, but it was shaken off. 'Michelle! It was an accident. She picked it right up.'

Hurriedly, Michelle turned her attention to her handbag. Rummaging through its contents, her colleagues thought she feared something had been taken, but her concern was quite the opposite.

Just as Michelle suspected, right at its bottom was a small scrap of paper that had been tightly folded. Once extracted, she hastily smoothed it against her shaking palm.

'A.M. One Beggar's Hollow,' she whispered, softly. '*Albertus Magnus.*'

A chill ran down her spine.

'What?' said Shaz, flatly.

'Eh?' said Gary.

Shaz attempted to look at the note, but Michelle screwed it into a ball and dropped it back within her handbag before she had the chance.

'I need a drink,' Michelle declared.

Instantly, her colleagues appeared horrified.

'Oh, Michelle—' began Gary, but Michelle was already headed for the bar.

Abandoning their table and weaving between seated punters, Shaz and Gary quickly pursued. Gary found this particularly difficult, having to ask several people to slide in their chairs, just so he could fit between them.

'I'm so sorry!' Shaz hastened apology – the first to catch up. 'I should have known better than to invite you to a pub.'

Her face was pleading.

'Then, why did you?' Michelle rudely quipped.

Elbows on the bar, Michelle was far too busy trying to catch the attention of the bartender to give Shaz the courtesy of looking at her. She felt cold, yet was sweating, profusely.

'I thought that the quiz might take your mind off things,' Shaz defended. 'I can see we made a mistake. But we can go somewhere else? We could get coffee?'

'I don't want coffee.'

'Water?' asked Gary. 'How about we get you some nice cold water – with ice. You look like you—'

'What? What do I look like?' Michelle sneered.

There was a momentary pause, wherein both Gary and Shaz exchanged looks of concern as Michelle shot daggers between them.

'You don't look well,' said Shaz, finally.

'Give the girl a prize!' Michelle exclaimed.

One shot. One shot, and Michelle would go home. Once there, she would locate her Dictaphone and head back out. Maybe she'd have two shots, or three? The sign behind the bar advertised a deal.

'What can I get you?' the bartender asked, turning to serve.

'Three shots of vodka, please.'

Shaz's face fell – Michelle could see it from out the corner of her vision. Gary buried his head in his hands.

As the bartender busied himself, fulfilling her order, Michelle kept her gaze forward. Consciously, she began scanning the bottles lined up along the back display. First of the month, and everything was decorated with the first seasonal decorations that Michelle had seen that year. Surrounded by a string of fairy lights, plastic sprigs of holly and mistletoe had been taped between them. A simple sight; it brought a tiny glimmer of hope. Michelle loved the holidays. She would usually – work permitting – travel down to Brighton to where her grandfather lived, and where her parents had moved to upon retirement also. Her heart sank as she realised that work would probably not pose an issue this year.

There it was: *the* bottle.

Short and stout, with a rectangular base, the picture of a clawed-hand graced its labelled sticker. *The Devil's Hand.* Inconspicuously nestled amongst the many others, it appeared just as Michelle had remembered it, and the image of Elizabeth Thackerall drinking from it only grew stronger the longer she stared. Its bright green alcohol shone with luminescence. Up until now – its discovery – and the colour had remained a mystery.

'What's that?!' Michelle demanded.

Abruptly, she tapped the bartender on the forearm – jogging him – as he finished pouring the final shot. Leaning over the bar, Michelle did her best to point at the bottle. Muttering under his breath, the bartender turned to look.

'That?' he asked, flatly.

Michelle vigorously shook her head and waved to the right. Taking to standing upon the railing at the foot of the bar, she leaned further.

'Oh, this!' said the bartender, taking the correct bottle down from the shelf. 'This is absinthe.'

He placed it in front of her and Michelle snapped it up. She was in wonderment. Since her suspension, Michelle had begun to doubt all she had seen, as well as herself, but this bottle – this *physical* bottle – that she held within her hands, was proof enough that her mind had not made the entire thing up.

Michelle stroked at the label with an index finger. At sixty-eight percent, even she would have been hesitant of consuming the alcohol. The image was not unlike the many drawings Michelle had obsessively sketched, but the hand had feathers. Only three, they jutted out from the palm. Each of its five fingers – or claws – was slightly retracted.

'Fancy a tipple?' the barmen tempted – misinterpreting Michelle's silence for that of a drinker on the verge of trying something new. 'Go on, shake hands with the devil.'

'Please – don't encourage her,' Shaz hissed.

'I'll take the bottle,' Michelle announced.

*

Outside of the pub, Fred checked his pager for what must have been the hundredth time. Darkness had long since fallen, and there was still no word from Zach or Ally. It had been almost four hours. Frustrated, he kicked a drainpipe next to him.

All the way through the ordeal that had been choir practice, Fred held onto his pager between sweaty fingers. It was on loud, but he dared not put it away for risk of missing that all-important message. Ros encouraged Fred to join in rehearsals, but he had vehemently refused. He'd never had any inclination to sing anywhere other than the shower, and today was not the day for that to change.

Fred had been sketchy as to what his 'project' entailed when Ros asked him, choosing to only vaguely answer that it was 'for R.E'. By concealing the truth, this was not an outright lie. Fred just didn't want to give Ros the opportunity to back out until it was too late for her to do so. The irony that he was not allowing her to form an opinion on the ritual, when he himself had had his own ignored by his friends, was not lost unto him, but at this stage, there were more important factors than what was fair.

'That was quick,' Fred observed, as Ros scurried out of the pub – she had only minutes ago walked in.

Much to Ros's apparent relief, Fred had chosen to wait outside. A place frequented by many of his underage peers, Fred disliked The King's Head with a passion.

'It was only a flying visit,' said Ros. 'Where to now then?'

She proceeded to peer in through one of the pub's stained-glass windows. Fred overlooked his classmate's eccentricities. It was nothing out of character.

'To Rye's house. I'm hoping we can meet her there.'

Fred had no idea how he was going to explain all this to Pris. He was just praying that Rye would somehow reappear and do so herself, so that he didn't have to.

'Frederick,' began Ros, cautiously, before asking again. 'What exactly is this project?'

Though sounding far from assured, she had already begun walking quickly away, seemingly keen on getting as much distance from the pub as possible.

'I'll explain on the way,' Fred breathed. He swallowed. 'You're an intelligent, trustworthy soul. I'm hoping you can help us.'

'I'll explain on the way,' Fred breathed. He swallowed. 'You're an intelligent, trustworthy soul. I'm hoping you can help us.'

- CHAPTER XXV -

Sunday 30th November, Again

<u>Sunday 30th November 1997, 20:27pm, SCIENCE ROOM 6, SCIENCE BLOCK, FIRST-FLOOR, ASHFIELD COMM-UNITY SCHOOL, ASHFIELD, LONDON.</u>
Ally, Zach, Rye and Anoch fell, spinning, into the Science corridor from ceiling height. All immediately separated upon entry, except for Rye and Anoch. The adjoined pair slammed against the wall, crashing into the metal bin beneath.

Balls of scrunched paper, drink cans and crisp packets cascaded out around them, as the stone – which had been held between Ally's fingers – skidded down the corridor, and into darkness. Ally reached after it, but it continued to gush smoke that masked its own trajectory.

Bewildered and confused, the demon scampered in the opposite direction to the stone, and thus parted from Rye. Like the others, Anoch too was regaining its bearings.

Rye's jaw dropped in response to the excruciating pain that seared from below her right collarbone. Shiny with sweat, the vein on her forehead popped out against the skin. Throwing her back to the wall, she instinctively reached deep into her lungs and let out an almighty howl.

Anoch's incision must have been half an inch at its deepest. Masterfully, the demon's claw had skewered the flesh above the breast. Rye did not want to look, but her skin had parted from itself, leaving a gash through to the muscle.

Ally wildly felt about the floor for the stone. She couldn't see anything – not even her friends. She had only heard Rye cry out in agony. Flat on her stomach, Ally slapped the lino with her palms. All of a sudden, her fingertips brushed up against something solid, and she stretched out a little further to pull whatever it was closer. It was Zach's hand. The smoke began to clear – slightly – and Ally could see that his face was drawn and queasy. He crawled towards her, arms open for an embrace.

Ally ignored the appeal, and instead physically pulled the boy up alongside. Together they crawled towards Rye's silhouette. Her form gained clarity upon approach.

It was then that Anoch ran at them through the clearing smoke. On all fours, the demon lunged for Rye's extended legs, catching her left shin with its right talon, just as Ally grabbed hold of her beneath the armpit, and dragged her into her lap. The demon's claw sliced the length of the bone, drawing blood. Rye would have screamed again, but the shock only made her gag.

As Anoch fell forward, its hind legs struggled to find grip. Its left talon slipped across Rye's right thigh, tearing her skirt, but missing the skin. The demon made another swipe and missed.

Ally – backside upon the floor – pulled a knee up to her chest before slamming her boot across into Anoch's snout. Her heel skimmed the top of Rye's chest wound, however, causing her to wince and gasp. Like kicking a brick wall, Ally's efforts had little impact. The demon only spluttered – drooling saliva over the leather.

Zach lifted the empty metal bin above his head and threw it down over the bodies of his friends. It collided with Anoch's skull with a low hollow clang, and the demon fell back against the neighbouring wall. The bin clattered to the lino, rolling down the corridor and past the open Biology room door.

Seizing their opportunity, Zach and Ally pulled Rye to her feet.

'Hello?' a voice spoke from inside the Biology room.

Zach looked at Ally, aghast.

'*Trinity*,' he mouthed.

Hurriedly, the pair heaved Rye along the corridor, but she staggered – pulling down heavily upon the sleeves of their blazers. Zach and Ally allowed her to stay limp and proceeded to slide her as she silently whimpered.

Thankfully, the door to the storeroom was unlocked and Ally barged it open with an elbow. Zach pushed Rye across the threshold, and she collapsed in a heap. Unceremoniously, he kicked her legs inside.

'Who's there? Don't think you're scaring me, 'cause you're not, alright?!' Trinity shouted, as she poked her head out from inside the Biology room.

Zach and Ally hastily stepped over their friend, just as the latter spotted the stone. Innocuously, it laid at the foot of the doorframe. Ally barely had time to whip it through before Anoch shot past and Zach slammed the door closed.

After dragging Rye a little further into the room, Zach and Ally – without discussion or hesitation – began ripping furniture away from the walls. Zach spun the desk nearest to him by ninety degrees and pushed it up against the door.

'I'm bleeding!' exclaimed Rye.

'I thought you – might – be,' breathed Ally, as she grabbed hold of another desk and, with Zach's help, turned it upside down to place atop the other.

'Rye – can you stand? We need you to get up,' Zach urged.

He was frantically throwing random objects from the cupboards onto the stacked desks. Ally wheeled out a small chest of drawers and shunted it up against the amassing pile, adding to their barricade.

From out of the darkness, towards the back of the elongated room, Mr Tumnus chirped a merry tune. Hardly distressed by the disturbance, the little bird was excited by the unexpected company.

Bang! Bang!

Anoch rammed itself against the storeroom door, which shuddered in its frame. The stacked furniture retracted a couple of inches, and Zach shoved all firmly back, just as the demon once again hurled its body.

'It – hurts,' squealed Rye.

She pressed her blazer down onto her torso, in the hope her skin would somehow glue itself back together.

Bang! Bang!

'I don't doubt that it does,' said Ally, fiercely, chucking a pile of textbooks onto their defences. 'Unfortunately, you don't have time to hurt.'

Rye pulled herself up on the filing cabinet behind, pushing all her remaining strength down to her legs. Rising, she steadied herself with a shaking hand. Her other was still firmly clasped to her wound. Grimacing, Rye continued to apply pressure.

Bang! Bang!

The beady eyes of the taxidermy – emotionless and stiff – bore down upon Rye. Nauseous and dizzy, she could see two of each animal. Her head swam. What with Anoch's unexpected reappearance and subsequent maiming of her, Rye had yet to even appreciate that the stone – and pentacle thereon – had delivered, just as promised, in transporting them all back to the night before.

'It's no use, it won't hold much longer,' said Zach, quietly.

Bang! Bang!

Anoch slammed home again, and the barricade lurched backwards once more. The brackets holding the shelf above the storeroom door then suddenly gave way, and the plywood – and all the objects stored upon it – came crashing down. Glass from the cabinets and jars that encased the taxidermy and pickled offal smashed, as they impacted the pile. Wedged in place, the shelf now served as a beam lock. Whether it had fallen by magic, or simply a consequence of Anoch's repeated efforts? None of them could be sure – not even Ally – but as the demon gave one last slam, all knew that any further attempts would be in vain.

'It's given up?' Rye murmured – hopeful – although she knew this not to be true.

Bang! Bang!

All three automatically looked to the storeroom door, but the sound was coming from further away this time. Having given up on the first point of entry, the demon had moved on in search of another.

'*Trinity,*' said Zach and Ally in unison, looking at one another.

Quickly, they turned and hurried for the adjoining door that led through to the Biology room. Zach collected a lab rag from the radiator as he went. Ally snapped a fire extinguisher away from its bracket on the wall. Obediently, Rye followed, wincing. Mr Tumnus hopped down from his perch and tweeted after them, as Zach cautiously eased the door open.

The Biology room was lit by half a dozen lights. Set into the ceiling tiles, only the ones towards the back of the lab were switched on – right above where the trio crept. With her back to them, Trinity stood in the central aisle. She was transfixed by the door against which Anoch was now throwing itself. Thankfully, she'd had the sense to shut and lock it, though it would surely not last much longer.

Bang!

Rye flinched as Trinity threw a stool at the door. Noisily, it fell to the floor. Zach lifted the lab rag, ready to pounce.

Bang!

All three flinched this time, as Trinity backed right up into another stool and angrily kicked it aside. Mere feet from Zach, she made a movement to turn around.

Zach successfully ambushed Trinity mid-turn, draping the rag over the girl's face as one might a bull. Ally dropped the fire extinguisher down by her feet before helping. All-the-while Anoch continued to throw its body weight.

Bang! Bang!

Rye could see the demon's gnarly face through the frosted glass – it had cracked, but the wire set between the panes had prevented it from shattering.

Pulling the rag taut, Zach moved around a flailing Trinity as she attempted to knee him in the plums. Ally grabbed hold of her wrists and forced back her arms.

Bang! Bang!

Zach furiously shook his head, gesturing Rye to the fire extinguisher. Unable to move, the boy was sandwiched between Trinity's backside and Ally's crotch – their captive's arms caging him in. Under different circumstances, he might have appreciated the position.

Rye let go of her wound to lift the extinguisher. Trotting wearily up behind Ally, the four of them formed an awkward and floundering conga-like line. Rye's friends teetered to one side as Trinity fought to keep her balance. Crouching, Rye navigated the forest of legs to smack the heavy metal into the back of Trinity's knees. The exertion was agonising.

With a yelp and sharp intake of breath, Trinity fell to the floor. Zach and Ally moved expertly with her descent, ensuring her face remained covered.

Bang! Bang!

Zach rolled Trinity onto her back, and she kicked out her legs, choking.

Bang! Bang!

As Zach and Ally dragged Trinity across the room, only Rye stole a glance back at the door. Evidently, it was much sturdier than the one to the storeroom, but appearing concave, the wood was beginning to splinter.

Their minds working in tandem, for Zach and Ally there was no question of their direction; together they bungled Trinity into Mr Vincent's stationery cupboard. Zach jammed a stool under its handle as an extra measure. As much as they all despised the girl, he didn't want to risk Trinity getting out, or indeed, Anoch getting in.

'Looks like we got to tea towel your bird after all,' Zach joked, looking over to Rye, his hands on his knees.

Unfortunately, all were unable to catch their breath for long, as a particularly loud bang thundered through the lab. Anoch had finally succeeded in splitting the door in half and ripping it from its hinges.

The demon came hurtling inside at speed. Leaping over the first two desks in a single bound – to send a pile of exercise books flying – it landed in front of the third, only to push off from its hind legs, ready to dive on top of them all. Instinctively, the three friends fell to the floor and ducked beneath the desk, just as Anoch came hurdling forward.

Scrambling out and up on the opposite side, Zach reached inside his pocket for a lighter. Although he was making up his plan as he went along, it was based entirely on what he'd already seen upon entering the very same room yesterday. He knew that he, Ally and Rye could escape – it was possible because it had already happened. Right now – as it was happening, however – he just needed to make it so.

Zach twizzled open the gas taps nearest to him. Hissing forth, he sparked them alight. Flaming jets streamed across the desk.

Anoch turned and, pushing off from the wall, careered like an ice-hockey puck beneath the flaming desk. Zach jumped to his right, as the girls hopped up onto the desk behind, knocking the last of Mr Vincent's exercise books onto the demon's head. Crashing through the mass of stools, Anoch slowed. Like an ugly Bambi on ice, it struggled to stand back upright.

Ally had already set about turning on the gas taps at the front of the lab, and so Zach threw her the lighter. Neither girl caught it, but Rye was quick to retrieve it from the floor after it struck the chalkboard. She stood and lit these taps also.

Depositing the lighter in Ally's outstretched hand, Rye then ran back around the desks and over to Zach by the windows, where he was turning on more taps by the second. The room was rapidly filling with propane – its smell repugnant and strong, like rotten eggs.

Ally ignited another tap, just as Anoch made a swipe for her. The demon's arm passed through the flame to singe the few feathers that sprouted from it. Howling, Anoch recoiled.

Ally threw the lighter once more, as Anoch turned – following its path with orange eyes. Zach realised just in time for him to catch it.

'I've got a plan,' he began, hastily lighting another tap. 'On the count of three,' he ordered, backing up against the windows.

Rye rallied beside him.

'What plan?!' she shouted, as the demon ran towards them, and leapt.

Rye looked the abomination dead in the eyes before tightly shutting her own. Zach wrapped his arm around her shoulder – his fingertips painfully digging down into her bloody torso.

'ONE!' Zach yelled, and pushed Rye to the floor.

A crash reverberated overhead as Anoch collided with the central window with the power of a demolition ball. A short pause and Zach and Rye could hear a thud, as the demon landed on the tarmac below, followed by the tinkle of glass fragments.

Ally jogged up to her friends and peered out through the void where the window had once been. Zach stood up beside her.

'Where is it? Can – can you see?' Rye demanded, unmoving.

Zach and Ally leant out as far as they dared, but there was nothing – hide nor feather. The demon was nowhere to be seen. No shadows were cast other than the cars' – Pris's included. Ally's eyes came to rest on the prize-giving ceremony that was taking place through the windows of the Main Hall opposite.

'We've got to go. *Now*,' she instructed. 'Before we come face-to-face with our past selves.'

Zach helped Rye to her feet.

'What about the gas – we need to turn them off – or else—' Rye spluttered.

'Let past-Rye worry about that,' said Zach. 'Ally's right, we have to go.'

Rye nodded her acceptance and understanding, then made a start for the Biology room door.

'Not that way,' said Ally. 'We're not leaving without getting what we came for.'

Rye slowly nodded again, and she trudged after Zach and Ally, as the pair headed back to the storeroom. Rounding its corner and her friends were already disassembling the barricade. Rye did not attempt to help them.

'I don't understand. Why are you—' she began, but her thoughts were laboured by the throbbing pain in her shoulder. Rye's blazer and blouse had become congealed to her wound, and she could feel the material tug upon it as she moved.

'Because this is the way we escape,' replied Ally, impatiently, as she helped Zach remove the shelf from where it was wedged. '*Kill the bird.*'

Mr Tumnus chirped happily – oblivious – from his cage beneath the window, next to where Rye was stood.

'How?!' Rye demanded, trying her best to block out the tune.

Her friends offered no advice, and so Rye – exasperated and desperate – was left to ransack the cupboards in search of some sharp object with which to undertake the budgie's execution.

In her haste, she pulled out a drawer with more force than was intended and it flew out onto the floor of the already messy room. As the contents spilled, Rye caught sight of a collection of brand-new, unused scalpels, that were bound together by an elastic band. She bent down to extract one.

'It's nothing personal, Mr Tumnus,' Rye whimpered, squeaking open the cage door. 'It's just, I think this is becoming a you-or-me type of situation, and I know that it's selfish, but—'

'Get on with it!' shouted Ally.

Zach murmured something similar between swears as he stubbed his toe.

Mr Tumnus hopped down onto Rye's hand. Affectionately, he nestled his downy head against her thumb. She palmed him back onto the lowest perch.

'God, forgive me,' Rye whispered.

Squeezing her other hand inside through the small opening, she clenched the scalpel like a pencil. Quick as a cat, Rye then held Mr Tumnus down and immediately the bird began squeaking and flapping its tiny wings.

'Ergghhhhh-ohhhhh!' Rye squealed, as she dug the blade.

Her eyes closed, Rye could feel the warm blood spurt – wet and slippery. Mr Tumnus's sounds of protest grew louder, and so she dug deeper until the bird's struggle slowed – its tiny heart faltering, as Rye's sped up. She opened her eyes.

The crimson pooled in her hand, glistening. Unable to make any sound herself, Rye's grip on Mr Vincent's pet slackened, and the bird fell to the bottom of the cage.

Horrified by her actions, Rye tried to push the pet's demise to the back of her mind. Desperately, she whipped her head from side to side, in search of a container in which she could deposit the 'blood of the Avem'.

Rye selected a test tube from a rack on the windowsill and carefully poured the blood as best as she could. Stoppering it with a rubber bung, her fingers left behind bright smears. Rye dried her hands on the hem of her skirt. She then slid the tube into her blazer's inside pocket. Wracked with guilt, she proceeded to remove the droppings tray out from the cage.

'What are you doing?' Ally asked, curiously – having turned.

Rye shuddered as she wrapped the feathered corpse delicately in the plopping-covered newspaper.

'I'd prefer that Mr Vincent think Mr Tumnus had escaped, as opposed to having been murdered!' Rye defended.

She dropped the bundle into the bin, concealing it, before replacing the tray.

'Sssssssh!' Ally then hissed, suddenly, pressing a finger to her lips.

Zach ceased his movements as the sound of running footsteps could be heard passing by the other side of the storeroom door. Gently, Rye leant out to the adjoining door and pushed it to a close.

'Why did you do that?' hushed Ally, rebuking.

Ally opened her mouth to further reprimand her injured friend's action but verbally stumbled. Could she really be mad at Rye for something she knew to have already happened? Something that yesterday she herself had seen happen. Ally was starting to lose herself in the timeline of events.

'Because, I—' Rye began, whispering, but was interrupted by herself.

'No! Splitting up only works when more than one person is useful! Don't be *stupid* – we're sticking together!'

Like hearing oneself on tape, hearing herself from the other side of the adjoining door was unpleasant. Rye's voice did not sound as she would have expected; she had a huskier tone than she'd ever realised.

Immediately Zach and Ally began kicking and shoving the last few objects away from the foot of the storeroom's door. Rye rocketed over to join them.

'Just don't open that door!' past-Ally hollered from the Biology room. 'We'll be right back.'

Zach kicked a desk into the centre of the storeroom before pushing the girls out into the corridor. Rye tumbled through first, followed by Ally – who clapped her hand over her blazer's pocket, to ensure she hadn't misplaced the stone during their kerfuffle with Anoch. Sure enough, it was still there. Zach slipped out last – shattered glass crunching beneath his feet, just as his and Ally's former selves entered the room, ready for a confrontation.

*

'Run faster,' Ally instructed, as the trio tore down the corridor.

'You've said that before,' growled Rye.

In the lead, Zach and Ally crashed through the first set of double doors that led onto the bridge. Their ribs still ached from the exact same battering less than twenty-four hours prior, which strangely enough, was seconds away from happening. They could hear past-Zach and past-Ally sprinting after them. They couldn't let them catch up. Except, they hadn't; Zach and Ally had witnessed their own escape. Could that change? None of them knew what would happen if it did.

Through the second set of double doors onto the stairwell and DCI Goodfellow's voice could be heard from the ground floor. He spoke louder and much clearer than the school's staff and governors.

Zach directed the girls onto the staff corridor. They all made a final sprint to its end, but with no escape, they were cornered – trapped – and moments away from an encounter with past-Zach and past-Ally.

'Have you – got the stone?' Zach panted.

Retrieving it from her pocket, Ally held it out.

'I don't know how to make it work!' she despaired. 'I'm not entirely sure how we made it work before.'

'"And thee must fill thy heart, and thy head, with thoughts" …' began Zach, quoting.

'How do we know it's a two-way trip?' whispered Ally.

'We weren't caught, were we?' Zach assured her. 'Not properly.'

'Where are we going to go?' Ally pressed.

'She's going to get us!' interjected Rye.

'"She" does have a name, you know,' Ally shot back.

Breaking huddle, Rye tentatively turned to face past-Zach and past-Ally. Their silhouettes unclear; they could be seen standing at the opposite end of the corridor.

'Do you reckon you could knock her out or something, before—' she began.

'Nope!' shouted Zach, as he grabbed both her and Ally by the arms, pulling them to one side.

He too had pre-empted past-Ally's offensive, but also knew it to be triggered by Rye's not-so-well-chosen last words. And so, he hauled the girls into Mr Bullen's office.

Zach slammed the door behind them, and all three dived to the carpet, just as the sound of chairs firing into plaster – like bullets from a machine gun – echoed all around. From their position, each turned their heads in time to witness four chair legs pierce through the door's wood.

There was silence, as all three gathered their thoughts.

'Now, why couldn't you have done that when we were facing off against Anoch, huh?' asked Zach, harshly.

Not knowing how to respond, Ally ignored him. It was a good question, but one she didn't have an answer for. Sitting up – cross-legged – she delicately placed the stone upon the floor before her.

'Where are we going to go?' she asked, repeating her earlier question. 'We all need to decide, because I don't know what will happen if we don't. I imagine it was pretty unanimous the first time.'

'Home. I want to go home,' Rye wailed.

The other two both nodded their approval. Zach held out his hands – one for each of his friends – and they were gladly taken. Ally then lifted the stone dramatically aloft her head – her eyes tightly closed. Black smoke erupted from the pentacle, and just as before, all three were folded inwards.

⚬❦⚬

<u>Monday 1st December 1997, 22:33pm, MICHELLE DAVEY'S</u>
<u>RESIDENCE, FLAT 1, 179A LONDON ROAD, ASHFIELD,</u>
<u>LONDON.</u>

Michelle Davey entered her flat and switched on the light. But recoiling from its brightness, she flicked it off again. She strode across her sitting room to the sofa, and perching on its edge, hesitantly lifted the short bottle of absinthe out from her handbag. *The Devil's Hand.* Michelle had not consumed its contents – why did she feel so dreadful?

She had been in a rush to leave The King's Head – Michelle could remember that much – but why? Discovering the bottle? There was a vague memory. There'd been another note – Michelle had found it upon the passenger seat of her Mini, after regaining awareness within Sullen Woods. That had surely been her reason for returning to Beggar's Hollow, yet again. But there had been nothing there, yet again. And nothing was all she could remember from the near three hours missing.

'Think, just, *think.*'

Striking her aching temples with her fists, Michelle goaded her brain into gear. *Wine.* She needed wine. That would clear her head – she was convinced of it.

Unsteadily, she walked through to the kitchen. Taking a scrunchie from off the counter, she tamed her untidy locks into a bun and opened a cupboard. Michelle returned to the sitting room, wine bottle in hand. She would drink straight from it – all her glasses were dirty.

Michelle crashed back onto the sofa and reached into her bag for her phone. Discovering an apple therein, she took a bite, washed down with a mouthful of wine. As Michelle resumed the search, a red flashing light caught her eye. Curiously, it did not belong to her mobile, but instead her Dictaphone. The light indicated the tape was full, and so Michelle – confused – extracted the device to press rewind.

It took nearly a complete minute until the tape ground to a halt, during which time Michelle finished off half the apple and another two inches of wine.

Before pressing play, Michelle solemnly placed *The Devil's Hand* upon the coffee table, squeezing it amongst the clutter. As if she were about to undertake a ritual, Michelle calmed her heart and composed her head, by fixating her gaze upon it, if only for a second.

Without taking off her boots, Michelle curled. Dictaphone in one hand – wine in the other – she pressed play.

❧❦❧

Monday 1st December 1997, 22:40pm, TURPIN RESIDENCE, 32 KYNASTON GARDENS, ASHFIELD, LONDON.
Zach, Ally and Rye came hurtling down from the ceiling of the Turpin's sitting room, with the invisible portal that had transported them having manifested itself somewhere close to the central light fitting. The mystical gateway spat them out, spraying the three teenagers in different directions.

Rye's body thumped down – as chance would have it – backside first into the vacated pink armchair. Zach landed by the gas fire, but rolled, due to velocity and the angle of descent, across the carpet and into two pairs of feet at the foot of the sofa. Ally, the last to appear, shot vertically downwards, her head cushioned by Zach's bottom.

'Rye!' cried Pris.

- CHAPTER XXVI -

Bullets Beat Bones

Bullet cracks; the heated nugget of metal is propelled forward. The noise splits all others so crisply in that fraction of a second, as the sound's waves ripple out through the darkness – through swathes of tall, still trees. Sparks erupt from the end of the gun; a fountain of fiery froth. Each one is minuscule and beautifully formed.

The bullet penetrates through the lowest leaf of an evergreen sapling. Singeing nature's tissue, it leaves behind a dark glowing ring. Relentlessly, the metal continues to fly, twisting and funnelling. Gracefully, it pirouettes through the air; hot but quickly cooling. Speeding, the tiny, deadly shot, reaches closer and closer to its unsuspecting target. This bullet has a name.

Like a meteor, the projectile hits, breaking the cranium into shrapnel. Bullets Beat Bones. Persistent; it continues to slip and slide through the internal components, emulsifying connective tissue and ripping fibrous membranes apart.

Death is instantaneous.

❧✋❧

<u>Monday 1st December 1997, 22:41pm, MICHELLE DAVEY'S RESIDENCE, FLAT 1, 179A LONDON ROAD, ASHFIELD, LONDON.</u>
The images of the bullet and its impact brightly shone upon the surface of Michelle's eyes, before being constricted to the size of a pinprick at her pupils' centres. Like an old television set being

switched off, the picture was sucked into an infinitely small and tiny dot.

'... the fact that you've yet come face-to-face with either demon, is extremely fortunate ...'

The cassette tape within her Dictaphone was still playing. Without having left her flat, Michelle had seen it all – the rest of the night, in all its gory and portentous detail. She pressed the tape to a stop. Michelle did not need to hear the rest of the recorded conversation, for she could remember it in its entirety. Michelle remembered everything. It was déjà vu all over again, and in every which way possible.

Swinging her legs from off of the sofa, Michelle tentatively put her weight down upon them to stand. She combed loose strands of hair away from her face, twisting them around her bun.

Flying into a rage, Michelle reached for the wine. With a soft exhale, the sofa's cushions expanded to fill the void left by its removal. It was as if they were sighing, as Michelle drew breath, drawing back her arm to fling the bottle across the room like a cricket ball. She'd even lifted her leg to get the maximum force behind the throw.

It instantly smashed on impact, splattering Cabernet Sauvignon majestically across the words she had defaced her wall with: 'The Death of Elizabeth Thackerall'.

Michelle screamed a full-bodied scream as her hair fell defiantly back across her forehead and cheeks. Fragments of dark-green glass rained down onto her carpet. Apart from the few shards that clung to its label, only the bottle's neck remained intact.

Her unsupported chest heaving, Michelle struggled to come to terms with what she had seen. She was enraged – incensed by the cruel irony of it all.

Steadily, the deep-red liquid began to trickle downwards. One offshoot met the photograph of Elizabeth, and – after pooling along the rim of the paper – dripped over the girl's face, allowing the inanimate image to cry tears.

The scene tugged at Michelle's heartstrings, beseeching to her very character. Calming herself as best as she could, this truly virtuous woman was now determined like never before. Michelle was certain of what she had to do – she had learnt the whole truth of what she was, and the part she must play.

∽❦∾

<u>Monday 1st December 1997, 22:41pm, TURPIN RESIDENCE, 32 KYNASTON GARDENS, ASHFIELD, LONDON.</u>

'Where have you been?!' Pris demanded. 'I've been worried sick!'

Dropping the cordless phone that she'd held to her chest, Pris strode around the armchair upon which her sister was sat, so that she could continue shouting face-to-face.

'I was just about to call the police! I'd have called them sooner, but Fred—'

'Don't shout at me,' Rye snapped. 'I'm injured.'

'Holy shit!' Pris exclaimed, stooping to inspect the wound. 'Rye, you're bleeding!'

Ally rolled herself from off Zach's lower-half and groaned. Fred and Ros shifted themselves along to make room for the pair.

'Try not to smash the sofa through the wall as you sit,' Zach whispered to Ally, jovially, as he relaxed back into it. His body felt like it had been crushed by a steamroller, but he masked it – as he did most things – with humour.

'Shut up,' Ally whispered back.

It was then Ally realised the stone was missing. She had not felt it between her fingers as she'd crash-landed, nor had she seen it fall. No-one questioned as she crouched back to the floor and began searching between her friends' legs and under the sofa. She had no luck, and so crawled over to the mantelpiece.

'What happened to you?!' Pris continued to reel.

Gradually, amid dramatic grimaces from both, she began to peel Rye's school blazer away from the hardening bloody mess.

'You mean Fred didn't fill you in?' Rye shot, rudely, across the room to him.

'He told me you went looking for trouble!' Pris scolded, as she wrestled her sister's arm out of the blazer. 'Honestly, Rye. What were you thinking?'

'So, you didn't discuss the demon that hijacked our little trip back in time to yester—' began Rye.

'Oh, believe me, we've discussed plenty. You've been missing for hours,' Pris rebuked. 'I know all about Anorak, the warehouse fire, and your nightmares of the dead girl. Oh, Rye, why couldn't you have confided in me—'

'Oh, you wonder why, do you?!'

Despite her body's protests, Rye sat forward in the armchair – words searing her tongue. Fred, Ros and Zach exchanged awkward glances, then took to looking at anything else other than the siblings' quarrel. There was no television set – not since Rye's birthday – but Ally crawling around behind its stand was as good enough to settle their collective gaze. Rye proceeded to fully remove her blazer unaided. She flung it across the room.

'You, my *caring* sister,' Rye sneered, 'saw with your very own eyes what happened the night of my birthday, and still you chose to bury your head in the sand! I have tried to talk to you, *confide* in you! Lord, knows, I have tried. Maybe I could have tried harder – I admit that much – but you weren't forthcoming, and you *did not* make it easy. Maybe if you'd have taken the time to *listen*, then you'd have heard all about this hell, a hell of a lot sooner!'

'Well, I can tell you I've heard it all this evening,' began Pris, standing. 'And I'm telling you that it stops—'

'Oh, then you know all about the ritual we're doing later then?' Rye goaded.

She knew that her question would only add fuel to the fire but that was her intention. Rye slumped back, eager for a retort.

'I do, and I forbid it. I won't allow—'

'You can't forbid it,' Rye interrupted, nonchalantly. 'We need five people we can trust for the ritual to work – other than myself. One, two, three, four—' she pointed around the room '— *five*. You're coming with us.'

With her finger settled upon her sister, Rye held it there, unwavering.

'I most certainly am not,' Pris spat, folding her arms.

'You have to – we – I,' Rye huffed. Taking a breath, she then altered her tone. 'Look, Pris, you really want to put a stop to all this? – So do I.'

Pris turned away from her sister, as Ally – unsuccessful in her search – crawled back to the sofa, her head low.

'This ritual is our only option,' Rye continued, pleadingly. 'There might well be others, but we're running out of time. Anoch won't stop coming after us – after *me* – until we're all *dead*. Please, Pris, we need you. *I* need you.'

Pris wiped away a tear.

'What do you say?' asked Rye.

'I say …' Pris breathed, heavily. 'I say that I'm going to get some bandages and antiseptic for your shoulder.'

And with that, the eldest Turpin went to walk briskly from the sitting room.

'Is that a yes?' Rye pressed.

There was no time for either of them to dance around the subject. Pris paused by the doorway. Turning to face her sister, it was clear she was stricken.

'I'm going to do what I've always done,' said Pris – her voice unfaltering. 'I'm going to protect you. So, yes. It's a yes.'

Before giving her tears time to properly form, Pris darted out into the hallway and through to the kitchen.

'Well, that's a relief!' exclaimed Zach.

'Is it?' asked Fred.

'Not much of one, I suppose,' Zach conceded, 'but at the very least, we have our five people now. Speaking of which – Fred, how did you convince young Rosalind here to join us?'

Zach peered around Fred's head, to look Ros dead in the face.

'Got a death wish?' he asked.

Ally angrily elbowed Zach in the ribs. Selfishly, she did not want him to perturb the girl. Though their peril was very real, the last thing Ally wanted was for him to lose them a participant after having just gained one.

'I told her the truth,' Fred admitted, dejectedly. 'I couldn't not, not really. It wouldn't be fair. Not if we're actually planning on going through with this.'

'I've always been a believer in God,' said Ros – herself seemingly calm. 'It makes sense to me that for good to exist in this world, then there would also have to be bad. And, if you guys need my help to defeat this bad, then I feel it's my duty to help.'

Rye rolled her eyes and Ally screwed up her face.

'Righhhhtttt,' said Zach, slowly. 'Works for me.'

'It doesn't work for me,' said Pris.

Returning from the kitchen – her arms laden with medical supplies – she'd overheard the entire conversation, and altogether disagreed.

'Rye said that you needed people you can trust for this 'ere ritual,' she explained, unbuttoning her sister's blouse. 'How can you be sure she's trustworthy?'

Rye was unconcerned by her friends seeing her bra – it was the least of the problems she'd face tonight. She gritted her teeth, as Pris began to peel away the blood-stained white cotton. No-one responded to Pris's open question, and so she continued.

'On your birthday—' she nodded to Rye '—the voice that spoke through you, said that "Goldilocks" was not all that she seemed. How do you know that wasn't in reference to her?'

Pris fired an accusatory look back at Ros, as she moistened a cotton pad with antiseptic from a bottle.

'He was probably referring to me,' Rye admitted. 'Seeing as I was the only one who could see Elizabeth up at the lake – agghh!'

Rye's face contorted in agony as Pris cleaned her wound. Still, she dared not look at it.

'Probably?' Pris repeated. 'Rye, I think you need stitch—'

'Well – ouch! As the only blondes in the room, Male-AL10 was referring to either myself, Ros or you? Are you hiding anything, sis? – OWW!'

Rye shrieked for her sister had daubed deep at the grisly incision.

'No, of course not,' Pris affirmed. For a moment, she considered revealing the truth of her hair's natural colour. Not that it wasn't blatant. 'We should take you to the hosp—'

'Are you?' Rye asked Ros, bluntly.

'No,' said Ros, ceasing chewing of her own blonde hair. 'Absolutely, nothing to hide.'

'There we go then,' Rye announced. 'We can't afford to waste any more time chit-chatting and second-guessing one another. Anoch is out there and could turn up at any moment. We need to complete the ritual, and fast.'

Having struggled to control her fingers, Pris ripped a bandage free from its cellophane. Its sound made everyone – herself included – jolt.

'Having enlightenment, or a revelation, or whatever, doesn't mean that we'll find it any easier to actually kill Anoch – for good this time,' said Fred.

'No. It doesn't,' Rye agreed. 'But it will, hopefully – *finally* – give some context to all of this. Context that might shed some light on how to defeat Anoch. If we know its intentions – its motives—'

'What made you pick this time?' Ally interrupted, directing her question at Rye, who looked confused. 'Twenty to eleven. It's been hours since we disappeared at the church. What made you choose this specific time to come back to? Because I was aiming for around the time we left. Someone's thoughts must have been stronger.'

Ally had grown tired of the conversational ping-pong – to which she saw little point – and so jumped in with a question that had been preying on her mind.

'I didn't,' replied Rye. 'I was thinking of – *aiming* for – eight o'clock.'

'Why eight o'clock?' asked Ally.

'It's the time *EastEnders* is shown,' Rye explained.

She cast her gaze forlornly over to where their television had once stood.

'We arrived at twenty to eleven,' Ally repeated.

Rye grimaced as Pris began binding her shoulder.

'Twenty to eleven is the time that *On Side* starts,' Zach replied, sheepishly.

'Oh, I see,' said Ally, flatly. 'I'm going to get changed.'

*

Reaching the top of the stairs, Zach walked across the landing to the bathroom, but movement from inside Rye's bedroom caused him to double-take. He took a step back to linger. Zach knew he shouldn't have – he hadn't even meant to – but he was mesmerised.

Through the half-foot gap between the door and its frame, Ally could be seen dropping her skirt to the floor. She stepped out of it and Zach gawped. Flipping her long dark hair over one shoulder, Ally turned, and Zach retracted. She did not turn to face him, however, only to profile. Loosening her school tie, she pulled the loop up and over her head and began unbuttoning her blouse.

Zach's mouth gaped open. Apart from Rye – only moments ago – Ally was the first female the boy had ever seen in a state of undress that wasn't from the pages of a magazine. This wasn't strictly true, but Zach discounted the time he had once walked in on his mother getting her stamp licked by the postman. That was a regrettable tale, and one he'd tried his best to forget. Needless-to-say, he found Ally a far more exhilarating sight than the others.

Zach looked to the bathroom. He knew it wasn't right to peep. The action was against everything he believed to be right – against everything his single mother had brought him up as.

'You can come in, you know,' said Ally, suddenly – snapping Zach back into reality. 'You don't have to lurk.'

In nothing more than her bra and knickers, she was looking directly at him now. Zach slapped a hand over his eyes.

'It's – I – erm,' he spluttered.

A tuft of black hair fell over Zach's clasped hand. His unruly mop had been growing longer of late, and he was not yet sure whether he liked it or not. But Ally did like it – a lot.

'I – I was just going to the – to the bathroom,' Zach garbled.

'It's only underwear, Zach. It's no worse than a bikini,' replied Ally, matter-of-factly. Still, the boy did not move. 'Oh, just come in.'

Hesitantly, Zach did as he was told. Releasing his hand from his face, he diverted his gaze to the laundry-strewn floor. His eyes fought to climb back up the scantily clad Scottish beauty, but he forced them down with him, as he sat upon the mattress.

'What are you? Some sort of peeping Zach now?' Ally jested, and Zach's bright blues shot straight up to meet her weary brown.

'No – I – I'm sorry,' he began. 'That's a great film, though – *Peeping Tom*. Terrible, what with the – the voyeurism – but ground-breaking in terms of the slasher genre. Although, of course, I don't condone—'

Ally laughed heartily, cutting his jumbled apology off mid-sentence.

'I'm only messing,' she chuckled.

Turning, Ally reached down to retrieve her midnight-blue minidress from the foot of the desk's chair. Zach only stole a snapshot of her bottom, before being immediately drawn to the large bruise that stretched from her right hip, all the way up to her bosom. Practically three-dimensional, the purplish contusion stood out ferociously from Ally's otherwise flawless skin.

'Holy crab cakes! Your ribs – are you OK? How – when did you do that?'

With the intention of inspecting her infliction further, he went to stand, but ultimately stopped himself.

'Who can say?' Ally replied – unfussed. 'Maybe it was running through the doors and using my body as a battering ram – either time. Or falling from the ceiling, and onto a hard floor – either time. Jumping over desks to escape a demon? Really, take your pick.'

Shrugging, Ally sat down heavily beside him. Dress held in her lap; she wistfully fondled its material.

'Does it hurt?' Zach asked.

He peered down at Ally's burst blood vessels, following the mark up across her ribcage to where it ended. His stare continued upwards to absorb every contour of Ally's body until softly resting upon her face.

'What do you think?' she replied, sarcastically. 'I mean, yeah, it does – a little. Nothing compared to Rye's war-wounds, though.'

'Why are you changing into that anyway?' Zach asked, nodding to the dress. 'Sure, it's fearless attire, but it's hardly practical for a showdown.'

He spoke kindly, but his concern was real. Zach wanted Ally to be able to move freely, especially if the night was to involve a lot of running – which he feared it might.

Ally laughed again. It was a far weaker laugh than before.

'If I die tonight, I want to look my best.'

Her voice was strained.

'You always look your best,' Zach flattered, unblinking.

Tickled by his cheesiness, Ally laughed a full-bodied laugh once more.

'What sort of a line is that supposed to be?'

'A rubbish one,' Zach admitted.

He puckered his lips and leant in to kiss her.

'Zach, what are you—' began Ally, pushing the boy away. Although taken aback by his forwardness, she did not find it unwelcome.

'What if we die tonight?'

Zach ran trembling fingers through Ally's silky hair, bringing them down to caress her cheek. His touch was as tender as his tone. Ally did not quash his advances a second time. Taking comfort from their physical connection, she closed her eyes and steadily exhaled.

Ally then reached out – her hand much less shaky than his – and pushed Zach's head forwards to hers. He didn't have a chance to pucker his lips this time. Zach was scared to lose his virginity, but he was far less afraid of that than dying.

*

'What's taking them so long?' Rye vented, angrily. 'We're wasting time!'

In only her bra and school skirt, she paced up and down the length of the sitting room. Her injury bound; Pris had attempted duct tape butterfly stitches, and a bandage had been wrapped around Rye's chest and neck, as to prevent the many cotton pads from slipping.

'I've just thought of something,' said Fred, with a start. 'You left Anoch behind. When you zapped yourselves out of Mr Bullen's office, you left it behind, right?'

Rye stopped pacing for a moment to address him.

'Yes, we left him behind, just like we left you behind. Did you see a demon come crashing down from the ceiling with us? No? Didn't think so.'

Rye was still furious with Fred, and as the minutes ticked by, she was mentally adding more bricks to the wall between them – much to his obliviousness.

'Then, that's to say there's been two Anochs running around in the timeline from yesterday evening until – well—' Fred consulted his watch '—roughly eight hours ago, when you guys got sucked into the stone. Why didn't either version of Anoch attack in the meantime? Even double-team us?'

'Rye, you said Anoch fell out the window. Maybe it was injured?' offered Ros.

'I doubt it,' Rye sighed – taking note that Ros was truly taking everything in stride. 'It wasn't a long fall. I'm running on guesswork now, but there was something Anoch said to me by the lake back in September – back when this all started. It was the way it spoke, but I reckon Anoch's just a pawn – a soldier. And a stupid one at that. I reckon Anoch knows it's screwed up, and—'

'It's in detention,' interrupted Ros.

'In a manner of speaking,' replied Rye. 'Tonight – *last night* – was the second time Anoch's failed to kill me – kill all of us – although I do admit, I am feeling a little targeted. I think it's because I'm the only one who can see Elizabeth. I just wish I knew how it's all connected.'

'You think Anoch reported back to its king, or duke, or whatever?' asked Fred.

'*General*,' Rye corrected – upon turn – and resumed pacing.

'You mean there's more than just one of them?' Pris uttered.

Horrified, she physically recoiled.

'Oh, Pris-*ter*,' Rye sighed. 'If Solomon's to be believed, they're hardly an endangered species. We can only hope that it's just the two that want me dead,' she laughed, hysterically. 'I just wish Zach would hurry up, 'cause I *really* need the can!'

At that moment, Ally entered the room. She unwittingly trod upon a creaky floorboard, and Fred leapt up from the sofa.

'Ally, is Zach still in the bathroom?' Rye asked, jogging on the spot. 'Do you know if he'll be much longer?'

'Oh, I'm sure he'll finish up *quite* quickly,' Ally huffed, taking a seat beside Ros.

'This is ridiculous!' exclaimed Rye. 'Can we just get tonight over and done with?'

*

Ten minutes later and Rye was furiously banging on the bathroom door.

'Zach! Would, you, hur-ry, up!' she shouted, matching every syllable with a frantic knock. 'I'm, gon-na, pee, my-self!' she projected, before growling in an agitated whisper, '... *again.*'

With both fists, Rye proceeded to hammer. The door suddenly opened, and she almost rapped Zach on the nose.

'Alright, alright,' he surrendered. 'I'm done.'

Pushing past her, it looked as if Zach had been crying, and Rye's own expression shifted from that of irritation to empathy.

'Zach, are – are you OK?' she asked, reaching out her hand to comfort him. 'We're all scared—

'I'm fine!' Zach snapped, batting her away. He took a calming breath. 'Look, I'm sorry. I just want to get this evening over and done with.'

'Don't we all,' Rye agreed, sadly.

Zach weakly smiled, and with that, Rye entered the bathroom. Almost instantly, she turned back around.

'Have you seen my blue shirt?' she asked. 'I could have sworn that I'd left it on the radiator.'

Zach shrugged.

'I haven't seen it,' he responded, unhelpfully, and sniffling, began his descent down the stairs.

'CHRIS!' Rye hollered and Zach flinched. 'Have you seen my blue shirt?!'

'Which one?!' Pris shouted up from the sitting room. 'And don't call me, "Chris"!'

Pris had the right to be irritated, for her younger sister had a habit of this. Immaturely, whenever Rye could not immediately lay her hands on something, she would accuse the whole world and their mother – usually Pris, her acting mother – of having stolen it. Rye's anger was wholly hypercritical, seeing as she had borrowed – and lost – Pris's heels the night of her birthday.

'The blue paisley one!' Rye screeched. 'It's not in the bathroom!'

'I haven't seen it! Maybe it's in your sty of a room!'

Rye scowled, then shut the bathroom door and bolted it.

'"Maybe it's in your sty of a room",' she mimed, pulling down her skirt.

Her shoulder objected to the abruptness of her action.

*

'Location is important,' Ally explained, and Ros nodded enthusiastically. 'We have to conduct the ritual in a place directly tied to the questions that *you*—' Ally pointed to Rye, as she re-entered the room '—want answering. Which in this case would be—'

'The lake,' Rye interrupted.

'Bingo,' confirmed Ally.

Having failed to locate her blue shirt, Rye's top half was clothed in a zip-up hoodie. She would have preferred to layer up under the garment, but her only other shirt – her school blouse – had been sliced and diced, and there was no way she'd have been able to comfortably manoeuvre herself into a T-shirt. She had not bothered to change out of her skirt. Rye perched on the arm of the chair now occupied by her sister.

'And here I was hoping you'd say we could just do the ritual right here in the sitting room,' bemoaned Fred. 'I just don't know how on earth we're supposed to *kill* Anoch, let alone its general – if it indeed has one. I mean, what are we all exactly? A girl who has nightmares, because she saw a dead girl this one time.' Rye narrowed her eyes at him. 'Another girl, who I'm pretty sure could do pretty much anything, except she doesn't know how she's doing it – or why.'

'You keep on saying the word "girl" like that, and we're gonna have a prob—' began Ally, but Fred ploughed forth.

'And then there's Zach and me. Zach brings sarcasm, and I bring …' he trailed off. 'We're the worst bunch of superheroes ever.'

'There's Pris and I as well, you know, Frederick.' Ros glowered beside him. 'I know we may just be *girls* but—'

'*You*,' Pris fired back at Ros. 'I still don't even know if we can trust *you*.'

'We've covered this!' Rye blurted, before Ros could retort.

'I'm not trying to be sexist—' Fred spoke over her.

'We know you're not, mate,' Zach sniffed, rubbing his red and puffy eyes. 'It's just, there's not one of us here that ain't already terrified of dying tonight. You don't need to rub salt into the wounds.'

As Zach spoke, Rye stared blankly, stroking her bandages.

'Salt!' declared Ally. 'We need salt to draw out the pentacle. Pris, do you have any in the kitchen?'

Pris nodded and got up from the armchair.

'We can't go in unarmed,' hastened Fred. 'If we stand any chance of survival, we're gonna need more than just condiments. Too bad you don't still have the stone—'

'Oh! So, now you *want* to use the stone,' said Rye – hardly able to stomach him. 'Besides, we aren't going in "unarmed"; we've got Ally.'

'Please, don't,' Ally begged her. 'You can't rely on me.'

'Then we suit up,' Zach concluded, quoting many a superhero.

It was then that Pris returned from the kitchen. A tub of table salt in one hand, she clutched two large knives to her chest with the other. Both blades identical; they were very much evocative of Casey Becker.

'Oooh, good choice,' beamed Ally, approvingly.

'Thanks,' Pris replied – far less enthused. 'I think we've got a hammer and a cricket bat under the stairs too.'

- CHAPTER XXVII -

The Midnight Tea Fairy

<u>Monday 1st December 1997, 23:35pm, ASHFIELD POLICE STATION, ASHFIELD, LONDON.</u>
Michelle entered the number into the keypad at the Police Station's side entrance. Her superior may have confiscated her badge, but he could not remove the access code from her memory.

Keeping her head low and shoulders high, the suspended officer passed several colleagues as she made her way, but none took notice and so did not greet her. For this, Michelle was thankful.

Entering the canteen, she sighed with relief. It was empty. But Michelle had suspected this. She strode across to the counter and removed five mugs from the cupboard above the microwave. The china clattered together as her hands shook. Michelle knew not precisely how much time she had before she was to be interrupted but knew it to be little.

Selecting five tea bags from the jar, Michelle dropped one into each of the mugs. Hands still shaking, she reached into the pocket of her trench coat. Her fingers tightened around the small cardboard box inside, and she looked back over her shoulder. Still, she was undisturbed.

Michelle whipped the box out. Fumbling at its opening, and all twelve sachets within scattered across the counter. Only when it was too late, did the action become familiar, and she chastised herself for not having pre-empted it. Emitting a panicked cry, Michelle rushed to gather them back up.

'OK, OK, come on.'

She hurried, tearing the first sachet open.

Atop the teabag, Michelle tapped the powdered contents into the first mug. She added another three before moving onto the next – adding four sachets in turn, to three out of the five mugs. The empty box was discarded in the bin beside her.

One at a time, Michelle filled the mugs with boiling water from the dispenser. She stirred two sugars into the first four, and a dash of milk. The final mug – her own – received neither.

It was just as Michelle had dropped the teaspoon into the sink – after removing the bags – that the door to the canteen squeaked open. Quick as a shot, she spun around to see who had entered. It was Kevin Gunn – just as anticipated.

'Oh, it's you,' he said – himself surprised to see her. 'What are you doing here?'

He marched over to the vending machine.

'Just – visiting friends,' Michelle replied – her voice strained. 'I miss the place – familiar faces, and all that.'

'Are you even allowed to be here?' Kevin asked, his fingers hovering over the machine's pad. 'I thought you were suspended.'

'Being suspended doesn't mean that I'm not allowed to be here.'

'I'd have thought that was all part and parcel of, you know, *being suspended*,' Kevin retorted.

With a loud thud, his chosen purchase fell, ready for collection. Michelle jolted at the sound.

'I find it odd that you choose to come into the station now, when before you didn't even bother to show up when you were supposed to.'

Kevin laughed as he bent over to collect his treat. If his oozing condescendence had not been enough to do so, the revelation of his bright pink socks boiled Michelle's blood.

'I told you,' she reiterated – her teeth gritted. 'I wanted to visit my friends.'

'At this hour?'

Turning to face her, Kevin unwrapped his chocolate.

'Well, I—'

'Doesn't matter. Who am I to question the sleep patterns of an …'

Speaking with his hands, Kevin let the end of his sentence hang, although it was obvious to Michelle what word filled the blank. Eyes wide, as if to encourage retaliation, he took an audibly wet mouthful of chocolate.

'It was Richard Simkins' sentencing today,' he continued, his mouth twisting into a smile. 'You probably don't remember.'

'Of course, I remembered.'

In truth, the date's significance had gone completely unnoticed to Michelle. How funny it was, that something she'd once held in such high importance, now even failed to register. The date gave context to Shaz and Gary's pub invite, however – they had been trying to distract her.

'How did it go?' Michelle asked, feigning interest.

'Knocked it right out of the park, of course,' Kevin enthused, striking an imaginary ball with an imaginary bat. 'He went down for seven years. "Top Gunn" strikes again!'

Michelle looked on, blankly.

'Well, after such a long day, you're more than deserving of a cuppa.'

Coolly collecting up the mugs, Michelle approached her nemesis. She gestured for Kevin to take one of the teas she offered with her right hand and a little sloshed onto the floor.

'No, it's alright, I—'

'Take it.'

Reluctant, but taken aback, Kevin reached out.

'Not that one – that's mine!'

'Bloody hell, Mich—'

'That's no milk, no sugar,' Michelle interrupted. 'It's also how I take my coffee. Although, you probably don't remember.'

She smiled innocently, as Kevin took a correct mug.

'Drink it whilst it's hot,' she advised, departing.

'T-Thanks!' Kevin hollered after her.

As she turned the corner and headed for the stairwell, Michelle smiled to herself. Revenge, like Kevin's tea, was best served sweetly.

*

'Knock, knock,' Michelle sang, prying open the door to the auditor's office a crack.

'Oh, it's you!' smiled Lauren, spinning away from her computer screen to face her. 'Oh, do come in! Come in!'

An unrelenting chatterbox, Lauren O'Donnell was harmless enough, but she was dull; she looked dull and so were her stories. Thankfully, the women did not get the opportunity to speak often.

'It's me! The midnight tea fairy!' Michelle announced.

Grinning from ear to ear, she pranced into the small room – three teas in hand – and merrily took the seat that was wheeled out for her. Michelle was beginning to find her antics rather fun – and so she should, for she knew that in less than an hour, the evening's frivolities would take a nose-dive.

'There we go, Elijah.' Michelle smiled, sliding one of the mugs across the opposite desk. 'This one's yours.'

Elijah – Lauren's only immediate colleague – grunted his caring and proceeded to tap away at his keyboard.

'I'm sorry, I don't have any biscuits,' Michelle apologised. 'I really should have bought some.'

'Don't be silly,' replied Lauren, with a wave of her hand. 'I think we've got some stashed around here somewhere – Oi, Elijah!'

The young woman clicked her fingers in his direction.

'Have a look in that drawer, would you?'

Elijah made a noise of disapproval but begrudgingly did as was asked of him. Michelle had always considered the man rude, and his failure to even properly acknowledge her presence only cemented this opinion.

Awaiting biscuits, Michelle surveyed the room. Cramped and clinical, it was painted stark white. A large window – its glass thick – took up most of the wall behind Lauren's desk. The small grill and hatch set within it provided a point of communication between the auditors' 'prison' and the station's armoury on its other side. Back here, there were no windows to the outside world. Comfort was provided in the form of a wind-up radio, perched atop a filing cabinet. Lauren had turned it down to an almost inaudibly low volume now, but before it had been blaring Sheena Easton's '9 to 5 (Morning Train)'. Michelle knew the track, but today it struck an altogether atypical chord within her – one of sorrow.

'It's so lovely to see you,' Lauren beamed, revealing a snaggle-tooth. 'What on earth are you doing – I mean, at this hour – it's so late.'

Unlike Kevin, Lauren chose to handle the subject of Michelle's suspension delicately.

'I couldn't sleep,' Michelle embellished, taking a sip of her own tea. 'I thought I'd swing by, catch up with a few people, you know? It's not like I have to wake up early for work tomorrow or anything.'

Both women laughed – Lauren more awkwardly so.

'I must say, it's a lovely sur—'

'Bourbons,' interrupted Elijah.

Lauren took the half-empty packet from him with a strained smile. Elijah's gaze remained glued to his screen.

'As I was saying,' Lauren continued, eyebrows raised, 'it's lovely to see you. We don't get many visitors down here. Except – you know – to check out ammunitions and what not. And, of course, they don't usually stay long.'

Michelle nodded emphatically, taking another sip of tea. Lauren mirrored her action. Extracting a bourbon, Lauren then crunched the biscuit in one.

'As 'm 'ure you can appre-ciate, the comp-any down 'ere can be *pre-tty* dry at the best of 'imes,' Lauren confessed. She swallowed, before musing. 'Much like that biscuit, actually. Would you like one?'

'Oh, none for me, thank you. I've had my fair share of bourbons recently.'

'Fair enough,' replied Lauren, and she disposed of the lot in the bin beneath her desk. 'You're not missing out on anything.'

'How's the baby?' Michelle asked, hurriedly.

Exhaling, her eyes casually flicked up towards the clock. She hoped the tea would take effect soon.

ஒ❦ஒ

<u>Tuesday 2nd December, 00:05am, OUTSKIRTS OF ASHFIELD, LONDON.</u>

Pris's grey Ford sped along the country lanes that led out of Ashfield. She was driving much faster than she had ever before, and for reasons she did not quite understand. If Fred's stories of Anoch were true – as Pris believed them to be – then she was surely only ferrying them to their deaths all the more quickly.

Driving was not the most direct way of reaching the lake, however. By taking the roads, they skirted back around, but would reduce the distance they'd all have to traipse through the darkness. Rye had mentioned there was a track – large enough to fit a car – that led down to the lake from a car park, and it was this that Pris hoped to find.

After changing gears, Pris reached across to give Rye's knee a squeeze. Sat in the passenger seat, her sister had spent the entirety of their short journey writing in her diary – or rather not writing, as the case was. Her pen had been hovering over its pages for a near five minutes, yet she had failed to write a single word.

'Zach,' Ally whispered, into the boy's ear. 'I'm worried. I'm worried that I won't be able to … make anything happen when I need to. *If,* I need to … It's just that, in the corridor, when I made all those chairs move, I was scared. But, in the Biology room, when Anoch was charging around, I was scared too, and there was … nothing.'

Zach said nothing. He simply gripped his bow and quiver ever tighter – his knuckles turning white. With himself, Ally, Fred and Ros, having all successfully squeezed into the back, his weapon of choice lay across all four of their laps.

Sarah Palmer had shown little concern over her son's short pit-stop by their home, as he'd covertly collected his prized bow. She had only voiced slight trepidation when Zach had kissed her goodbye, for it was the first time in a long while.

This was in great contrast to Fred's mother, Caroline, who had sent him seven messages over the course of the evening so far. And as his pager flashed with the eighth, it was only now, that Fred sent a reply:

'At Rye's. Staying over. X'

'Zach,' Ally whispered again. 'When all this madness is over, can we start over? We could go on a date, maybe. I mean – if you wanted?'

Zach turned to her this time. Without a word of warning, he nudged his face the five inches it took to reach hers, to give her a peck on the cheek.

Finally putting pen to paper, Rye began to write:

Tuesday 2nd December, 00:07am, OUTSKIRTS OF ASHFIELD, LONDON.

Dear Diary,

I'm writing this as Pris, Zach, Fred, Ally, ~~Zach,~~ Ros and I are driving to Sullen Woods. I apologise for the handwriting – Pris's driving is still dodgy, and I'm scared. I don't think I've ever been so scared.

I'd like to say that at least one of us is putting on a brave face, but I can't. This whole thing is so ~~messed~~ fucked up. Demons … I don't even like to write the word. All I can hope for now is that I survive – that we all do. Please, just let me get through tonight – through all of this.

Please. Please. Please. Please. Please. PLEASE. Oh, God, PLEASE.

And I pray. I pray that if we do survive the night, then that'll be the end of it all. I hope this isn't my last entry. But if it is … well, just wish us luck. And if Louie is ever to read this, then I want him to know that I cared. I really cared.

Rye Turpin. Aged 16. x'

*

'And then, Stephen only went and put cloves in the Spag Bol!' Lauren creased up, sharing the anecdote. 'He thought he was adding cumin, but—'

A soft, shallow fart emanated from Lauren's backside, and the sound caught her off guard. Michelle's ears pricked. Appearing mildly alarmed and red-faced, Lauren rushed on with her story.

'But it wasn't cumin, it was cloves. Still, we dished it up – didn't want it to go to waste. Oh, but the taste, Michelle – it was ghastly—'

Another parp ripped through Lauren's sentence. Much louder than before, the flatulence reverberated upon her chair, rescinding into a high-pitched, wet squeak. Lauren laughed a laugh of an equal pitch – clearly embarrassed by the behaviour of her bowels. Still, Elijah did not turn away from his computer. He simply wrinkled his nose.

'I – erm – I'm sorry.' Lauren smiled, nervously. 'I have no idea where that came from.'

'So, what happened next?' Michelle pressed, her heart racing as the laxative took effect. She had lost track of all conversation long ago.

'We binned it all – had to … ordered pizza …'

Deep in concentration, Lauren's expression slowly contorted into a horrific grimace. The subsequent and final fart to grace the air was the loudest and wettest by far. Lasting a full five seconds, Michelle could see the horror of realisation flood, as it was exuded. There was no doubt that the poor woman had shat her knickers.

'Bloody, damn hell, Lauren!' Elijah bellowed. 'That stinks! What the fuck?! My God!'

Without any acknowledgement, excuse or goodbye, Lauren jumped up from her seat and half-ran, half-waddled, to the door. Michelle knew she should feel guilty, but she didn't. Her initial reaction had been one of laughter and she struggled to stifle it by way of covering her mouth, as well as her nose. At just under three pounds a box, the laxatives were a steal from the twenty-four-hour supermarket, and they had worked a charm.

The door slammed shut and Michelle's chuckles subsided. She immediately turned her attentions to Elijah, who had stood to inspect the damage Lauren had inflicted to her swivel chair.

'You know,' Michelle said, rising from her seat to walk the three short paces over. 'You really shouldn't take the Lord's name in vain.'

Elijah looked puzzled, finding her proximity to him uncomfortable. He opened his mouth to speak, but in one swift movement, Michelle head-butted him right on the forehead.

He crumpled to the floor. His body limp, the side of Elijah's face missed Lauren's shit-stained seat by a mere inch. Michelle rubbed her aching frontal, then resigned the throbbing sensation to the back of her mind.

'Only a warm-up,' she reminded herself, with a heavy heart.

Michelle stepped over Elijah's unconscious form to then lift his arms. Heaving, she dragged him across the small room to the only other door out of the auditor's office. This door led directly into the armoury itself, and the biometric scanner that locked it required the fingerprints of two authorised personnel for it to open.

Holding Elijah up from under his shoulders, Michelle fought to stretch his forefinger to the scanner at the door's side. Pressing it hard against the reader, the light turned from red to amber, and she dropped Elijah to the floor. Heart racing ever faster, she then pressed her own to the scanner, and the light turned from amber to green.

The door made a clicking noise, indicating its unlocking, and Michelle burst through with all her weight against it. Thankfully, despite her suspension, at least her accesses remained.

Michelle stumbled across the armoury. She was no longer exhilarated, but angst-ridden. The last shelf on the right – she knew it well. Her hands shuddered as she lifted the Glock 26 pistol down from its allotted sill. Turning, she glanced up to the CCTV camera.

Michelle darted across the room to its opposite side. Third drawer down – she knew it well also. She grappled for the handle and flung it open. Fingers shaking, she removed two American Eagle 9mm calibre bullets from their labelled box. *Two bullets* – that's all she needed.

Michelle slammed the drawer back shut. The bang caused her to flinch. Returning to the other side of the armoury once more, Michelle proceeded to collect a magazine from the lowest shelf. She then ran for the exit, stealing one final glance of the CCTV camera.

Seeing as the laxative-laced tea had worked so excellently on Lauren, there was no reason to believe that it hadn't on David. By now, he was almost certainly burning the enamel off a toilet – or, so Michelle hoped. David Harries had been the unfortunate officer tasked with monitoring the cameras that fateful night, and she had been sure to pay him a fleeting visit.

Ramming the exit door's release bar with her side, Michelle fell out into the night.

- CHAPTER XXVIII -

The Ritual

<u>Tuesday 2nd December 1997, 00:09am, SULLEN WOODS, ASHFIELD, LONDON.</u>

Slowing the car, Pris turned left off of Beggar's Hollow. The narrow track was ridden with pot-holes that tested the Ford's suspension and bounced all its passengers uneasily in their seats.

Rye peered up at the tall trees on either side of them. Their forms mostly bare, reached high into the sky – stark and unyielding. The beams from the car's headlights did little to penetrate the undergrowth that surrounded them. Whatever dwelt beyond was shrouded in complete, pitch blackness.

Pris slowed the car further – to all but a creep – as she carefully lined up the vehicle so that it could fit between the two metal poles hailing the car park's entrance. For a moment it was touch and go, and all six persons collectively held their breath. The pole to their left missed the wing mirror by a hare's whisker and as the car's wheels graced the cattle grid, Rye laughed. The only one to do so, Pris shot her sister a disapproving look. But Rye did not care – it may have been the very last time she was able to laugh.

Driving into the car park's centre, Pris turned them back around to face the exit, before pulling up the handbrake and cutting the ignition. There was only silence. All but dark, the only light was from that of a run-down toilet block.

'What are you doing?' Rye asked.

'It's too muddy,' replied Pris. 'If we take the car any further, we'll stand no chance at getting it back up the slope.'

'She's right,' said Zach – from behind. 'And you guys will need a quick getaway if this all goes tits up, as I expect it will.'

'What do you mean, "you guys"?' Ally questioned him, sharply. 'Don't speak that way.'

Opening the car's door, Zach ignored her. Cold air quickly flooded the vehicle.

'Come on,' he urged. 'We'll go the rest of the way on foot.'

❧

<u>Tuesday 2nd December 1997, 00:21am, A STREET CLOSE-BY TO ASHFIELD POLICE STATION, ASHFIELD, LONDON.</u> Back within the security of her Mini, Michelle slotted the two bullets into the Glock's magazine. Her hands had never shaken whilst loading a gun before – not even her first time, not even when out in the field. She'd always boasted a clear and level head, even when confronting dangers unknown. Maybe it was because Michelle knew exactly of the dangers this time. She knew unto whom these two bullets were destined – she had seen it. And she was scared.

With a clack, Michelle slid the magazine into the gun's casing before pulling back the slider with a definitive click – her forefinger on its frame. She dropped the loaded gun into her handbag that sat upon the passenger seat and turned her key in the car's ignition. It was time. Releasing the handbrake, she shunted the gearstick into first, and, revving the engine, swung out into the centre of the road.

*

Having slid and squelched their way down the slope, the group – minus Ally – stood huddled beside the lake's edge. Closely entwined, the Turpin sisters both gripped a large kitchen knife in hand. Every so often, one of them would nestle their face down by the other's neck and tightly close their eyes – imagining they were anywhere else other than where they were.

Fred grasped a cricket bat up to his chest and kept glancing out over the lake's surface. It was completely still. He actively chose not to look back up along the track – his eyes had played enough tricks on the way down. The only one to have tumbled; a muddied streak stretched all the way up Fred's school trousers, from his ankle to the hip.

Zach held his bow's string loosely between the fingers of his right hand – arrow loaded, but not drawn. Scanning the tree line, he was ready to fire at any disturbance.

Ros did not clutch onto her weapon – a hammer. Its handle stuck out of a blazer pocket, its weight pulling down upon the material. She watched, intently, as Ally crawled around on the ground, to draw out the pentacle in table salt.

Ally had weighed down the printed sheet – illustrating the Fifth Pentacle of Jupiter – with stones she'd pulled from out of the mud. There was no wind, but she did not want to risk their only hope of revelation blowing away. Eking out the condiment, she had been copying the intricate – and overall large – design for over ten minutes.

'OK, I think I'm done,' she announced, finally.

Tapping out the last few grains from their container, Ally realigned the pentacle's central writings with a finger, before standing, to reveal muddy knees.

'Neil Buchanan eat your heart out,' observed Zach.

'Ally, I can hardly see it,' Rye quivered, taking a tentative step away from her sister, and up to the pentacle.

The salt Ally had precisely poured was already turning – rendered translucent by the sodden earth. Some patches were invisible.

'It should still work,' Ally reassured, stepping out from within. 'Just because you can't see it doesn't mean it's not there.'

About to make a joke unto Zach's genitalia, Ally thought better of it. The others were still unaware of their all too brief indiscretion, and this was not the time – nor place – for that particular revelation.

'Alright, so what do we do now?' asked Pris, sidling up beside her sister.

'Rye sits at the pentacle's centre, and we five—' Ally gestured around '—sit at equal-distant intervals around its outside. Now, Rye, so long as you remain within the pentacle, nothing can harm you – careful!'

Ally raised her voice as Rye began to unsteadily tiptoe between the salted lines.

'I'm being careful!' Rye snapped, plonking herself to sit.

Rye had no choice but to cover the design's centre with her bottom and could already feel the wetness seeping through her skirt and knickers to her skin. Agitated and angry, she stabbed her knife into the mud – its blade easily sliding three inches inward. She looked up at the old oak tree to her left and shuddered. By choosing to face the lake, she had her back to the track's opening and immediately regretted the decision.

'Well, come on then!' Rye hastened.

Zach lowered his bow. The next to take a position – fronting Rye – he ensured a clear view up the track. Ally passed him a candle, and he begrudgingly relinquished his bow to the ground. Pris placed herself a few feet around to Zach's right and crouched. She gave her sister a weak smile. It was similarly returned. Ros trotted obediently past Pris, to sit cross-legged as the next person along.

'Fred, I said "equal-distant",' Ally reminded him, sharply, pulling the boy to his feet, and thrusting him a candle. 'Shift it.'

Having not entirely absorbed Ally's instructions, Fred had sat right beside Zach. Taken aback by his handling, he shunted himself around the circle by a few feet, scowling.

Ally navigated herself around the pentacle, surveying her handiwork as she did so, and comparing it one last time to the printed sheet, before crumpling its paper into a ball that she disposed of over her shoulder.

Taking a seat between Ros and Fred, Ally too had a view of the lake, and it was at this moment that she eyed the others' weapons with jealously. She tossed a candle to Ros and Pris, proceeding to light her own. The flame flicked up high, and its glow transfixed her for all but a second. Ally then passed the lighter anticlockwise around the circle. In turn, each threw or stretched in a relay, until all five candles were lit.

'Now what?' Rye asked, about to turn.

'Don't move!' Ally barked. 'For God's sake, Rye – you'll smudge the pentacle!'

Rye seethed at the order and began stabbing at the mud with her knife.

Ally sighed and took a deep breath.

'You must combine your blood, with the blood of the Avem,' she instructed. 'You do still *have* the blood, don't you?'

'Of course, I still have the blood,' Rye hissed, removing the test tube from her hoodie's pocket, and holding it aloft her head so that Ally could see. 'How do I combine my blood?'

'You've got a knife,' Ally pondered. 'Just slice a bit of you open and mix it up a little.'

'Slice a bit of me open! Are you serious?' Horrified by the prospect, Rye turned her head as best as she could. 'Like I haven't had enough of me sliced open already!' she raged.

'That doesn't sound very sanitary,' commented Pris.

'And you think Anoch ripping her shoulder open, with its claws, was?' Ally shot back.

'Guys, please, let's just all remember to whisper,' Fred reminded everyone.

Rye yanked her knife clear from the mud, regretting her actions of dirtying its blade. She wiped it clean upon her sleeve, then turned her left hand's palm upward. After counting down from five in her head, she decidedly slid the metal across – her teeth gritted.

Yelping from the pain, Rye dropped the knife. She clenched her hand into a fist and allowed her blood to dribble out and pool upon her right palm. Un-stoppering the test tube, Rye grimaced, pouring its contents; her overexposure to bodily fluids that night had not made her immune to the sight.

'Now, repeat after me,' Ally began. 'As I was among the captives, by the river of Chebar.'

'As I was among the captives, by the river of Chebar,' Rye repeated, slowly.

'The heavens were opened, and I saw visions of E-lo-him,' Ally concluded – careful as to annunciate the final word clearly.

'The heavens were opened,' Rye repeated, looking up to the inky sky. 'And I saw visions of E-lo-him.'

She scrunched up her face in concentration. Ten seconds easily passed, wherein each of the ritual's participants on the outside of the pentacle exchanged looks of apprehension. Rye was the first to break the silence. In a huff, she looked back to Ally.

'How will I know if it—'

A brilliant shaft of white light erupted forth from the pentacle's innermost six-pointed star to engulf Rye's body. Crackling with electric-like energy, the tunnel shot upwards, high past the treetops and straight into the sky.

Caught off guard by the ritual's effect, Ally, Pris, Zach, Fred and Ros, all fell backwards. Both Pris and Fred's candles fell to the mud – their flames now extinguished. It hurt their eyes to look directly at the tunnel's light, and so all shielded themselves from its glare.

Distracted as they were, not one noticed the materialisation of the two others by the lakeside. And it was only as the sound of crackling energy subsided, that one of the demons spoke.

'What a collect-sion you all make.'

The voice came from behind Zach, and so he was the first to stand. Backing into the pentacle's innermost circles, he suddenly found himself thrown forwards, and onto his knees. The salt – as Ally correctly predicted – had acted as a barrier, protecting Rye, and the shaft of light that concealed her. From the ground, Zach looked up at the demon.

Visually similar to a centaur, only this demon's torso and face were humanoid. Two antlers sprouted from its head, and the bone-like material that formed them extended down to the waist as an exoskeleton. In place of forearms, the abomination displayed flint-like swords. A snake slithered itself out and around empty eye sockets – its tongue flicking menacingly. The demon continued to speak through the serpent, to address them each in turn.

'What a collect-sion indeed,' it hissed. 'The orphan-s who mourn their long-dead parent-s.'

Pris took to her feet.

'The whore.'

Ally stood also.

'The would-be s-odomite.'

Fred reached for the cricket bat before wriggling back around the pentacle and over to Ally.

'The boy, who des-pite being s-urrounded his friend-s, ha-s never felt more alone.'

Quiver still strapped to his shoulder, Zach whipped his bow up from off the ground.

'And, *you*,' the demon concluded, turning its head – as well as that of the snake's – to look directly at Ros.

∾❦∿

Tuesday 2nd December 1997, 00:31am, SULLEN WOODS, ASHFIELD, LONDON.

Michelle's Mini skidded as it screeched to a stop. In her unwillingness to slow, she'd smashed her car's left-wing mirror upon one of the metal poles at the car park's entrance. Michelle had seen the tunnel of light reaching high above the woodland from the road. She just hoped that she wasn't too late.

Leaving the engine running and headlights full beam, Michelle was quick to exit her vehicle. She pulled her handbag over from the passenger seat, removing the pistol from its depths.

Gun grasped tightly in her right hand, Michelle flung her heavy handbag over a shoulder. She then ran across the gravel in the direction of the light, leaving her car's door open.

*

'Who—' Zach wavered.

'Who am's I?' the snake spoke, coldly. 'I am's Anoch'-s commanding General. I am's Pheanex.'

Anoch crouched beside its master, cowering.

'Pheanex?' Zach repeated, drawing back his bow's string. 'Sounds more like a brand of tissue, yer bloody wet wipe.' The snake stuck out its tongue. 'Oh, please. Am I supposed to say, "please, don't kill me"? Like I'd want to make more than just a cameo in the sequels anyway.'

Arms shuddering, Zach fired. The arrow shot past Pheanex's lower body, missing the demon by a fair few feet, to soundlessly pierce the lake's surface.

'What are you doing here?' Pris questioned – herself backing up the slope. 'What do you want with my sister?'

Beside her extinguished candle, Pris's knife lay forgotten.

'I am's here, to kill-s her,' Pheanex replied, simply. 'S-omething Anoch here s-hould have accomp-lish-ed, week-s ago.'

The serpent lurched forwards as the demon reared to kick Anoch. The much smaller creature whimpered in its shadow.

'Oh, so it's a "and he would have managed it too, if it weren't for you pesky kids" type of situation, is it?' Zach retorted, pulling back another arrow.

Just as before, the projectile fired straight past Pheanex and into the lake. Zach's aim was proving significantly below par – a fact that anyone, other than himself, could have forgiven him for.

'Lay your prim-sitive weapon down, ignorant child!' the snake spat – distorted and strained.

'You shan't save the girl's soul!' piped Anoch, standing to full height. 'She shall remain—'

Pheanex turned this time to kick Anoch down to the muddy ground with its hind legs.

'You want Elizabeth's soul? Is that it?' asked Ally. 'What – what do you do? Collect them? Torture them?'

'Collect-s them? Yes,' Pheanex hissed. 'Torture-s them? No. That's S-atan's prerog-sative, and I would hate-s to take that privilege away-s from them.'

'Satan?' Pris whispered. 'Is he here? Now?'

Immediately, she turned to scan the tree lines, expecting that at any moment, an even greater evil would join them.

'Satan is missing,' Ros startled everyone, by speaking. 'No-one – not even, the Almighty – knows where they are, and that's saying something, believe me. Satan is lost.'

'"Them"? "They"? Why are you all talking in the plural? Ros—' began Fred.

'It's called, preferred pronoun-s, fag!' hissed Pheanex, angrily, taking a step towards the group and pentacle. 'I thought your s-pec-ies were approach-sing a new millennium!'

Fred flinched.

'If Satan isn't even here to torture these souls, then why are you collecting them?' asked Ally.

'They're lost without them,' spoke Ros. 'There's no real hierarchy. They're in disarray without a leader – biding their time, waiting – not knowing. All are hoping to gain future favour. This is all just hijinks to them.'

'To welcome back the future sovereign—' Anoch began to sing, but Pheanex hoofed the soldier in the underbelly, and the demon recoiled once more.

It was at that moment Zach heard a crack from within the tree line to his right. The only one to catch it, he quickly drew his bow. The figure in amongst the undergrowth appeared human, however, and so he slackened his stance. A sudden crackle of energy from the light's tunnel and the figure was illuminated. If only fleetingly, it was enough to reveal their identity to Zach; Michelle drew a finger up to her mouth to shush him. She carefully moved parallel to the track, down the slope, and towards Pheanex and Anoch.

Zach turned his attention back to the demons also. If he was to help the police officer get close enough, then he needed to keep the hell-beasts talking.

'Why is Satan missing?' Zach demanded.

'You ask, a lot of question-s,' Pheanex hissed – snake writhing. 'They s-uffered downfall – *obv-siously*. Doe-s no-one read the damned script-sure-s, anymore? They wa-s defeated by the s-on.'

Ghost-like – for it looked no more than inhabited – Pheanex's body then raised both its sword arms and began to canter up the slope towards the group of humans.

'Freeze!' shouted Michelle, and Pheanex halted.

Appearing from the shadows, she held out her pistol with outstretched arms.

'Identify yourselves!' Michelle ordered, looking from one demon to the other.

Pris, Fred and Ally, all drew a sharp intake of breath. Ros's eyes widened.

'Look-sy here,' Pheanex hissed – tail flicking between nasal aperture. 'The failing, depre-ss-ed officer has finally s-hown up to; TAKE! US! DOWN!'

The demon's denouncement was deep – almost autotuned – in sound. Skull tilted to the heavens, only the serpent's mouth opened to a cackle.

'The arrogance of your s-pec-ies, never fail-s to amaze me.'

'*The arrogance,*' repeated Anoch, in a whisper.

'I know my part to play,' Michelle replied, fiercely, and focusing her aim. She then closed her eyes.

The gun's hollow boom echoed out all around them, across the lake and through the trees. Nesting birds took flight, scattering into the night. Two flew straight into the tunnel of light that encased Rye and their bodies fell limp to the mud beside the pentacle.

Pheanex did not fall, however, nor did the demon even flinch. Instead, it was Michelle that fell back into the undergrowth. Somehow, the bullet had been turned around on the officer.

Without thinking, Zach ran down the slope and across Pheanex's path to kneel beside Michelle. He inspected her wound and winced. The bullet had hit her clean in the forehead.

'She's dead!' Zach declared. 'You've killed her!'

Pheanex expelled another howl of laughter and its snake gleefully extended feet out from the skull; no-one could be sure how much of its length lay coiled up within the body's cavity. The demon reared again.

'The Spiritist killed herself!' Anoch sang.

For the first time, Ally could feel something powerful coursing through her veins. Embracing the feeling, she walked out from around the pentacle – much to the others' protests. She felt connected – could feel the earth turn beneath her feet, and it made her giddy. Her body felt light, yet her head was crystal clear. Gone were the feelings of sickness that had dominated the last few times she had knowingly used her abilities.

Ally raised both her hands and the tree roots beneath the track wriggled themselves free from their earth-bound prison.

Twisting and contorting, nature creaked against its will, as Ally bent it with ease to her own. Becoming fluid, the roots began reaching – twirling – up and around all four of Pheanex's hoofed legs. As they slithered upwards, they tightened, restricting.

'How quaint, your trick-s are – witch!'

Shaking its body, the demon stamped angrily upon the ground. Within seconds it had successfully turned the creepers to dust.

'COME!' Pheanex demanded, and the snake's head retracted into an eye socket.

Ally was transfixed by the demon's command. Within the space of a heartbeat, all that had flowed through her dwindled into nothingness. Zombie-like, she began her descent towards Pheanex. She had no choice but to obey.

'RUN!' yelled Zach – directing his own command over to Pris, Fred and Ros. 'I'll look after Ally – GO!'

Fred grabbed hold of Pris's arm, pulling at her to follow.

'I'm not leaving Rye!' she screamed, unmoving.

'Ally said she'd be protected,' Fred urged, pulling at the older girl again. 'We're not. *Come, on!*'

Fred grabbed Ros's wrist, but she shook it away.

'*Ros!*' he pressed, as Pris now pulled at him to leave.

Still, Ros did not move. She too appeared transfixed.

'*Zach?!*' Fred hollered down the slope.

Herself, wasting no more time, Pris turned to make haste back along the track.

'I said, RUN!' Zach shouted – he was already loading another arrow.

After hesitating, Fred bolted up the slope after Pris, catching up and overtaking her. They followed the track for several dozen feet before diverting off into the woods.

'Anoch,' Pheanex whispered. '*Fetch.*'

An arrow shot between its antlers and the demon hissed a sound of boredom.

*

Fred ran, blind. Cricket bat gripped tightly in hand; his legs complained as they threatened to buckle against the incline. Thorns ripped his uniform to scratch his flesh. Glancing over his shoulder, and he stumbled slightly. Pris wasn't far behind.

Nature's obstacles slowed their progress, but they fought onwards. As the brambles grew denser, Fred dared push back towards the track. He snapped a branch away from a rotting tree and the car park was revealed. Swallowing freezing air for breath, blood thumped through his head.

Equally exhausted, Pris appeared by his side, clutching her gut. Fred held out his free hand, and she took it. Together – and without looking back again – they ran ahead. Pris already held her car key.

*

Zach willed for his aim to be on target. Though, even if it was, who was to say his fate would not be the same as that which had befallen the fallen officer? But he had to try – Ally was close to being in sword's reach. Zach closed his eyes, and prayed, drawing back the bow's string.

'*Please*,' he whispered.

A seemingly direct hit, the arrow fired straight for Pheanex's torso. Just as with the bullet, however, and the projectile's path was altered mid-flight. Zach's arrow pierced his own ribcage. He fell to the ground with a thump, his arms falling limp over Michelle's lifeless body.

Ros tearfully recoiled.

In the split-second that it had taken for Pheanex to redirect the shot, the demon's hold on Ally had been broken, and regaining her senses, she looked around. Upon seeing the arrow sticking vertically upright from Zach's chest, Ally began to run over to him, but Pheanex raised its right sword, and she froze.

'Tell me, witch,' the demon hissed, and Ally swallowed. 'Can you-s fly?'

Bringing down its black, flint-like sword, Pheanex did not strike Ally, but she was thrown, nonetheless. Yanked sideways from the hip, it was as if a rope had been attached to her waist. Ally soared across the track – narrowly missing the first line of trees – before colliding with the trunk of the oak tree. She was out cold.

*

Pris wrenched the car's door open with force. Fred was already at its passenger-side – ready for her to lean across to unlock it. Pris did so, and he jumped in.

'Where are we going?' he asked – unsure of their exact plan.

Pris's fingers fumbled with the key as she struggled to line it up with the ignition.

'Pris?!' Fred pressured.

The older girl dropped the key to the floor of the car.

'Je-sus!' she exclaimed.

Bending over double, Pris frantically felt around in the darkness.

'It's not Jesus,' Fred replied – his mouth dry, and eyes staring. 'Definitely, *not* Jesus.'

To the left of Michelle's abandoned Mini – it's lights still on and door open – Fred could see Anoch. A solitary shadow in the track's opening, the demon stood upon its hind legs. Fred's grip tightened on the cricket bat, as Pris grunted and gasped. She was no closer to retrieving the car's key.

'*Pris*,' Fred breathed, and tugged at her coat.

His breath condensing into mist upon the side window; panic began closing Fred's throat. He turned to face his friend's sister, but had to double-take, as upon first glance, the driver's seat appeared vacant. Pris was bent so low to the floor of the car now, that everything from her waist up was completely hidden beneath the wheel.

Anoch's body heaved, and Fred was sure that the demon had sniffed. Even from forty feet away, he was certain that it could smell their fear. Then, back on all fours, Anoch galloped towards them.

'Pris!' Fred shouted.

*

'Look-s like it's ju-st you and me,' Pheanex sneered, triumphantly trotting up the slope to confront Ros. 'You and I, we aren't all that diff-serent, not really. I knew it, from the very moment, I laid eye-s upon you. We both s-erve.'

Ros did not back away. Standing tall, she met the demonic General's snaked-skull, head-on.

'I mu-st admit,' Pheanex continued. 'I was s-urpri-s-ed to see you out-s in the field. Don't mo-st of your kindred work behind clo-sed door-s? *Hidden,* door-s?'

The serpent's head protruded sharply outward before then ducking back within – its tongue flicking.

'I'm not "most of" my kind,' Ros spat.

Hands held behind her back, white light of a brilliance equal to that which engulfed Rye, sparked between Ros's fingers, as she twitched them.

'S-till, let the mortal-s die,' the demon coerced. 'Out-s in the open, maybe, but s-till let-s them die! Your heavenly father's chils-dren—'

'Leave!' Ros bellowed. 'I won't tell you again.'

'We're not-s going anywhere,' Pheanex snarled, through hollow sockets. 'We s-ubject-s, can't sit idle, s-imply awaiting your former comrade's return—'

Ros whipped her arms out from behind her back – her blonde hair flowing with the back draught, caused by the stream of purest light that fired forth from her hands. Its sound, terrific and fizzing, eclipsed that of the pentacle's tunnel.

As expected, Pheanex had pre-empted her assault, and the demon shielded itself by crossing swords across its chest. The light Ros emitted sparked unto the ground.

*

'Got it!' Pris announced, triumphantly – holding the key aloft her buried head.

At that moment, Anoch collided with the passenger door, buckling the metal inward and shattering the window into a thousand shards. The key shot upwards, before beginning its descent in seemingly slow motion. Fred leapt backwards onto the gearstick as Pris flailed out her arms. Somehow, she succeeded in catching the key – blindly – from beneath the car's controls.

Teeth bared, Anoch's face was halfway through the window. Hunger encapsulated the demon – wild, unadulterated and raw desire. Its scab-ridden talons clawed at the window's frame, to wrap around. The demon was either about to rip the door from off the car's chassis or attempt to clamber through the void. Fred could easily distinguish between the demonic ranks now. Pheanex was far more reserved – pretentiously intelligent. Anoch was feral.

Fred sent several kicks flying in the direction of Anoch's face and swung the bat, violently. All-the-while Pris squirmed beneath him, as he inadvertently held her down.

Anoch caught Fred's right foot and pulled. Sliding some inches before grabbing the steering wheel for tether, Fred dropped the bat to Pris's feet – into the car's footwell, and out of sight. From Fred's new position, however, Pris was able to sit upright once more, to take hold of the boy from beneath his shoulders. She pulled him, as the demon pulled back harder, and a tug of war ensued.

Fred's vision – much like his face – appeared drained of colour. His perception felt slowed, yet somewhat heightened – juxtaposed and disjointed – all at the same time. Their struggle and Pris's screams sliced across the car park's silence like a rusty knife.

Then, Pris's grasp of Fred vanished, forcing him to take the full strain of Anoch's greedy strength, all on his own. His sweaty palms losing hold on the wheel, Fred was slipping.

Above his head, the plastic lid of a metal canister flew off with a pop; aside from the key and cricket bat, Pris had discovered something else upon the car's floor. She gave the de-icer two sharp shakes before vigorously spraying a thick fog into Anoch's face, orange eyes and open jaws.

Immediately, the demon began to shudder and twinge. As if having a seizure, Anoch was spasming. Still, Pris persisted to spray. Fingers forcibly pressed down; her knuckles had turned white. Anoch let out a high-pitched cry and disappeared from view.

Both knew Pris's act of heroism could not have bought more than a few precious seconds, and so she hastily slid the key into the ignition. The engine juddered and faltered.

'Come on! Come, on! *Please!*' Pris pleaded.

Herself choking on the spray, she twisted the cold metal between her trembling fingers. The engine roared into life, and Pris and Fred yelped, as a loud thump emanated from the car's bonnet. The entire car shook, as its suspension contracted. Anoch was crouched right in front of them.

'OK,' Pris muttered, slamming the clutch. 'Little *shit.*'

She shoved the gearstick into first, and her foot hit the gas. The engine thundered, and the car shot forward.

Unable to see anything beyond the demon, Pris steered randomly as she tried to shake it off. Though initially perturbed by the vehicle's sudden movement, Anoch continued to scratch and tear at its metal exterior – its eyes glinting.

Trees cast ominous shadows across the windscreen, and Fred closed his eyes tight, as Pris careered her Ford towards the only other car in the car park. Appearing deranged – her hair quite dishevelled – she swung the wheel abruptly to her right – her prominent features contorted in a mixture of grimace and wild enthusiasm. It was only by sheer luck – and the smallest of distances – that Pris missed a collision with the Mini.

Suddenly, both she and Fred were thrown forwards from the force of a separate impact; their car had hit a tree.

*

Another of her blasts deflected, Ros ducked. She had no plan – no real offence or defence. Ros leapt back from a sword's swipe. She was outmatched – she knew it, and so did Pheanex.

'You're fighting, a lo-sing battle,' the serpent chided – unexhausted by the movements of its bodily shell. 'S-atan will return, and when revelation occur-s, all will be lo-st.'

His groans inaudible, Zach bore sole witness to the showdown, although he could not hear the words exchanged. His head woollen, his thoughts were fragmented. For the past few minutes, he'd been in and out of consciousness more times than even he knew. What he did know, however, was that if something was not done soon – if there was no intervention – Ros would surely die by Pheanex's swords.

Zach's hand felt out around him – the process laborious, for he kept blacking out. His chest quaking, he followed Michelle's arm down to reach her hand. Her pistol was still nearby – Zach knew it. And sure enough, after weakly patting the area surrounding the police officer's hip, he found it.

Zach strained for breath – his face pained yet determined – as he channelled all his remaining energy into lifting the firearm from off of the mud. Keeping his wrist low – for he could lift it no higher – Zach outstretched and squinted, fighting the urge to close his eyes completely once more.

*

Pris held her hand against her forehead – it had slammed into the wheel. Not allowing this – or their disorientation – to distract them, she and Fred scrambled out of the car. Its bonnet crumpled; it was a write-off.

Quietly, they absorbed the wreckage and their situation. Just because they could no longer see Anoch, it did not mean the demon was dead. Fred reached back inside the car to reclaim the bat – their only remaining weapon.

They had no chance of outrunning Anoch. Both knew this to be true. Their best option would be to barricade themselves someplace, as to shield from immediate danger. The dim lights of the toilet block flickered at the car park's opposite end.

Bang!

The second shot fired that evening echoed out, and Pris and Fred jolted at its sound. Whoever had been the second person to fire the gun – and to potentially get hit – would now, for them, remain a mystery, although they yearned for the knowledge.

Forcing the bullet to the back of his mind, Fred beckoned to the toilet block – his eyes teary – and Pris nodded, wearily. Supporting each other, they limped towards its light.

Their progress was infuriatingly slow but steady. Still, Anoch was nowhere to be seen, yet neither dared look behind them. It was a silent agreement that both would prefer to not see the demon coming, if it was to deliver their deaths, whilst at their most vulnerable.

Pris and Fred were just under the block's porch when they heard it – a sound so full of anger and hatred. Evidently, Anoch was informing them of its displeasure.

'It survived the crash,' Pris wailed. 'What if it can't die?'

Ignoring her obvious observation and unanswerable question, Fred crossed the toilet block's threshold. Pris hobbled after him.

Moths danced above their heads as the strip lights flickered. The floor – a brown tile – was covered in a thick film of grime and gave off an unbearable stench of urine. Her trainers cached with mud – that oozed from the fabric – Pris slipped. She grabbed hold of Fred, who slipped also, but steadied himself against the wall.

Concluding that their only defence could be a cubicle, Fred ushered Pris into the nearest one. He pushed her in first, before quickly following, shutting the door behind them.

'There's no lock,' Pris whispered, as Fred's hand hovered over where one should have been.

'I doubt—' he swallowed '—that it'll make a difference.'

She whacked him in the ribs and the pained momentum was all Fred needed to fall back out. Leading, he hurried them along to the one adjacent.

Pris climbed atop the toilet seat as Fred bolted the door. Raising the bat up level with his head, it swayed back and forth with every beat of Fred's heart. He could feel his pulse in his fingers. Pris crouched – her hands clasping his shoulders.

They waited. They listened.

Moments passed – neither knew how long exactly, but when Anoch did enter the block there was little further delay.

Pris let out a full-bodied scream as the cubicle door was torn clean off – its bolt buckling – and Fred's eyes widened. The car crash had impaled a tree branch right through Anoch's torso. Its orange eyes blood-shot, the demon's expression was pure fury.

'MAGGOTS!' Anoch growled. 'You have no comprehension of—'

Thwack!

They did not hear the rest of Anoch's sentence, for in one – swift – movement, Fred had swung the bat through its head. Parted from its body, it burst and splattered like a watermelon against the cubicle's partition. Astonished, Fred looked back at Pris. Neither could believe their luck. Their relief was only short-lived, however, as a loud bang brought them back down to earth.

Mere seconds after Anoch's head had been severed from its body, a fountain of maggots exploded out from the base of the demon's neck. Hundreds, upon hundreds of miniature larvae, shot feet into the air – far more than Anoch's body could possibly contain within its capacity.

Fred scuttled backwards, precariously joining Pris atop the toilet seat. They palmed the walls, whilst clinging onto each other for balance.

Still, the maggots erupted. A constant stream, they fired up at the ceiling, ricocheting off, before falling back to the floor. Ever deeper, they began to pile. A heavy, viscous and orange fluid began pouring amongst them, dribbling thickly from out of Anoch's windpipe. Gelatinous chunks tumbled down the demon's sporadically-feathered hide, as its carcass collapsed in upon itself. All tissue bubbled and burned until all that was left of Anoch was a hot and sticky mess.

Pris and Fred gaped as the liquid continued to pour forth from seemingly nowhere; spreading, and taking on a force of its own. It corroded the walls, and the water pipes, sending powerful jets shooting in all directions. The wash basins – now unsupported – fell from off the walls and into the ankle-deep torrent before being consumed – their structure melting away to nothingness.

'Duck!' shouted Fred.

Pris did as instructed, and Fred rammed the cricket bat into the small letterbox window above their heads. After several powerful blows, he broke it, then cleared the fragments from the frame.

Without further instruction, Pris climbed the toilet's tank. She squeezed her arms, and with an added boost from Fred, was able to pull her upper body through the narrow opening.

By now, the toilet was threatening to topple. It too was falling foul to the murkiness that lapped at its base – at least two inches had been stolen from it already. Himself unsteady, for Fred it felt as if he was surfing.

Pris whimpered as she landed with a squelch upon the ground behind the toilet block. Fred hurried to follow her. The toilet disintegrated the moment his foot left it, and he was left hanging – half-in, half-out of the window. With all his remaining might, Fred wriggled himself through the void. Breathless, he fell to the mud beside Pris. It was lucky that both were so slender.

They looked back at the block, entranced. The acidic substance was beginning to leak out from between the joins in its brickwork.

'Do you reckon – we ought to—' began Fred.

'Back up?' Pris interrupted. 'Yeah.'

Stumbling away, they crumpled onto the embankment behind. Foundations weakened; the building's timbers creaked. One final groan and the block collapsed completely, with a tremendous crash. A mass of smoking brick and wood, the structure's components came to settle, and all was silent. Pris looked up towards the heavens; it had started to rain.

CHAPTER XXIX

The Sky Garden

<u>Tuesday 2nd December 1997, 00:30am, SULLEN WOODS, ASHFIELD, LONDON.</u>

Rye's eyes suddenly snapped closed, as her chin was forced up. Her thoughts were swimming with smoke, and she felt heavy. From the smoke, colours dripped – pooling – then formed lines and shapes. Their vividness growing, the constructing scene forced itself into the consciousness of Rye's minds-eye. And it was painful.

'Oh, no,' she breathed.

Finding herself on the pavement of a residential street, the road's sign confirmed Rye's location: Dragnell Lane. The sun was so bright in the cloudless sky that she had to shield her eyes.

Tentatively, Rye took several steps along the path, testing the solidity of the ground beneath her. Then, she froze. A girl with beautifully curly, auburn hair and wearing a black lace dress, dropped to the ground from a drainpipe outside of number 23, to Rye's immediate left.

Rye watched – her eyes wide – as Elizabeth Thackerall slung a holdall over her shoulder and proceeded to hop over the wall of the small front garden. She walked straight for her, and Rye breathed in to flatten herself. Elizabeth took no notice of her, however. She jogged on past to a car that had pulled up several houses down.

Rye opened her mouth, about to holler a greeting, or warning – the words of which she was unsure – but the scene before her changed, in one loud snap. As if Dragnell Lane had been all but a painting dropped into water, its colours ran to diffuse, and new shapes were created, to sharpen.

A green bottle fell in slow motion from off a glass-topped table. *The Devil's Hand.* Rye fell with it. As if she'd tripped within a dream, her heart faltered, as her body plummeted. As Rye hit the floorboards, along with the glass, the splash crashed the visual into fluidity.

Another snap – akin to the clicking of fingers – and colours swirled to take on the form of a new location, and people – lots and lots of people. All around Rye, figures were walking. Their chatter grew in volume as her surroundings focused. Next to a baggage conveyor, Rye was stood in an airport.

Turning on the spot, a shiver reverberated throughout Rye's entire being and she bent double. A large woman, dressed in a sari, had passed right through her apparent, non-corporeal form.

Rye retreated to take refuge behind a pillar. Cautiously, she peered out.

'Ally!' she shouted, instinctively.

In afterthought, she clasped a hand to her mouth, but she needn't have. Rye's outburst – exactly as her presence had – went quite unnoticed to those around her, including her friend, who was running full pelt towards the baggage conveyor. Ally dived headlong onto its moving belt, just as the airport was snatched away from Rye's sight.

Snap!

Once again colours pooled, but quicker. Reforming a familiar scene, Dragnell Lane was recreated, although this time, it was night. Rye stood in the road's centre as rain poured. She held out a palm, but as precedent had set, the droplets passed through her skin, causing her whole body to buzz with the sensation of pins and needles. Her shins felt numbed also, and as Rye looked down, she realised the entire road was flooded to knee height.

Surveying, she immediately spied a woman. Dressed in a trench coat, this woman was stood in the road's centre also, by the side of a parked car. She was punching its driver's side window. Though Rye could not be certain, she suspected this to be the same car that she'd only moments ago witnessed Elizabeth approach – it was in the same spot. Rye remained vigilant as the downpour worsened. Its pellets stung.

After looking around herself in a panic, the woman turned to her left, to wade over to a builder's skip. She heaved a chunk of masonry from out of it before hurriedly returning to the car. Rye squinted – the woman was Detective Inspector Michelle Davey.

Rye moved closer to the car – easily, through the water – and saw what Michelle apparently could – what was responsible for her frenzy. It was Elizabeth Thackerall, and she was on fire. Sat within the car, facing away, her scratched and yellowed – translucent – form hammered away on the glass. Like a television, Elizabeth flickered. But, why? When Rye herself had seen – and indeed been touched by – the deceased teen at the lake, her hands had been bloated and rotten – solid.

Michelle struggled to hoist the masonry over her right shoulder but ultimately succeeded in flinging it at the driver's side window. Rye watched as the car disappeared in the blink of an eye, a half-second before Dragnell Lane did also, with another loud and decisive snap.

Her surroundings changing yet again, Rye felt woozy. She had hardly seen the colours melt and merge.

Within the English corridor of her school, Rye knew the boy before her – even from the back of his head. It was Fred, and he was walking away so fast that she had to jog to keep up with him. Overtaking her friend, Rye proceeded to run backwards. Fred's eyes were red and puffy, as were his cheeks. He'd been crying.

'What's wrong?' Rye asked, taken aback, but knowing he would not hear her.

As Fred increased his speed, Rye staggered to the side of the corridor. She was in no hurry to relive the unpleasantness of another human passing through her. In these scenarios, she was very much the ghost. Deciding instead to trail him, Rye remained hot in pursuit as Fred sharply turned a corner.

He stopped dead, and momentum carried Rye forwards into his back, and out through his chest. Shivering from the exact feeling she had been trying to avoid, Rye then flinched. She was face-to-face with Liam Pritchard – the reason for Fred's abrupt halt.

'What're you crying for, gay boy?' Liam sneered, and Rye raised an eyebrow. 'Thought you liked it when other boys touched you?'

Liam's fist travelled right through Rye's head, and straight into Fred's nose. Both recoiled from the action in unison.

The scene snapped with dissolution. And feeling rigid and tight, yet without human form, Rye herself was the black oil pastel that pressed down hard upon the heinous subject of her own artwork – the china doll with auburn ringlets, black lace dress and black eyes. The pastel painfully snapped clean in two, only to reform and snap again, and again. There was a flash of the chalkboard: 'FEAR.'

Snap!

Reeling, Rye found herself staring into the faces of at least two hundred people, as they stood, clapping. She tensed, before remembering no-one could see her, and so relaxed once more.

'Huh?' Rye breathed – slowly adjusting.

It was the evening of prize-giving – *again* – and from her position atop the stage, she attempted to spy herself within the audience as they re-seated.

'And f-f-finally, in recognition of Detective Chief Inspector M-Malcolm Goodfellow f-for his—'

'Fire! Look – up there! Fire!'

The elderly gentleman's outburst, as he remained standing, cut across Mr Bullen's speech. One-by-one, members of the crowd stood to extend their necks in the direction of the high windows. As chaos quickly ensued, past-Rye climbed onto her chair.

'I don't understand,' Rye whispered.

She acknowledged and understood each scenario the ritual had so far conjured – well, mostly – but their selection seemed random. And, perhaps, they were.

Snap!

Rye's head began to thump, as fresh images forced themselves through the very synapses of her brain, in an explosion of dark colour.

Clawing at her temples, Rye recognised her vision's latest arena all too well. She was beside the lake, on the very same night that her current, physical form was located. The Fifth Pentacle of Jupiter drawn out upon the mud, a brilliant shaft of white light was erupting forth from its centre. Rye was unable to see her own body from within its blinding, whirling vortex. Her sister and all four friends stood, looking directly at her.

'What are you doing here?' spoke Pris, backing away, and Rye spluttered. 'What do you want with my sister?'

'I am's here, to kill-s her,' an unknown voice hissed reply, and Rye turned – cold. 'S-omething Anoch here s-hould have accomp-lish-ed, week-s ago.'

Rye screamed. Inches from her face, a snake slithered out from an eye socket of a hollowed and humanoid skull. Its tongue flicked, menacingly.

Snap!

Rye did not have time to grasp the events that were unfolding around her physical form, for she again had been transported against her will. Now, within a dingy toilet cubicle, she was squashed against its partition. Two others – Pris and Fred – were already cramped inside. The latter brandished a cricket bat, as the former crouched atop the toilet's seat. Both were dressed in the same clothes as when Rye had last seen them.

Taking a side-step to her left, Rye looked into Fred's eyes. Unblinking, they were a deep well of fear. The cubicle's door was unexpectedly ripped clean off its hinges, and—

Snap!

Rye's surroundings blurred into a colourful rainbow. She hadn't had time to scream, though her jaw had instinctively dropped to do so, and as her body felt plunged, she garbled.

The gardens of Ashfield Crematorium. Names on a stone:

'Neal Arthur Turpin, 18th September 1934 – 1st November 1983. Jean Barbara Turpin, 24th April 1942 – 1st November 1983. Beloved parents.'

Snap!

In a sitting room that she didn't recognise, Rye sat opposite a woman she did not know. Her intimidating facial features exacerbated by jet-black hair, set into rollers, blood-red fabric stretched valiantly across the woman's heavy bosom.

Still fearing for Pris and Fred's safety, Rye anxiously looked about herself, feeling nauseous. With its curtains drawn, the room was dated, cluttered, and filled with furniture from the thirties. The woman was perched on a coffee table. Rye was sat upon a shabby sofa. No, Rye was sat *inside* another – a girl – judging by the chest that rose and fell to cross the outline of her own, spectral one.

The woman in red leaned closer; her eyes appeared yellow.

'Well, hello,' she then mused in an American accent, furrowing her pencilled brow. 'What do we have here?'

Rye could have sworn that the woman was addressing her, as opposed to the girl whom she inhabited.

Snap!

Rye only caught a glimpse of her vision's next segment – a glimpse of shimmering gold. Shaped as the letter K, it was – what

Rye believed to be – a necklace. Like staring into the sun, the image imprinted itself. And she cried.

Snap!

There was Fred again. A huge rucksack on his back, he was running through a covered car park. It was night. Rye was thankful that he, at least, had lived to escape whatever was to happen within the toilet cubicle – but what about Pris? Fred's foot splashed a puddle as he passed by her and its water seared Rye's ankles.

Fred was not alone, however. Another boy, similar in age – and dressed like an extra from a production of *Oliver!* – sprinted after him. Chasing, or trying to keep pace? Rye wasn't sure.

Snap!

A crib in the corner of a darkened room was draped with a dust sheet. From a distance, Rye saw herself readying to remove it. A quiver on her back and a bow slung over her shoulder, this future-Rye also held a pistol in her right hand.

Snap!

There was a prison cell with glass walls. The girl – or woman – inside was stripped naked, and on the floor. Her face was hidden from view.

Snap!

Rye's body moved like tracing paper atop that she was stood within, and as they lifted a hand, there was blood on their palm. There was blood on the edge of a table also. That's all Rye could see, before—

Snap!

There was a statue. It wore a crown. Its subject; human?

Snap!

A Tarot card, displaying 'THE DEVIL' was turned over by a manicured hand—

Snap!

Snap!

'No!' Rye screamed. 'Wait!'

Snap!

Snap!

Snap!

The time between images now lasting no longer than a split-second, it became too difficult for Rye to differentiate between them.

Snap!

Snap!

Snap!

'Aaaagh!' Rye screamed.

Snap.

This latest snap was much heavier – deeper – than before, with the image conjured significantly slowed. It was as if the ritual had finally heeded Rye's cry for deceleration – either that, or it was about to play itself out.

Rye felt floaty as she glided through a tunnel of the London Underground, manoeuvring her unseen form over, past and between commuters. Their fashions were different from those she was used to. Men's suits appeared tailored slimmer, and the women's attire more fitted to flatter. The posters and advisements were modernised also – some were moving as if they were television screens.

Snap …

The final snap revealed an image so terrible that Rye felt paralysed by it. Behind the glass at the top of a tall skyscraper, the City of London sprawled before her at sunset. Carnage; that was the only word Rye could pluck to describe the spectacle. Streets and buildings flamed, as materials that she thought were incombustible burned. Tower Bridge – which she could see to her left – was all but a ruin, and the Thames flowed as red, hot lava.

All of London was amok. Overrun, it swarmed with beings of varying shapes and sizes; stomping, scurrying, wading and climbing everything that there was. Even in the sky, some flew to navigate fire whirls. The visual was akin to an apocalyptic disaster movie but displayed far more movement, detail, and scope than anything Rye had ever seen on screen. This was hell on earth.

Impossible to take in, Rye stepped back. Tears streaking her cheeks, her heart raced whilst sinking. She hit something solid and turned to see a swanky dining table sway. Before Rye had time to steady it, the champagne glasses fell to the floor and smashed.

Rye braced herself with the table's top – shocking herself as she did so. Yes, she'd been sat upon a sofa within an earlier segment of her vision, but she'd still very much been a spectator. This was the first time Rye had made a physical impact on her surroundings.

Rye slapped the table's surface. It remained solid to the touch. With a hand, she brushed a plate onto the floor. Like the glass, this too, shattered. With a foot, she then crunched its pieces into smaller fragments.

Fear spiking, Rye scanned the level. A sky-high restaurant and bar, the venue was beautiful, and clearly not a place for those strapped for cash. Plots and borders of plants and trees rose with the steps that led up from the dining area to another viewing deck. An oasis in the sky; flowers bloomed beneath a glass ceiling and unseen water could be heard trickling.

Sensing movement behind her from shadows, Rye turned to face the windows once more. To her utmost horror, hordes of demons were climbing the skyscraper's outer glass. Unobservant or uncaring of Rye, they went by her to ascend further.

Every demon was as hideous as the next, but no two were the same. A jig-saw of random parts, each had been constructed as if from a reject pile – spare or faulty. A Bosch painting brought to life; animal heads and tails were stuck mismatched, and in varying numbers, onto forms.

A demon parallel with Rye – a crab-like creature, with three human heads and a set of oversized butterfly wings – let out an audible growl, as it hovered behind the blanket of climbers.

Rye screamed, and the window shattered. Its shards turned fluid as they flew towards her face. The metal girders of the skyscraper became wobbly and blurred, as the entire structure then popped like a balloon into a sea of colour, that dissipated as smoke upon an intangible breeze.

The next thing Rye felt was the cold mud on the side of her face, accompanied by the smell of damp earth.

- CHAPTER XXX -

The Recoil

<u>Tuesday 2nd December 1997, 00:54am, SULLEN WOODS, ASHFIELD, LONDON.</u>

'Call an ambulance!'

Ally's voice was the first thing Rye heard when coming to. Her stomach in her mouth, her stomach's contents covered the front of her hoodie. She rolled over onto her back. The stars in the night's sky were blurry and spinning. It felt like she had fallen from a building, as opposed to simply toppling over.

'They'll trace the number!' spoke Ros – her voice panicked.

'I don't care!' shouted Ally.

Rye rolled onto her side and looked over in their direction. Ally knelt several feet away; she cradled another's head in her hands. Immediately freaked as to the other's identity, Rye willed her vision to focus. She saw no peroxide hair – it was not her sister.

'Do it!' Ally screamed. 'Now, Ros!'

Ros backed away, producing a pink mobile from her blazer's inside pocket.

Panic flooding over her weakened mind and body, Rye forced her limbs into cooperation. She pushed herself up onto her knees and crawled across the mud and down the slope towards Ally. To her utmost horror and heartache, Zach's motionless form was laid out before her friend. An arrow stuck up from his torso.

Rye's tears were instantaneous, and they choked her.

'I can't – I can't find a pulse!' Ally wept.

Deeper into the woods, Ros's forefinger hesitated over her phone's keypad, as she absorbed Ally's declaration. Taking a deep breath, she then relented to opening her contacts folder, and dialled the only entry held there, labelled, 'A.M.' The line rang three times before being answered.

'Yes – yes – I know – I know!' Ros fought to speak. 'We did the ritual and—'

Ros held the mobile away from her face, waiting impatiently for the berating tones she'd invited to subside.

'There was a hitch,' Ros began, tentatively – seizing the opportunity presented by the recipient's pause. '*Two* hitches, actually …'

Rye reached out and took Zach's hand in her own, feeling around the boy's wrist for a pulse that Ally had been unable to find at his neck. With every watery blink, Zach's form divided and became two in her vision.

'I – I can't find one either,' Rye whispered. 'What – what happened? Where did the demon go?! Where's Pris?!'

'Zach shot it – with the gun!' wailed Ally, unquestioning of Rye's knowledge of Pheanex.

Snot dripped from Ally's nose – a long globule hanging low, before conjoining with her lips. It rippled unattractively, as she spat her next words.

'The noise – I was knocked out, I think – but, the noise— '

'I need to find Pris,' Rye proclaimed.

Her thoughts suddenly full of her sister and Fred cornered in the toilet cubicle, Rye's agitation grew. She turned her head to look back along the track and made a movement to stand, but gravity felt heavy and she slid, collapsing in a heap beside Zach once more.

'I don't know – I don't know where they went! Pheanex threw me against a tree and – and when I came back around, they – they were gone!'

Ally's nose was red and flared as she spoke. She looked over her shoulder before speaking again – angst-ridden and snarling.

'Hurry up! For fuck's sake – HURRY UP!'

'They're in the toilets – I think – in the car park,' Rye struggled – sounding, and feeling confused. 'I have – I have to find them.'

Pushing herself up from the ground with both hands, Rye stood. She turned too quickly on the mud, however, and slipped. Falling, her wounded shoulder slammed into the earth. Proceeding to cough and splutter, a warm trickle of gastric vomit dribbled out from between Rye's lips. It stung her throat and watered her eyes. The colour and consistency of tar, it was so far in the digestion process, it was near faecal, and clung to her chin.

It was then that Pris and Fred emerged from out of the shadows, hobbling down the track's slope. They were breathless and dirtied, but very much alive. As Fred limped, Pris supported him.

His eyes hurriedly exploring the scene that greeted them, Fred could identify both Rye and Ally from a distance. He then saw a third person, whom he deduced to be Zach, and broke into a laboured sprint.

'Zach?! ZACH! Oh, my God. Oh, my God!' he cried, skidding over to Zach's side, and falling to his knees also.

'Pris – Pris?' Rye panted, weakly.

Catching up with the group, Pris pulled Rye to her feet and into a hug. Rye's legs gave way at the knees, but her sister's firm embrace prevented her from falling. It took all of what was left of Pris's strength to hold on, but there was no chance of her letting go.

'What happened to the demon?' Pris asked.

She, too, was fighting tears.

'Zach shot it,' replied Ros, flatly, as she reappeared. 'What about Anoch?'

It was obvious that Ros had been crying also, but her eyes were now dry.

'It's dead,' whispered Pris. 'Where's Pheanex's body?'

'Dissolved to dust,' Ros confirmed, with a far-off look.

'Did you call an ambulance?!' Ally pressured – her hands shakily stroking Zach's hair. 'Fred – there's no pulse!'

'Don't say that – don't you dare say that! Zach! Come on, Zach! Breathe!'

Wailing, Fred unfastened Zach's duffle and flapped the material back as far as the arrow would allow. Sodden to his touch, the once white cotton of Zach's school shirt appeared dyed black.

'Oh, my god … there's so much blood!' Fred recoiled. 'We – we need to put pressure on the wound—'

'We can't remove the arrow – he'll bleed out!' Ally squealed, pushing Fred's hand away from its shaft. 'How long until the ambulance arrives?'

'I didn't call an ambulance,' Ros replied, calmly.

'What?!' exclaimed Ally.

'Why not?!' yelled Fred.

'Zach doesn't need an ambulance, neither of them does.' Ros sighed. 'They're dead. There's nothing that can be done.'

'W-We've g-got to keep him warm,' wavered Ally.

'He's *dead*,' Ros said again, and knelt beside her.

Fred gave Ros a withering look before directing his reply to Ally.

'W-what with?' he asked, feebly, wiping his nose.

'Use her jacket,' Ally insisted, pointing to Michelle's body.

'Don't touch it!' shouted Ros, just as Fred moved to do so. 'He's *dead*, and we have to leave.'

'What do you mean, "leave"?!' Fred shouted back. 'We're not leaving! We're not going to leave him here!'

'There's no pulse,' Ros repeated.

'But if we just – if we just—'

'He's *dead*, Frederick.'

'He can't be,' Fred sniffled – strained. 'He isn't! We just have to find a way—'

'Zach is dead. Michelle is dead. It's horrible, and it's tragic, and it *should not* have happened, but we *need* to leave—'

'Who made you the leader?' Ally stung.

Standing, she angrily stared Ros down.

Next to Ally, a bird fell limp from its treetop perch. *Dead* – it slapped into the mud beside Zach. From a few trees further back, two more fell, then another, and another. With every tear Ally shed – that rolled down her cheeks and off her chin – a bird plummeted.

Seemingly unaware or uncaring of this, Ally bent down and prised the gun from out of Zach's hand. She stood and slowly walked around his body to Michelle's. All-the-while she kept eye contact with Ros, daring the girl to challenge her.

'Everything you touch will be covered in your DNA,' warned Ros.

'I'm not touching anything that I intend on leaving behind,' Ally snapped.

Another six birds came crashing down. One after another they quickly plopped, and Pris ushered Rye back into the centre of the track.

Being very careful of what she was touching, Ally extracted Michelle's handbag from off the woman's shoulder before shunting it up over her own. She dropped the empty pistol inside.

'What – what are you doing?' asked Rye.

'She was a police officer. She had a gun,' Ally stated, simply. 'And seeing as it ultimately succeeded in killing Pheanex, we're keeping it.'

'Are you mad?' Fred objected. 'That gun got her killed!'

Dramatically, he threw his hand out in the direction of Michelle.

'Bullets beat bones,' Ally replied, steely. 'As do arrows.'

Another bird fell to land atop Michelle's torso.

'I'm so sorry,' Ros apologised – her eyes cast down to the fallen officer. 'I should have done something sooner. It just all happened so fast—'

'And what exactly did you do anyway, Ros?' Fred spoke up, coldly.

'Shut up! All of you – just, shut up. This isn't helping,' Pris piped. 'Ros is right – we need to leave. If anyone shows up – there's no way that we can explain this.'

'Who's gonna show up?' asked Ally. 'It's the middle of the night!'

'This isn't the United States. Police officers don't usually carry guns here,' explained Pris. 'So, if there's any chance that she told anyone else what she was doing, or where she was headed, who's to say how much time we have. We need to leave and get our stories straight.'

'We – we could tell the truth?' suggested Rye.

'The truth is a far too bitter a pill to swallow,' replied Pris.

A long silence followed in the wake of her words, as each of the group processed the reality of their situation.

Ally then collected Zach's bow and quiver. The latter was much harder to remove than Michelle's bag had been, but she did so delicately. She thrust them across to Fred. Then, without saying another word, and without taking another look back at Zach's body, Ally began making her way up the track.

Rye squirmed to pull herself free from her sister. She lurched over to Fred and plonked herself down beside him. Zach's eyes were already closed, but she caressed his eyelids with her fingertips anyhow.

'I'm so sorry – I'm – I'm …' she rasped.

Rye flapped the material of Zach's duffle back across his wound. She patted it and leant in to kiss him on the forehead – goodbye, for the last time.

'Come on,' urged Pris, softly.

Rye stood and backed up into her sister's open arms. Together they set off up the slope after Ally, with Rye crying onto her sister's shoulder. Rye trod on a forgotten candle, and its wax snapped beneath her feet. The sound startled her, but Pris rubbed her back, and they continued their ascent in silence.

'We have to go—' began Ros.

'Shut up,' hissed Fred.

He moistened his dry lips with his tongue, looked up at her, then whispered:

'Just give me a minute.'

Ros nodded her understanding and walked back over to the lake's edge. Fred paid no attention to her direction, or to the fact that she was now sweeping the area of candles, knives, lighter, et al.

'Listen,' Fred hushed, lowering his mouth to Zach's ear. 'I know you can hear me. After all we've seen in the last couple of months, I *know* you can hear me.'

Fred swallowed, then shut his eyes.

'I love you. I have *always* loved you – and I don't mean in *that* way.' He laughed a little. 'Just, always know … always remember … wherever you are, know that I love you. I'll carry a piece of you with me forever. You'll forever be a part of me – and – and then, you'll never really be gone. Because, if you're never forgotten, how can you have ever really left?'

CHAPTER XXXI

Frederick Bateman & Zachery Leith

<u>Monday 14th August 1989, 12:16pm, SULLEN WOODS, ASHFIELD, LONDON.</u>

It was the height of a sweltering summer, and families – comprising mostly of mothers and their children – sat about lazing and playing on the hills at the edge of Sullen Woods. Amongst them, on a picnic blanket, was Caroline Bateman and Sarah Leith.

'I wonder where the boys have gotten to?' Caroline mused. She shifted onto her knees and raised her head to scan the parched grasses.

'Honestly, Caz, you worry too much!' Sarah scolded, half-heartedly. 'No harm will come to them out here.'

Caroline detested being called 'Caz', but it was a nickname she had persisted to endure for the past seven and a half years, and one that Sarah would seemingly never cease to use. Caroline was about to voice yet another protest at the dismissal of her concerns, but Sarah had descended into giggles, for a pooch had come bounding out from the taller grass behind them.

The panting pup gave Sarah's bare feet two licks before turning its attention to their food. Caroline waved her hands in an attempt to shoo, and it did so, but only after it had stuck its tongue into the potato salad and filled its mouth with a sausage roll.

Much slower than their canine companion, four youngsters appeared, running out of the same tall grasses. One child, the eldest – with auburn ringlets – threw a Frisbee, as the smallest fell to face-plant the ground.

'Your dog ruined our picnic!' Caroline reprimanded.

The children – unperturbed – tore off in pursuit of their pet around the bandstand, and Caroline sighed. She picked up the pack of sausage rolls, and huffed, then dropped them back to the blanket with an upturned nose.

Reclining, Sarah cackled with laughter. The pair were chalk and cheese; one large, the other stick-thin. One's hair was naturally waved and untamed, the other's bubble permed, albeit similar shades of brown. But they shared a solid friendship.

'Well, it's certainly good to hear you laugh again,' Caroline admitted, rearranging her mouth into a smile.

She flattened out her denim dress and repositioned her oversized sunglasses. Sarah sat up with a start – a devilish grin creeping over her face.

'How about we crack open the bubbly?' she smiled, wryly.

'It's a bit early for that, don't you think?'

'It's after twelve,' Sarah defended.

Caroline shook her head – reluctant. She had disapproved of Sarah's decision to bring the bottle of Buck's Fizz along in the first place and hoped – naively – that its presence had been forgotten. Caroline was all for a drink but deemed there to be a time and a place. Yet, for Sarah – of late – that time had been any time, and that place, any place. Caroline was the sort of woman who brought fruit and carrot sticks to a picnic, not cheese puffs, chocolate mini-rolls and Buck's Fizz.

'It's only four percent, Caz. Lighten up!' Sarah laughed. She reached into the hamper to remove the bottle and two plastic cups. 'It would make me happy, and I've been ever so down lately. You want me to be happy, don't you, Caz?'

'Of course, I want you to be happy,' Caroline affirmed, weakly, and took the cup offered to her.

She quietly observed that the cocktail was a supermarket's own-brand – a cheap one, no doubt. Caroline did not consider herself a prude, just that some things ought to be done properly, or not at all.

After filling both cups to the brim, Sarah held her own aloft in a toast.

'To Ian – the fucker! And may he fuck as many Avon ladies as he cares to, now that he's single, because he sure as hell ain't getting his hands on this—' she jiggled her left tit with a hand '— ever again. I swear it – on my son's life.'

'To Ian,' Caroline reciprocated, raising her cup also.

Whereas Sarah took a satisfyingly huge gulp, Caroline sipped.

'I don't see the attraction myself,' she admitted, grimacing – referencing Sarah's soon-to-be ex-husband, although she could easily have been referring to the Buck's Fizz. 'He's overweight. Balding before thirty. It's not even like he has any money! And he's lazy.'

Caroline sucked in her waist as she spoke, enviously eyeing the mini-rolls. In truth, she was jealous of Sarah's jeux de vie. That despite being heartbroken, she could still be humorous. It was an outlook Caroline could never emulate.

'He is charming though …' pondered Sarah, reclining further. 'Charmed the thong right off Renata, and into our laundry basket, that's for sure!'

'Oh, to hell with the diet,' Caroline muttered, angrily, helping herself – rather aggressively – to a mini-roll.

'That's right, Caz,' Sarah encouraged. 'You live a little!'

Caroline was careful to finish chewing before speaking. She combed her fingers through her heavy perm and washed her food down with another sip of Buck's Fizz. It tasted better upon the second try.

'You can be sure of one thing,' she said, reassuringly. 'Your son is better off without that scumbag for a father. He'll grow into a man that'll put Ian to shame – I'm telling you.'

'Damn right,' Sarah chuckled, and nodded, sharply.

*

'En garde!'

From beneath the old oak, Zach's playful cries resonated out across the lake. He and Fred were alone, though the distant sounds of other children playing could be heard. The shade was a relief down by the water but hadn't been what the two boys had sought on their adventure.

Brandishing a plastic sword, a seven-year-old Zach leapt forward, chasing Fred across the cracked dirt.

And Fred ran – screaming – around the lake's edge. Rounding a particularly sharp corner, he hopped down onto a gravelly beach beside the rotting skeleton of a tree. Soil eroded from its base; a bare network of roots had been left exposed. These roots reached down to fill the void between the trunk and the beach, to form a cage, and in that instant, both reimagined this as the dungeon of their make-believe castle.

'I must protect my prince!' Fred exclaimed, majestically raising his own plastic sword into the air.

Their fantastical tale had grown organically over the course of twenty minutes, with each boy spontaneously adding their own part to their story as they went along.

Jumping down next to Fred, Zach scrunched up his face.

'Don't you mean, princess?' he asked, incredulously.

'No,' Fred clarified, certain. 'She screamed and ran off ages ago.'

'OK!' Zach accepted.

The short battle that ensued was brutal by children's standards. Fred whacked Zach on the thigh with his lightweight sword, as Zach jabbed his own. Dodging the move, Fred skipped back, and so Zach bounded forwards again – slapping his sword down upon his opponent's forearm. Fred retaliated by poking him in the gut.

Lunging forwards once more, Zach took aim at Fred's torso – but he ducked – and the tip of the plastic caught him in the eye.

'Ouch!' Fred squeaked.

He dropped his sword, and immediately covered his face.

'I'm sorry!' Zach apologised, instantly – guilt freezing him. 'Please, don't tell your mum – I didn't mean to.'

'Yes, you did!'

From under Fred's palms, tears streamed. Their manifest was not a vie for attention, or sympathy, but simply a reaction to the stinging.

'I'm sorry,' repeated Zach.

Wracked with regret, he trotted over to his friend, but Fred turned his back and ran around.

'I don't want to talk to you, Zachery!' he whimpered, emulating his mother.

'Fine!' exclaimed Zach, then repeated again, 'I'm sorry!'

Ignoring him, however, Fred had already begun climbing the trunk of the precariously angled tree that adorned their 'dungeon'.

'Get your arse down here!' Zach called after him. Mimicking his own mother now, he was quoting a phrase he'd heard shouted to his father only a week prior. 'Well, if you don't want to come back down, I'm gonna slay your prince and – and marry his sister!'

'My prince doesn't have a sister!' sniped Fred, climbing higher.

'Yes, he does!' Zach shot back, before elaborating. 'She was thrown out the kingdom as a baby, because she was a witch, and her parents were scared of her! That's why your prince doesn't know her!'

Grazing his knee upon a gnarly protrusion, Fred decided he would climb no further. He inched out across the nearest branch and looked down at Zach from the top of his 'castle'. He had secretly proclaimed himself king.

'If my prince has a sister, where is she now?' Fred asked.

'Erm …'

Zach stabbed at the gravel with his sword, deep in thought.

'In the lake, of course!' he declared, suddenly. 'She's being held prisoner by the sea hag that wants to turn her evil! I have to save her!'

And with that, Zach hastened to clamber up onto the bank. Fred watched as his friend ran further around the lake.

'How can she breathe — underwater — how can she breathe?!' Fred shouted.

'Magic!' Zach shouted back.

His little legs carrying him as fast as they could, Zach then spotted something that excited him, and so skidded to a stop.

Fred looked on in awe as Zach began crawling out along the trunk of a tree that had fallen across the lake's surface. His mouth open in admiration, Fred stuck a finger up his nose and pulled out a long, wet bogie. He wiped it casually on the bark.

Cautiously, Zach balanced himself into a crouch, before then standing to his full tiny height. The task was made all the more difficult by the fact he'd taken his plastic sword with him.

Certain Zach was about to fall, and inevitably be taken by the sea hag, Fred gasped — nearly falling from his tree.

'Be careful, Zach!' he hollered. 'Don't let the hag get you!'

'She doesn't stand a chance!' Zach hollered back.

Regaining confidence, Zach flourished his sword at an invisible foe and charged forwards with a war cry. Fred cackled a long burst of machine-gun-like laughter.

'Die, hag, die!' Zach cried.

Taking a running jump from the end of the trunk, Zach drew his legs up to his chest, and with a tremendous splash, bombed into the murky water. He had not planned on taking a swim, and his decision to do so had been an impromptu one – spurred on by the narrative, as well as the heat.

'I'll save you, Zach!' Fred panicked. 'I promise, you won't die!'

Half-jumping, half-falling out of the tree and fearing the worst, Fred darted off around the lake, and over to the scene. His response was an overreaction, for Zach was a strong swimmer, but his reasoning was real. Displaying far more confidence and daring than even he himself thought possible, Fred then edged out onto the fallen tree. He did not risk standing but instead chose to slide his backside.

'Zach – don't die!' Fred squealed. 'Please, don't die, Zach! Zach!'

As he approached the tree trunk's end, Fred scrambled to peer into the dark water. His features fearful; he sloshed at it with his fingers.

'Zach?!'

Faux fears of the sea hag having long since dissipated, Fred began contemplating risking his own life to attempt a rescue, until a terrific whooshing noise took him by surprise. It came from behind him and caused Fred to fall back against the tree in fright, where he cowered, clinging.

'Boo!' bellowed Zach.

Having pushed himself up and out of the water, he'd lowered his voice to an unnatural – somewhat demonic – level. Fred screeched, and tightly shut his eyes.

'That's not funny!' he scolded – his chest heaving.

'Yes, it is,' replied Zach, simply.

He pulled himself up beside Fred.

'I thought you had died.'

Sitting upright, Fred shuffled himself around to face Zach – his mouth downturned in disapproval. Again, this was an unconscious mirroring of his mother. Zach beamed at him, triumphantly – proud of his success in scaring.

'It'd take more than a sea hag to defeat me,' Zach affirmed.

He placed his hands on his hips and puffed out his chest in a mock-superhero stance. Zach proceeded to fish his sword out from the lake before it floated away. He closely examined it before shrugging and smiling. His clothes were soaking wet and covered in algae, but he was unconcerned.

'I thought you'd died,' reiterated Fred, glumly. 'Thought you were gone forever, just like grandma. I didn't believe Dad when he said she was gone, but I haven't seen her in ages.'

In February that year, Stan Bateman's mother had tragically passed just before Fred's birthday. Admitted to the hospital for a routine hip replacement, the elderly lady had succumbed to an infection and ultimately met her maker. The direct consequence of this was that Fred had been unable to attend his own joint party with Zach – a reality that he'd been embittered towards, until the harsh truths of life had slowly filtered through into his young mind, over the months that followed.

'I don't know why she had to leave.' Fred sighed. 'Where does life go, when it can't no longer be kept in a body? Like it's been able to escape somehow.'

'Sometimes people just move on, and there's nothing we can do about it,' replied Zach, shrugging. 'That's what Mum said, when Dad left.'

'But your dad didn't die.'

Maybe it was for the dread Fred had recently experienced at the prospect of losing his friend, but for the first time since his grandmother's death, he could feel his brown eyes well up.

'No,' Zach agreed. 'But I don't think I'll ever see him again. He's a liar, and a cheat, and I'm better off without him; that's what Mum said.'

'I do miss Grandma though,' Fred mused. 'She used to give me sweets.' He chuckled, his face beaming once more, and devilishly steepled his fingertips.

'I'm gonna ask Mum if we can get some—' began Zach, energetically.

'What do you think happens when you die?' asked Fred.

'I dunno,' said Zach. 'Go to heaven, probably.'

- CHAPTER XXXII -

The Lady in the Lake

'There are times that you want to split the world open with your cries. Somehow, make such a racket — a tantrum — that everyone can hear. There are other times, when there are no more cries left to come out. There'll be nothing left to give — nothing left to get. You'll hope for that elusive solitude, in that hard to come by silence.'

❧❦❧

<u>Saturday 6th December 1997, 13:14pm, BATEMAN RESIDENCE, 52 BELLAMY AVENUE, ASHFIELD, LONDON.</u>
Snaked between cardboard boxes, Fred lay beneath his bed. A pillow squashed around his head, it muffled the background noise of the world around him — the traffic, passers-by, and his mother on the landing.

Caroline Bateman had been hovering on the other side of the door for the past ten minutes. What she was doing there? Fred did not know or care. He just wished she'd desist.

Sleeping — or hiding — under his bed was a habit Fred had occasionally indulged since childhood. Surrounded by dusty, long-forgotten toys, he felt safer here. He felt protected.

In his left hand, Fred clutched an umbrella. He had not let go of it for hours. If he had to, he could fight off intruders with it — like a sword. Futile and feeble a weapon as it was, the symbolism of his act was very telling, for Fred was broken. He was exhausted. He was emotionally drained, and he was reminiscent.

A knock sounded upon his bedroom door, and Fred's eyelids flickered open. He exhaled, loudly.

'Go away!'

Fred pushed the pillow harder to his ears.

Ignoring – or unhearing of – her son's request, Caroline Bateman opened the door a crack, and peeped inside. Fred shuffled backwards, recoiling from the shaft of light his mother had let into the darkened room.

'I've just come back from Sarah's,' she spoke, softly.

Fred absorbed this information, but only vaguely. He was far more transfixed by his mother's feet and ankles. For the first time in Fred's recollection, his mother had failed to adhere to her own rule that no shoes be worn inside the house.

'The poor woman's a state,' Caroline continued. 'I've never seen her like that before. She wanted to know if you'd be happy to give a reading at Zach's funeral.'

'Would I be "happy" to give a reading?' Fred breathed, heavily.

Suddenly fired up, he relinquished his grip of the pillow. Apart from being pissed at her choice of phrase, Fred was angry at his mother for wearing her shoes inside the house – much angrier than he should have been. The act was so incredibly hypocritical, especially when considering the countless times Fred had been yelled at for the same felony. He stared daggers at the black peep-toed heels, directing all his rage at them, as he qualified a response.

'I can assure you,' he choked, 'that giving a reading at my best friend's funeral, does not appear anywhere on the scale of things that would make me "happy".'

Caroline said nothing.

Fred's bedroom door opened a little wider, and another pair of legs appeared – purple polka-dotted leggings, and zebra patterned socks. His sister's sudden presence was even more unwanted than his mother's.

'Please, come out, Freddums,' said Mollie. 'I miss you.'

To Fred's utmost horror, his sister then crouched down on the carpet and wriggled out across to him. Uncomfortably close, she smiled, sadly.

'I don't know why *you're* upset,' Fred spat, rudely. 'Zach wasn't your friend, and you hate hanging out with me.'

Immediately, Mollie burst into tears, wriggled back out, jumped up and ran from the room. Fred watched as her socks disappeared through the door and listened to the sounds of her gallop down the stairs. He was glad – glad she was gone, and glad he'd made her cry. He rolled his eyes, awaiting a telling off.

'You're not the only one who lost him, Freddums,' Caroline sighed. 'Zach was very fond of your sister. He used to bring her sweets, remember?'

'Zach didn't like her,' Fred lied, scratching at the wooden slats of his bedframe. 'Can you leave now?'

'Please, don't be harsh,' Caroline whispered.

Having spent the entire morning at Zach's mother's, Caroline was sapped. Never in her life had she had to console another mother after the loss of a child. It was proving an incredibly difficult and altogether traumatising experience, and one that brought forth a wealth of unexpected emotions. Fred had forgotten that he was not the only person to have known Zach since the day of his birth.

'Please *leave*, and I'll stop being harsh,' Fred replied.

'OK,' Caroline relented. 'But later, we need to talk. I need you to tell me exactly what you said to the police—'

'I've told you everything,' Fred lied again.

'I know ... you did,' Caroline wavered. 'It just doesn't make any sense. Why Zach would leave you all at Rye's the way he did? Why he'd steal her sister's car, I—'

'You're right, it doesn't make any sense. *Please* ... could you just go,' Fred implored.

To his relief – despite a twinge to his heart – Fred's mother took heed of his wish. He watched as her patent heels backed out over the threshold. And, with the door closed, the room was dark once more.

Fred reached for the photo album he had stashed beneath his bed the day before – stolen from the shelf downstairs. Carefully labelled by a white sticker and biro, its cover read, simply, '1991'. With numb fingers, Fred began to flip through the pages for what must have been the hundredth time within twenty-four hours. The first five pages displayed pictures of his and Zach's joint ninth birthday. They had gone bowling.

 торт

<u>Saturday 6th December 1997, 13:25pm, TRAFALGAR SQUARE, LONDON.</u>

Sat on the steps at the base of Nelson's column – in the shadow of the Christmas tree – Ally re-read the advert she had circled within the classifieds of the *Metro*:

'COVEN of the RISING SON.
Our warm and welcoming coven are seeking new,
or experienced, witches with an open mind and
spirit. All backgrounds and ages welcome.
Females ONLY. Meetings twice weekly.
For details please call Angelica on:
07778566991'

The days following Zach's death, Ally had found herself unable to sit still. Unlike Rye, she could not remain cooped within the confines of 32 Kynaston Gardens. Instead, each day she had gone somewhere and someplace different. Without any plan as to where she was going, or what she was doing, she felt lost and wandering – taking each hour and minute as they were presented to her. Ally's discovery of the advert in the newspaper was a perfect example of this. She had not sought it out, but it nonetheless threw up an inviting prospect.

Bending its front page back upon itself, Ally folded the newspaper and placed it under her left armpit. She had no desire to be reminded of – nor to re-read – its cover story. Today's running headline was: 'THE LADY IN THE LAKE'.

For three consecutive days, the murders of both Zach and Michelle had made local, as well as national headlines. The media was in a frenzy and it made Ally sick.

'Can – take – picture?'

Ally had been so wrapped up amid her own thoughts, that she had not noticed the man approach. His question – spoken in broken English – however, brought her crashing back down to the bustling capital. The tourist waved a camera, and Ally stood, abruptly – almost defensively.

'I'm busy,' she excused. 'I'm really late – I'm sorry.'

Without looking at the man – or his female companion – Ally then bounded down the steps. She stumbled a little with her speed, breathing heavily, and suddenly feeling anxious. Not knowing where to go next, she felt lost once more.

Choosing a direction at random, Ally walked briskly back around Trafalgar Square and up past the side of the National Gallery. Between tourists and lunching Londoners, she weaved. Every so often, she'd mutter an apology, as she pushed past those she deemed too slow.

For a half-second, Ally had considered entering the galleries, but her legs kept moving. A pub to her right provided another possible sanctuary, but it too appeared busy. For another half-second, she internally debated whether to steal a passer-by's wallet, just for the hell of it, but she didn't.

Ally passed by Leicester Square tube station. She had only arrived at Charing Cross less than an hour before but considered the option of returning to Ashfield anyhow. There was still the option of getting on a train and going *anywhere* – Ally had no real ties to Ashfield, nor to any individual there, not really. She could start her whole life over in a heartbeat. But the mere thought of such was enough to drain her limbs of energy. She didn't know where she wanted to be. And was worried if she were to stray much further, it would require too much effort to return. Ally slowed.

'Excuse me, miss, got any change?'

Huddled in the doorway of a casino, the teenage boy who'd addressed her sat under a blanket, shivering. Ally ignored him, yet in that moment of eye contact, something struck a chord deep within her. The fact both were close in age? The fact Ally was cold also, although did have a home to return to, if she wished? The fact Ally had lived a similar life, and not that long ago? The answer to all three questions, was yes; Ally had lost sight of who she was, and where she'd come from.

Ally stopped dead and a woman carrying a collection of high-end shopping bags walked into her back. The woman tutted, and Ally swore at her. She then turned and headed back to the homeless boy.

'What's your name?' Ally asked, crouching.

The boy – his hair scruffy – looked shocked by the unexpected question.

'Red,' he replied. 'Red Arain.'

'Here, take this,' said Ally. 'It's all I have.'

Reaching inside her leather jacket, Ally produced three pound-coins and a ten pence piece.

'Thank you—'

'I'll get more,' Ally promised – deciding at that moment to put her own street-smarts to good use that afternoon. 'Give me an hour or two, and I'll come back with some more, and a coffee – do you drink coffee?'

⋰⟊⋱

Saturday 6th December 1997, 13:51pm, TURPIN RESIDENCE, 32 KYNASTON GARDENS, ASHFIELD, LONDON.
The local newspaper's chosen headline took up almost the entirety of its cover, with only the smallest of introductory paragraphs

squeezed onto the bottom, before the story was continued on page four.

Still dressed in her pyjamas, Rye was sat at the kitchen table and wrapped in her duvet. Along with her body, she had dragged it down the stairs with her. A half-eaten slice of toast lay forgotten upon her plate. Rye hurriedly read through the article with a mixture of apprehension, sadness and guilt:

'Ashfield Gazette
Saturday 6th December 1997
ASHFIELD MURDERS: TWO FURTHER BODIES FOUND
The remains of a male and female – identified as Nikos Castellanos, 32, and missing teen Elizabeth Thackerall, 18, from dental records – have been recovered from the bottom of the lake within Sullen Woods. Cont. page 4.'

Paper rustling, Rye flipped the cover and first sheet. Four photographs – two on either side – adorned the double-page spread. Lined up like mugshots, Rye was immediately drawn to the first, not just because it was first, but because it was Zach's. Well acquainted with it, she had seen this picture many times before. A school picture, Zach had obligatorily hated it, for it captured a forced smile.

Next, was Michelle. Much like Zach's portrait, she too sat in front of a blue screen and was dressed in a uniform. She appeared somewhat younger than when Rye had known her, leading her to assume that it must have been taken during the early years of her career.

On the adjacent page was another picture Rye had come to know well – that of Elizabeth Thackerall. The newspaper had chosen to recycle the same beaming photograph of her at dinner, that had been used within their summer articles.

The final portrait showed a man beside a pool that Rye did not recognise. Attractive, he was tanned – those were her first observations. The caption beneath confirmed this was Nikos Castellanos. Mouth open in a smile, all his pearly whites were on display. Rye's stomach churned, as she thought these to be the same teeth that had been key to identifying him: *Male-AL10*.

Rye read on:

'The discovery – made by officers yesterday – has only brought forth more questions than answers with regards to the open investigation into the homicides of Detective Inspector Michelle Davey, 42, and local schoolboy – Ashfield Community pupil – Zachery Leith, 15, whose bodies were found by a dog walker early Tuesday morning. It is not yet clear whether their deaths are linked to those of Mr Castellanos and Miss Thackerall, although a source has disclosed that Detective Inspector Michelle Davey had taken it upon herself to re-open the case into Miss Thackerall's disappearance, in the weeks leading up to her own death.

An officer, who has spoken to us off the record, described Detective Inspector Davey as "unpredictable" and "erratic", claiming that their colleague had been a long-term sufferer of alcoholism and depression.

Miss Davey had resided in Ashfield – alone – since 1989, when she had moved from Harlow, Essex, to take up the position of Detective Inspector. Her parents now live on the south coast and have yet to give a comment on the news.

Miss Davey suffered a bullet wound to the front of the head, and Mr Leith with an arrow to the chest. The weapons that inflicted both deadly shots have yet to be located, and it was only because divers had been searching the lake for these, that the bodies of Mr Castellanos and Miss Thackerall were discovered.

At present, no cause of death for Mr Castellanos, or Miss Thackerall, has been released, although it has been confirmed that both bodies were found locked inside a Renault 5 hatchback. The car had been resting on the lake floor.

Elizabeth Thackerall was last seen on 24th July 1997 – this date also having been her birthday. Miss Thackerall's parents were contacted yesterday for comment – four months after their daughter's disappearance – but our request was declined.

Miss Thackerall was reported as a missing person within the local media during the weeks after 24th July, but due to her age, and the lack of any leads, the case was purportedly back-benched by investigating officers.

Miss Thackerall's former headmistress – Mrs Theobald, of St Anthony's College, Hatfield – described her ex-pupil back in August as, "an exceptionally bright and funny girl". Miss Thackerall had been due to start a degree course at De Montford University, Leicester, in October, to study Creative Writing.

Mr Castellanos' brother – Thierry, 27 – spoke of his shock and sadness late last night. He had not seen or heard from his elder brother since July also, but had not been concerned for his welfare. Apparently, it was not unlike the deceased to holiday at short notice, and for long periods of time.

The news of Mr Leith's death has sent shockwaves throughout the local community, as well as the school at which he'd been a pupil. The headmaster of Ashfield Community – Mr Andrew Bullen – took the decision to close the school, with immediate effect, until this following Monday, when it will re-open with a vigil. Mr Leith's single mother – Sarah Palmer – has also declined our request for comment.

At this moment in time, the Metropolitan Police are unsure what exactly connects the deaths of all four of these victims to one another. Most of Sullen Woods is expected to remain cordoned off for at least another few days.

The Metropolitan Police have made an appeal for witnesses from the night of Monday 1st December and urges anyone with information to come forward. Ashfield Police can be contacted on 0181 772 6467, or Crimestoppers can be contacted – anonymously – on 0105 623 267.'

Rye concluded the article, quietly absorbing the information she had read. After taking one final look at Zach's photograph, she stiffly closed the paper and shunted the print across the table – pushing it beyond her toast. She retracted her hand, her eyes tearful.

'Would you like some risotto?' asked Pris. 'I'm just about to—'

'Why couldn't I see him?'

Changing the subject, Rye turned to face her sister, where she was stood in the doorway. Rye was unsure quite how long she'd been there.

'I don't – what do you mean?'

'When Zach … died, why couldn't I see him? I could see Elizabeth, even when I closed my eyes – when I slept – I could see her, but him …'

Unmoving, Pris appeared to think very hard as to her response before committing.

'I won't pretend to be an expert, Rye, but you saw Zach die.'

'I didn't—'

'But you knew what killed him.'

'I killed him,' wept Rye in a flurry. 'If I hadn't been so hell-bent – if I hadn't seen – I only wanted to – I needed – but, he didn't have to – why did he have to – ergh-OW!'

She suddenly clasped a hand to her shoulder, as her body convulsed.

'Oh, Rye! Is it your wound? I knew I should have taken you to the hospital!'

Rye's stiff posture dissolved, as she then fell limp over the kitchen table. Instinctively, she wrapped an arm around her head, as if to shield herself from further concern. Tears rushed down Rye's cheeks, moistening her dressing gown.

The sisters had argued over the subject of a hospital visit every day since Rye had been injured. Pris had never approached the topic angrily, yet it had always been twisted by Rye into a slanging match. Deep down, Pris knew she could not take her to see a professional, for it would risk drawing further attention to themselves, though at times, she did not care. Without proper medical treatment, Rye's lesion was left to heal with only the aid of cream, bandages and a truckload of painkillers. Thankfully, it was only crusty and did not appear infected, but without surgical sutures would scar, horrifically.

'I can't believe we just left him there!' Rye sobbed.

She could feel her sister's arms around her waist now – fighting to find a way in beneath the duvet.

'There was nothing you could have done – none of us could,' Pris attempted to soothe her. 'He was already … he was already dead—'

'In the mud – in the dirt. *Dead.* Yes, I remember!'

'I know it's hard. It's awful. It's the wait … between now and the funeral. That's the hardest part. But I promise you, after, things will slowly start to get better, and … and we'll finally be able to put all this behind us. Grieve, yes, but … move on.'

Pris had just started to succeed in her efforts, but her final words had not been taken well, at all.

'*Move on*?!' Rye's voice broke, and she threw up an arm to throw Pris off. 'Even after all you've seen – after Zach's *death* – all you can think of is *moving on,* letting go and forgetting about it?'

Unable to push back her chair, Rye instead shoved the table forwards, dropping her duvet to the floor. Seething, she turned upon her stunned sister.

'We are so far from moving on!' Rye continued. 'Do you not get that?! What I saw in those visions – this is just the beginning!'

'I – I didn't mean – I didn't know—'

'You didn't ask!'

Rye knew this rebuke was not entirely fair. It was true that Pris had not asked, but neither had the others, and Rye had not been in a hurry to share.

'Please – tell me now. I'm listening,' Pris pleaded.

'No,' Rye dismissed, simply – her voice quiet again. 'After Zach's funeral. After … *after* …'

Unable to look at her sister any longer, Rye whipped the newspaper up from the table and marched out of the room before stomping up the stairs.

Once in her bedroom, she dived onto her mattress, proceeding to punch and kick it as violently as she could. The springs twanged and squeaked in protest to the beating, as Rye let out all her anger upon them, all-the-while wailing like a banshee. She kept this up for several minutes until her voice grew hoarse and her appendages ached – ultimately, until her shoulder could take no more. It felt as if she'd ripped her wound open once more, but as for whether she had? Rye did not check. The pain that seared from it was welcomed – physical pain, distracting from the emotional.

In one final fury, Rye flung her pillows from her bed. They hit the window and fell behind the desk with a soft and unsatisfying thump.

Clambering onto all fours, Rye swiped for her Walkman. She covered her ears with its headphones, and, as her breathing levelled, pressed play. The mixed tape that Fred had made for her birthday spun in the deck. Sarah Polley's 'Courage'; goosebumps spread down Rye's body, from head to toe. Numb, but warming, she felt nicked all over. The song, lifted from the soundtrack to *The Sweet Hereafter* held a special place in Rye's heart, for she, Fred and Zach, had watched the film together. It was a good memory, although in itself melancholic.

Rye flipped through her diary. The majority of its pages now filled – most within the last few days – she flicked by many illustrations. When it had come to detailing her vision's multiple segments, Rye had found this medium of expression far more efficient than a written description.

As she thumbed past a particularly unnerving rendering, her blood ran cold. All of Rye's other drawings had been devoid of colour, but not this one. This woman's robe was red, and her yellow eyes pierced forth from the page with as much intensity as when they had pierced Rye.

At the next clean sheet, she proceeded to flatten her diary back against the mattress. Rye then snapped up a pair of scissors and set to work cutting out the article from that day's, *Ashfield Gazette*. Being far bigger than her diary's pages, she attached tape along only one of its sides, folding the remainder inwards. When closed, it would no doubt add considerable depth to the overall thickness.

Rye then flicked to her diary's final page. She had stuck Zach's obituary to it only yesterday:

'Zachery Dennis Leith,
18th February 1982 – 2nd December 1997
It is with sadness that we announce the death of Zachery D. Leith, 15, of Ashfield, who passed away this week. The son of Ian Leith & Sarah Palmer, he was currently a pupil of Ashfield Community School where he excelled at sports, and a member of Ashfield Archery Club. He is survived by his parents. The funeral will be held at 11am on Friday 12th December, at Ashfield Crematorium. In lieu of flowers, the family asks that you consider donations to the registered charity, The Crimestoppers Trust.'

A sad-looking caricature of a rose accompanied the short, epitaphic summary. The image was simple and crude – standard, stock and ordinary. *Unworthy.*

Rye wiped away a tear – that would otherwise become another stream – and thumbed back to the first of her drawings; a badly sketched and ill-proportioned Elizabeth, halfway down a drainpipe. Rye had never been very gifted at drawing people.

Studying the drawing, between thoughts of self-deprecation and reflection, Rye wondered if she would ever learn the truth of the exact circumstances surrounding the death of Elizabeth Thackerall.

CHAPTER XXXIII

The Death of Elizabeth Thackerall

'There are places where your life can change forever, for better or worse. Usually, they're the ones least expected – the mundane – that will ultimately hold the most significance. Children's adventures, a first date or sanctuary; whatever's experienced there, forever shapes the mind's perception. A location can represent something different for everyone. But a time, a moment – even if long since forgotten – can be revisited, in just a blink of an eye, or snap of a finger.

North London, 1997. Specifically, Sullen Woods; the place where I died. The lake there bore witness to the concluding paragraphs in the final chapter of my life, that I'd unknowingly already started. I, Elizabeth Thackerall, had hoped to become an author. And this is my story. It always had been. But every chapter has a beginning, and so – like a tape – we'll rewind.'

<u>Thursday 24th July 1997, 19:54pm, THACKERALL RESIDENCE, 23 DRAGNELL LANE, ASHFIELD, LONDON.</u>
I hated birthdays – always had – not sure why, exactly. Maybe if I'd known that my eighteenth would've been my last, I would have made more of an effort to enjoy it. That's easier said than done, however, for hindsight is a godsend, and if you're not enjoying something at the time, there's usually a reason – or multitude of reasons – for why you're not.

It was just before eight o'clock when I'd run upstairs to my bedroom – my face stinging. My mother had slapped me. The only time, ever, she had chosen my first day of adulthood – and last day alive – to do so. We had argued, but I wasn't angry at her. I was angry at him. How my father could have cheated on my mother? I will never understand. How he had the audacity to lie about it? I'll never understand that either. But the day will come that he will be judged for his sins, as it comes for all of us. As it came for me. I went through my father's mobile without permission. Nonetheless, I had my suspicions. I don't regret it.

'The beauty or ugliness of a character lay not … in its achievements, but in its aims and impulses; its true history lay, not among things done, but among things willed.' Thomas Hardy, *Tess of the D'Urbervilles*, 1891.

That's a quote from my favourite book. Anyway, I digress.

When I entered my room, I slammed the door and dived onto my bed, taking a customary foetal position. It was then my laptop gave off a loud squeak – like a broken trumpet – and startled me. My heart fluttered. I knew who this noise was synonymous with. It's here that, I might add, I'm not embarrassed by my actions, just … I only craved understanding and affection. *Hindsight is a godsend*, and it's in hindsight, that this could well have been the title of my final chapter.

I sat up, cross-legged, and excitedly flipped open my laptop. An ugly thing, really – it was clunky – but I thought it was fantastic. At a time when personal computers were expensive, I was very lucky to have been bought one. Why did I think it was fantastic? Simply, it gave me an escape. I'd always found it hard to connect with people, on a personal level, you know? Not that anyone would have thought that. To everyone else, Lizzie Thackerall was a social butterfly; 'an exceptionally bright and funny girl.' I never saw that in myself.

In the months leading up to my death, I had actively tried to distance myself from the people who referred to me as a friend. And I'd rebuffed any suggestion they'd made that I should celebrate my birthday. In truth, I resented everybody. It may sound incredibly shallow, but I felt they held me back from becoming the person I thought myself to truly be. The friends I had made, aged eleven – out of fear and loneliness – I no longer had anything in common with.

'You have 1 new message.'

The notification flashed up in red lettering – the text bold and basic, as was the aesthetic of the chatroom. I wondered what message, 'Male-AL10,' – or Ryan, as he'd become known to me – had sent. Ryan always managed to make me feel better. He would always say the right things – the most perfect things. For example, the first time I'd sent him a picture, he declared my auburn hair beautiful and that he had, 'never liked those blonde, bimbo, goldilocks-types.'

Ryan's message this time was:

'I should leave soon ... bout 15 mins, then I'll head over. So glad I can wish you happy birthday in person bbes xxx.'

His words elated me beyond belief – more so than usual – for my birthday was the day we were to meet for the first time, face-to-face. Little did I know; it would also mean *knife*-to-*gut*.

Some of you might be wondering why I chose to meet with him – a stranger, purportedly a near-decade older than myself. *'How could Lizzie have been so ignorant? Foolish? Naïve?'* And to those people, I offer three alternative words: Lonely, hopeful, *and* ... naïve. I was a stranger to him also, and don't all soulmates start off as strangers? I thought. He would have no preconceived views of me, other than those I'd allowed. He needn't ever know of the time I vomited on the Year Seven school trip to the Buddhist temple. Or when I'd first gotten my period at the swimming pool. The internet gave me the platform to act a character, with only the baggage I wished to carry. I could easily filter myself – drip-feed information – emit and exaggerate. Trouble is, Ryan was playing the same game. Hindsight is a godsend.

'Ok :) can't wait to meet you for real! I'm just gonna finish getting myself ready! Xxx.'

I had to edit my reply several times because I kept making spelling mistakes – as was my eagerness and nerves. I had hoped to spend at least an hour getting ready but the argument with my mother had left me severely behind schedule.

I had bought a new dress in anticipation of the meeting. I felt the need to make the right first impression in-person, and to live up to the carefully selected pictures I had shared. I had to look beautiful. A black and intricately lacey affair, I'm glad I never saw my mother's face whilst wearing it, for I can only imagine what she'd have said: 'That's far too grown up for you, Lizzie! Looks like something your grandmother would have worn to a funeral!' Never mind, Mother, I wore it to my own. Then, the fact she certainly would not have approved, only made me like the dress more.

Awaiting Ryan's arrival, I changed out of my jeans and Mickey Mouse sweatshirt. I deliberated over shoes but settled on a pair of kitten heels. I applied foundation to my face, and thighs – not wanting him to see the self-inflicted scars normally concealed there. The long history of these scars is a separate side-story, but one I will spare you from. I wasn't proud of them. No-one knew about them. They were another escapism.

My body squeezed into the dress, which I secretly knew to be too tight, I slinked back over to my bed and popped a Disney tape into my cassette player. As I set about taming my hair, I sang along – albeit, very badly – to 'Part of Your World'.

I had always related to Ariel. I had everything – everything materialistic – yet felt empty. All I really wanted was freedom. I was due to start a university course – Creative Writing, at De

Montford – in October, but I wasn't going. Though, of course, no-one knew that. College had forced me to make the choice regarding my future, and I had done, but only because they offered no alternative.

As the song reached its crescendo, I picked up the birthday card from my bedside table. From my parents, I had read it that morning, but as my mind wandered, I intended to study it with an increasingly critical eye:

'Happy 18th Birthday, Lizzie. Lots of love, Mum and Dad xxx.'

It was unlike them to write anything soppy or un-necessarily long and my heart sank upon re-reading the short inscription. I now know how they loved me – *dearly* – because, what is hindsight? My parents weren't psychic. They weren't even that blindsided. I chose to never tell them of my depression. I even hid it. How were they to know? Yes, there are signs, but they're not always obvious. They can be subtle.

The birthday card was pink, however, and depicted a kitten. I was more of a dog person and preferred black. So, I dropped it into the bin.

I moved across to the window. With my bedroom at the front of the house, it was easy for me to spot Ryan's arrival. I just had to patiently wait and hope he wouldn't use the horn. In an act of spontaneous thought, it was then I decided to pack a bag – a change of clothes, my laptop, mobile and chargers. I had not arranged to stay over, nor was I so presumptive as to assume that I could, I just wanted the option to change back into my sweatshirt and jeans, if that scenario arose. I was still a virgin. And I never planned on having sex with Ryan. Nonetheless, I was about to go on a date – an adventure. And sex did not scare me.

A car pulled up – a dark-blue, Renault 5 hatchback – and I threw my holdall out of the window. I didn't wait to see if it was Ryan, for as I said, I didn't want to risk him using the horn. I proceeded to shimmy down the drainpipe. I had never done this before but found it surprisingly easy. I must have looked fearless. After all, what sort of obstacle was a drainpipe in the pursuit of true love? See, *naïve*.

I hopped over the garden wall and walked quickly down to meet him. I didn't dare look back at the house. If my mother had seen or heard me, I sure as hell would have known about it.

It was whilst getting into the car that I noticed Ryan looked a little older than his pictures. His dark hair appeared a little thinner and his belly a little fuller. You'd have thought that this alone would've been enough to start alarm bells ringing, and for me to get straight back out of the car. It didn't. Who doesn't choose the best pictures of themselves to use online? I was guilty. Guilty of squeezing my tits together. Guilty of choosing the best lighting. It never occurred to me Ryan had lied about his age.

'You look beautiful.'

I think that's what he had said. It had been something along those lines. His voice was soft and nurturing – sexy, and foreign. All I managed in reply was a nervous giggle. I began twisting my hair tightly around my index finger – intentionally, as I'd hoped to appear coy.

'Alright then, gorgeous, where do you wanna go?'

We had not finalised a plan, only thrown around a whole bunch of ideas, and so I replied by telling him that I wasn't sure and didn't mind.

'No worries, babe. I know the most beautiful place,' Ryan said, and winked a brown, twinkling eye. 'Oh, and Happy Birthday.'

He shifted the gearstick into first and with a crank of the radio, we were away – pulling out of Dragnell Lane to the tune of Fontella Bass' 'Rescue Me'. Oh, the irony.

20:23pm – I checked my mobile for the time – but it died, right there and then. I asked Ryan where he was taking us, but he said it was a surprise and remained elusive. Whilst turning the volume up further, he made some excuse for the music – that the cassette player was broken, and the radio's station stuck.

I didn't mind the retro tunes. My mother had a large vinyl collection and I'd been raised on a musical diet consisting largely of classics. Despite Ryan's excuses, I think he was secretly enjoying the music too.

He apologised for his clothing. Apparently, he'd come straight from work at the garage and didn't have time to go home and change.

'It's OK,' I said. '"Great men are seldom over-scrupulous in the arrangement of their attire".'

Ryan looked confused and questioned my quote. I responded by confirming it as Charles Dickens and jested he wasn't such a great fan, if he didn't recognise it. He looked a little hurt by this, so I lied by conceding that *The Pickwick Papers* was not Dickens' finest, that he hadn't missed much by not reading it, and the author's stories had gotten better with subsequent works.

I studied Ryan's face out the corner of my eye. A few lines had developed under his, and the skin beneath them looked heavy, though this did nothing to dim their sparkle. I then worked my way down his body, taking in every detail. For each negative I found, it only took a small chip out of my child-like adulation for him.

Ryan's torso was not as tight and muscular as the topless snap he had sent me a few weeks before, sure. But his arms were quite magnificent. I began mentally undressing him for thirty seconds or so. I thought of his dick. Anyone saying they wouldn't, would be a liar.

Turning another corner, a drink's can rolled out from the footwell. His car was filthy – full of fast-food wrappers and plastic bags. A tiny figurine of Jesus was tacked to the dashboard, and his little head bobbled along to the music – more so whenever we hit a bump or pot-hole. Ryan had never claimed to be religious and I found its presence funny, if not a tad strange.

All in all, I considered this a modern-day fairy tale to rival any other. Next to me was a man that liked and wanted me. He was to be my saviour, or so I thought. Take note, girls – and guys – this is not a healthy outlook.

'It's great to finally meet you in the flesh,' I beamed.

'So, how's your birthday treated you so far?'

'Oh, Ryan,' I began, and launched full throttle into a rant about my day.

I found it just as easy to speak to him in person as I had online. That was probably because he was someone other than my parents, or friends – someone who had already given me the time and patience over three months, to listen. In reality – during that car journey – Ryan gave me no reassurance. He was only present and let me unburden.

I bemoaned my mother's 'stupidity'. And I labelled my father a 'martyr' – with as much sarcasm as I could accentuate the word with – explaining how he would only effuse this attitude to use it 'as a smokescreen'.

'That bastard,' Ryan spewed.

I was taken aback by the ferociousness of his retort and so fixed my gaze upon the bobbly-headed Jesus once more. We were headed out of Ashfield, yet that fact did not perturb me. I knew Ryan lived in Hatfield, and that was where we appeared to be headed. It was a bright evening – full of opportunity. No matter what, I was grateful to be freed from the ties that bind.

'Open the glove compartment.'

I obeyed.

'There's a bottle in there,' Ryan elaborated. 'Have a sip. Sorry, it ain't Malibu – that's what girls your age usually drink, right?'

My immediate thought was how I wasn't a drinker – at all – and so I wavered. I'd had the occasional sip of alcohol, but the teenage rite of passage of getting drunk had so far completely passed me by.

The bottle was short and stout, with a rectangular base. *The Devil's Hand* – that's what it was called, and I remember its label, vividly. There was a large, clawed-hand in its centre, like a woodcut. I didn't recognise the brand, but bright green, I knew it as absinthe. My aunt had brought a bottle back from Prague once and opened it at a family barbecue. Another side-story; the less said about that, the better.

This bottle was smeared with grease. I didn't want to drink it, and my apprehension must have been obvious, because Ryan then said:

'I'm not asking you to get drunk!'

I replied by confidently unscrewing the cap – far more confidently than I'd felt. The idea of drinking it neat did not appeal. I had seen people's faces after they'd taken a gulp of neat spirit, and it looked rough. My aunt had drunk it diluted, and with sugar.

There was a ring of pink lipstick hidden beneath the cap, engulfing its opening. Now, that did cause my heart to sink. What other girls had he shared this bottle with? Maybe it had been with a friend? Everyone's allowed friends. Or sister, even? I had only ever heard of a brother. Realising the length of my pause, I quickly wiped away the smear. I was, however, non-too subtle and Ryan interjected.

'What you doing that for? I'm not infected.'

I would have been taken aback by the harshness of his words then also, had he not laughed. I raised the bottle to my mouth just as the car jolted over a bump. Jesus shook his head, and I – unintentionally – swallowed far more than I had hoped. Instantly, I pulled a face and recoiled.

'Fuck me, that's strong!' I spluttered, coughing.

Ryan then began laughing, heartily.

'What's so funny?' I asked, or, 'Why are you laughing?'

Embarrassed and defensive, I was somewhat aggravated by his reaction.

'Nothing. Just an interesting choice of phrase,' he replied.

In retrospect – in *hindsight* – his own choice of phrase was highly disturbing. At the time, I was still recovering from the absinthe to really acknowledge it. Defiantly, I took another swig – an intentionally longer swig, this time – knocking the bottle back as if it was water. It burnt my throat. I fought the urge to spit it out. I hated the taste of liquorice.

'You drink like a man.' Ryan smiled.

Playfully, I hit his side, telling him to go screw himself. Again, I'm not sure of the exact insult, but it was said in good humour. I offered out the bottle, and Ryan said he'd already had some – that he'd needed to calm his nerves before meeting the girl of his dreams. Attempting to flirt, I joked whether anyone had ever warned him of drink-driving.

'Didn't anyone ever warn you of meeting strangers?' he replied.

His voice was deadly serious, but I laughed anyway. I thought he was joking too, and that his delivery had just been particularly bad. My mother had always said men were worse at flirting than women. My mother had indeed also warned me of meeting strangers. I had romanticised the risk, however; I see that now. I hadn't given any real thought to putting my heart on the line, let alone my life. That's why I wore my heart on my sleeve with Ryan. He, on the other hand, would see to it that I wore my insides on my dress.

Life is *not* a fairy tale. Except, Hans Christian Anderson originally had the Little Mermaid's new legs hurt with each step. If she did not marry the prince, she would turn to sea foam. And, spoiler alert; he chose another.

We pulled into a car park, in Sullen Woods, and continued down a dirt track. I remember there was a toilet block in the car park itself. But it appeared run-down. I would have rather peed in amongst the trees. And so, I would.

Ryan's promise of a beautiful place was just that. We got out of the car just as the sun was setting and went for a walk around the lake. It was still, and perfectly mirrored the oranges, pinks and purples of the sky.

We took *The Devil's Hand* with us and shared it – sparingly. I was already beginning to feel tipsy. The sensation latched itself onto the ecstasy emanating from my heart and made me giddy. We talked about an all manner of things – his job, the expectation of me to go to university, television shows and music.

After several laps of the lake, Ryan leant in for a kiss – which I received, willingly – and we embraced. His action was not unexpected, for we had been growing physically closer throughout the hour, and been holding hands. The taste of his tobacco-ed lips on my mine was electrifying. I knew he was a smoker, but this only appealed to my increasingly rebellious attitude. I yearned for him.

I then ruined the romantic scene by declaring that I was desperate for a pee. Behind an old oak tree, beside Ryan's car, I pulled down my knickers. I laughed, scolding him, as he pretended to look.

Sitting by the lakeside, we spoke until it was dark. Even though we had only met – for real – a few hours earlier, it was as if we'd known each other forever. Ryan did genuinely make me laugh that evening – although that may have been more down to *The Devil's Hand* than his actual personality. I found him funny. When compared to his online persona, he was odder in person, but I explained it away. I found his quirkiness endearing.

As it grew chilly, we got back into the car and Ryan turned on the ignition so that we could listen to the radio. The clock on the dashboard read seventeen minutes past eleven. I had another couple of swigs of absinthe.

Ryan started to unbutton his shirt, and when he'd gotten halfway down, he looked at me. My entire body numbed with the strength of a thousand goosebumps. A sliver of bare chest; yet Ryan had given me the most erotic moment of my life to date. Man, did it go downhill from there, and fast.

I smiled, I think – I must have – for he moved his hand to my thigh, grasping it, before moving it up higher.

We smooched, using our tongues. Girls at school used to practice French kissing on their forearms and I remembered thinking how they'd discussed it in such over-complicated detail. Maybe it was the stress of trying to ascertain a standard that made me pull away. Maybe, it wasn't. But whatever it was, Ryan seemed unbothered. It was only when he unbuckled his belt and shimmied down his trousers, that I said:

'I'm really sorry, but I can't do this.'

I was beginning to feel light-headed – *drunk*. I had never experienced the feeling before. I wasn't used to it, and it panicked me. And I hated myself for what happened next, I really did.

I thought Ryan would stop getting undressed, but he didn't. He didn't even seem to hear my declination, and so I repeated myself. Again, he gave no reaction, and I quickly realised he did not care.

Ryan – his name I now know to have been Nikos Castellanos – shoved my face to the car's dashboard. It collided with a smack, busting my lip, and once more Jesus shook his head. It hurt but the pain paled in comparison to my fear. He ripped my dress up to the hip.

Nikos raped and murdered me that night.

The first act in his defiling of me took a while. It was a struggle – I struggled – as the car's handbrake kept getting in the way of his thrusting. Low down in the car, I felt very claustrophobic. I closed my eyes, but his breathing – his groaning. It was as if time had stood still.

I kicked out with my legs, but they were held open by his. I knocked a few buttons on the central panel of the dashboard, inadvertently turning up the volume of the radio and – as I would later discover – pressing down the cigarette lighter. No-one was around to hear, but I had drowned out my own screams with Sheena Easton's '9 to 5 (Morning Train)'. If I was to have chosen a song to be my last, I would have preferred Alanis Morissette. Unapologetic; the gut-wrenching cheeriness of this track felt like being dragged across concrete.

Nikos let out an almighty groan, screwed up his face and shuddered. He collapsed on top of me – his weight crushing me. I hate to say it, but I was waiting for this moment, and I seized it.

I grappled for the door's handle, wrenched it forward and fell back with it. I managed to roll over and clawed at the stony ground. As Nikos pulled me back inside the car by my legs, my fingertips were drawn across the surface of an almost perfectly circular and flat black stone. I remember it well, for at that moment, it seemed to symbolise my lifeline – out of reach, and impossible to cling onto. Nikos slammed the car door back shut. It whacked into the top of my skull, trapping some of my hair within the frame.

I'll try to spare you most of the gory details of what followed – I'll be frank, but factual. Nikos locked the car's doors and – as the song hit mid-chorus – stabbed me thrice. I only caught a glimmer of the blade and have no idea where he had produced it from.

Knife in my gut, I scrabbled around on the floor of the car for something to hit him with. Finding the half-empty bottle of absinthe, I smashed it over the side of his head. The neon green splashed across my bare legs and doused the dashboard. Ignited by the cigarette lighter, the alcohol went up in an instant.

Flames leapt between us and Nikos reached out for his own door – to unlock it and make an escape. But, ripping my hair free, I threw my body through the fire and onto his naked lap – consequently, driving the knife further into my belly. He tried to push me off, but I wouldn't allow it. If I was going to die — as I most surely was — then I was taking him with me.

I can't tell you what Nikos was thinking, exactly — throughout any of this, in fact — but I imagine he was just hoping to put the fire out as quickly as possible, for he pushed a hand down between my thighs to release the handbrake and shunted the gearstick into first. I heard his foot slam and the car lurched forwards. Together, we roared towards the lake. The car flew off the bank. It managed to fly a fair distance airborne, considering the short run-up, and that we had moved from a standstill.

The car landed, almost flat. Nikos's head hit the wheel as water was displaced — thrown up — around the body of the vehicle. All around us, geese took flight, escaping — just as I wanted to. I couldn't hear their squawks, for the radio was still loudly playing.

Almost immediately, the lake began flooding our metal prison with dirty, smelly water that poured in through Nikos' window, that had somehow broken during the impact. This caused the car to capsize at an angle. The water hissed out the flames, but gravity swayed my attacker's unconscious form over his side window, and door release also.

I removed the knife, and screaming, slammed my bloodied fists into the passenger window. In hindsight, I probably should have fought my way across to the broken window, but I was not exactly thinking logically. I'm sure you can sympathise. My inflicted blows to the glass left streaked red smears but did nothing to break it.

The final bars of Sheena Easton's track could be heard until water drowned the speakers to a gurgle. With my face pressed up against the roof of the car, all then became silent. Time seemed to slow, as I became hyper-aware of even the tiniest of details. Each grain of silt and every weed. The smell of the felt — perfumed, yet smoky. Water lapped up beside my cheeks and I took one final breath of stagnant air. I didn't close my eyes. Beneath the surface, the murky water had turned a dark shade of pink, as blood from my abdomen swam readily out through the slits in my dress.

I don't remember drowning, and for that I am glad. I'm not sure why I don't, but my best guess is that it's all part of the transitional process. And it's all fragmented from there onwards, until now.

When I was raped, my mind was full of questions such as, 'how could I have been so stupid?', and statements like, 'this is all my fault'. I placed more blame and guilt upon myself in those moments than I had in my entire life up until that point. I thought of all the awful things that had ever befallen me, every incremental choice made that led me to here. Only now – in hindsight – do I realise that I cannot be held accountable for the aims and impulses of another, for that is where the true beauty, or ugliness, of a character lies. It lies in these moments.

There are moments that change your life forever, and this moment ended mine. There are times that you want to split the world open with your cries. And there are places – even if overlooked – that can be reanimated. In just a blink of an eye, or snap of a finger.

END OF ACT THREE.

VOLUME II

Power & Control

<u>Thursday 1st January 1998, 00:28am, 6 EDGEHILL STREET, MUSWELL HILL, LONDON.</u>

London's night sky was alive with fireworks that crackled overhead, illuminating the horizon with brilliant colours. Cheers and yells accompanied each explosion – some near, others far. From here – Muswell Hill – the whole of the capital could be seen and heard, celebrating the first hour of the New Year. There was, however, one girl that wasn't.

Summer Murphy banged loudly upon the door of a house that appeared like any other. There was no immediate stir from within, and so she banged again.

'Open the door!' she shouted. 'Angelica, open the door!'

Backing away, Summer descended the steps. Her legs were unsteady. Looking up from a distance, a light could be seen to switch on from within the master bedroom; its glow dimmed behind heavy curtains.

'Angelica!'

Racing forwards, Summer proceeded to bang upon the door as before – her pale face screwed up in anguish. From under lank black hair, sweat beaded her forehead.

The sounds of revellers making their way down the street only hastened her already frenetic knocking. Summer tried her best to ignore their approach but as her paranoia grew, her posture stiffened. And as the group grew level, there was the unmistakable noise of bone hitting concrete. Summer – against better judgement – turned.

One of the seven – a man – had landed backside first upon the pavement, directly in front of Angelica's house. He had tried, and failed, in vaulting over a bollard. The man's friends descended into rapturous, drunken laughter. The group's halted progress had Summer frozen to the spot. A deer in the headlights; she watched them with glassy eyes.

One of the young women took it upon herself to try and help her friend to his feet. Tottering over, she offered out both hands, whilst clasping a bottle in an armpit. The man took hold of her wrists, but it was evident from his limp form that the effort would nosedive, as it did. She fell forwards to land atop him, skirt riding high to reveal her thong. The bottle emptied.

The pack fell about in hysterics. One of the men removed a can from a plastic bag and cracked it open. Taking swigs between fits of chortling, it was inevitable that some came back out through his nose. Another of the girls – dressed in plunging tiger print – leant in to give him a snog. It was upon withdrawing from the embrace, that this woman clocked Summer's statue-like presence.

'Hey! How're you doing, babe?' she hollered. 'Wanna join us in town for a few?! We're headed to The Highwayman!'

Her voice caught in her throat, Summer only mustered a sniffle in response – as was her shock at being addressed directly. Oh, how she wished Angelica would hurry up and open the door – what was keeping her?

'She looks 'omeless, Mand!' slurred the man with the can.

Mand – whom he'd just smooched – loosely smacked him with a forearm.

'Go away!' Summer managed.

Her attempt to sound intimidating was lacklustre.

'Oh, ignore him, babe!' Mand shouted back, snatching the can. 'He can be a right ol' wanker sometimes!'

'What the fuck?' the man retorted. 'She's obviously 'omeless. I mean, look at the state of it! Like she crawled out from under a bridge.'

Of all the things this stranger could have said, he'd chosen not once, but twice, to utilise the singular word that affected Summer the most. She would make him wish he hadn't. Flying into a fit of rage, Summer strode barefoot down the garden path.

'*Leave,*' she strained, before bellowing, 'Go away! Get out of here! Leave me alone!'

'You what? *What?!*' the man jeered. 'Calm yer tits. *Freak.*'

Spitting to the pavement, he narrowly missed Summer's feet.

'Go away, or I'll – I'll—' Summer trailed off.

'Or you'll what, darlin'? Lamp me one?' the man goaded.

'She's a woman, Tom,' Mand scolded. 'Why you gotta act like a prick?'

The man – revealed as Tom – snatched back his can. Smirking, he took another sip. The rest of the group remained silent.

Fighting back her tears, Summer's body trembled, and it was this action that seemingly set off the next, as Tom's can was crushed in upon itself by an invisible hand. Skin nicked between the metal; he dropped it, with a high-pitched shriek.

'What the fuck?!' Tom began, flicking beer from his soaked hand. 'What—'

Tom then slapped himself around the face – hard and heavy. Appearing as if she too had been slapped, Summer blinked. Tom's jaw protruded angrily out from his face and his eyes narrowed.

'You little mare! How—'

Tom's other hand smacked himself in the mouth. Cautious and confused, he began backing away down the hill. Mirroring the movement, Summer backed through Angelica's front gate, closing it. She flinched, as Tom's left hand lifted once more to slap him around the forehead.

Decidedly, Tom then turned on his heels to run away, full pelt. The rest of the group hastened after his disappearing silhouette as he continued to self-inflict injuries to his face with alternating hands. The last to leave was Mand, who exchanged a final look of uneasiness before departing also.

Summer watched – her chest heaving and face twitching – until all sight of them had vanished. She then ran up towards the house.

'Angelica, please! Let me in!'

Crouching, Summer flapped open the letterbox, and to her surprise, was greeted by a pair of yellow eyes. She did not recoil past the point of initial shock, however, for she knew to whom they belonged. The eyes blinked and a nictitating membrane was drawn transparently across them.

'Open the door, Tez,' Summer demanded. 'Open the door, before I break it down.'

Illogically, Summer had no quibble in speaking to Tez this way. In truth, she found the demon far easier to challenge than humans – her dislike of him was simply that strong.

Tez silently did as instructed. He whipped open the door, and in doing so, revealed himself not much taller than the height of the letterbox itself. The demon stood stoically – goblin-like – to the side of the hallway.

Without further prompt or invitation, Summer marched through, past, and right up to the foot of the stairs. Tez closed the door. As he strolled after, his enormous phallus – dirtied and calloused – dragged behind, between perpetually bowed legs. The demon had far more penis than body. Its glans also bore a face – reversed, as it was heaved. Cruder than the other, its expression was of a vacant smile. Tez lingered beside Summer.

'Angelica! Angelica, please! I need your help! Please!'

Summer placed a tentative foot upon the first stair but was quick to remove it, for Tez had coughed – by way of warning. She had never seen the upstairs of Angelica's house and was wary of venturing without permission. Summer turned to eye the demon's genitals with a look of revulsion and abhorrence, then tilted back her head.

'ANGELICA!'

'In the name of all that's unholy, would you be quiet!'

Appearing at the top of the stairs, a woman's shadow – sweeping and striking – posed dramatically, with her hands drawn up to her ears.

'Sweetie,' Angelica continued, in an American accent, 'would you, please, *compose* yourself?'

'I've killed him!' Summer began to offload. 'I've killed my Pops!'

Angelica remained still for several seconds, during which time Summer's heart continued to pound against her ribcage. Having not yet told a soul of the evening's unfortunate turn in events, Summer's admission – out loud – of her actions, made the circumstances in which she'd found herself even more real.

Gracefully, Angelica glided down the stairs, and her concern was illuminated. A cross between a thirties' Hollywood movie star and Morticia Addams, Angelica was the epitome of classic beauty. Everything from her pencilled brows, to her flawlessly pale complexion and jet-black hair – currently set into rollers – had been carefully constructed.

'What do you mean you've "killed him"?' she asked.

Summer opened her mouth to elaborate, only for Angelica to hold up a hand.

'On second thought, go on through to the sitting room,' she directed, by way of another gesture. 'We're not having a conversation of such proportions standing in the hallway. Go on through to the sitting room, and we can discuss … *this* … in there.'

Like a reluctant child, Summer obeyed. Angelica patted Tez affectionately upon his hairless head, as she went to follow her protégé. He trudged after them both, muttering something offensive – yet inaudible – under his breath.

Summer sat down heavily upon the moth-eaten sofa. Shaking uncontrollably, she began swaying back and forth. Angelica flicked the light switch and the Edison bulb – shade-less – rattled into life. Though far from bright, Summer shielded her eyes from its glare.

'Would you like an ice cream soda?' offered Angelica – hovering.

'What?' questioned Summer. 'No.'

'So be it,' Angelica whispered, huskily – taking a perch on the coffee table, opposite. 'Tell me all.'

Tez plopped himself down in the armchair by the window.

'I'm not talking with *that* here,' Summer spat.

Angelica sighed and fluttered her eyelids theatrically.

'So be it,' she relented. 'Tez, my darling, wait upstairs.'

Obediently, Tez stood. His hunchback form – and penile head – had barely crossed the threshold, before Angelica turned on Summer.

'Tell me, how did it happen?' she asked, between rouged lips. 'I thought we'd agreed you wouldn't go back there.'

Her apprehension was tinged with awe.

'We were arguing – about money – about me getting clean – and he—'

'Never mind that,' Angelica dismissed, rudely. 'How did you kill him, *exactly*?'

'*Knife*,' Summer whispered – a far off look in her eyes. 'A knife to the heart. I didn't mean—'

'TEZ!' Angelica screeched.

Her lungs – squeezed in at the waist by a crimson robe – fought against the fabric that constricted them, as Angelica made the exclamation.

The demon shuffled back into the sitting room at his name's call. Apparently, he had not made it far past the doorway, and Summer – assuming he had been eavesdropping – shot him daggers.

'Take this,' Angelica ordered.

Standing, she handed Tez a bejewelled athame from atop the mantelpiece.

'Take this and put it under my pillow.'

Athame in hand, Tez left the room once more. Angelica twirled on the spot – analysing the entire sitting room, for any other object that could obviously be used to inflict bodily harm.

'And, Tez!' Angelica called, and the demon popped his penile head around the doorframe. 'Be sure to shower before coming to bed.'

Nodding, the length retracted, and Tez could be heard to slink up the stairs. Regaining composure, Angelica retook her seat.

'I told you, you should have moved in here, with me, permanently. I don't know what you were thinking going back there – he was never going to accept you.' Angelica shook her head, dismally. 'If only you'd have heeded—'

'Help me,' Summer begged. 'You said that you'd always be here for me – that I could ask you for help whenever I needed it. Well, help me, *now*. Help me bring him back.'

Angelica indulged a moment's pause to steady her tongue. She fluttered her eyelids – whilst simultaneously rolling her eyes – before lifting Summer's lowered head with a hand. Angelica looked directly into her eyes as she next spoke, as to ensure she needn't repeat herself.

'Yes, I did say that, and I will always be here for you when you need me. But you never ask me that again.'

As Angelica took her hands in her own, Summer thought she could feel every bone. She unhooked her eyes from Angelica's gaze before quickly withdrawing from her grasp.

'But, please—'

'NEVER!' Angelica boomed; her patience having had worn thin – as thin as the fabric that struggled to contain her heaving breasts. 'I'm sorry, Summer – *sweetie* – but you know, that's not something that can be done.'

Her unnecessarily large sleeves billowing, Angelica re-arranged the front of her robe. Summer began running her fingers through her hair – the action growing ever more violent and unfocused with every stroke.

'Help me somehow then! Don't just sit there. We both know I can't control my abilities, and it's getting worse every day!'

'Learning to relax is all part of your self-control.'

'I can't fucking *relax!*' screamed Summer.

'It's the only way you'll ever learn, honey,' Angelica scoffed, rattling off the unhelpful guidance – her voice dripping like nectar.

'I've killed him, Angelica! I killed Pops and he's never coming back. I loved him! I loved him, and I killed him! I couldn't stop it – I couldn't – I didn't—'

Appearing wild, Summer was breaking down. Completely ruled by the emotions inside of her, all she could do was scream at the world, and demand reprieve.

'Summer, I can't help you, unless you concentrate, and list—'

'All I've ever done is listen to you – for months now! What else can you tell me that you haven't before?' Summer dismissed. 'God, what have I done?'

Angelica looked on – wide-eyed – as the sofa Summer was sitting on slowly began to shudder and lift itself from off the carpet. The whole room then began to shake – powered by teenage angst but taking on a life force of its own.

Its doors flapping, the cabinet to Angelica's left slid across the floor. As if pulled by elastic, the solitary teacup upon the coffee table shot through the air. Smashing in the gas fire's hearth, its fragments magically turned to dust – rotting away into the ether. The spilt liquid bubbled to a boil, turning black and thick like tar.

All ritualistic paraphernalia and dusty objects then took flight from their carefully placed positions – whipped up in a spinning vortex. All-the-while, Summer grasped the sides of her face. Eyes strained, they were turning bloodshot, as her hair flowed out on a storm-like wind.

'ENOUGH!' Angelica boomed.

Instantly, all the floating objects – including the sofa – fell back down to earth with an almighty bang. The two doors of the cabinet gave one final slam at Angelica's word – one door so abruptly that it broke away from its hinges and crashed to the floor, along with everything else.

'Very impressive …' Angelica pondered. 'Now, I will *show* you control. Close your eyes.'

'*Control?*' Summer whispered. 'Like what you have?'

'Yes, you'll be just like me.' Angelica smiled, as her eyes began to glow yellow. 'Close your eyes.'

Summer sniffled. She closed her eyes whilst wiping her nose along the back of her hand. Though appalled by her unintentional trashing of Angelica's sitting room, she was far from shocked by her magically charged and emotionally fuelled destruction.

'Well, hello,' Angelica then mused, unexpectedly, furrowing her pencilled brow, as she leant closer. 'What do we have here?'

THE END.

Special thanks:

D Bird, Information Rights Unit. N Smith, Freedom of Information Caseworker, College of Policing.

L Foroze, my writing pal, for your endless support. To bounce ideas around with you is a beautiful thing.

The reader, for selecting this book. If you've enjoyed what you've read, why not leave an Amazon review to help THE DEVIL'S HAND reach a wider audience. Perhaps order another copy from your local major / independent book retailer as a gift for a friend or loved one. Everyone loves gifts!